THE TRUEST THING

A HART'S BOARDWALK NOVEL

SAMANTHA YOUNG

THE TRUEST THING

A Hart's Boardwalk Novel

By Samantha Young

Edited by Jennifer Sommersby Young

Cover Design By Hang Le

ALSO BY SAMANTHA YOUNG

Other Adult Contemporary Novels by Samantha Young

Play On

As Dust Dances

Black Tangled Heart

Hold On: A Play On Novella

Into the Deep

Out of the Shallows

Hero

Villain: A Hero Novella

One Day: A Valentine Novella

Fight or Flight

On Dublin Street Series:

On Dublin Street

Down London Road

Before Jamaica Lane

Fall From India Place

Echoes of Scotland Street

Moonlight on Nightingale Way

Until Fountain Bridge (a novella)

Castle Hill (a novella)

Valentine (a novella)

One King's Way (a novella)

On Hart's Boardwalk (a novella)

On Dublin Street: The Bonus Material (a novella)

Hart's Boardwalk Series:

The One Real Thing

Every Little Thing

Things We Never Said

Young Adult contemporary titles by Samantha Young

The Impossible Vastness of Us

The Fragile Ordinary

Young Adult Urban Fantasy titles by Samantha Young

Tale of Lunarmorte Trilogy:

Moon Spell

River Cast

Blood Solstice

Warriors of Ankh Trilogy:

Blood Will Tell

Blood Past

Shades of Blood

Fire Spirits Series:

Smokeless Fire

Scorched Skies

Borrowed Ember

Darkness, Kindled

Slumber

Drip Drop Teardrop, a novella

Titles Co-written with Kristen Callihan:

Outmatched

Titles Written Under S. Young

True Immortality Series:

War of Hearts

Kiss of Vengeance

Kiss of Eternity: A True Immortality Short Story

PROLOGUE

EMERY

Hartwell
Present day

THE NUTTY, smoky, caramelized smell of coffee lingered with me long past my day at work. It was a good thing I liked the scent. It made me feel content, in control, and safe. Because it usually meant I was in my favorite place.

My bookstore café.

Standing at my Mastrena high-performance espresso machine, I wasn't feeling so content. I tried to focus on making my customer's cappuccino and not on my immature behavior earlier.

Bailey wanted to invite Ivy Green into our friendship circle.

And because I wasn't comfortable with the idea, the girls had decided not to.

Like we were in middle school.

I groaned under my breath, feeling my cheeks heat. As I handed over the coffee, took the money for it, and moved on to the next customer, only half of me was in the store. The other half was locked in my head and would be for a while. Whenever I did something bothersome, I'd chew on it for a long time. Even when I would finally move on, I'd never *really* let it go, because it would come back to annoy me months later, just for the hell of it.

Ivy Green was Iris's daughter. Iris was one of my favorite people. She'd been the only person I was close to until Jessica Huntington—now Lawson—vacationed in Hartwell and ended up staying. There was something about Jessica I instinctively trusted, and trust was difficult for me.

I'd trusted Iris too.

And this was how I repaid her friendship? By using my influence with my friends to cut her daughter out of a pretty fantastic group of women who could help her through an arduous time?

By arduous, I meant that Ivy used to live in Hollywood as a screenwriter and was engaged to a big-time director, Oliver Frost, who sadly died of a drug overdose. Ivy returned to Hartwell a complete wreck, only for Deputy Freddie Jackson to hold her at gunpoint to extort money out of her, all after he murdered local businessman, Stu Devlin. My other good friend, Dahlia McGuire, took a bullet trying to protect Ivy. Ivy then cracked Freddie Jackson over the head with an Oscar statuette to protect Dahlia from getting shot again.

Welcome to Hartwell, folks!

We've had a lot going on these last few years.

Iris had worried about her daughter before Oliver died, especially after Ivy broke contact with her parents during the relationship. I'd counseled Iris about it, continually prodding her to reach out to Ivy. But the woman was stubborn. Now I knew she regretted that stubbornness.

Iris would want Ivy to have support. She needed excellent friends. I couldn't stand in the way of that, even if I was afraid someone new might change the dynamic of our group, a group that had become my family. I was a little possessive over the girls.

That was no reason to shut someone out.

I sighed. The girls wouldn't make a move now. Jessica said they were just going to let things work out naturally. Perhaps Ivy needed more effort than that.

It would be up to me to approach her and bring her into the fold.

The thought made my stomach knot.

I wasn't good with giving people any kind of power over me, and what if Ivy rejected my offer of friendship?

And yet, I'd let Jess, Bailey, and Dahlia in, and it had been my best decision ever.

Now I was a part of their lives. I was a bridesmaid in Jess and Cooper's wedding; I'd be a bridesmaid again when Bailey and Vaughn tied the knot at the end of summer. Moreover, I had a front-row seat to the reunion of Dahlia and Michael, which was magical to watch considering the painful years they'd spent apart.

The icing on the cake: Jess had recently informed us we would be aunts! She actually said the word "aunts." I was going to be an *aunt*. Jess was twenty weeks along, and I'd already started shopping online for baby gifts.

There was so much goodness in my life because of these women. Who was to say Ivy wouldn't just add more goodness? If she was anything like her adoptive mother, Iris, then she absolutely would.

A customer yelled from the raised seating area near the fireplace, asking for a clean spoon. I was a staff of one, and although I knew I should hire some help during the high season, I enjoyed keeping busy. It would be great, however, if customers would read the signs that pointed to the cutlery tray so they could help themselves. This was not a restaurant.

I excused myself from the line of customers waiting for

coffee and hurried from behind the counter to grab a spoon for the guy. He didn't even say thank you.

Asshat.

Not that I'd ever dare call him that to his face.

Even Bailey, the most forthright, ballsy woman I'd ever met, wouldn't call a customer an asshat. To his face.

As I rounded the counter again, the bell above my door tinkled and I looked over at it. My stomach dipped like I was on a roller coaster.

Jack Devlin.

I wrenched my gaze from his intense expression, my heart skipping a beat, and tried to concentrate on my other customers. Still, I knew I was blushing, and I knew he'd know he was the cause.

Always the cause of the damn blushing!

I cursed my fair complexion on a daily—no, strike that —*hourly* basis.

What was he doing here?

Jack hadn't come in for coffee since last summer, since "the incident."

That's what I was calling it.

It was better to call it that than the hottest—and most humiliating—moment of my life thus far. I bet you didn't know those two sentiments could go hand in hand.

Respectful of my request to leave me alone, Jack had avoided me since then. He'd even given up my coffee, which I knew he loved since he used to come in every morning for an Americano.

But last summer wasn't the last time we'd interacted.

I hurt for him as I remembered that moment between us.

"I gave you ten dollars."

The aggravated voice brought me out of the memory. Christine Rothwell, the chair of the board of licenses in Hartwell, glowered.

"Excuse me?"

She pursed her lips before replying. "I gave you ten dollars." She spoke obnoxiously slow, as though I was too stupid to understand. "The coffee"—she pointed to her cup—"was four dollars. Are you with me?"

Must not insult customers to their faces. Must not insult customers to their faces.

"Yes."

"You gave me back a dollar."

"I'm sorry." My cheeks bloomed even redder knowing Jack was witnessing my fumble. I handed over a five-dollar bill, which she snapped from my hand before marching out of the store. The bell above the door tinkled aggressively with the force of her departure.

My next customer gave me a sympathetic smile. "Someone forgot her manners today."

I returned the smile, relaxing a little. Well, as much as I could relax with Jack in the room.

Which wasn't a whole heck of a lot.

My hands trembled as my line depleted and Jack grew closer. No new customers had come in after him.

Pulse racing, I threw back my shoulders to face him as he stepped up to the counter. What was he doing here?

One of the most confusing things about Jack's decision to go work with his father and be involved in the nefarious plotting of the Devlin family was his obvious disgust of them. You only had to look into Jack's eyes to know he wasn't a rotten person. In fact, he had the kindest eyes I'd ever seen.

And when he looked at me … he *looked* at me. Jack stared so intently at my face, as though he didn't want to gaze at anything else. It was hard to resist that kind of open intensity.

And I couldn't.

Consequently, he'd broken my heart last summer. And not for the first time.

It was something I'd kept to myself. Not even the girls knew about the secret interactions between me and Jack Devlin.

However, those kind eyes that could morph into a smoldering gaze, and the tortured, brooding hero thing he had going on would no longer appeal to me. Jack had a dreadful habit of pulling me in and then pushing me away. It wasn't deliberate. I knew that.

But I was over it.

I'd offered him support on the beach three months ago because, no matter what, I hated to see him hurting.

That's as far as it went.

I wrenched my eyes from his, determined not to be pulled in. "What can I get you?"

He hesitated a moment. "The usual, Emery."

I loved Jack's voice. It was deep and smooth. Like whisky-flavored caramel. And it caused a physical reaction in me.

Dammit.

Turning away, I started on his coffee and kept my back to him.

I could feel his eyes all over me and tried not to hunch my shoulders against his perusal.

"Busy today," he noted.

I shrugged.

"Anyone buying books or just your coffee?"

Stop trying to make idle chitchat.

"Yeah," I answered vaguely.

Jack let out a huff of irritated laughter. "Was that an answer?"

I didn't respond.

By the time I returned to the counter with his coffee, his expression had darkened. "Is this the way it'll be from now on?"

I slid the coffee toward him and he swiped his card over the card machine.

Jack scowled. "Em, are you seriously going to give me the silent treatment?"

"I'm not giving you the silent treatment." I took a deep breath, my focus wandering past him to the book stacks. "I asked you not to come here. Nothing's changed in that respect. I'm going to suggest, *again*, that you find somewhere else to get your coffee from now on."

"Look me in the eye when you say it, and I might take that advice on board."

I determinedly met his eyes. His expression veered between anger and concern.

His head dipped toward mine. "Look, Em—"

"Don't." I jerked away.

"I wasn't going to kiss you, sunrise," he murmured.

I ignored the ache of hearing the endearment he'd started using years ago. "I know. But you were going to lean in close and try to soften my resolve, and I don't want you to."

"Em—" A shrill ring sounded from somewhere on Jack's person.

He sighed, placed his coffee on the counter, and reached inside the inner pocket of his suit jacket for his cell. His expression told me we weren't done as he moved away from the counter, phone pressed against his ear.

I didn't want to want to listen in, but I couldn't help but watch him.

He had a strong, angular jawline covered in prickly stubble. The unshaven look started just over a year ago. And I knew that because I'd personally felt the prickle of it against my skin a year ago.

I flushed and looked down at the counter.

"She did what?" Jack's angry voice brought my attention back to him.

He glared at my wall, a muscle ticking in his jaw as he listened to whomever was on the other end of the call. "Fuck," he bit out. "Okay, I'm on my way." He ended the call and turned to me.

My heart hammered at what I saw in Jack's eyes.

Fear.

"What is it?"

"Rebecca."

Rebecca was Jack's sister. She'd been living in England for the last few years, in a form of exile from the Devlin family. "What about her?"

"She came home two days ago … that was Sheriff King on the phone."

"Jack?"

He leaned his hands on the counter, bowing his head.

Worry flooded me. "Jack?"

"She … she just turned herself over to the police."

Oh my God.

I reached for his hand.

He lifted his head, his tortured gaze locking with mine.

I knew what this meant.

I knew something no one else knew about the Devlins.

I knew the real reason Jack went to work for his family and why he'd betrayed Cooper, his best friend.

I knew it all.

And it had everything to do with protecting Rebecca Devlin.

"Oh, Jack," I whispered, heartbroken for him.

1

JACK

Hartwell
Nine years ago

It didn't matter if it was high or low season, Cooper's Bar was always busy in the evening. Creedence Clearwater Revival played from the jukebox, fighting to be heard over the football game on the bar's two flat-screen televisions. Football season had just started, and a lot of the locals came to Cooper's to eat, drink, and watch their favorite game. As Delaware didn't have an NFL team, most folks in Hartwell were Patriots fans.

Jack split his time between eating his burger, watching the screen above the bar, and talking to Coop while his friend served customers.

There was nothing atypical about the evening.

Jack was foreman of his own construction company, a job usually done by someone older. But Jack had worked in construction since he was fourteen years old. He'd hired Ray English, the guy he'd learned everything about construction from, stealing him away from the competition. He and Ray were more like co-foremen.

They'd closed the site they were working on earlier than usual. It was a private development of a small community of homes, out near Jimtown. Jack tried to keep the weekends free, but sometimes when a client offered a lot for overtime, it was hard to say no. Not only was his team not working the weekend, but with permission from their clients, he'd given them Friday off so they could enjoy the kickoff game with a few beers the night before.

His guys had been working flat out all summer and deserved the extra day. As for Jack, he was looking forward to doing some work to the home he'd bought six months ago in North Hartwell, near Coop's house.

Yeah, there was nothing out of the ordinary about Jack hanging out at Cooper's Bar, eating, drinking, and shooting the breeze with his buddy and their local friends.

Old Archie sat at the end of the bar, dressed immaculately from head to toe, despite the fact that he'd probably been drunk for forty-eight straight hours. His real name was Archibald Brown, and he was from old money. He was also an alcoholic whose wife had left him twenty years ago and had taken the kids with her.

People had tried to help. Jack had tried.

It was no good.

Old Archie didn't want help.

Jack had to learn to let the guy be.

"The Saints are looking good." Old Archie gestured to the screen.

Jack nodded. They were playing the Minnesota Vikings. "Yeah."

"Where's Dana, Coop?" Old Archie asked. "She's usually here for the first game of the season."

At the mention of Cooper's wife, Dana, Jack flicked his

buddy a look. Cooper was pulling a pint, not looking at Old Archie as he replied, "She wasn't feeling it tonight. She's at home, watching some shit romantic comedy and having something she called 'self-care time.'"

Jack looked up at the game, afraid the derision he felt was obvious. Self-care time? The woman worked eight hours a week at the salon as a receptionist and then did nothing else. She didn't help Coop around the house. She didn't help him at the bar. And she didn't provide the guy with any kind of support beyond what she gave him in the bedroom. She bought shit Cooper had to work his ass off to afford, and Jack was afraid one day Dana would bury Coop in debt.

Or worse.

It would be fair to say Jack Devlin did not like Dana Kellerman Lawson.

In fact, she'd caused the first real argument between him and Coop.

Sometimes, Jack still couldn't believe Cooper had disregarded Jack's opinion.

For years, they'd joked about Jack's superpower—his ability to smell bullshit on someone from a mile away. Perhaps it was growing up in a house like the one he had with manipulative bastards around every corner. But Jack had instincts about folks, and he wasn't often wrong. He couldn't remember the last time he'd been wrong about someone.

And when Dana Kellerman came back to Hartwell from college and set her sights on Cooper, Jack tried to make his friend see sense. However, Coop couldn't see past Dana's beauty or that falsely sweet smile. Or the way she seemed to rely on him entirely, something that fed the protective, alpha-male shit Coop always had going on with the women in his life.

However, Jack saw right through Dana. He saw past her movie-star looks and what did he find?

A whole lot of nothing.

That woman only wanted Cooper because other women wanted him, and *they* failed to nail him down.

It probably didn't hurt he owned lucrative property on the boardwalk.

She wanted a handsome husband who bought her nice stuff and took care of everything and that's what she got in Cooper. Seriously, she didn't lift a finger to do a damn thing. They even had a housekeeper to look after their average-sized, three-bedroom house, something Cooper complained about because his mom had raised him to clean up after himself.

Worse, whenever Cooper had a problem or was worried about the bar, Dana didn't want to hear it. So Cooper laid that shit on Jack. What was the point of having a wife if it wasn't a partnership, a support system? Jack had asked this, and Coop shut him down every time, so he stopped asking.

After he'd warned Cooper not to propose to Dana, calling her shallow as a kiddie pool, he and Cooper hadn't spoken for days. Jack finally had to apologize, knowing he'd lose his friend if he didn't just let him do what he needed to do with Dana.

Still, standing up as his best man at the wedding had not been an outstanding day for Jack.

Cooper was more brother to him than his own brothers, and Jack wanted the absolute best for him.

He deserved better than Dana, something that was becoming more apparent with each passing year.

She'd realized Jack didn't like her, and Dana didn't know what to do with that. She expected all men to fall at her feet in worship and the fact that Jack didn't was a challenge.

Dana had been getting in his face lately, and Jack had been working overtime to avoid her, which wasn't easy when she was married to his best friend.

"Self-care?" Old Archie snorted. "What the hell does she need self-care for? The woman spends all day every day self-caring."

Jack's lips twitched around his beer bottle as he stared determinedly at the screen.

"She works," Cooper said easily. "At the salon."

"For one day a week and only to catch up on the latest gossip." Iris's voice sounded behind Jack and he glanced over his shoulder. Iris Green, along with her husband, Ira, owned Antonio's, an Italian pizzeria on the boardwalk. They weren't Italian but their food certainly was. Jack lifted his chin at Iris.

She smiled and patted his shoulder before looking at Cooper. "You got that table for three I reserved?"

"Yeah, reserved you a booth." Cooper nodded to the back of the bar. "You going to introduce us?"

Wondering who Coop meant, Jack leaned so he could see past Iris.

He spotted Ira standing next to a tall woman with pale-blond hair that spilled down a slender back in attractive waves. She wore a long, dark blue dress made of a material that clung to her body. And what a body it was. At least from what he could tell from the back. Narrow waist, gentle roundness to her hips, and the dress clung to an ass that made all the blood in his body travel south.

Fuck me, he thought. *Turn around so I can see that face.*

"Emery's kind of shy." Iris's words pulled his attention from the new woman to her.

"Emery?" Why was that name familiar?

"She inherited the Burger Shack," Cooper said, leaning on the bar.

"The woman who's turning it into a bookstore?" Jack had heard about her. Everyone had. Property on the boardwalk was prime real estate. His father, Ian Devlin, owned a lot of property in Hartwell. What he didn't own was boardwalk property. Jack endured Sunday dinners at his parents' house every second week and when news of Emery's arrival hit, his father was disgruntled, to put it politely. "Some little upstart from New

York inherited the Burger Shack from her grandmother and won't sell it to me because she's planning on running a business there. Idiot child. You know she's moving here under a false name. Thinks the businesspeople here are too stupid to do a background check. But she's not who she says she is. She's a society princess with more money than brains. Woman is worth a mint."

When Cooper told him about Emery Saunders converting the place next door, Jack hadn't told him that the woman was from money. No one needed to know her business, and while he trusted Cooper, he didn't trust his friend wouldn't tell Dana.

And if Dana knew, everyone would know.

"And when I say shy"—Iris leaned toward them conspiratorially—"I mean *shy*. We need to break this one in gently."

Jack snorted and shot the woman another look. "She's not a horse, Iris."

"Trust me, Jack." Iris sighed. "I know what I'm talking about."

It was then, as Jack flicked another look at Emery, that she turned around.

And his typical evening at Cooper's Bar went completely atypical.

His heart raced like he'd just run a marathon. His mouth felt dry.

Holy shit.

Emery Saunders was the most beautiful fucking woman Jack Devlin had ever seen.

"She's only twenty," Iris said. Her voice filled his ears as his eyes locked with Emery's startling light blue ones. A blush stained her pale, smooth cheeks, and her lips parted as if she were surprised.

His gut tightened.

"And if the way she reacts around men is anything to go by, the girl is innocent as Snow White." Iris tapped Jack's shoulder and he reluctantly pulled his gaze away. She smirked at him.

"She's not a tourist you can mess around with—you hear what I'm saying?"

Jack frowned at her but before he could respond, Iris was walking away. She led Emery and Ira across the bar to their reserved booth. Emery shot Jack another shy, quick look over her shoulder before sliding onto the bench seat, her long hair swaying across her slender back.

"She's a beauty," Old Archie observed.

Swallowing hard, wondering why his heart wouldn't slow down, Jack tore his eyes away and stared unseeing at his half-empty plate.

"Jack?"

He looked up at Cooper. His friend was amused.

"You might want to wipe your chin. You got a little drool right there."

"Fuck off," Jack muttered good-naturedly.

However, as the minutes passed, Jack couldn't get back into the game. Instead, he kept looking toward his right shoulder, wanting to glance at her.

Finally, he lost the struggle and looked across the bar at her.

She was smiling softly at something Iris said.

Jack itched to get off his stool and cross the room to introduce himself.

He'd never been one for settling down. He'd expected to later, maybe in his thirties, which was only a couple years off. He wanted kids eventually. Someone to come home to.

But since the age of thirteen, he'd been content to play the field. Jack had enjoyed his and Cooper's standing in high school. They were on the football team. Girls thought they were good-looking. He'd never had a problem getting a date.

Living in a tourist town was excellent for a guy who didn't want to settle but also didn't want to hurt a woman's feelings. Born with a natural charm that he used to his advantage, Jack would see an attractive woman, approach, and make easy conversation that would eventually lead to a sexual relationship lasting only as long as their vacation in Hartwell.

He firmly steered clear of local women.

However, staring across the bar at Emery Saunders, Jack did not want to steer clear. The opposite, in fact. Some caveman-bullshit need to scoop her up before any other bastard got to her fired his blood.

"Jack."

He wrenched his attention away, turning to face Cooper.

His best friend's amusement was replaced with disbelief.

"What?"

Cooper flicked a look in Emery's direction and then back to Jack. Understanding dawned, and he grinned. "Really?"

Feeling like he'd been caught doing something wrong, he shrugged, rubbing the nape of his neck, which was weirdly hot.

Cooper leaned on the bar, lowering his voice. "Woman is beautiful. Iris is taken with her, which says a lot. You know she doesn't suffer fools easily."

True.

"But you heard Iris. Pure as fucking Snow White." He raised an eyebrow. "You don't fool around with a woman like that."

No. You didn't. And Jack wouldn't.

As he remembered the calculating look in his father's eyes that Sunday he talked about Emery, he knew he couldn't approach her—even if he wanted to get to know her with a fierceness he'd never felt before.

What no one else knew—what Ian Devlin was keeping close to his chest probably to use in the future—was that Emery Saunders was actually Louisa Emery Paxton. She'd inherited the majority shares in her deceased grandfather's company, the Paxton Group, a billion-dollar corporation that owned airlines and an aeronautical company.

If Jack attempted to insinuate himself into Emery's life, Ian would only use him to get to her.

Tightness clawed at his chest as it always did when he thought about his father and brothers. Jack had tried his best to break away. Now and then, one of them would hound Jack to come back into the fold. And Jack did whatever he could to avoid fucking up and giving Ian something he could use to blackmail Jack.

All this time he thought he'd made it out. Free and clear of Ian.

But Jack realized now that he hadn't.

When he finally settled down, it would have to be with a nobody. Someone Ian couldn't use.

It couldn't be with a woman as wealthy as Emery Saunders.

Disappointment that seemed out of proportion to the situation, considering he hadn't even spoken two words to Emery, flooded him.

Cooper must have seen something in his face because concern furrowed his brows. "You all right?"

"I'm fine." Jack's voice was flat. "Just realized you're right. I'm not ready to settle down."

His friend gave him a slow nod, but there was suspicion in Coop's eyes.

Avoiding him, Jack looked up at the flat screen.

For the next two hours, he did his best to ignore the urge to look across the bar at Emery. He tried not to look at her when Iris and Ira came over to say good night while she hung back a little. If Iris hadn't told him she was shy, Jack would think the New York princess was aloof.

She didn't look like a New York princess in that long, clingy dress.

Christ, the image of her in that dress was imprinted on the back of his eyelids.

As the Greens departed with Emery at their back, Jack's willpower fled, and he looked.

Just as Emery glanced back over her shoulder at him. When their eyes caught, she blushed again.

She made his chest ache.

Fucking ache.

Then she was gone.

His chest ached harder.

Jack's reaction was an overreaction. But he couldn't deny it *was* how he felt.

And for the first time in a long time, Jack got very, very drunk that night.

2

EMERY

Hartwell
Nine years ago

STANDING behind the counter of my bookstore café, I gazed in wonder at the space. No one would have believed the compact building that had housed the Burger Shack could look like it did now.

When my grandmother died, leaving me everything, including the rental properties she'd obtained up and down the East Coast, I'd spent weeks poring over it all with her business manager and financial advisor, Hague Williams. Hague was now in his late fifties, sharp as ever, and as devoted to me as he was to my grandmother.

I knew I didn't want to live on her estate in Westchester. The house was too big and lonely. I'd had dreams of opening a bookstore since I was a child, and I wanted as far away from society life as I could get. Like my grandmother before me, I had to trust in other people to run the Paxton Group so I could pursue my own passions.

My grandmother's interest had lain with real estate. She liked to travel the country looking for buildings that were unassuming but lucrative. For instance, the Burger Shack in a small beach town called Hartwell in Delaware's Cape Region. Technically, Hartwell was a city, but it was tiny.

She bought the building to rent out because boardwalk property in the tourist city was worth a lot of money.

When I started investigating her properties, I did it physically. I went out to all the locations that interested me. And I knew as soon as I arrived in Hartwell that it was the place for me. I gave the tenants of the Burger Shack three months to make other arrangements and included a hefty compensation for their troubles, against Hague's advice. I had to soothe my guilt somehow, though. I was kicking someone out of their business so I could launch mine.

"You own the building, Emery," Hague had said, exasperated. "It belongs to you. Not them. It's in the rental contract that you can end the contract with only six weeks' notice."

I knew that. But still.

After that, I began the hunt for a place to live. By sheer luck—or at least it seemed like luck—a beach house, minutes' walk from what would become my bookstore, came up for sale. It was a sizable beach house with an open-plan living space, a wrap-around porch, and three bedrooms. I fell in love immediately. Mostly because the previous owners had attached a stunning porch swing that was almost like a bed. I could sit curled up on it every morning with coffee in hand and watch the sun rise above the ocean.

Perfect.

It cost a lot of money.

But it was worth it.

And now, I was actually here.

As you entered the store, to the left was a large counter and behind it, coffee machines. To the right, the bookstore, its walls painted in a soft gray against the white woodwork. Ahead and up a few steps was a seating area filled with cute little white tables and chairs. To the left of those, comfortable armchairs and sofas were arranged near an open fireplace. I'd placed some Tiffany lamps from the house in Westchester around the store to give it a cozy vibe. Behind the counter was the door that led to my office and a private restroom. The customer restroom was behind a door on the opposite wall of the fireplace.

I bit my lip as I took in the store—*my* store. The gray was exactly the sedate color my grandmother would've chosen. Maybe when it needed refreshed, I'd go for something punchier —like teal or turquoise. I was also thinking about selling sandwiches for people to enjoy with their coffees. I could make them up in the morning before the store opened. I'd have to get a permit for that but it was worth considering.

Emery's Bookstore and Coffeehouse had been open for a week.

That first weekend had been very busy with tourists and locals. It was an extremely difficult few days in which I'd wondered if I'd made a colossal mistake. I was a shy person—there was no getting around that. Not only did I find small talk uncomfortable but I had trust issues a mile long, which made it hard for me to make myself vulnerable enough to befriend most people.

Since moving to Hartwell two months ago, I'd befriended Iris and Ira Green. They owned Antonio's, the boardwalk pizzeria. I'd trusted them almost immediately. There was just something so genuinely good about them, even if Iris was blunt. She reminded me of my grandmother a little, minus the cold ruthlessness. She'd even aided me with the tradesmen that helped create the look of the bookstore and coffeehouse. She tried to teach me how to be more assertive with them, to tell them exactly what I wanted done.

I think she saw how panicked I was when she popped into

the store that first weekend. Her brief pep talk calmed me down when she reminded me it wouldn't be like this all the time. People were just curious about me.

And she was right. By the end of the week, the store was quieter. Most people who popped in were tourists and since it was hot, they were usually there to buy a beach read and iced tea. I had some regulars already appearing in the morning for coffee, but today's caffeine rush had just ended.

"I have my own business," I muttered as I picked up the paperback I was reading and sat down on the stool behind the counter. I didn't take the rare and blessedly quiet moments of free time for granted. There always seemed to be something to do, even after hours, so I had to get my reading in when I could.

The bell above the door rang, drawing my attention.

The man striding into the store caused my breath to catch.

Jack Devlin.

Iris had told me his name when she caught me looking at him for the hundredth time when we were at Cooper's Bar weeks ago.

Jack was tall. I hadn't realized how tall until I saw him around town. And now, as he walked to the counter with a slight smile on his face, I realized he had to be about six four. Which was perfect for me because I was five ten.

Not perfect for me, I reminded myself.

Iris said he was a player.

I'd had enough of those to last a lifetime.

Not that I would get involved with a Devlin. Or that I was ready to get involved with anyone. My business was my priority.

Yet, staring up into Jack's handsome face, it was hard to remember any of that. It had been like this from the first moment I saw him. He wore jeans, a plain white T-shirt, and tan construction boots. I was used to men wearing suits or preppy clothes.

Jack and his best friend Cooper dressed similarly, and together they were unfairly hot.

Jack alone was … wow.

He had these beautiful, expressive eyes, and he was now close enough that I could see they were a dark bluish gray, striking against his naturally tan complexion. His hair was dark blond, thick, and disheveled like he was always running his fingers through it. Jack Devlin wasn't as in your face handsome as Cooper, but to me he was even sexier. It was his height, his loose-limbed walk, the exaggerated power of his broad shoulders against his lean build. And there was something about his eyes and the mischievous quirk to his mouth that was difficult to resist.

"Emery, right?" Jack stopped in front of the counter as I stumbled off my stool to greet him.

My cheeks and neck felt like they were on fire, so I knew I was blushing like crazy, which only made me more embarrassed and increased the flushing.

His lips twitched as his eyes took in the sight.

"I'm Jack Devlin." He held out his hand for me to shake.

To my shock, I didn't even have to think about it. I wanted to feel his hand against mine, so I reached for him. As soon as I did, he clasped it tight. Our eyes locked, the breath leaving me as goose bumps rose across my arms.

Jack's eyes narrowed and his grip tightened.

He didn't shake my hand.

He just held it.

This caused a swooping sensation in my gut and I let out a little sound of surprise.

Jack's eyes dropped to my mouth, and I watched as his jaw clenched.

Quite abruptly, he released my hand, and I had to stop my arm from hitting the counter.

He cleared his throat and looked swiftly around the shop. "You settling in okay?"

I was grateful for the question.

It allowed me time to remember that Jack was a Devlin and his father, Ian Devlin, was to be avoided at all costs. This wasn't just because of the information Iris and Ira had provided me with about everyone in town.

I'd known about Ian Devlin before I moved to Hartwell.

He'd tried to buy the Burger Shack when he learned of my grandmother's death.

Hague had dealt with him but had warned me to avoid Devlin. He said he was an unscrupulous businessman, and he'd used private investigators to discover my true identity. It made me uncomfortable that someone here knew who I was, but Hague seemed convinced it wouldn't be in Devlin's best interest to tell the entire town about me.

From Iris's account, his eldest sons Stu and Kerr worked for Ian and were just as disliked around town. She said the exceptions were his daughter Rebecca and his second youngest son Jack. They took after their mother, Rosalie, who'd been well liked until she became more and more reclusive. Jamie, the youngest Devlin, was a late baby and it was too soon to tell which way he'd go.

As for Jack, Iris had nothing but good to say. But she'd warned me that he was the town player and only "dated" tourists.

He wasn't for me.

Even if I wasn't a shy, bumbling twenty-year-old with trust issues.

"Yes, thank you," I replied to his question, studying his strong profile.

He turned to me and I blushed harder for being caught staring at him.

Jack's lips quirked into that mischievous smirk. "How are you liking Hartwell?"

Small talk.

I was awful at small talk.

I nodded. "I like it."

This made Jack grin. And just like that, it knocked the breath out of me.

Oh boy.

He had the best smile I'd ever seen. It gave him these sexy crinkles at the corner of his eyes. It was a boyishly naughty smile, the smile of someone up to no good and at complete odds with the kindness in his eyes. The overall effect was detrimental to my heart.

A person could melt a marshmallow on my cheeks.

His eyes actually *twinkled*. "We're glad to have you here, Emery."

The sound of his deep voice saying my name caused another swooping sensation in my belly. I exhaled and stammered as I turned to point at the price board behind me. "C-coffee?"

At his silence, I glanced back at him.

He was looking at the silver bangles on my wrist.

Strange.

His eyes flew to my face and his voice sounded rougher when he replied, "Americano."

Grateful to have something to do, I turned from him and made his coffee. Neither of us spoke again.

When he handed over cash, I touched the five-dollar bill by the tip of it so our fingers wouldn't brush. I slid his change across the counter.

"Thanks."

I forced myself to meet his gaze again. "You're welcome."

"See you around."

I nodded.

Jack tipped the to-go cup toward me and turned to stride

out of the store. I held my breath the entire time. The bell tinkled above the door and then he was gone.

I let out air like a deflating balloon and sagged against my counter.

Typical me, I thought. *I would have to develop a crush on the one guy I shouldn't want.*

3

JACK

Hartwell
Seven years ago

WAKING up to a phone call from Ian was not Jack's favorite thing in the world. He answered it because he knew Ian would just keep calling until he did. He answered it even knowing what the call would be about. Every two months or so, Ian liked to call and berate Jack for not coming into the family business. Jack didn't know what Ian hoped to accomplish with these phone calls other than to irritate his son.

There was a cure to Jack's current mood, however, and it was on the boardwalk.

Sure, Emery's coffee was the best in town and he'd taken to going every morning, Monday to Friday, before work to grab himself a coffee. On the mornings he and Cooper ran on the beach, they'd go to Emery's together and the buffer of Cooper was much appreciated.

Cooper found Emery's shyness awkward as fuck. If it weren't for her coffee, he'd probably avoid the place.

Not Jack.

Jack thought every blush, every stutter, was so adorable, he couldn't stand it. There was something mysteriously feminine about Emery Saunders. He wanted to know all her secrets. He wanted to make her laugh, to know what it sounded like.

And he wanted to be the one to discover if she blushed all over.

In the two years Emery had lived in Hartwell, no one had learned much about her. The people of Hartwell understood that she was painfully shy, so it wasn't like they disliked her. It was just that they would always consider her an outsider while she didn't participate in town events and befriend folks.

It annoyed Jack. Someone should make more of an effort. He'd talked with Bailey Hartwell about it, and she'd tried to approach Emery, but it had backfired. Bailey's lack of filter had led her and Jack to deduce that she was a little too intimidating for Emery.

Someone more reserved needed to approach the shy newcomer. He'd asked Cat, Cooper's sister. Although she was as blunt as Bailey, she didn't have Bailey's overwhelming energy or reputation as the town princess.

Cat, unfortunately, was like her big brother and was uncomfortable with Emery's timidity.

She was also suspicious of Jack's motives, as were Cooper and Bailey ... so Jack stopped asking folks to look out for Emery.

He'd just have to do it himself, but from a distance.

Little did he know he'd have to do it that morning.

Jack pushed open the door to Emery's, a smile prodding his lips at the mere anticipation of seeing her. That smile disappeared at the sight of the man aggressively shouting at Emery.

"I bought it yesterday. I should be able to return it!" the man waved a book in her face.

Emery was scarlet with embarrassment and concern. "S-sir

… as I've—as I've tried to explain, the book is damaged. You've clearly read—"

"I want my money back, moron, end of story!" he yelled, making her flinch back in fright.

Furious, Jack pushed past the guy waiting in line and grabbed the aggressor by the scruff of the neck to shove him away from the counter. He stumbled, almost going to his ass.

"What the fuck?" He glared at Jack as he straightened.

Jack glowered down at the tourist. "You do not get in the face of any woman in my town, asshole."

The man waved his book at Jack. "The bitch won't give me my money back."

Oh, he really wanted to hit this loser. Jack took a step toward him. "You watch your mouth, or I'll make you watch your mouth."

He swallowed. "Look, there's no need for threats. I just want my money back."

"No need for threats? You don't think screaming at a woman in her establishment is threatening for her?" Jack looked at the book in his hands. The spine was bent to shit, the pages speckled in sand. "This isn't a fucking library. You bought the book, you read the book, end of fucking transaction. You got me?"

"I—"

Jack moved right into his space, shutting him up. "I don't care what your problem is, why you need to treat a woman like shit to make yourself feel like a big man. But you're not a big man. You're a bug. A bug I'll squash if I see you in here or anywhere near Emery again. Got me?"

Despite the rage flickering in the man's eyes, cowardice won out. Without another word, he marched out of the store, slamming the door behind him.

Dick.

Jack turned back to Emery who seemed a little dazed. "You okay?"

She nodded slowly.

Jack gestured to the man waiting in line who looked embarrassed too. Probably because he'd just stood there while that guy tore into Emery. Once the customer got his coffee, Jack was alone in the store with her.

He loved and hated these moments of aloneness.

She was pure temptation.

He couldn't have her.

But, fuck, did he want her.

His blood was up after dealing with that little shit, and it was harder to ignore the urgency of that want.

Drifting to the counter, he enjoyed the way she watched him. Anytime he saw her around town, she had a faraway look on her face, as if she was somewhere else. She was like this when she served her customers. But not with him. Jack always got her entire focus.

And he liked that more than he could say.

"You sure you're all right?" he asked as she began making his and Cooper's Americano without him having to ask.

She nodded, glancing over her shoulder at him. "Thank you."

"That happen a lot?"

"The angry customer?"

"Yeah." Jack didn't like the thought of her being alone in here all the time. She needed to hire someone else to work along with her. He'd thought she would. But it had just been her for the entire two years she'd been here.

"Now and then, but rarely, customers can be unpleasant." She set his coffee on the counter. "But nothing like that. I'm sorry you had to deal with it. I wish I were better with confrontation."

"I'm not sorry. I'm glad I could be here. That asshole has anger problems. It wasn't about you."

She nodded again.

His concern for her frustrated him. "Why don't you try to make more friends in town?"

There she went, blushing again. The white dress she wore beneath her short apron had a V-neckline so he could see even her chest flushed. Jack tried not to look. He always tried not to look. The dress had tight sleeves at the upper arms and then they puffed out from the elbow to the wrist where the fabric was tight around the wrist. The bodice was tight, hinting at perfect breasts and a narrow waist that flared at the hips. Jack couldn't tell with her standing behind the counter if the dress was long or short, only that it loosened around the hips.

Silver jewelry dripped off her, and her hair was tied in a fancy-looking side braid, hanging down over her right breast.

Emery Saunders was like a fairy princess come to life.

Or an angel.

Yeah. A goddamn angel.

Jack, at once, wanted to protect her from everything, arm her with a metaphorical sword and teach her to fight for herself, and he wanted to dirty up those angel wings by rolling around in bed while she wore only her silver jewelry. He wanted to hear it jangle so badly, it hurt.

Christ, he was so lost in his lustful thoughts, he momentarily forgot what he'd asked her when she replied, "It's not that easy for me."

Remembering he'd asked her about making friends, he leaned his hands on the counter, bringing them closer. Her eyes dropped to his mouth and his gut clenched.

Jack knew Emery was attracted to him.

That knowledge made avoiding temptation extremely hard.

Literally.

"Why isn't it easy?"

"I … I find small talk difficult."

"You're small talking with me."

"I …" She frowned. "I don't think talking about my shyness is really considered small talk."

"Okay." Jack leaned away, crossing his arms over his chest. "Emery, it's a beautiful day today, don't you think?"

Her lips twitched with amusement, making Jack feel about fifteen feet tall. "Yes, it's very nice today."

"Has the shop been busy?"

"It's busy every morning. People need their coffee. Are you on your way to work?"

Elated that she'd asked him a question, Jack grinned. "I am. I'm on my way to a restaurant we're renovating in Dewey Beach."

"Do you like your job?"

"I do. Do you like yours?"

"Surprisingly, yes. I thought when I first opened, maybe it was a mistake … you know, with the whole small-talk thing being hard for me. But I like it. I love being surrounded by books." She gestured to the stacks behind him, those silver bangles tinkling around her wrist.

"How long has this affair with books been going on?"

She grinned at him now, and Jack felt that smile like a punch to the gut. It was the sweetest smile he'd ever seen. That smile was like the sunrise across the ocean. There was nothing more beautiful to Jack than watching the sun start its languorous climb in the morning. The way it moved across the water as the sky transformed through shades of purple to pink to orange. Jack had never seen anything as awe-inspiring as the sunrise over Hart's Boardwalk. Until Emery Saunder's smile. Jesus Christ, she was so beautiful. And she had no idea. The complete opposite of Cooper's wife, who knew she was a beauty and used it to get what she wanted.

"Since I was five. But it became something of an obsession when I turned twelve."

"Why?"

Her gaze lowered. "That's when my parents and grandfather died. I went to live with my grandmother." Her eyes flew to his, like she couldn't believe she'd told him that.

Of course, Jack had looked her up and knew from the articles that her family died when their private plane crashed.

"I'm very sorry for your loss, Em."

Her eyes widened, perhaps at his use of a nickname. "Thank you. It was a long time ago."

"I'm still sorry."

After a few seconds of studying Jack, she asked, "Have you and Cooper—"

The bell above her store stopped her in her tracks, and she turned to look at the incoming customer.

Jack glanced over his shoulder, annoyed by the interruption and even more so by who'd caused it.

Dana.

Tall, slim, and tanned with an athletic body and sweet tits, Dana walked with a confidence that would've been sexy on any other woman. Jack understood from a purely visual perspective what Cooper saw in his wife. She had lots of silky, light brown hair and ice-blue eyes that tilted like a cat's. Perfect little nose and full, luscious lips. High cheekbones. Great skin.

She strutted across the store, her icy gaze flicking between Emery and Jack. He barely noticed what she was wearing. She was always showing off her figure in a summer dress that looked the same to him, if not for the variation in color.

"I thought it was you I saw as I was passing." She came to a stop at the counter, eyeing him and Emery with a narrow smile that didn't reach her eyes. "I'm Dana Lawson."

Emery shifted uncomfortably but nodded.

Dana raised a perfectly plucked eyebrow. "Do you speak?"

"Dana," Jack warned.

"It was just a question." She smirked at him. "I actually came in to ask if you like brisket, Jack. We bought a slow cooker and

Cooper was thinking of trying brisket for dinner this Thursday. He wanted to invite you."

"Yeah, sure."

Dana made no move to leave, even though Jack's look was pointed.

She pushed up off the counter. "I'll walk you to Coop's."

Realizing his progress with Emery had been well and truly blocked by his buddy's annoying wife, Jack sighed. He looked at Emery who watched them both with those intelligent eyes of hers. He handed her the money for the coffees.

"You have a great day, Emery." He gave her a small smile.

She returned it as she took the cash. "You too, Jack."

It was the first time she'd said his name.

And he would not lie—he felt it in his gut and his dick and in the sudden increase of his pulse.

The urge to shout "Fuck it!" and grab her by the nape so he could kiss the hell out of her was an almost uncontrollable itch beneath his skin. Instead, Jack swallowed the impulse, raised his coffee to her in salute, and walked out of the store with Dana trailing behind.

As soon as they were out on the boardwalk, Dana snorted. "Please tell me you weren't flirting with her."

At his silence, she huffed. "Jack, you can do so much better than a shy bookworm."

"I'm not going after Emery Saunders," he bit out as he yanked open the door to Cooper's. "You know I'm not the settling-down type."

Dana seemed satisfied. Too satisfied.

Lately, she'd been a little too concerned about who Jack had in his bed. It worried him.

The sight of Cooper coming around the bar to accept the coffee Jack held out, while wrapping an arm around Dana's waist, soothed him somewhat.

Dana snuggled into Cooper's side, smiling up at him like she actually did love him.

Maybe Jack was being paranoid about her.

He could blame growing up with Ian Devlin for that.

Cooper took a sip from his cup and sighed. "That girl can certainly make a good cup of coffee."

Dana snorted. "That's about all she can do. People think it's shyness, but I think maybe she's a little dumb."

Cooper rolled his eyes. "I doubt it."

"C'mon. I said hello and she just looked right through me."

"I think that's because she's the opposite of dumb." Jack turned heel and walked out before either of them could call him on his sly insult.

No one would say shit about Emery Saunders around him.

Ever.

4

EMERY

Seven years ago

AFTER WEEKS of Iris's not-so-subtle hinting about Hartwell's annual, midsummer music festival, I gave in and agreed to go.

I'd closed the store for the afternoon and walked along the boards toward Main Street. Passing Cooper's Bar, the building next to mine, I saw it was open, which probably meant the bar staff were running it. According to Iris, Cooper wasn't the type to miss out on town events.

Beside Cooper's was the Old Boardwalk Hotel, the largest and tallest building on the boardwalk. Built at the turn of the century, it was a red-brick building with small, white-framed windows. Every time I passed it, I marveled at its history but also thought it was sad there was no vantage point from any of the rooms to enjoy the spectacular ocean view.

The owner didn't live in Hartwell. He was a real estate mogul from Florida and relied on his staff to take care of the place. I'd been inside out of curiosity, and the slightly musty-smelling hotel needed a revamp.

Iris said Bailey's place, Hart's Inn, at the north end of the boards, was always fully booked because people would rather stay at her establishment before choosing the Old Boardwalk. I didn't blame them. The inn was a stunning New England–style home with white shingles, a wrap-around porch, and a widow's walk overlooking the water.

Next to the Old Boardwalk Hotel was George Beckwith's gift shop where he sold tacky souvenirs the vacationers loved. Beside his store sat Antonio's, which was open and would be managed by Ira today, since I was supposed to meet Iris on Main Street in ten minutes.

I passed the pizzeria, the surf shop, and Mr. Shickle's Ice Cream Shack and approached the bandstand at the top of Main.

A band was setting up under the covered stage. The town had hired several musical groups for the day while businesses set up stalls to sell everything from music memorabilia to jewelry.

A plaque on the bandstand spoke of the legend of Hartwell and explained to tourists why locals called it Hart's Boardwalk. Back in 1909, Bailey Hartwell's great-grandmother's sister Eliza was the darling of Hartwell. The founding family still had money and power, and Eliza, being the eldest, was expected to marry well. Instead, she crossed paths and fell in love with a steelworker from the Station Railroad Company based outside of town. Jonas Kellerman, Dana Kellerman Lawson's ancestor, was considered beneath Eliza—and a noted con artist. They were forbidden to marry.

Instead, Eliza was betrothed to the son of a wealthy businessman. On the eve of her wedding, a devastated Eliza walked into the ocean. By chance, Jonas was up on the boardwalk with friends, saw Eliza, and went in after her. Legend said he reached her, but the waves took them under, and they were never seen again. Jonas's sacrifice for his love was said to have created magic. For generations since the deaths of Eliza and Jonas, people born in Hartwell who met their husbands or wives on the boards stayed in love their whole lives. It told tourists that if they walked the boardwalk together and they were truly in love, it would last forever, no matter the odds.

As tragic as it was, I loved that the town was built on such a legend. It spoke to my romantic soul ... and may have factored into my decision to stay in Hartwell.

Staring out at bustling Main Street, at the crowds gathered around stalls, mingling and talking, I again wondered about my decision. Two years I'd been in Hartwell, and I'd still not made any progress in forming relationships with anyone beyond Iris Green.

And even then, I gave her only what I was comfortable with. Which wasn't a whole heck of a lot. Melancholy suffused me.

Time and perspective had taught me that my shyness no doubt originated from my parents' behavior. As a child, when I spoke to them, they ignored me, were obviously bored by me, or sometimes even belittled me. It got to the point where I didn't want to speak for fear of being mocked or considered insignificant. It was easier to be invisible than to have them *make* me feel invisible. I was shy with them because I cared what they thought of me.

At the opposite end of this behavior was the way I'd acted with the house staff, including my nanny. I was not shy with them. I was angry. In fact, sometimes I wasn't an amiable child at all. That happened when you were given everything you could ever want—except your parents' love and attention.

Neglected and ignored by the two people who were supposed to love me most, I took out my anger and frustration on the staff they'd surrounded me with.

I flinched.

They must have hated me.

Living with my grandmother changed all that. She wasn't the warmest person in the world, and she believed in class, status, and staying within your own station. While she thought our family superior over others, she also believed in treating everyone, including her staff, with the utmost respect. The first time she heard me snap at her housekeeper, my grandmother not only made me apologize in front of the entire estate staff but she made me stay in a guest room devoid of all entertainment. When I came home from school, I was allowed to do my homework and eat, but then I was sent to that room to languish from boredom for two weeks.

Strangely, I appreciated that my grandmother cared enough to teach me some manners.

I never spoke to a member of our household like that again. I grew shy with them instead as I began to care what they thought of me. And I cared what my grandmother thought of me.

As much as I loved my grandmother, she had not been an easy woman to live with. Beneath her hard exterior was a broken heart, and she was terrified of losing the only family she had left. So, I was *protected.* I wasn't permitted to do any extracurricular activities unless the lessons took place at the estate. No boyfriends, no school trips, no plans for college unless it was somewhere in New York State. She didn't even allow me to attend my debutante ball, something I knew my father had attended as an escort for my mother on her debut into society.

Being excluded from any semblance of a normal teen life made me an outsider with the kids at my private school. The mocking and bullying started, and, just like it'd been with my parents, I found it difficult to speak for fear of the response. So I withdrew into myself. I made no plans to attend college. No plans for any future at all.

Tripp Van Der Byl had only made things worse.

I threw him from my mind as soon as he entered it.

It had been three years since my grandmother's death, and I still didn't know how to break free of the wall of defense I'd built around myself when I was twelve.

The urge to turn around was strong, but I'd promised Iris I would meet her. Scanning the crowds, I finally spotted her by a stall, talking to two women I recognized.

Damn.

Behind the stall was a stunning brunette with smooth olive skin. She was short in stature with a beautiful, curvy figure.

Dahlia McGuire.

She'd smiled and said hello whenever we passed on the street, but I didn't know much about the young woman other than that she owned Hart's Gift Store next to Bailey's inn. Unlike George's place, Iris said Dahlia sold unique pieces, including the jewelry she crafted. I thought it was wonderful that Dahlia was a silversmith, and if I hadn't been avoiding townspeople and all their inevitable questions, I'd have investigated her store long before now.

I didn't want anyone to find out who my family was.

People treated you differently when they knew you were worth billions of dollars.

That's why I went by Emery Saunders. Emery was my middle name and Saunders was my mother's maiden name. Yes, it wouldn't take a genius to find out who I was (as proven by Ian Devlin), but the name Paxton would definitely draw attention.

If it had been up to me, I'd have sold the majority shares in the company back to the other shareholders, but I'd promised my grandmother I wouldn't. That promise weighed on me.

I didn't want the responsibility.

Moreover, the legacy of the Paxton Group had taken so much from me. The company had always been more important to my parents and grandfather. It meant a lot to my grandmother, but not as much as I did. Still, out of respect for her husband's hard work, my grandmother made me promise.

Feeling a flutter of nerves in my belly, I made my way to Iris once she caught sight of me and waved me over. Standing at Dahlia's stall with them was Bailey Hartwell.

Bailey was this larger-than-life character everyone seemed to adore. Her parents had recently retired and left the running of the inn to her, and according to Iris, Bailey was in seventh heaven.

The slender redhead was one of those women who became infinitely more attractive as you conversed with her. At first, she seemed like the girl next door with her peaches-and-cream complexion and the smattering of golden freckles across her nose and cheeks. However, once you spent time with Bailey, the "hometown girl" description seemed entirely too mundane. She was charismatic, friendly, outspoken, and had the most glamorous smile.

She was so outgoing, I found her more than a little intimidating. Mostly because Bailey had no filter and asked all the personal questions I wanted to avoid answering.

So, I avoided Bailey.

Until Iris coerced me into situations like these.

Dammit.

Muttering under my breath, I forced myself to keep walking.

"There you are!" Iris called out as I approached.

I gave her a pained smile, and she chuckled knowingly.

"Emery, hey!" Bailey peered past Iris's shoulder and beamed at me. "You came!"

I offered another pained smile. The wink of metal at the stall drew my eyes, however, and the jewelry on Dahlia's table monopolized my interest.

I stepped closer.

"Hey, I don't think we've been formally introduced."

I looked up from the jewelry. Dahlia held her hand out to

me. I noted she had an accent and remembered Iris telling me Dahlia was originally from Boston. I shook her hand. "Hello."

"I'm Dahlia."

"Emery." My attention returned to her jewelry.

She was very talented. I saw at least five pairs of earrings I wanted.

And I wanted all the rings.

"You like your silver, huh?"

Said silver bangles jangled on my wrist as I tucked my hair behind my ear.

My jewelry had been my only rebellion against my grandmother. She believed in pearls and diamond-stud earrings. Simple elegance.

I believed you could never wear too much jewelry. And when I turned eighteen, I embraced my own style.

Grandma used to curse the sound of my bangles jangling as I walked around the house, but secretly I think she appreciated my stubborn refusal to give up this stamp of identity. It was the one thing that was all mine.

I nodded.

"I thought we'd lose her to your jewelry as soon as she got here," Iris joked at my side.

"It's beautiful." I glanced shyly up at the gorgeous brunette. "You're very talented."

Dahlia beamed. "Hey, thanks."

"I'll take those." I pointed to a pair of long silver earrings sculpted like a teardrop with an amethyst stone clutched between silver prongs. And then the same design, but with jade. "Those too. And those. And … those. And all of these." I gestured to a row of beautifully hammered bangles that would look great as a set.

"Are you serious?" Dahlia asked.

"Yes."

"But … but that's like a thousand bucks' worth of stuff."

"Dahlia, why are you trying to talk the girl out of buying your jewelry?" Iris teased.

"Fine, fine. Thank you." Dahlia held out her hand to me again and I shook it, even though I was sure my skin was the color of a lobster.

"I had a feeling Emery would make a great customer." Bailey leaned against the table at my side as Dahlia gift wrapped all my selections. "You have a wonderful sense of style."

"Thanks," I muttered. I wasn't very adept at accepting compliments either.

Frustration bubbled inside me at my inability to converse like a normal person. At my inability to feel comfortable in social situations.

I wanted to leave.

I wanted to take my new jewelry and leave so badly, it was a physical pain.

"Hey, Coop!"

I flinched at Bailey's loud yell and kept my eyes trained on Dahlia as she worked.

Cooper Lawson made me nervous. Not as much as Jack did, but Jack made me nervous in a different way. Bizarrely, I actually liked the way Jack made me feel.

Cooper just made me want to hide behind my bookshelves.

He grimaced every time I blushed, which just made me blush harder out of sheer self-directed frustration.

I made him uncomfortable. He made me uncomfortable. Therefore, I preferred avoiding him.

And his catty little wife.

I did not like how Dana Lawson stared at Jack when she'd interrupted us in my store a few weeks ago. She'd looked at him with the possessiveness of a girlfriend, and that made me uneasy, considering she was his best friend's wife.

Handing my credit card to Dahlia, I hoped to keep my back

to Cooper but hearing his voice grow closer, I knew it would be unforgivably rude for me to do so.

Clasping tightly to the bag now weighed down by my exciting purchases, I stepped to the side of the stall and turned to look at the new additions.

Cooper was holding his nephew Joseph in his arms while his sister Cat stood at his side. I hadn't been around for the gossip that spread through town when Catriona Lawson got pregnant. Iris told me all about it and what a tough time Cat had dealing with it. She'd been in college and returned home for summer vacation her junior year. Rumor was, she had a one-night stand with a tourist whose name she couldn't even remember, and nine months later, Joseph "Joey" Cooper Lawson came along.

Watching Cooper dote on his three-year-old nephew was one reason I wished I could act like a normal person around him. Everyone seemed to love the guy, which meant he was probably a wonderful man.

But he was the kind of handsome that flustered me.

Cat shared Cooper's coloring, and there was no denying the relation. She seemed equally uncomfortable in my presence.

As Bailey took Joey from Cooper's arms and said something that made him giggle, I felt a rush of envy as the group chatted easily. Like always, I was an outsider.

Then Cat stepped forward and held out her hand. "It's been awhile. I'm Cat, remember?"

It was nice of her to reintroduce herself, but it was also a terrible reminder that after two years of living in Hartwell, I'd had so few interactions with her.

Trying not to berate myself into an agitated puddle of mush, I shook her hand. "Emery."

She gave me an uncomfortable smile. "Nice to see you here."

"Emery just nearly bought out Dahlia's entire store."

"That doesn't surprise me." Cooper surprised *me* by offering a teasing smile.

I wanted to say something funny and cute in response. My brain tripped over itself trying to find the words, and an awkward silence prevailed.

Cooper cleared his throat and reached for Joey, taking him from Bailey's arms. "Well, we said we'd meet Dana at some stall. She's got her eye on a purse she likes."

Everyone said goodbye, including Joey who kept yelling, "Bye, bye, Bail-Bail!" as Cooper carried him away. I felt awful for chasing them off.

I threw Iris a pleading look. *Please let me leave.*

She patted my arm in sympathy but gave a slight shake of her head and a "you can do this" expression. Iris, Bailey, and Dahlia chatted about the bands that were playing this year, and I tried to look like I was listening when really, I was plotting my escape.

As I glanced from them to the crowds enjoying the festival, my attention snagged on a particular someone.

Someone who made my heart beat fast.

At his height, Jack was easy to spot.

And he was talking to Cooper and holding Joey.

My stomach flipped at the sight of him holding Joey above his head and blowing raspberries on his tummy, making the toddler squeal with delighted laughter. He kicked out his legs, almost catching Jack on the chin.

"Well, if I wasn't already in love with Tom, I'd be transferring my old crush on Cooper to Jack Devlin right about now," Bailey said dryly, and I noted her eyes were on Jack too. "That man looks good with a kid in his arms."

"That man just looks good, period," Dahlia opined. "I curse his no-locals rule."

Realizing Dahlia meant she'd sleep with him if he didn't have a rule against sleeping with local women, a spike of awful jealousy sliced through me.

That jealousy only grew as Jack handed Joey back to Cooper

and slipped his arms around a woman I hadn't even noticed. I didn't recognize her. She was a tourist, a tall brunette with enormous boobs and a tiny waist.

So that was his type.

That wasn't crushing.

Okay, I lied. It was unbelievably crushing.

As Cooper, Cat, and Joey strolled away, Jack turned to the brunette and murmured something in her ear as he held her by the hips.

And then he kissed her.

Not just a mere brush across the lips.

But a kiss.

Devastation that was way out of proportion to the moment crashed over me. Iris had told me about Jack and his tourist conquests.

However, this was the first time I was seeing one live in front of me.

I felt betrayed.

Which made no sense at all.

"Lucky lady," Bailey said at my side.

I was transfixed by the scene that hurt so much to look at.

When Jack broke the kiss, smiling as he tucked the woman into his side and turned, our eyes locked as he lifted his head. He seemed to pause, the smile abruptly leaving his face as we stared at each other.

Yanking my gaze away from his, the first one I met was Bailey Hartwell's.

And she was examining me like she could see into my head.

Like she knew I had a massive crush on Jack Devlin and the news delighted her.

This … this was why I avoided Bailey Hartwell. She was nosy.

"I have to go," I muttered. "Sorry, Iris." I brushed past her and hurried through the crowds.

My heart beat triple time as I marched down the boardwalk toward my beach house.

I wanted to cry.

It was foolish and childish and made no sense.

But the image of Jack kissing that woman how he did … yeah. It made me want to cry.

With significant effort, I sucked back the tears and let myself into my house. Hidden inside, I made myself a cup of peppermint tea and opened all the jewelry boxes to appreciate Dahlia's work.

In another life, she and I would be friends. She'd maybe even let me watch her work because I'd love to see that.

In another life, I wouldn't blush like an idiot every time Cooper Lawson spoke to me.

In another life, I'd be sophisticated and witty and Jack Devlin wouldn't be able to resist me, local woman or not.

"In another life," I whispered to myself.

5

JACK

Five years ago

How did you tell your best friend that his wife grabbed your dick?

Jack's heart raced hard.

Not even the sound of the waves gently lapping the shore could calm him as he gazed out at the water from the sand-encrusted boards.

An hour ago, Dana had called Jack to tell him she was concerned about Cooper and could he come over. That they needed to talk. The last person Jack ever wanted to talk to was Dana, but he was worried about Cooper too.

His friend had been closed off lately. Worried about something. And whenever Jack tried to talk to him about it, he blew him off. Hoping Dana might have some insight, and relieved that she cared enough about her husband to call his best friend, Jack had gone to her.

She started with the crocodile tears. They were having problems getting pregnant and Cooper was taking it out on her. As soon as she said that, Jack knew she was up to something. There was no way Cooper would blame his woman for that shit. How stupid did Dana think Jack was? Knowing something was definitely wrong, he moved to leave. She stood in his path and then to his horror she grabbed his dick and tried to massage it through his jeans.

Furious, he pushed her off and stormed out of the house.

And now … now he had to explain this shit to his best friend and hope Cooper believed him.

"He'll believe me," Jack muttered to himself, knowing it was true. But it was messed up either way because Cooper was the one who would be hurt.

Dana Fucking Kellerman.

It was the one instance Jack hated that his instincts about that woman had been on point.

He took a deep breath and pushed away from the railing. The bar would close soon. Jack needed to tell Cooper and get it over with.

A flickèr of white on the beach drew Jack's attention, however, and he grew still at the sight of the tall figure walking along the shoreline in the dark. The moonlight gleamed across her hair and the white sweater she wore. She held it closed with her arms wrapped around her waist.

Emery Saunders.

His heart changed beat for a different reason.

Without thinking, his feet were moving him in her direction. Perhaps it was procrastination at its finest. Or perhaps she'd shown up just when he needed her to.

Four years, he thought as he hurried down the beach to her, sand getting in his shoes. He didn't care about the sand. Emery had lived in Hartwell for four years and in that time, she'd kept to herself. As far as he was aware, the bookstore and coffeehouse owner had no friends, no family, and no interests beyond the store.

Jack had tried to get over whatever it was that pulled him in Emery's direction, but as the years passed, it had gotten harder to ignore what she made him feel. He didn't know her and she made him *feel*.

He still went nearly every morning to her store to buy a coffee to start his day. Sure, she made the best coffee in town, but he went out of his way for one because he got to see her blush at him every day. Four years and she still blushed at him. He loved when the pink stained her cheeks anytime he smiled at her. And that sweet smile she gave him in return. The way she'd flush redder when he deliberately touched his fingers to hers when he took the coffee. Jack wondered if she felt the tingles rush up her arm the same way he did.

After that moment at the music festival two years ago, when Emery saw him with the tourist whose name he was ashamed to say he couldn't even remember now, the progress he'd made with Em halted. He'd watched her hurry away after seeing him with that woman and for some stupid reason, he'd felt like a jackass. Like a guy who had just cheated on his girl. It made no sense. But he got the distinct impression he'd hurt Emery's feelings that day. Maybe he just wanted to believe that.

He told himself that was just wishful thinking.

Until he went in for coffee the following Monday and she would not look at him. Sure, she blushed, but she didn't respond to his questions and not once did she make eye contact.

That went on for weeks.

Wearing on Jack's nerves.

Yet he was a masochist who just kept going back for more.

Until eventually, she talked to him again. Two years later, he reckoned he was about the only one other than Iris who could get an actual conversation out of Emery Saunders. And she was cute and funny when she let her guard down.

It made him want to unwrap her slowly, find out what else went on in that mind of hers. Stephen Hawking once said the quietest people had the loudest minds. Jack suspected that of Emery. He suspected there was lots of fantastic stuff to discover about her.

"It's late," he said as he approached her.

Emery startled from her spot on the shore.

His eyes flickered down her body, and he swallowed hard. She usually wore long dresses or jeans and tops with lots of fabric on the arms. Not tonight. Tonight, she wore pajama shorts beneath her oversized sweater and Jack glimpsed her gorgeous long legs for the first time.

Jesus Fucking Christ.

Of course, she had the finest pair of legs he'd ever seen.

Everything about the woman was made specially to torment him.

Jack came to a stop beside her. Emery was tall for a woman, but he still had to look down at her. She stared up at him, a little wide-eyed, swallowed hard, and looked out at the ocean.

"You okay?" he asked.

She nodded, tucking a loose strand of her beautiful hair behind her ear. Silver rings sat on nearly every one of her fingers and long silver earrings hung from her ears. They were accompanied by two more piercings—little diamond studs that winked in the moonlight.

The woman was always jingling and jangling with jewelry.

Jack still imagined the sound of her jewelry making their song for a whole different reason—with every thrust of his body into hers.

Arousal flushed through him and he cursed inwardly. Every time he was around her, he felt like a fourteen-year-old boy with no control over his hormones. Jack looked away, watching the calm ripple of the waves.

"Are you okay?" Her soft voice filled the space between them, causing his skin to prickle with awareness.

He answered honestly. "No, I'm not okay."

"Oh." He could feel her looking at him, so he turned to meet her gaze. That ache in his chest only she caused made itself known. "Can I ... help?" she asked.

It seemed to take a lot for her to ask him. Jack turned his body toward her. "If ... if ... okay ..." He blew out air between his lips. "Say you have this friend. A good friend. And this friend has a husband."

Emery nodded. It felt good to be the recipient of her undivided attention and focus. "So say you have this friend, and her husband—who you've made it clear to your friend that you don't trust or like—makes a pass at you."

Her eyes widened slightly, and she gave him a gentle nod to continue.

"You tell your friend, right? You tell her what he did? Even if she blames you for it?"

To his shock and pleasure, Emery placed a hand on his arm. Her brow creased with concern. "Yes, Jack. You need to tell him. Cooper. You should tell him if Dana did that."

A huff of dry laughter escaped him. Not because what she said was funny, but because he realized then that Emery paid a lot more attention than people thought.

She winced and dropped her hand, moving to retreat.

Jack reached for her, taking hold of her slim biceps to stop her. "No, I'm not laughing *at* you. I just ... I guess I shouldn't be surprised that you see a lot more than you let on."

Her eyes lowered, and not for the first time, Jack marveled at the length of her eyelashes. "People assume things about me."

"It's hard for them to do anything but assume if you won't befriend them," he told her gently.

"I don't make friends easily. I told you that. I find it hard to converse with people I don't know very well."

"I get that." Jack stepped closer until their bodies almost brushed. "But you seem to be able to talk to me. We practiced. And here we are."

Emery studied his face for a second, her focus so intense, Jack's heart hammered harder in his chest. "It wasn't just practice. It's your eyes. You have the kindest eyes I've ever seen."

Fuck, but he wanted to kiss her so badly.

"Emery …" His voice was hoarse with that want.

She seemed to sense the change in him and instead of pulling away, she swayed a little closer.

For four years, he'd convinced himself he couldn't have this woman because of his father's machinations. But Ian Devlin hadn't so much as lifted a finger against Emery Saunders, and Jack suspected that was because she had way too much money and influence, too many connections for it to be smart.

Which meant … maybe … maybe she wasn't entirely out of Jack's reach after all.

He was so sick and tired of wanting this woman. He thought it would go away. That he'd get over her. But he couldn't. So why wasn't he making his move?

"Jack, it'll be all right," she promised. "I've seen how you and Cooper are, and Iris talks about you both all the time. I know you're closer to him than you are to your own brothers. Cooper will believe you. It'll hurt him … but he'll be grateful for the truth in the end. He deserves better than a wife who would try to cheat on him with his best friend."

It was the most he'd ever heard her say.

And she said it with passion. Concern. Like she cared.

Yeah, Jack was done waiting to have what he'd fucking pined for, for four very long years.

"Em," he said, loosening his grip on her biceps and smoothing his hand down her arm until he held her hand.

She looked down at their clasped hands, her eyebrows raised.

"Em … I'd like to take you out. On a date."

Her eyes flew to his, lips parted with surprise. "You? A … a date?"

Hearing the disbelief in her voice, he almost growled in frustration. He cursed that day at the music festival. She thought he was a player.

Okay, he wasn't exactly *not* a player.

But not with her.

She was all he could see.

"No fucking around," he promised. "I mean a real date. To be followed by another. And another and another …" Until there was no doubt in anyone's mind that Emery Saunders belonged to Jack Devlin and Jack Devlin belonged to her.

His pulse raced with excitement at the thought.

He could tell he'd shocked her.

She tugged on his hand and he tightened his grip.

"I would never hurt you." He made his second promise.

Taking a shuddering breath, Emery studied him again, gazing deeply into his eyes, as if she could unearth all his secrets. She could. She had that power over him. Then, just as he worried her shyness would ruin any chance between them, her lips twitched just a little. An almost smile.

I want to make her laugh, he thought. Jack had never heard her laughter, and he wanted to more than anything else.

"Okay."

Euphoria flooded him. "Okay?"

This time she grinned, and he saw the pink stain her cheeks. "Yes, I'll go on a date with you, Jack Devlin."

He wanted to kiss her. He wanted to haul her into his arms so badly and kiss the breath out of her … but he stopped himself.

It had to be slow.

Jack had to prove to her that he wanted more than just her gorgeous body.

He wanted everything from Emery.

Jack trusted his instincts. He knew he'd never meet a purer heart than the one that belonged to this beautiful woman.

Her goodness shone out of her.

She was an angel.

She was a beautiful sunrise dawning on a hope-filled new day.

Christ, this woman was turning him into a fucking poet. And a bad one at that. He smirked inwardly to himself.

Jack squeezed her hand and gently released it. "Friday night. I'll pick you up from your beach house at 7:00 p.m. There's this great seafood place about twenty minutes down the coast. We'll have more privacy there. That work for you?"

She bit her bottom lip, looking so shy and adorable he wanted to kiss the shyness right out of her. She nodded, seemingly trying not to smile too hard.

Jack smiled hard enough for the two of them. "Good. Great. It's a date."

Emery nodded again.

"Have I stolen your ability to speak?" he teased.

She nodded.

Jack laughed, disbelieving she could make him feel this good when his gut was in turmoil.

Emery smiled.

They studied one another for a tension-filled time.

Jack regretfully took a step back. "I better go. I need to go talk to Cooper."

"Good luck, Jack. And remember …" She started walking backward in the direction of her house. "Trust in him."

"I will, sunrise." The endearment slipped out before he could think on the wisdom of being so familiar with her.

"Sorry?" she squinted at him in confusion.

"Sunrise," he repeated. "That's what you remind me of."

To his relief, Emery seemed to understand his sentiment without explanation. The surprised but soft expression on her face suggested she liked it. As did the way she ducked her head bashfully before giving him a little wave. Jack watched her turn on her heel to walk home.

He watched her for a while.

Then, with a shuddering sigh, he made his way up the beach to the boardwalk. At least he knew he had something to look forward to beyond the gut-wrenching task of telling Cooper about Dana.

Feeling more nauseated the closer he grew to the bar, Jack's irritation increased as his cell rang in the back pocket of his jeans. He took it out and saw it was Rebecca.

It was late for a call from his little sister.

"Becs, what's up?" he asked, coming to a stop outside the bar.

"It's not your sister. It's your father." Ian's brittle voice sent an icy shiver down Jack's spine.

"Where's Becs?"

"Something's happened. Your sister is in serious trouble. I need you at the house."

Trepidation filled him. "Is she okay?"

"Just get to the house." Ian hung up.

Jack threw the bar a regretful look and jogged down the boards to Main Street where he'd parked his car.

The truth about Dana would have to wait.

6

EMERY

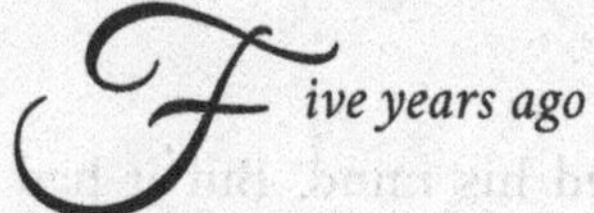

ive years ago

Not for the first time in my life, I felt like a naive fool.

Jack Devlin hadn't shown up to take me on that date he'd promised. I'd sat on my porch swing overlooking the water, waiting. And waiting.

At fifteen minutes past seven, I wondered if he was late because of work.

At seven thirty, I wondered if we shouldn't have exchanged phone numbers.

But by eight o'clock, I knew I'd been stood up.

Maybe I was wrong about Jack.

Maybe his kind eyes were a trap.

Maybe it had been like that time at Daltry Prep when Lucinda Weymouth told me she'd set me up on a date with her brother, Logan, who was a beautiful senior boy I'd crushed on forever. When I'd risked my grandmother's wrath and snuck out of the estate to go meet him, Logan, Lucinda, and their friends did an egging drive-by on me. They literally threw eggs at me as they drove by in their expensive SUV. Apparently, they'd gotten the idea from some teen movie.

It was not only humiliating but I was covered in bruises from those goddamn eggs. Getting hit with an egg when the thrower was on the rowing team hurt like a mother. In more ways than one.

The prank had been the talk of the school for weeks.

Plus, I'd had to return home covered in egg yolk and my grandmother officially grounded me for a month. It seemed pointless to ground me. My entire life was one big grounding.

Was Jack playing a cruel joke on me by asking me out and then standing me up?

That didn't seem like him.

There was a possibility he'd changed his mind. But it had been almost a week since he stood me up, and I hadn't seen or heard from him. He usually came in for his coffee every morning.

Jack was definitely avoiding me.

I cursed the flush of heat that crawled across my skin at the thought and said goodbye to a customer who'd bought an entire pile of beach reads.

Sighing as the bell tinkled above the door announcing her departure, I rested my elbows on the counter and stared unseeingly at the stacks of books opposite my coffee counter.

For four years, I'd watched Jack Devlin from afar, and my stupid crush had only intensified. I'd often wondered what it was that I found so attractive about him. I mean, of course, Jack was handsome, but it was more than that. When I talked to him, he went from handsome to the sexiest man I'd ever met. He just had that thing. That je ne sais quoi. He brimmed over with charisma and a genuine charm.

Not that disingenuous, smooth kind of charm like I'd encountered before with Tripp Van Der Byl and only realized was disingenuous after the fact.

Perhaps what fascinated me about Jack had more to do with my own feelings than Jack himself. Until I moved here and met the black sheep of the Devlin family, I'd honestly thought something had broken inside me. That Tripp had broken something. He seemed to have hit the kill switch on my attraction for men. I felt nothing. Zip. Zero. Nada.

Until Jack.

Suddenly, everything was zinging in all the right places again.

No way did I think I'd ever have the courage to agree to a date with him.

But I couldn't help myself. There was something about Jack that made me want to be brave.

Silly of me, really. I'd confused the town's love for him as something I could trust over the fact that for four years, I'd watched in painful longing as he made his way through a smorgasbord of female tourists. Jack was *not* the settling-down type, no matter what he somewhat promised me on the beach ten days ago.

God, I wished I could stop thinking about him.

Someone who stood me up and then didn't tell me why was not worth wasting thought and energy on.

The bell above my door tinkled and I straightened off the counter, a warm, welcoming smile prodding my lips as Iris Green stepped inside the store.

"Hey."

"Hey, sweet girl." Iris came to a stop at the counter. "Ira is in the mood for one of your lattes today. I'll have one too."

Noting the crease between her brow and the preoccupied way she avoided my gaze, concern hit me. "Are you okay?"

Her eyes flew to me. She studied me a moment. "Did you hear?"

"Hear what?"

"Jack handed over his company to Ray English. Just handed it over." She threw her hands in the air, frustration furrowing her brow. "Who does that? And what's worse … he's gone to work for his old man. Ian Devlin. Jack hates Ian!"

Despite my lack of friends in town, Iris had filled me in on the social dynamics of everyone as the years passed. And I people watched. A lot. I felt like I knew everyone, even though we rarely talked.

I turned away to make Iris's and Ira's coffees.

"And he won't talk to me about why. He won't even tell Cooper! And moody! That boy has never been ill-tempered with me in his life and he actually told me to back off. And he used the F-word. I thought Cooper would swing at him for that one. No, something not good is happening with Jack. Something very not good."

My breath caught.

Was this "something not good" the reason he'd stood me up?

Ugh.

That's incredibly self-involved, Em.

"What do you think is going on?"

"Don't know." Iris sighed heavily. "But I'm worried about him."

I slid the coffees across the counter and waved off her attempt to pay me. "Free coffee for life, remember?"

She gave me a sad, soft smile. "You're a good girl." She shook her head. "You know, I once had hopes for you and Jack. Stupid thought. Even more stupid now that he's acting like a jack*ass*."

I blushed at the notion of Iris attempting to match me and Jack and changed the subject. "I'm sure there's a reason for his behavior."

"I'm sure you're right. I'll just need to keep pushing. Ivy always said, the worst thing about having me as a mom is that I'm like a dog with a bone when I think something's going on I should know about."

I laughed. "I don't think that's a bad way to parent."

Iris patted me on the arm. "Thanks, sweetheart. Okay, I'm off. We're still on for dinner Sunday night, right?"

"I'll be there," I promised.

Once Iris left the store, I let my mind reel.

What on earth was going on with Jack? If something was wrong ... should I be brave? Perhaps approach him to see if I could be of help?

BY THE TIME I gathered enough courage to approach Jack, it was too late.

One Friday, a month after my talk with Iris, the news was all over town.

Cooper Lawson had caught Jack and Dana having sex on his couch. I couldn't process how the man who'd come to me for advice could then cheat on his best friend with his wife!

None of it made sense.

Cooper was devastated, and my heart hurt for him.

Everyone shunned Jack and Dana.

Iris was heartbroken and sure that something had happened to Jack to make him do this.

I wanted to believe that. I did.

For a while, *both* Iris and I did.

She suspected that even Cooper hoped for an explanation. However, more months passed, and more ...

And Jack got further away from who he used to be until we all started to forget.

Now he was just another one of the Devlins.

Not to be trusted.

And I couldn't understand why that hurt so much more than it should, considering we'd never even had that first date.

7

JACK

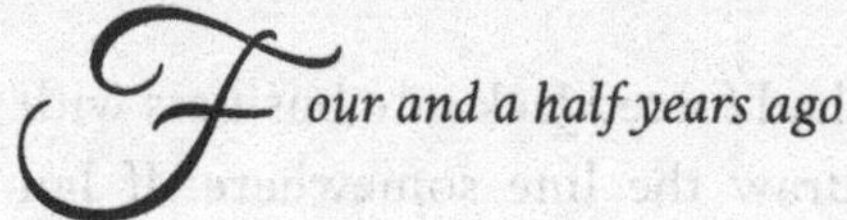

Four and a half years ago

LIFE FOR JACK was a daily exercise in going through the motions, compartmentalizing the shit he knew about Ian's dodgy business dealings, and the sour attitude of people who'd known him his whole life. Everyone hated him for betraying Cooper.

Jack despised himself.

Some nights he closed his eyes and all he could see was the look on Cooper's face when he walked into the house and caught Jack thrusting into Dana.

He hadn't even wanted her.

But he'd taken what she offered and poured all his frustrations into hate sex.

Rationally, he knew it was for the best.

But it didn't mean it didn't fucking hurt. It was like grief. Every day was moving through the weighted fog of mourning.

Jack grieved for the guy he used to be. However, he mourned Cooper more.

His cell was connected to his car and it rang, jerking Jack out of his heavy thoughts. Ian's name showed on the screen and he sighed, hitting the answer button on the steering wheel. "What is it?"

"Good morning to you too."

Jack didn't respond.

Ian sighed. "I'm just checking you're on your way to Bill Succoth's place in Millton."

"Yup. I'm on my way to drop off the contract."

"Do it with a gentle reminder."

"I will fucking not."

Ian sighed again.

Events beyond his control had forced Jack into business with his father, but Jack had to draw the line somewhere. If Ian wanted to blackmail people into doing business with him, he could get Stu or Kerr to do that shit for him. Jack would play errand boy, but he wasn't blackmailing anyone.

Bill Succoth owned a catering company in Sussex County. He catered to businesses all over, to great success. Ian Devlin wanted Bill to make sandwiches and snacks to be sold at a bakery he'd bought in Aspen Meadows. But Ian didn't want to pay what everyone else was paying. So, he had Kerr follow the poor guy, discover he was cheating on his wife with a pretty young thing in Essex, and used photographic evidence to blackmail Bill into catering at a discounted rate. And by discounted rate, Ian had barely left any room for the guy to make a profit. It was repulsive.

Just one of many repulsive ways Ian Devlin ran his business.

"Fine. Just get that contract signed."

Jack hung up before Ian because it gave him a small satisfaction to hang up on his father. He needed to find those moments wherever he could these days.

Parking his car in the lot behind Bill Succoth's kitchen, Jack grabbed the contract and got out to knock on the rear entry door. It had gotten easier over the last few months to be the cold son of a bitch he needed to be. Because he was frozen. Through and through.

"Oh, it's you." Bill glared at Jack as he pushed open the back door to the kitchen.

Jack held up the contract.

Without a word, Bill gestured him inside. Jack ignored the two other people in the kitchen preparing food. He waited in the doorway as Bill washed his hands and strolled back to Jack. He held out the papers to the man, along with a pen.

Bill snatched them out of his hand and placed the paper on the door beside Jack to lean on it. As he signed, he muttered under his breath, "You and your entire family are bottom-feeding scum, you know that, right?"

Jack didn't flinch. He was way past used to this kind of disdain.

Bill huffed as he handed over the signed contract. "If you were my only business, you'd cripple me with this contract."

He waited patiently for the man to move aside.

"Nothing to say?"

"I think all that needs to be said has been said. Now move out of my way."

"Cold son of a bitch," Bill murmured, stepping aside to let Jack out.

The kitchen door slammed behind him, and Jack drew a deep breath. As he did, a flash of blond hair across the street caught his eye.

He tensed at the sight of Emery Saunders marching down the street. She wore a long coat over what looked like a cream dress, a big blue scarf wrapped around her neck. The tails trailed behind her as she strode with purpose. She disappeared into a brown stucco building before he could have his fill of looking at her.

Emery.

Jack's pulse picked up and suddenly his feet were moving in that direction.

What was Emery doing in Millton on a Monday morning? Why wasn't she at the bookstore? Having avoided her the last six months, Jack didn't know what she was up to these days. He'd barely seen her around town, catching one or two glimpses of her now and then. Glimpses that made him feel temporarily warm and alive.

As he approached the building, he noticed the signage and frowned.

BALANCE: Counseling Center for Children and Adults.

What the hell?

Blood pumping for the first time in months, Jack wrenched the door open and stepped inside the building. It was toasty, making his cold cheeks flush warm. The reception area was empty except for a young man behind a desk whose eyes were glued to the pages of the paperback in his hands. Jack ignored him and strode down the wide hall in search of Em.

A burst of laughter brought his attention to double doors at the end of the corridor. Stopping outside, he peered in through the glass panes and he zeroed in on her. She'd taken off her coat and scarf and was lowered to her haunches in front of a young boy of about seven or eight years old.

Emery beamed that beautiful smile as she talked, and the boy burst into laughter.

Other kids approached her. Awe moved through Jack as he watched her engage with the kids in a way he'd never seen from her. She was like a totally different person, and the kids seemed to gravitate to her, even though she wasn't the only adult in the room.

"Uh, can I help you?"

Jack startled at the voice and turned to find the young man from reception standing next to him.

He hadn't even heard him approach, he'd been so focused on Em. "What is this?" he pointed to the room.

The young man frowned. "Why?"

Jack glowered fiercely at him.

A flicker of unease moved over the guy's face, and he swallowed hard. "Well, uh, it's a playgroup for children who either have cancer or have loved ones who have or are dying from cancer. It's a form of therapy and togetherness but in a normalized environment."

"And why is Emery here?"

"You know Emery?" The guy's entire face brightened at her name. "Oh, she's one of our volunteers. She's a total sweetheart. Comes every Monday morning to play with the kids. They love her."

The information moved through Jack in a painful ache as he turned to watch her.

It was like losing his chance with her all over again.

He mourned her.

He mourned her and what could have been.

But this … this evidence of her goodness just reminded him how far out of his reach Emery Saunders had become.

Jack's chest tightened. It was too tight. His skin too.

Without another word, he marched out of the building. He sucked in a giant gulp of crisp, chilly air and rested his hands on his hips as he tried to get himself together.

He was shaking, for Christ's sake.

Glaring across the street at the fancy car he now drove, Jack tried to force himself to move toward it. There was no reason to stay. There was no reason to engage in conversation with her. That's what he told himself.

Yet, he couldn't move.

Jack stood outside that building for an hour until people,

presumably parents and guardians, arrived to pick up their kids. Most of them came back out not long later with children in tow.

Then she was there.

She stepped outside as she wound her scarf around her neck. He watched as she moved to the side, her mind elsewhere, and pulled her long hair out from underneath the scarf. It fell down her back in thick, silky waves and slim braids, and Jack imagined for the millionth time what it would feel like to run his fingers through her hair.

"Emery."

Her head jerked in his direction, her expression one of surprise.

But for the first time since he'd known her, Emery didn't blush upon seeing him.

Her surprise turned to utter blankness.

And that fucking killed him.

"Jack." She nodded at him.

And then walked right by him.

As if he didn't exist.

As if he hadn't waited for over an hour just to see her.

But what else had he expected?

He'd stood her up and then weeks later screwed his best friend's wife.

Jack turned to watch Emery walk away.

It hurt.

It hurt a fucking lot.

Good.

It's only what I deserve.

Taking a deep breath, Jack turned from watching Emery and strode across the street to the fancy car he hated. He got in, making sure not to wrinkle the fancy suit he hated, and he drove back to South Hartwell to the fancy house he hated.

By the time he got there, he felt nothing but cold again.

8

EMERY

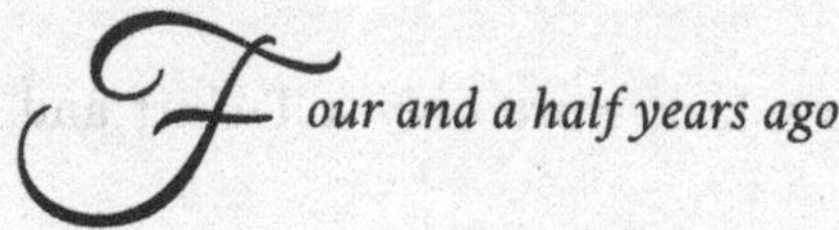

Four and a half years ago

THERE WERE many advantages to owning a beach house, but that morning, it was seeing Jack running along the shore.

Two days ago, when we'd acknowledged each other's presence outside the counseling building where I volunteered with the kids, my hurt manifested into coldness that I regretted as soon as I got into my car. Ahmad, the receptionist, had said a guy was in asking for me at the beginning of the playgroup, but it wasn't until I reached my car that I realized it must've been Jack.

Jack had waited outside that building for an hour for me.

Why? I didn't know.

I knew I had every reason to be mad at him … but when he looked at me with those soulful, sad eyes, a voice inside told me something was not right. Iris had said it months ago, before Jack cheated with Dana.

But I'd let my hurt control my response outside the building.

Now, seeing his expression in my mind over and over again, the guilt ate at me.

What if something had happened? What if Jack needed someone to talk to?

Was I a fool to even offer him that kind of compassion or benefit of the doubt?

All questions fled as soon as I saw him running past my house.

I moved.

I slid my coffee cup onto the porch table, kicked off my fuzzy slippers, and hurried down the steps and through the private gate that offered beach access. It was winter in Delaware, so I was wearing thermal pajamas and an oversized knit sweater.

It mildly concerned me that Jack wore only a T-shirt and jogging pants.

But he was running, so I guess he was warm.

"Jack!" I called, struggling through the sand in my cold, bare feet.

He kept going.

Dammit.

"Jack!" I yelled louder.

This time he glanced back over his shoulder. Catching sight of me, he stopped and turned to me. I hurried as fast as I could, despite the obstructive sand.

"How do you do this every day?" I huffed as I approached him.

Although his eyes moved over my face, there was a cool blankness in them I didn't like.

Moreover, his hair was beautifully disheveled, a flush rested high on his cheeks, and I was desperately trying not to stare at his corded throat or muscular forearms or basically any part of his profoundly attractive physique.

Which meant there was nowhere I could look that didn't

make me blush.

And quite abruptly, the blankness melted from his expression and something warm moved through him.

I relaxed a little.

"Em, what are you doing out here in your pajamas?"

I ignored the flutter in my belly at the nickname. "I came to apologize."

Just like that, his expression grew stony. "Not necessary."

"But I was—"

"Em, leave it." He turned to go.

And even more abruptly, I was mad. I'd trusted him enough to approach him despite his past behavior. "You know how hard this is for me?"

Jack halted and heaved a sigh. He glanced back, frowning. "Em, you don't owe me anything."

"No, but you owe me." I surprised myself.

I think I surprised him too.

Jack wiped the sweat off his forehead with his arm, and I tried not to notice the way his T-shirt rose, revealing a flash of hard abs. My eyes darted upward and my cheeks prickled with heat against the icy ocean breeze.

Jack's lips twitched with amusement, which was better than the coldness, so I'd take it.

"I'm sorry I was rude to you in Millton."

He shrugged. "I understood why."

"It doesn't excuse my behavior."

"It actually does." He shook his head at me. "Em, you're too good for your own good."

Despite what sounded like a warning in his words, I took another step toward him. A flicker of wariness crossed his face, but I boldly took another step until we were almost touching.

"Will you tell me why you stood me up?" This man made me inexplicably brave. I wished whatever it was about him that made me feel stronger could be bottled so I could have it with me through the rest of my life.

Jack's eyes searched mine before moving down my face to my lips and then back to my eyes. "I wish I could, sunrise."

There was that endearment again.

I reminded him of the sunrise. It was probably the best compliment anyone had ever given me. Sweet and surprisingly poetic from Jack.

"You can't tell me or you won't tell me?"

"I can't tell you."

Hmm. What on earth had happened?

"You can always talk to me, Jack," I offered. "I'm a vault."

He chuckled unhappily, and the sound hurt my heart. "Why do you assume I have anything I need to talk about?"

"Because I don't believe you just decided to join your father's company and betray your best friend for the hell of it."

The muscle in his jaw ticked. "Well, you'd be the only one."

"I don't think that's true. But"—I bravely placed a hand on his arm, feeling a tingle in my fingers at the connection—"the longer this goes on, the less likely people are to forgive you."

Jack abruptly stepped away from me, his expression shutting down. "I'm not asking for forgiveness."

I deflated.

Embarrassment held me frozen as he turned and walked away.

What a stupid woman I was to assume that I could coax the truth out of Jack when no one else could.

I was about to retreat to my house when Jack stopped and spun back around. He marched through the sand, a fierce expression on his face. And my heart leapt into my throat when I realized he wasn't slowing down as he came at me.

Then he was there, reaching for me, one hand clasping my nape in a demanding grip as he hauled me against him. His mouth captured mine as his other arm wrapped around my waist. My breasts crushed against his chest.

And he kissed me.

It was no simple brush of his lips across mine.

It wasn't anything like the kiss I'd seen him give that tourist two and a half years ago.

This was the hungriest kiss I'd ever experienced in my life.

Jack's tongue swept over mine in a dance that consumed. His kiss was deep. Thorough. I could taste coffee on his tongue. And his mouth was hot. So hot, his kiss scorched me from the inside out. I wanted more. I wanted everything. I kissed him back in open invitation, my fingers biting into his shoulders as I pushed into his mouth for more. His grip bruised as his groan vibrated down my throat, and I swear I felt seconds from fainting.

He was hard against my stomach and I whimpered, my lower body melting against him in mutual need.

Then, just as suddenly as he'd pulled me against him, Jack pushed me away. But he didn't let go. He held me by the shoulders as he tried to catch his breath.

As we both tried to catch our breaths.

I knew.

I'd known from the moment I talked to Jack Devlin that his kiss would be the kind I'd waited for my entire life.

He squeezed my shoulders, his expression warring between desire and affection. "I had to do that." His voice was hoarse, his tone almost apologetic. "I had to do that just once in my life."

Then he released me.

He walked away.

And tears filled my eyes.

Because his words suggested I'd never experience a kiss like that again.

9

JACK

wo years ago

He'd like to believe Ian was only going after Cooper because he was next on the list to harass. Nearly everyone had been tormented by Ian Devlin at some point in the last twenty years regarding giving up their prime boardwalk real estate. And this would not be the first time Ian had gone after Cooper's Bar.

However, Jack got the distinct impression Ian was doing it to anger his son. No matter that his blackmail had worked on Jack, he'd never respect his father. He'd never give him his loyalty willingly, and that bothered Ian Devlin more than he'd like anyone to know.

Going after Cooper was about punishing Jack.

He thought Jack would balk at dealing with Cooper in this matter, but as much as Jack didn't want to face his old friend, he needed to be the one in control of this situation. He'd have to find a way to make sure nothing happened to Coop's bar without Ian finding out Jack was the reason.

It did not make heading down the boardwalk to Cooper's that morning any fucking easier.

His palms were clammy, for Christ's sake.

Shaking it off, Jack reminded himself that this wouldn't the first time he'd spoken to Cooper in two years. They lived in a small town. They bumped into each other.

However, it would be the first time he deliberately approached his old buddy.

As he got closer to the bar, his attention was drawn past it to Emery's as Cooper stepped out of her store with a to-go cup in his hand. Jack's gut twisted. He hadn't spoken to her in two years.

Two fucking years.

But he'd kept an eye on her, and he did not like what he saw.

Em had lived in Hartwell for seven years, and she was still alone. He knew she went to her kids' playgroup every second week, but that was the extent of her social life. She didn't have friends. She didn't have family.

She didn't date.

A sick part of him was relieved he didn't have to watch that, but the better part of him grew steadily more concerned every time he saw her. Emery wasn't happy.

A little sadness had always existed within her, but it was growing.

And watching that happen killed him.

It made him hate his father more than he thought possible for trapping him in this life.

Stupid jealousy twisted in his gut at the sight of Coop drinking Em's coffee. His old friend got to speak to her whenever he liked. Petty to be jealous. But there it was.

Cooper's steps faltered as he walked toward his bar and spotted Jack.

Just like that, Jack watched the cold aloofness that had

become familiar wrap around Coop. He always looked ready for a fight whenever he saw Jack.

Not that he blamed him.

Even though a harsh part of Jack still felt like he'd done his ex-friend a favor by showing him Dana's true colors.

"Here on business." He held up his hands in surrender before Cooper could tell him to fuck off.

He admired Cooper's blank expression. It must've taken some restraint to master his reaction. As they stopped outside Coop's bar, facing each other, his friend sipped his coffee with an air of casualness Jack doubted he actually felt. "And Ian thought it was a good idea to send you?"

C'mon, man, you know Ian likes to inflict as much damage as possible on any given day. "I gave up trying to work out how my father's mind works a long time ago."

"And yet you work for the bastard?"

There it was. The thing that Jack had destroyed a friendship to avoid discussing. "He's upping his offer on the bar."

Anger and frustration flickered across his old friend's expression, and Jack wanted to punch Ian for doing this. Cooper took a step closer to Jack; it was meant to be aggressive and intimidating.

There was a part of Jack that wanted Cooper to hit him.

He'd hit him when he'd caught him with Dana.

But it had been one punch.

Not enough.

Not what he deserved.

"You tell your father what I've told him every year since the bar became mine … I. Am. Not. Selling. And while I've got breath in my body I never will. You tell him if he ever comes back here with another offer, he and I will have a serious problem."

It wasn't anything less than what Jack had expected.

Ian would escalate things against Cooper now. He'd try

something shitty and underhanded. Already attempting to figure out how he could put a stop to anything Ian might initiate, Jack gave his old buddy a tight nod and walked away.

~

Several months later

Every few weeks, Jack found himself at Germaine's. It was a trendy bar on Main Street where locals and tourists hung out on the weekend. On the nights Jack didn't feel like sleeping alone, this was where he came.

Tonight, he needed a warm body to take his mind off Ian's latest machinations.

Losing the Beckwith property on the boardwalk to that fancy chef had pushed his father over the edge. He'd been easing up on his plans to fuck with Cooper, but now they were back in motion.

And Jack had just learned that Ian had greased the palms of someone on the board of licenses. Cooper would not get his liquor license renewed this year. Or the next.

He would be out of business.

It took everything within Jack not to swing for Ian when he'd told him.

No, when he'd taken *extreme delight* in telling him.

Jack sipped his beer as his eyes wandered the bar. He had to find a way to warn Cooper. However, he had to do it in a way that wouldn't get back to Ian, or his sadistic bastard of a father would take it out on him through Rebecca. Or his mom.

Movement near the bar entrance drew his attention, and Jack tensed.

Jessica Huntington.

Cooper's new woman.

The blond doctor walked through the bar with George Beckwith, of all people. Jack drew his gaze down her body and back up again. When they'd bumped into each other weeks ago at the music festival, it was deliberate. He wanted to look into her eyes, get a feel for who she was and if she was good enough for Cooper. Everyone in town had welcomed her into the fold so quickly, Jack thought that said excellent things about her. He was glad Cooper had found Jessica. From all accounts, she was exactly the kind of woman his friend deserved: smart, kind, warm. Jack was inclined to like her because since her arrival, she'd made friends with Emery. Everyone was talking about it. The shy bookstore owner was finally opening up to someone.

Jack was grateful to the doc for giving that to Em.

But now, word on the street was that she and Coop had broken up.

And Jack knew why.

Because his father was a dirty fucker, Jack knew things about Jessica that no one had a right to know. Horrible, shitty things. Her past was not an easy one, and although he didn't know her, he couldn't help but admire her from a distance. His father had blackmailed Jessica to get her to push Cooper to sell the bar.

Instead, she'd broken up with Coop, which meant she would sacrifice herself to save his ex-best friend.

Jack could trust her.

His gut told him that.

But Jessica needed to trust Cooper. There was no way in hell Cooper would turn his back on her if he knew the truth.

Maybe I can kill two birds with one stone here, Jack realized.

Waiting impatiently, Jack found his opportunity when Beckwith left Jessica alone. He moved through the bar and slid onto George's vacant stool.

The doc blinked in surprise at his appearance.

Jack studied her face, stared into her eyes, and tried to get another feel for her. There was intelligence there, but she was closed off. In fact, she was giving him massive fuck-off vibes that pleased him. *Definitely still loyal to Cooper.*

"What do you want?" Her tone was cold.

Jack was used to that from anyone who cared about Coop.

"Just saying hello."

"Hello. Now you can leave."

Jack almost smiled. "Last I heard, you and Cooper were broken up."

"So?"

"So that means we can talk."

"No, it doesn't."

"You're still loyal to him?"

"So loyal that if you don't get your ass off that stool I'm going to make you."

Jack would like to see that. Laughing inwardly and feeling fucking pleased for his friend, he glanced around the bar as he tried to work out how to warn Jessica about his father. And then a woman with Dana's coloring threw him a smile across the bar, reminding him of something else Cooper *and* Jessica needed warned about.

Dana Kellerman.

That selfish cow was also working behind the scenes to fuck things up for Cooper.

That was, if Cooper and his woman hadn't already fucked things up for themselves.

Maybe giving Jessica a reason to see Cooper would help things along in that department.

He looked back at the doc and found her glowering fiercely as ever. It was hot. He absolutely understood what Cooper saw in her. "You know, Dana came to me awhile ago. Just after the music festival actually."

She wrinkled her nose in disgust. It was cute. "I don't care what you and Dana get up to."

"Just thought you might find it interesting that the reason she came to me was you."

"Oh?"

"She wanted me to seduce you." Jack wasn't even lying. The bitch had come to him at the festival and proposed he break up Jess and Cooper. She really was dumb as a post. "Seduce you. Those were the exact words she used."

He knew by the furious flash in her eyes that Jessica understood what he was trying to tell her.

Watch out for Dana Kellerman.

Seeing she got him, he moved on. Beckwith would be back any second, and he didn't need anyone witnessing this conversation with Jessica in case it got back to Ian. "My father isn't going to use what he knows about you."

The color leached out of Jessica's face, and Jack instantly felt like a prick. When he saw her fingers tremble around her glass, it took a lot not to place a comforting hand over hers. He wanted to tell her she had nothing to be ashamed of, not like Ian was making out.

She wouldn't invite that, though. What Jack really wanted to do was shake her and tell her to stop being stupid and tell his old friend the truth. Cooper was not a guy who would judge her for that shit.

Instead, he waited impatiently for her reaction.

"And why is that?" she asked, not looking him in the eye.

"You broke up with Cooper. You're no longer of any use. That doesn't mean my father doesn't know a good resource when he sees it. He'll keep that information on a back burner until it proves useful again." *So, fucking tell Cooper the truth.*

"You son of a bitch. Both of you."

Yup. No arguments there. He shrugged as if her words didn't touch him, and then he caught sight of Beckwith making a return.

Time to go.

Jack slid off the stool but rounded the table so all Jessica could see and focus on was him. "Cooper's liquor license," he warned.

She frowned in obvious confusion. "What?"

Frustrated, Jack bit back a curse. "Cooper's. Liquor. License."

Jack watched the understanding dawn on Jessica's face and relief moved through him.

He'd leave it up to the doc now to take care of his old friend.

10

EMERY

*ne year ago*

While the rain came down in sheets outside the store, the fire in the grate crackled, giving the space the cozy vibe I'd always hoped for. A few years ago, I'd made the bold decision to repaint the store in a rich teal that made all the white wood stand out in stark relief. I thought it looked great.

It looked particularly great right now because my friends were sitting around the fire eating the lunch I'd prepared for them.

My friends.

Who would have thought it?

But meeting Jessica Huntington had changed my life.

The doctor came to Hartwell for vacation, fell in love with Cooper, and stayed, and along the way, we'd connected. From the moment we met, I'd sensed a rare kinship. Her presence was soothing, she was unintimidating, and she didn't push for details of my past. Maybe that was why I'd let her in. Jess was almost as private as I was, and she explored a friendship with me without treating me like I owed her details about my life in exchange for her companionship.

My relationship with Jessica wasn't the biggest surprise. With Jess came Bailey and Dahlia. Bailey was Jess's best friend and Dahlia was Bailey's. They were a package deal. But the best thing was, they took their cues from Jess and never pushed me for information about my life before Hartwell.

Well, not too much.

I'd spent the last year getting to know all three women better. Bailey stopped by the store every morning to pick up coffee for Jess and Dahlia, and we'd chat. We were at a point now where I was almost as comfortable around Bailey as I was around Jess.

And it was nice.

Lovely, in fact, to have friends. Finally.

I studied Bailey as she moaned around a mouthful of the crabmeat canapé. I'd closed the store for our lunch to give us privacy. I thought perhaps, after everything Bailey was going through, she'd want to talk.

A few weeks ago, she'd discovered her long-term boyfriend, Tom, with another woman. They'd broken up after ten years together. Of course, that was a big life change, but I was more concerned about the things Bailey wasn't willing to acknowledge.

Anyone with eyes and ears knew about the antagonism between Bailey Hartwell and Vaughn Tremaine. He'd bought the Old Boardwalk Hotel four years ago, razed it to the ground, and started over. In its place he'd built a towering, modern building called Paradise Sands Hotel and Conference Center. It looked great. But Bailey had fought him the whole way, thinking he would ruin the aesthetic of the boardwalk.

They exchanged barbs often. Sometimes it was entertaining. Other times it was hard to watch. Like last year when I'd offered to supplement everyone's income if we boardwalk owners had to shut down in protest against the corruption amongst our bureaucrats and Ian Devlin. Tremaine hadn't been happy with me for letting everyone know about my money situation, and I'd felt a little silly for being open to trusting people only to be scolded. The scolding was tempered by Tremaine's obvious desire to protect me, which was nice. What wasn't nice—and was in fact upsetting—was watching how hurt Bailey was when Vaughn said, in front of everyone, that he didn't like her.

Foolish man.

Anyone who was paying attention (and I, the constant romantic, was always paying attention) could see the way Vaughn looked at Bailey when she wasn't aware of it.

Longing.

Pure longing.

And I suspected Bailey was equally attracted to Vaughn.

I just didn't know how that would play out and if it should so soon after Bailey's breakup with Tom. Yet I was eager to find out. But with Ian Devlin turning his evil plotting toward Bailey now that he assumed she was vulnerable, her romantic entanglements were the least of her concerns.

Ian Devlin.

He really was the devil.

"I can't believe Devlin called your parents and brother," Jessica said. Ian had gone behind Bailey's back and made overtures to her parents and her brother Charlie who owned shares in the inn. He voiced his concerns that "Bailey wasn't able to cope with running the inn at this juncture" and might be better off selling it.

Asshole.

"It sounds like he's planning something. This is how it started when he was coming after Cooper."

Bailey didn't appear all that worried. "It'll be fine. Emery, what are in these?"

"It's a secret," I teased, knowing how much she liked to know everything.

She reached for another, shooting me a mock glare. "You're lucky you're cute."

I warmed at our teasing.

It was so nice to be myself and not worry about offending or upsetting or chasing people away with my shyness. It had taken Jess's influence to show me that I could trust Bailey and Dahlia to accept me just as I was.

"Hey." Dahlia playfully pushed Bailey's hand away. "You've had more than your share of those."

"But I'm too skinny. I want a bigger ass and boobs."

Dahlia rolled her eyes at her friend, and I assumed it was because Bailey didn't actually mean it. I'd never met anyone as confident or self-assured as Bailey. She seemed to like herself wholly, and I admired that so much about her.

Not that I had self-image issues. I was content with what I saw in the mirror. I'd been told I was my mother's spitting image, and she was hailed as the diamond of her debutante ball. But I wished I had Bailey's sense of self. She liked herself. I didn't completely dislike who I was. Yet, I knew I could be a better version of myself. Braver. Like Jack once had, Bailey inspired me to be braver.

"What's with the sudden scowl?" Dahlia's voice brought me out of my musings. Her question was directed at Bailey.

"Just thinking about Devlin and his never-ending need to be a pain in the ass."

"You should tell Vaughn," Jess suggested.

"What?" Bailey's eyes widened, and something guilty crossed her expression. Like she'd been caught doing something she shouldn't. "Tell him what?"

"That Devlin is gearing up to bother you."

Relief flickered in her expression.

Hmm.

What on earth did she think Jessica had meant?

"Vaughn told Cooper that he wouldn't let Devlin cause trouble for us and I believe him. I know you have your issues with him, but this is bigger than that."

Issues. Right.

"I'm not telling Vaughn." Bailey glanced between me and Dahlia as if looking for backup. However, I agreed with Jessica. Vaughn was our current shield against Devlin. I truly believed he wanted to protect the boardwalk owners from Devlin's evil plotting.

"You're all crazy. Vaughn would rather see my place go under than do anything to help me."

I opened my mouth to disagree, but Jess beat me to it, sounding as exasperated by Bailey as I was. "That's not true at all. I wish you and he would just admit you're attracted to one another and stop acting like children at recess."

It took everything within me not to applaud.

As I'd said, anyone with eyes and ears could see through Bailey and Vaughn's antagonism.

Struggling to suppress my smile, I watched Bailey slump in her seat, shock slackening her pretty features. "That was almost mean. And he's not attracted to me."

"Aha!" Dahlia grinned gleefully. "But you're attracted to him?"

"What? No. What?"

Liar, liar, pants on fire.

"You just said he's not attracted to me when Jessica said you were attracted to one another. You made no mention of you not being attracted to him, just him not being attracted to you," Dahlia said.

"But I meant that. That thing you said. About us both. I am *not* attracted to Vaughn Tremaine."

"Methinks thou dost protest too much." Dahlia voiced my thoughts. I grinned behind a canapé.

"Methinks thou no longer deserves the last canapé." Bailey swiped it off the plate, and I laughed inwardly at Dahlia's crestfallen expression. Next time, I would make more canapés.

"I still think you should tell Vaughn," Jess continued.

"To have him laugh in my face? No thanks. Subject change!" Bailey clapped her hands as if we were in class. "Where will we start? Jessica and Cooper and wondering when he's going to get off his ass and get down on one knee, or Emery and man lessons?"

Oh no.

I shrank in my chair, hoping to disappear into it.

The other day Vaughn and his father had come into the store while Bailey was there, and she'd watched me blush my way through the interaction. Afterward, she offered to teach me how to talk to men. I'd really hoped it was something she'd forgotten about.

"Man lessons?" Dahlia asked.

"Yes—teaching Emery how to speak to men without wanting the ground to open up and swallow her whole."

"That would be nice, I suppose," I muttered. Despite how mortifying it was to require man lessons at my age, there was no denying I *did* require them.

"So lessons it is."

My cheeks flushed hot at the very idea. I wanted to be brave and make a change to my life. I truly did. But I wasn't sure man lessons was the way to go. And certainly not today. "Maybe some other time."

"Bailey," Jessica's tone held a note of warning. It was why I loved her. She never pushed me.

"Oh, come on." Bailey ignored Jess. "You're among friends, Em. No one here wants to humiliate you. We just want to help," she pushed. And as I saw the genuine affection in her expression, I realized maybe I did need to be pushed after all. Somehow eight years had flown by, and I was not where I expected to be in my personal life. "I don't want you to be alone forever. But if you do, then that's great, that's fine. I'll leave you alone to that decision because I just want you to be happy."

Her words rang with sincerity and filled my chest with heat.

The truth was, I didn't want to be alone. I wanted to find that special someone I could trust to erase the past. As the years flew by, my loneliness increased and I felt like I ... well, I guess, no matter how content I was with my life in Hartwell, I was always a little sad.

I didn't want to be sad and alone anymore.

And I realized that for the longest time, I'd allowed myself to stay frozen in one place because I hadn't quite let go of hope.

Hope that one day Jack Devlin would reveal himself to me. That he would change his mind. For months now, after years of avoiding me, he'd come into the store for coffee in the morning. I didn't know what prompted his return, but with it flared all my hopes again. Every time I saw him, I remembered that kiss on the beach and the words he'd said before he left me alone.

Yet Jack never said or did anything to give me hope when he came in for his coffee.

It was all small talk.

But I read too much into the way he looked at me.

I knew that.

And I needed to get over him.

"I don't want to be alone," I admitted. "Man lessons. But ... not today. Later, okay?"

My three friends grinned with excitement. "Later," Bailey agreed.

Gratitude swelled inside me.

For these women. My friends.

"Well," Jess said, "if we're not doing any lessons ... we could talk about the fact that Cooper proposed and we're planning to get married at the end of the summer."

Joy for Jessica flooded me as we all burst into a chorus of

delighted cries. Although I wasn't sure of the details, I suspected Jess had been through a lot in her life, and I was absolutely thrilled she'd finally found what she needed here in Hartwell. That knowledge eased my melancholy as we peppered her with questions about Cooper's proposal.

JACK

"You want me to what?" Jack practically growled, not sure he'd heard Stu correctly.

"You heard me." His brother sounded smug through the phone.

"You want me to prostitute myself?"

"If you consider fucking a prime piece like Vanessa Hartwell prostitution, then that's your problem. I'd do it. In a heartbeat. But Dana doesn't want me dipping my wick in anything else while we're screwing around, and Vanessa Hartwell might be sexy but she's no Dana Kellerman. And anyway ... Vanessa has made it clear she thinks I'm scum."

"Probably because you hit her sister in the face." Jack was still not over that. In fact, a seething rage had lived under his skin since the moment Bailey approached him in Lanson's Grocery to tell him Stu had attacked her in her inn.

She couldn't prove it was Stu.

But she knew.

And Jack knew it, too, because Ian had been harassing him and his brothers to come up with a way to get the inn out of Bailey's hands. He'd alluded to them breaking into her office to find something in her accounts that would help them.

And fucking Stu had broken into her inn when he was high on coke.

"How many times do I have to apologize for that shit? I was

off my fucking face. You know I never meant to do it. She startled me. I wasn't thinking. And anyway, I took your beating for it. Fair is fair."

"Unless you want me to tear out your throat with my bare hands, I'd shut up now, Stu."

"So sensitive, bro. Anyway, you're up with Vanessa. She'll sign over her inn shares if you grease those wheels, if you catch my drift."

Jack hung up and launched his cell phone into the ocean.

He heaved an angry inhalation and then cursed himself.

Now he'd have to buy a new goddamn phone.

Turning away from the water, he made his way back up to the boards, the moonlight and lights from the boardwalk leading the way.

When Vanessa Hartwell had approached Ian about selling her Hart's Inn shares, Jack couldn't believe it. He knew Vanessa and Bailey weren't close, but to snake her sister like that? And the greedy, conniving witch was playing with the Devlins. She was dangling the inn over his father like bait, all the while coming on to Jack whenever they met to discuss business.

So now he was to prostitute himself?

Fuck that.

He wouldn't touch Vanessa Hartwell with a barge pole.

Anger burned in Jack's gut as he moved up onto the boards. He was used to the anger. It was a constant part of him now and growing steadily worse. He was becoming someone he didn't even recognize.

The boardwalk was busy this time of night. Jack shoved his hands in his pockets and tried not to look at Emery's as he passed. Her store was closed. A familiar ache flared in his chest at the sight of her name on the signage and he glanced away. For some stupid reason, he'd started coming back into her place for his morning coffee.

When he was around her, Jack didn't feel so angry. It

soothed him for the few minutes he got to see her. And she still blushed when he came in. God, he was addicted to seeing that blush. There was no denying it.

Shaking his head at himself, he didn't look at Cooper's at all.

His best friend was getting married at the end of summer, to the right woman this time.

And Jack wouldn't be the best man.

He wouldn't even get an invite.

The loss cut deep.

Too deep to contemplate.

Right at that second, when he needed it most, a blond-haired angel came in the form of distraction.

Emery.

Jack's steps slowed as he watched her walk out of Antonio's with an ice-cream cone in her hand. She wore a dress like the one he first saw her in. Spaghetti straps, long, all the way down to her feet, made of a clingy material that left nothing to the imagination.

Emery Saunders really had the sweetest ass he'd ever seen.

Obviously, she had no idea what she did to a man looking the way she did in a dress like that.

Need, hot and heavy, flooded his groin, and Jack swallowed a grunt of irritation.

She still made him feel like a teenager.

Blissfully unaware of her effect, Emery leaned against the boardwalk railing and licked at her cone as she gazed out at the water.

"Fuck me," he muttered, his footsteps taking him to her without his permission.

Then suddenly, there was a guy beside her, and Jack slowed to a stop.

Was Emery seeing someone?

A knifelike pain cut through his chest at the thought.

Until he realized Emery had jolted away in surprise. And the guy was now holding out his hand for her to shake.

Who the fuck was this guy?

Jack walked faster now.

His eyes narrowed as Emery used her free hand to tentatively shake the man's.

As he grew closer, he saw her cheeks were flushed but she wasn't smiling, and she was holding her body away from this stranger. Her body language screamed "back off," and this guy wasn't getting it.

Jack's pounding heart leapt when Emery caught sight of him and her eyes widened.

"You okay?" he demanded, coming to a stop beside her. He faced the guy.

He was a little shorter than Jack. Definitely younger. Way younger, in fact. He looked like he might still be in college. And he had that good-looking, preppy thing going on that made Jack curl his lip in annoyance.

The young guy shoved his hands in his shorts pockets and stared unintimidated at Jack.

"This guy bothering you?" Jack asked Emery.

She opened her mouth to answer, but the kid beat her to it.

"I wasn't bothering her. I was introducing myself." His dark eyes moved to Emery. "I couldn't *not* introduce myself to such an angel."

Even though Jack had attributed the same description to Emery, he snorted in derision at the compliment.

"Move along, pal."

"Apologies." The tourist nodded his head in an old-fashioned kind of gesture. "I didn't realize the lady was spoken for. Have a good night." He wandered casually back into Antonio's.

"You okay?" Jack turned to Em. His chin jerked back in shock at her expression.

She was glowering.

Like full-on, appeared to want to rip off his head glowering at him.

Shit.

Without a word, Emery strode away, her strides inhibited by the tight, clingy dress. She dumped her half-eaten cone in a trash can and tried to hurry away.

Fuck.

Jack jogged after her. "What did I do?"

That blush of hers reached right down to her cleavage, something Jack was trying very hard not to notice. Especially since she was pissed at him and he didn't like it. Not one bit. She shot him an incredulous look as she tucked a lock of hair behind her ear. There were new piercings along her cuff. He wondered when she'd gotten those. "You … what did you do?" she huffed in exasperation.

"I thought I was helping you out. I thought that tourist was bothering you. I know you're shy, Em … I know you're uncomfortable around strangers." *That, and I was jealous as hell.*

"You don't know me," she hissed, wrapping her arms around her waist. "I was perfectly happy for the extremely well-mannered tourist to talk to me."

The jealousy tightened his chest. "It didn't look that way to me."

"Oh, really? You discerned my discomfort in the two-point-five seconds you *allowed* our interaction before interrupting us?"

"You don't date. I don't know why you don't date, but you don't. So, I thought I was helping."

Her pale-blue eyes were the iciest he'd ever seen them, and it cut Jack to the quick. "You don't know if I date. You don't know anything about me."

"So, you date?" Who the hell was she dating?

"That's none of your business. Now stop following me."

A couple threw them a concerned look as they passed, and Jack decided he was done having this conversation in public.

Grabbing Em's upper arm, he pulled her down the lane between her building and Cooper's. She protested, but he didn't stop until darkness almost completely shrouded them. Light over the bar's back door was the only reprieve, casting a yellow glow over Em as he maneuvered her against the wall of her shop.

"What are you doing?" She gaped up at him.

"I'm sick of chasing you down the boards." Something light and sweet and floral filled his nose, and he realized it was Em. He leaned his hands on the wall on either side of her head, blocking any escape. Jack was careful, however, not to touch his body to hers.

He'd lose his mind if he did that.

Emery swallowed hard, and Jack studied every flicker and nuance of emotion on her face, fascinated by her.

Why her? he thought. Why did she have to be so beautiful to him in every way?

It fucking hurt.

It would be best if she hated him too. But the very idea … Jack was sure if Em hated him, he'd be done for. The anger eating away at Jack would consume him.

"Don't be angry at me," he said gruffly, studying her expression. "I thought I was helping you. I promise."

"Were you jealous?" she blurted. Her eyes grew round, like she couldn't believe she'd asked.

She was so goddamn adorable, it killed him. Because she was everything. He didn't know one woman could be so much. Smart. Kind. Oblivious. Perceptive. Sexy. Beautiful. Classy. Awkward. Graceful. Innocent. Wise. And cute as hell. Jack huffed out an aggravated burst of laughter.

It would be so easy, he thought, weary to his bones, *to just give in to her*. Jack bent his head, breathing her in as he rested his forehead on her shoulder near the crook of her neck.

"Jack?" she whispered.

He could feel her chest rising and falling faster as his nearness affected her.

Jesus.

She smelled so good. What would it be like to lie with her skin to skin, wrapped up together, just breathing each other in? To confide everything and have her be a safe place to fall?

Jack turned his head so his nose pressed to her skin and he groaned, melting deeper as images of losing himself in her filled his mind. He buried his head in her throat, feeling her pulse flutter wildly against his lips. He brushed his lips against the flutter. Another brush, her skin soft and warm. Then he touched his tongue to her pulse, and her whimper of need was like a lightning bolt down his spine and straight to his dick.

"Jack," she breathed his name. It was a plea.

And he lost his mind.

He lifted his head, looked into her desire-filled eyes, and lost his fucking mind.

His lips crashed down over hers as he wrapped his arms around her, drawing her from the wall and against his body.

She kissed him back. Just like she'd kissed him on the beach all those years ago.

Emery Saunders may have been a good girl.

But she sure as hell didn't kiss like one.

She kissed him like she couldn't breathe without those kisses. Hungry, deep, savage kisses that fired his blood. Her hands were just as hungry. Searching. Touching. Caressing.

He returned the favor, thrilled at the sound of her bracelets jangling in his ears as she wrapped her arms around his neck.

Then he zeroed in on the one place he'd wanted to touch since the moment he'd seen her.

Jack slid his hands down her slender back and cupped her ass. He groaned down her throat at the feel of her. Firm, supple, round cheeks that he wanted to bite.

He wanted Em naked on her knees, that beautiful ass in his hands as he fucked her. They stumbled back against the wall as the images made him more desperate, starving. His dick was rock hard against Em's belly.

All Jack would have to do was lower himself just a little and then press up, and he'd be right between her sweet thighs.

As if his body had a mind of his own, it did just that, his dick pushing against his jeans and the fabric of her dress between her legs. The dress was in the way. Swallowing Em's breathy moans in his kiss, Jack fumbled for the material, bunching it in his fist, pulling it upward.

"Jack!" she gasped, breaking the kiss, her hands pressing against his chest.

For a moment he was confused, still lost in the fog of lust.

Then her hands covered his where he was pulling up her dress.

"Not here."

Realizing he was mauling at this angel like she was a quick dirty fuck in a back alley, Jack stumbled, his stomach feeling sick.

What was he even doing touching her?

Selfish bastard that he was.

He was a *selfish fucking bastard* and no better than his father.

"Jack?" Em pushed down her dress and fidgeted with her hair as she stared unsurely up at him.

He squeezed his eyes closed, remorse flooding him.

Remorse and anger.

Because she'd never be his, and he was a dick for touching her. Again.

"I'm sorry." He looked at her now. "I'm so sorry, Em. This won't happen again."

Hurt and rejection flashed across her face.

Jack moved to her, but she held up a hand against him.

"You deserve better than me," he explained. "You deserve a hell of a lot better than me."

Emery tilted her chin stubbornly. "Isn't that up to me to

decide?"

He smiled at her naivety and couldn't help but reach out to stroke her cheek. "Not this time."

"Jack." She tried to capture his hand, but he withdrew it. "Jack, why won't you tell me what's going on with you? What's been going on for years?"

Just like that, he was ice again.

Because no one he cared about could ever know the truth. It was too dangerous for them. "I'll walk you home."

Hearing the chill in his tone, Emery's expression closed down. "No, thank you. I can see myself home." She walked out of the lane without a backward glance. Jack followed at a slow pace.

He followed until he saw her disappear along the sand dunes and then watched from a distance as she let herself into her beach house.

Assured she was safely home, Jack retreated.

As he strolled down the boards, he tried to find the numbness that kept him moving through the days.

He struggled.

He struggled because he could still feel Em's warmth.

And that's when he knew what he would do.

Jack left the boards in search of Vanessa Hartwell.

He couldn't let her sell the shares to Bailey's inn to his father, so he had to control that situation. Had to manipulate her to protect Bailey. If that meant sleeping with Vanessa, then fine. She'd numb him to his bones, just like he needed.

And eventually Em would find out.

And she'd hate him.

Maybe that would crush Jack.

No maybe about it.

It would.

But it would be the best thing for Emery.

That was all that mattered.

11

EMERY

*ne year ago*

I'd lied to Bailey. Right to her face.

It happened two days after Jack had scared off a potential suitor on the boardwalk and then proceeded to kiss the life out of me only to turn cold *once again*. For some inexplicable reason, he'd come into my store while Bailey was there. Remembering our kisses in the alley, I was sure I'd turned redder than a stop-light. I hadn't wanted to touch or talk to him. I'd just wanted him out of there before Bailey noticed anything unusual between us.

Too late.

She'd pounced on me about Jack. So, I'd lied. I'd pretended Jack and I didn't even know each other. I'd told her I wouldn't jeopardize my friendships by pursuing a Devlin. The truth was, however, I wouldn't jeopardize my sanity by pursuing Jack Devlin.

He was the one man I'd decided to trust in almost a decade, and once again, I'd chosen the wrong man.

I knew that for a fact now.

Jack was sleeping with Vanessa Hartwell. He was using her as part of his father's manipulations to get his grasping paws on shares of Bailey's inn.

The thought made me sick.

I tried desperately to not let thoughts of Jack invade during Jessica and Cooper's wedding, but it was not the easiest of tasks. I was elated for Jess, overjoyed watching her marry the love of her life. And I was so honored to be a bridesmaid with Bailey and Dahlia.

As expected all eyes were on Jessica and Cooper… until they were on Bailey and Vaughn. Why? Because Vaughn punched out some guy at the wedding who, once upon a time, had broken Bailey's heart.

It was all very romantic and entertaining.

But then everyone started mingling again, and I was overwhelmed by attention from guests who wanted a chance to speak with me. Yes, I'd made a lot of progress in my friendships, but being surrounded by this many people was still out of my comfort zone.

Dahlia seemed to catch my deer-in-the-headlights look as Kell Summers, a councilman and town event planner, hinted about Emery's Bookstore and Coffeehouse hosting a stall at Winter Carnival this year.

"Hey, Em." Dahlia sidled up to me, wrapping her arm around my waist. It was a comical embrace as her head barely came to my shoulder. "Jess was looking for you."

"She was?"

"Uh-huh. Why don't you go check that out?"

The stunted quality of her tone alerted me that she was lying to rescue me, and I smiled gratefully. "I will do that. Excuse me." I gave Kell a polite smile and hurried away.

And by away, I mean I hurried right out of Paradise Sands Hotel where the reception was being held.

It was nighttime, the boardwalk lit up. I shivered as the ocean breeze swept over the boards, carrying with it the scent of sea salt that did nothing to mask the smells of popcorn, caramel, and burgers that pervaded every inch of the esplanade.

Goose bumps prickled down my arms. I was wearing the strapless teal bridesmaid dress Jess had picked out.

I'd heard horror stories about bridesmaid dresses, but Jess had great taste. We'd all worn the same color but in a style that suited our individual figures.

"Em."

The deep voice drew my attention. Jack. He leaned against the hotel, a bottle of beer in his hand. His hair was a sexy mess. Instead of the stylish suit he usually wore, he was in a T-shirt and jeans.

Images of him with Vanessa at this very hotel filled my head and chilled my bones.

Vaughn had caught them. He'd seen Jack and Vanessa disappear into a hotel room, all over each other, just minutes after the morning he'd come into buy *two* coffees when Bailey was there to witness our interaction. Had he been sleeping with Vanessa when he kissed me?

How could I have been so wrong about him?

For years, I'd held on to the belief that Jack Devlin was a good person beneath his mysterious transformation.

What a blind fool I'd been.

Jack pushed off the building, taking a swig of beer. He walked closer, and it took everything within me not to run.

Then the light from the hotel hit his eyes, and my breath caught.

Grief. His eyes were dark with grief.

"Jack?"

"Coop and Jess tied the knot, then?" His eyes flew to the hotel doors.

And that's when I understood.

"Yes."

Jack's gaze came back to mine. All tortured, making my heart ache for him despite him having hurt me. Damn him. "He's happy?"

I nodded. "I've never seen a man happier."

"Good." His eyes brightened, and he took another long drink of his beer. It seemed like an attempt to get a hold on his emotion.

There was a long silence between us and then his eyes drifted down my body and back up. "You look beautiful. But then, you always do."

I didn't blush. Not this time. "You should go home, Jack."

His lips quirked in derision. "You heard."

"About Vanessa. Yes."

The muscle in his jaw ticked and he stared out at the ocean.

"Were you sleeping with her when you kissed me?" I had to ask. I had to know.

He didn't look at me. "Does it matter?"

Pain flared across my chest, a hurt so deep, a little gasp escaped me.

Something like remorse flickered over his face.

Or maybe that's just what I wanted to believe.

Angry, I took a step toward him. He watched me warily. "I won't let you hurt Bailey."

He huffed. "So now you're finally starting to believe I'm not a good guy?"

"Sleeping with Vanessa Hartwell because your father wants Bailey's inn is not the action of a good man."

Jack glowered at me.

Tired of this dance between us, I shook my head in exasperation and turned to go. But his hand wrapped around my arm, halting me. I could feel the heat of his touch everywhere, not just on my bicep. "Let me go," I whispered.

Those blue-gray eyes of his were bright with intensity. "I would never let anything happen to Bailey. I know what I'm doing." Then he cursed, letting go of my arm. "What the hell do you do to me?" he breathed quietly, shaking his head as if in disbelief.

I hated that I cared that he was in turmoil.

But I couldn't trust him anymore.

"Go home, Jack. If you're here to make amends with Cooper, tonight is not the night."

"Amends." He scoffed, throwing me a "you're joking, right?" look. "Sunrise, you can't make amends for what I did to him."

"I don't know if that's true. What *is* true is that you can stop making things worse. Do you know that before Vanessa, Bailey never gave up on you? She believed, like I believed, that there was a reason for all you've done. But Vanessa was a step too far, even for Bailey. You're spiraling, Jack. Please stop before you lose the chance to come back from this."

Jack's eyes lowered to the ground. I thought he wouldn't respond but then he bit out, "And for you? Is Vanessa a step too far for you?"

The question pierced me. Painful and sharp. "I … I guess she was just a reminder."

"A reminder?"

"Of how you see and treat women. I'm not special to you, Jack."

His expression turned baleful. Furious.

That only made me madder. "In fact, some might say flirting with the town's shy bookstore owner whenever it strikes your fancy makes you kind of a dick." I was as stunned as he was by my honesty. But I was also proud of myself. "I'm done letting you toy with me whenever it amuses you." I turned from his shocked expression and marched back into the hotel to escape him.

Shaking, I hurried to the restrooms.

As brave as I'd been with Jack, it was enough for one evening.

I hid in the ladies' until it was safe to go home.

JACK

HE'D WANTED to get drunk that night because his best friend was finally marrying the right woman, and he wouldn't be there to see it.

However, as Emery's words echoed around in his head, Jack found himself getting drunk because of her.

It was one thing suspecting what your actions might cause … it was another experiencing the consequences.

Not only did Em hate him for sleeping with Vanessa, now she thought all their interactions over the years were just him fucking around with her.

He tried to tell himself it was for the best.

But he couldn't stand it.

He couldn't stand the awful pain in his chest, in his gut. Everything fucking hurt.

So he went home and cracked open the whisky.

He wanted nothing but oblivion now.

12

EMERY

*ne year ago*

I'd just changed out of the bridesmaid dress and into pajamas when I heard the growl of tires on gravel at the back of my house.

The alarm clock on my bedside table read 01:16.

Who on earth ...

I hurried to the window that looked down on my driveway and watched as a large figure pushed open the door of a Mercedes.

A Mercedes I recognized.

Jack?

He practically fell out of the car.

Oh my God.

Hurrying downstairs and out onto the porch, I watched as Jack stumbled on the gravel, steadying himself against the hood of the car. He snort-laughed under his breath and cursed.

He was drunk.

"Jack," I hissed, hurrying down the porch steps.

He looked up from watching his feet and gave me a wobbly smile. "Em, how did you get here?"

Jesus Christ. "Jack, you're at my house. You drove to my house. Drunk." I was furious.

He moved toward me and I rushed to put my arms around him as he stumbled.

Holy hell … he was *drunk*.

"Yes, I nee-needed to see you." He didn't slur his words but drawled them out like someone who was falling asleep.

Concern overcame my shock and with great difficulty, I helped him up the porch and into the house.

"You smell so good." He tried to bury his nose against my neck as I grunted beneath his weight. The man was huge! "You feel fucking good too." His hand slipped down to my ass and I yelped as he squeezed it. "You have the greatest ass in the world. I've fantasized a million times about your ass."

Flushing hot, I neared my sectional and pushed him to it.

He flopped heavily onto it and stared up at the ceiling. A few seconds later, he asked, "How did I get on the floor?"

"You're on the couch," I snipped. "I'm going to get you some water."

"Don't leave, Em."

He sounded so forlorn, I felt more than a prick of sympathy. Damn him! "I'll be right back."

When I returned, he hadn't moved and his eyes were still glued to my ceiling. "Jack, take this." I sat near his head and held out the glass of water.

He didn't take it.

"You hate me," he said instead, sounding distraught and not at all like the self-possessed, thirty-seven-year-old man I knew. He sounded young. And lost. "You're supposed to hate me. It's for the best. But I hate that you hate me."

Tears brightened my eyes. "I don't hate you, Jack."

"The real Emery does. She hates me."

"The real Emery?"

He turned, pushing himself up just enough to lay his head in my lap. I studied his handsome face, the length of his lashes that cast shadows over the crest of his cheeks. And I ached for him. Hours after finally telling him off, and here he was, and here I was.

Right back at square one.

Goddamn him.

"Jack."

"You're not the real Em. You're Dream Em."

I frowned. "Jack, you're drunk and you're really here at—"

"I'm just trying to protect you."

I stopped, biting my lip. He was drunk. And I shouldn't take advantage of that. I shouldn't. "Protect me from what?" I winced. This was so unfair of me.

"You know what," he said, as if exasperated with me. "Rebecca. The murder. The same reason I pushed Coop away."

The murder?

He was joking, right?

This was drunken silly talk.

Right?

Trepidation crawled through me and all thought of playing fair dissipated. "Tell me about it again. It'll help."

He took a deep breath. "I'm tired, Em."

"It'll help to talk to me about it ... since you can't talk to me in real life." I was going to hell.

Head still on my lap, he looked up at me now. His pupils were dilated. I stroked the hair back from his face, hoping he didn't feel the tremble in my hand.

"It was the night we made the date. Do you remember?"

How could I forget? "I remember."

"Ian called right after." His drunken words were slow, languorous, and I itched with impatience for him to reveal the truth. "I'd been on my way to tell Cooper that Dana came onto me." His gaze moved to the ceiling as he remembered. "Rebecca had brought a tourist back to the pool house. Some guy she barely knew. And he attacked her. Tried to rape her."

The words ricocheted around my living room and finally clipped me in the heart. "Oh my God," I breathed, shocked to my core. "Poor Rebecca."

Anger shrouded Jack's words. "She fought back. She hit him with a dumbbell a few times and she accidentally ... she killed the guy."

Of all the things I expected Jack to reveal, this was not among the possibilities.

"Stu and Ian covered it up. But they pulled me into it. Used it against me. Rebecca isn't Ian's, you see. My mom had an affair."

It was like an air raid of bombs of explosive information.

"He doesn't give a shit what happens to Rebecca. He sent her away and covered up the murder, but he's got it rigged for her to go down for it if I don't play my part in the family. I had to sell the business, go work for him. Sometimes I just drive around Hartwell, wondering where they buried the body. Knowing it's out there somewhere. It fucks with my head. It's fucked with my head for years.

"Cooper knew something was up. Something big. Knew I was haunted, just didn't know by what. He kept trying to figure out the truth. He couldn't know the truth. I couldn't make him party to murder. Couldn't have him wondering every time he drives on the outskirts if the body's in a particular spot he rests his eyes on. I couldn't have this sickness touching his life, just to protect my sister. To protect me. And Dana ... she was a disloyal piece of shit, and I ..."

Understanding dawned. "You deliberately set it up for Cooper to find you with her."

"Yeah."

"Two birds. One stone," I whispered.

"Exactly. He deserved better."

Tears spilled down my cheeks as I realized how much Jack had sacrificed for his sister. The depth of his father's evil was shocking. All this time I'd thought Devlin was a ruthless son of a bitch. But he was more. He was worse.

"Oh, Jack." I bent over and pressed a kiss to his cheek, flinching at the overwhelming scent of whisky wafting from him.

Our eyes met as I pulled back.

The sick feeling in my gut grew and grew as I considered how he'd feel if he remembered this in the morning.

"I'm a vault, Jack. I won't tell anyone." I wouldn't. I would never jeopardize him or his sister like that.

A murder.

I could barely wrap my head around it.

"Of course you won't," he whispered, his eyelashes fluttering closed. "You're just a dream."

I groaned as Jack's soft snores drifted into the room.

He would be so pissed in the morning when he realized what he'd done.

Or should I say … what I'd manipulated him into doing.

13

JACK

ne year ago

He was a coward.

Jack had never felt that more than when he woke up in a house he didn't recognize, saw a photograph of Emery on the wall with an older woman, realized it was her house, and high-tailed it out of there before she appeared.

Waking up fully clothed on Em's couch was one thing. Seeing his car parked right up against her porch, wheels turned out, proving he'd driven here drunk, was another.

Wondering what he'd said to her didn't bear thinking about.

Even though he shouldn't have, he drove back to his place.

He promptly threw up in his bathroom, thanking God he hadn't thrown up at Em's. He hoped. Downing Tylenol and one of the smoothies he drank after a workout, Jack sat for a bit to keep it down. And he tried to think. Tried to remember.

Nada.

Getting ready for the day with the hangover from hell was

difficult. His hands shook as he showered and trembled as he dressed, and his legs didn't feel steady. Part of Jack wasn't even sure if it was just the hangover.

What the hell had he said to Emery?

Jack remembered their encounter on the boardwalk. She'd cut him to the quick. He'd gone home, cracked open the whisky. Fucking downed a ton of his best bottle. Eighteen-year-old Macallan in a sherry oak cask.

That shit was expensive.

Groaning at the thought, Jack checked his phone, which he'd left at home while he was doing whatever he was doing at Emery's. There were missed calls from Ian, Stu, Kerr, and Vanessa.

Two missed calls from Vanessa.

An image of Emery's face flashed across his eyes. Her expression when he approached outside the hotel—he'd known right away she knew about Vanessa.

"I ... I guess she was just a reminder."

"A reminder?"

"Of how you see and treat women. I'm not special to you, Jack."

Not special to him.

He was enraged she'd said that ... but then what the fuck else was she supposed to believe?

Ignoring the missed calls, Jack stuffed the phone in his pocket and set out to run on the beach. Maybe it would help with the hangover. Maybe it would make it worse.

He didn't care.

As he took off from his house, he did so tentatively at first because every pound of his feet on the sidewalk was a beat of pain in his throbbing head. After a while, he picked up the pace and soon he was on the beach, the sand creating resistance.

That's when the memories came back in fragments.

He saw Emery on her porch, coming toward him.

He saw her above him, like he was lying with his head in her lap.

What the hell did he say to her, though?

Her sweet voice filled his head. *"I'm a vault, Jack. I won't tell anyone."*

That wasn't from last night, Jack argued with himself. Emery had said that to him years ago. Right?

"Of course you won't. You're just a dream."

Uneasiness built in Jack and he ran harder, faster, the sweat soaking his shirt as his body pushed out all the toxins from the alcohol.

"You deliberately set it up for Cooper to find you with her."

"Yeah."

"Two birds. One stone."

Fuck! Jack stumbled to a halt, bending over, hands on his thighs to catch his breath as it came back to him. Emery helping him into her house. Putting him on the couch …

Coaxing the truth out of him.

Horror slammed through Jack as he bit out a curse, running his hands through his sweat-soaked hair.

He'd told Emery everything.

Suddenly, he was running again, but this time with a clear direction. It was too early for her to open the store, so she'd be at home. Jack ran miles down the beach to her house, jumping over the locked private-access gate and taking her porch steps two at a time.

He pounded his fist against her screen door.

Not even a minute later, she appeared through the hazy screen, her frown disappearing when she realized it was him.

"Jack." She opened the door, standing before him in nothing but a tiny tank top and short shorts. Her hair was piled on top of her head, but long strands fell around her neck and face. It was also clear from the slight pebbling of her nipples that she wasn't wearing a bra.

Jesus Christ.

The whole visual was sexy as hell, but he wasn't in the mood to be distracted. He pushed past her without waiting for an invitation. Em's place was exactly how he'd imagined. Open plan, modern, elegant but comfortable. He stopped in the space between her dining and living rooms, glowering at the huge sectional he'd woken up on.

Jack didn't know whether to be pissed at her or pissed at himself.

Because he remembered everything.

Emery had manipulated the truth out of him.

He heard her close the door and turned to face her.

Her cheeks flushed a rosy pink and her eyes widened ever so slightly. "You remember."

"Oh, I remember." Jack took a step toward her but stopped when she retreated as if wary of him. "Fuck," he bit out. Was she afraid of him now? Did she think because he'd covered up this murder, he was capable of hurting her?

"I won't tell anyone, Jack," Em promised.

His eyes narrowed. "Because you're afraid of me, of my family?"

Her lips parted in shock. "I would never be afraid of you. I won't tell because I won't destroy you and your sister over a stranger who tried to rape her."

Surprise flickered through him. "Some people would call that morally wrong."

"Those people would be right." Em crossed her arms over her chest. "But I'm not obligated to do what's right for 'people.' I'm obligated to do what I believe is right, period."

Rage flooded him. "But now you have this secret, Em. You tricked this fucking secret out of me, and now you have to live with it."

Her expression softened. "I did trick you. And I'm so sorry. That was wrong. And now these are my consequences."

"And you feel sick to your stomach?"

"For you, yes." Her eyes brightened with an emotion that made his throat thicken. "I'm incredibly sad for you, Jack. I'm sad you've had to sacrifice so much for your sister ... and I'm in awe of you."

Fuck!

Jack bowed his head, not able to see that look on her face. He felt her words. He felt them all over, and as much as he didn't want to feel them, they were like salve on a festering fucking wound.

Someone *saw* him.

Not the shitty, horrendous actions he'd taken in the name of his father or the self-destructive ones that were a tool to push away the people he cared about.

Someone saw through it all to the truth.

And not just anyone.

Emery.

It was a relief that Jack didn't want to feel.

"So, you'll keep this quiet?" he asked, staring at the floor, his voice hoarse.

"Yes. I promise."

And he believed her.

His eyes flew to her and saw she'd crept closer.

Whatever she recognized in his expression made her face crumple. "Oh, Jack." Tears slipped down her cheeks seconds before she threw her arms around him.

He hesitated a second before realizing resistance was futile.

Jack wrapped his arms around her. Tight. Crushing her against him. He buried his head in the crook of her neck and breathed her in. She smelled of faded perfume and coffee. Em shook a little as she cried for him, and the ache in his chest expanded until he could barely breathe through it.

Eventually her shaking eased, as did her tears.

Then she turned her head, and Jack's breath stopped altogether at the feel of her lips on his neck. He moved to lift his head away but her lips caught his throat, the tip of her tongue teasing his skin.

Jack groaned as heat flooded his groin.

His fingers clenched at her tank top, pulling the fabric up until he felt her soft skin beneath.

"Em …" He meant to stop her. To push her away.

He did.

But she pressed her beautiful mouth to his and he tasted the salt from her tears in her kiss, tears she'd shed for him. And Jack was lost.

He let himself drown in their fiery, hot kisses, his hands disappearing under her top, caressing the smooth skin of her back, itching to rip the damn thing off. He felt the tug of Emery's hands on his T-shirt and he was being pulled forward.

"Couch," she huffed breathlessly.

Not wanting to break the kiss, Jack shifted his hands to her ass and prompted her to hop up into his arms. Her long legs wrapped around his waist and his dick grew impossibly hard with the need to be inside her.

His mind was a haze. Thoughts, rationale, all completely overwhelmed by her scent and the soft, supple feel of her in his arms.

And her kisses.

Fuck, the woman could kiss.

He hit the sectional and they fell onto it, his dick pushing between her legs with the movement.

"Oh!" she moaned, breaking the kiss, her eyes dilated, her cheeks flushed.

Jack thought he'd lost it before.

Now he *lost* it. He kissed her deeper, dirtier, hungrier as he rubbed his dick against the heat between her legs. His skin was on fire, and every time she whimpered, he swallowed it in his kiss and he got one step closer to spending himself like a fucking prepubescent kid.

Needing more of her, Jack took hold of the hem of her tank top and tugged it upward. Em scrambled to sit up halfway to help, taking over and pulling the thing off, her full breasts bouncing with the movement.

"Holy fucking Christ," he muttered hoarsely as she laid back on the couch, waiting for him, her chest rising and falling with anticipation. Her beautiful face was soft with need.

She was perfect.

She was so fucking perfect, it was a wonder she was real.

His hands itched to reach out and cup her, to fondle and squeeze, to hold her to his mouth so he could taste and suck. But his reason was returning. Slowly, through the haze of desire, he was remembering why they couldn't do this.

Then Em sat up, reaching for the waistband of his jogging pants, her hand dipping inside before he could stop her, brushing his dick.

Jack bit out a curse and grabbed her hand, holding it away from him.

She winced and he released her, realizing he was holding on too tight.

Emery blinked at him, confused. "Jack?"

Pushing off her, swallowing hard, trying to ignore the pain between his legs, Jack reached for the blanket she had thrown over the coach and he held it to her.

This time when she blushed, he felt like hell.

Her gaze lowered in humiliation as she used the blanket to cover herself.

"I'm sorry." He stood, turning away from her, afraid if he kept looking, he'd just say fuck it and take what he wanted. "This can't happen. Ian would use you against me."

"What if we kept it a secret?" She sounded hopeful.

Jack squeezed his eyes shut. His voice was gruff when he finally replied, "We can't."

He already suspected Ian was keeping tabs on all his sons. If he found out about Emery, he'd find a way to screw with her. And even if he didn't, what kind of life could they have? She'd finally found friends in Jessica and Bailey and Dahlia. She was part of Cooper's inner circle, and she was flourishing there.

If she chose Jack over them, she'd lose all that. And she'd have to stand by his side while he did shady shit for his father and just accept that she was with a guy people couldn't stand to be around.

He wasn't worth her losing everything she'd taken so long to build.

"Can't or won't?"

She'd asked him something similar before.

Forcing himself to turn, he found her flushed and disheveled and half-naked beneath the blanket, and even though he'd gotten her hot only to stop *again*, Em still looked at him like he was something more than he was.

"Some might say flirting with the town's shy bookstore owner whenever it strikes your fancy makes you kind of a dick."

It was time to end this. For good. For her sake.

"I'm attracted to you, Em. You obviously know that." He flicked a hand impatiently at her. "But I don't want you … permanently." He choked out. "I'm not that guy. And I might be an asshole, but I'm not enough of an asshole to screw around with the feelings of a good woman."

Understanding dawned on her face and she clutched the blanket tighter. When she spoke, she surprised and crushed him with her honesty. "I don't know if that's the truth or if you're just hell-bent on self-destruction for the rest of your life. Either way, the constant humiliation has grown tedious." Her words were clipped. Cold. So unlike her. "I'll preface this by saying that your secret is still safe with me. But now I'd like you to leave,

Jack. And I would appreciate it if you stayed the hell away from me. For good."

Shards of pain splintered through his chest.

It took him a moment to recover from the initial agony.

But finally, he gave the woman he was pretty damn certain he was in love with a tight nod and strode out of her house.

Out of her life.

On the silent promise that it was for good.

14

EMERY

hree months ago

Main Street was abuzz with anticipation and excitement for Winter Carnival.

And for once I was there and didn't feel at all uncomfortable. It was true what they said: Life was kind of like riding a bike. It was alien and weird and tricky at first, but once you got the hang of it, it started to feel natural.

I stood at Dahlia's stall, manned by Bailey. Vaughn was at her side, and I was at Jess's, Cooper at hers. We were waiting on Dahlia's arrival so she could take over from Bailey. It didn't surprise me Dahlia was running late. She'd been flustered ever since she returned from a trip home to Boston and her ex-boyfriend Michael Sullivan followed her back.

Michael, a.k.a. Detective Sullivan, was working for our new Criminal Investigation Department under Sheriff Jeff King. Interestingly, Dahlia used to date Jeff, and everyone knew *she* broke up with *him* and he hadn't been happy about it. I would've thought an interesting love triangle might unfold—until I had drinks with my friends.

While I no longer blushed and stammered shyly around Vaughn and Cooper, Michael was brand new. And he was charming in this rugged, tough-guy, Bostonian-cop kind of way.

Seeing how Dahlia lit up like a Christmas tree around him despite her determination to keep him at bay, I knew Jeff didn't stand a chance.

I didn't think Dahlia stood a chance either.

Michael seemed very determined to win her back.

It made my romantic soul extremely happy.

"Oh my God, there she is." We followed Bailey's gaze.

My lips twitched.

Walking toward us, dressed as Snow White, was Dahlia. It was the perfect character for her coloring. However, with her envious curves, it was impossible for anything to look demure on her. Especially not a dress with a sweetheart neckline.

Jess and Bailey wolf-whistled and catcalled as she approached, making Coop, Vaughn, and me chuckle.

Rolling her eyes at our teasing, Dahlia halted behind the stall. "Oh yeah, my puffy sleeves are so sexy." She squeezed Bailey's shoulder. "Thanks, babe."

The carnival parade this year was Disney-themed, hence Dahlia's costume. Kell Summers had tried valiantly to persuade me to dress up as Elsa from *Frozen*. I may have come far with my social anxieties, but the idea of taking part in a parade, being front and center, was nauseating.

While I was awkward with adults, I wasn't at all awkward with children. Their innocence and honesty cut through my shy armor. With kids, you always knew where you stood. I never had to guess or wonder if they found me tedious or wanting. I enjoyed being around kids for that very reason, which was why

I still volunteered at the counseling center in Millton every second Monday.

It was this affinity that probably drew Cat's son Joey to me. However, Cat was convinced it was because I looked like Elsa.

Either way, I didn't care. Joey was exceptionally bright and talented and a true joy to be around. I'd been disappointed to not see them with Jess and Cooper this morning.

"I sold a ring with peridot." Bailey informed Dahlia.

"Great." Dahlia glared at us. "You guys will put people off hanging around like this. You're intimidating in a group."

"Gee, thanks." Jess snorted. "And here we came over to ask if you'd like anything to eat or drink."

"Hot chocolate," Dahlia replied. "And a churro would not go amiss."

Deciding that sounded good, I followed Vaughn, Jess, and Coop as they ventured off to find food.

"Where's Cat and Joey?" I asked Cooper as we strolled across Main Street to the food vendors.

"Cat said something about them running late this morning. They should be here later."

"Yeah." Jess nudged me and grinned. "Joey wouldn't miss a chance to see you. You know he publicly declared his love for you, right?"

I laughed at the thought. That kid was so cute. "Did he?"

Coop shot me an affectionate smile. "Said he's going to convince you to wait for him until he's old enough to marry you."

Oh my gosh. My heart. I grinned. "Well, I am truly honored."

We stopped at a vendor and procured Dahlia's hot chocolate and drinks for ourselves. Vaughn tried to pay for everyone but Cooper wouldn't let him. Jess and I stood back while they argued, holding up the line.

"I can pay for my own," I tried to interject.

Jess shook her head at me, as if to say it's not worth trying.

"Fine," Cooper said to Vaughn. "You pay for Bailey's and Dahlia's, I'll pay for Jess's and Emery's."

Vaughn agreed to this, but there was still a stupid tension between the men as we moved on to a food cart. They split payment the same way again and the tension eased as we wandered back to Dahlia's stall.

Jess and I trailed at the back and she mouthed "men" with a roll of her eyes.

I bit back my laughter.

My steps faltered a little when I saw Michael was now at Dahlia's stall. He seemed to have ingratiated himself quickly with our group. It turned out that Michael and Cooper were becoming friends, running on the beach together in the mornings.

The image of another man jogging on the beach flickered at the edge of my memories, but like always, I pushed it out.

And it was like that mere flicker conjured him.

I'd been listening to my friends but also watching as Main Street got busier. As my eyes moved through the crowds, I spotted him.

Jack.

Waiting at a burger stand with a petite brunette.

I was hit with a wave of déjà vu.

And sadness.

And frustration.

Jack turned his head and met my gaze.

Longing slammed me deep in the gut.

Since the humiliating morning I'd offered myself to him on a platter and he'd refused, Jack had done as I'd asked and stayed far away.

I missed him. I didn't even know why since we hadn't spent that much time together over the years. However, the time we did spend was loaded with so much emotion and truth.

He was the person I wanted to trust completely. The person I wanted to tell everything to. I'd been ready to that morning.

I still wasn't sure if Jack had pushed me away to protect me like he had Cooper, or if he was telling the truth when he said he didn't want me permanently. My heart said it was the former. My hurt clung to the latter. Especially seeing him continue to sleep around with tourists like the brunette at his side.

Either way, Jack hadn't wanted me enough to even try, and I was done.

"Emery, what are you staring at so hard?" Jessica asked.

Afraid of being caught, I pulled my attention from Jack. "Nothing," I mumbled.

"What are you looking at?" Vaughn asked.

I glanced up, thinking he was insisting upon Jess's query, but he was talking to Bailey. She shot me a knowing, excited look that made me want to disappear. Then Dahlia nudged her, glowering, and Bailey glared back.

Oh no.

Did my friends suspect I had feelings for Jack?

Suddenly, the carnival held no appeal for me. I didn't want to see Jack here with another woman. Moreover, Bailey was a good friend, but she lacked subtlety. And the last thing I wanted was for Vaughn or Cooper to know about my crush on Jack Devlin. I'd never had male friends before, and I may have once been willing to lose their friendship over Jack, but not anymore. If Jack didn't want to fight for what was between us, then I certainly wouldn't jeopardize hard-won friendships for it.

Glum, I said, "I … uh … I think I'm going to call it a day."

"Oh, don't go," Bailey replied.

"She can go if she wants to," Dahlia argued.

"I don't want her to go."

"It doesn't matter what you want, especially when your head is in cloud cuckoo land."

Dammit. They did know. And reading between the lines, Bailey was for my crush on Jack, and Dahlia was not.

Mortified, I backed away from the stall. No one was paying attention. They were too busy wondering what on earth was going on between Bailey and Dahlia.

Seeing my chance to escape, I turned and hurried through the crowds.

I was so focused on trying to maneuver through people as quickly as I could that I didn't see him coming.

At once, Jack was there, and I stumbled into him. His hands curled around my arms as my palms fell against his chest.

I pushed away as if burned, but he didn't release me.

"Em, are you okay?" He bent his head to mine, eyes dark with concern.

I glanced at his side and saw the brunette was nowhere to be seen.

Heat flashed through me, being this close to him, heat I resented that in turn caused me to resent him. I attempted to pull out of his grip but he held on. "I'm fine, Jack. Let me go."

He scowled and reluctantly released me.

We shared a wary look before I moved past him, disappearing onto the boards.

A few days later ...

THERE WAS a lot to be said for living in a tourist town. There was a lot more to be said for living in a coastal town during low season. I loved walking along the quiet beach at sunset. Yeah, it was breezy, but I liked the wind whipping around my legs. And I loved the feel of the cold, wet, mushy sand sinking beneath my feet and squishing between my toes.

To avoid being whipped in the face by my own hair, I'd piled the mass of blond waves onto the top of my head, and I held my oversized sweater closed with my arms wrapped around myself.

Usually I was content here. But for a while now, I'd felt a disquiet. A dissatisfaction I didn't understand, considering mine was a pretty good life.

Not to mention the events in town lately were more than a little unsettling.

Even though I shouldn't be, even though he'd hurt me, I was worried about Jack.

We'd all known that Deputy Freddie Jackson was a bad egg. He used his position as a police officer to intimidate people, specifically for the Devlin family.

Yes, Jack had hurt me. Yet that didn't change the fact that his eldest brother had just been murdered by Freddie Jackson.

I wondered how Jack was feeling. He didn't get along with his brother. He'd laid him out a few times in the past. He'd helped trap Jack into a life he didn't want. There were moments when I'm sure Jack hated his brother. But Stu *was* his brother.

And he'd been murdered.

I couldn't even imagine the mess Jack's emotions were right now.

My chest felt tight with pain for him.

And suddenly he was there.

Catching sight of the lone figure standing on the beach, staring out at the ocean, my steps faltered. He was wearing running clothes, including a hoodie with the hood up, and yet I knew it was him.

I'd know Jack anywhere.

The closer I got, the clearer his profile got, his face peeking out from his hood.

Tall, lean but muscular, it didn't matter what Jack wore, he wore it well. He was just that guy that made clothes look great. Even jogging pants and a hoodie.

If it had been anyone else, I'd have chickened out and walked away. But Jack Devlin gave me the courage to push through my insecurities. He always had. And even though it had led to the kind of hurt I'd been avoiding the last nine years, I slowed to a stop at his side.

He barely turned his head. Just flicked me a look. If he was surprised by my approach, he didn't say anything.

The turmoil in those blue-gray eyes devastated me.

Jack looked back out at the water and I turned, my hand almost brushing his to gaze out at the ocean too. I heard his breath shudder a little and fought the urge to throw my arms around him.

I couldn't give him that. But I could give him this.

I stood with him, watching the sun lower beyond the horizon.

Time passed.

Until there was only a flare of orange and pink where the sea met the sky.

Gathering my courage, I reached for Jack's hand and clasped it in mine.

He squeezed my hand.

Tight. So tight.

I waited for him to let go.

He took awhile.

But eventually his grip eased.

I brushed my thumb along the top of his hand.

And then I released him.

I knew I didn't imagine his eyes on my back as I strolled down the beach toward my house.

I always knew when Jack was watching me.

I always had.

15

JACK

resent day

FIVE MINUTES AGO, the thing weighing most heavily on him was his selfish inability to leave Emery Saunders alone. He'd been doing well. He'd stuck it out and avoided her like she'd asked after he fucked up last summer. But ever since she'd approached him on the beach three months ago, to comfort him over Stu's murder, it had been a daily battle to stay away from her.

Jack was pissed at himself for going to her store and unfairly pissed at her for her coldness.

Now, for the first time in a long time, Emery had been shoved to the back of his mind.

Ian had allowed Rebecca to return home for Stu's funeral, but then he'd sent her right back to England. If Jack didn't already hate the man who'd spawned him, he'd hate him for that. Anyone could see Rebecca was a shadow of who she used to be. Worried about her, Jack had kept in contact with her almost every day since she'd returned to London. And when she'd asked him to arrange her secretive return to Hartwell, Jack didn't think twice. He did it.

Rebecca had been living in his house for the past few days. She'd been quiet, introspective. Jack was trying to give her space while she got herself together.

It didn't occur to him that she'd go to the police now that Stu was dead and couldn't be charged for covering up Rebecca's crime.

Heart pounding, Jack hurried down Main Street to the sheriff's department.

Almost five years ago, Rebecca had murdered a guy she thought was a tourist, but in self-defense while he'd attempted to rape her. Stu came in after she'd hit the guy over the head with a dumbbell and convinced Rebecca to help him bury the body and the weapon. Stu told Ian, because he told his father everything, and Ian forced Rebecca out of the country to school in England. Then he'd used her crime to blackmail Jack into the family fold. Ian said he'd tell the police where the body was if Jack didn't work for him ... and that he'd make sure it was Jack who went down for covering up the murder, not Stu. After all, it would be way more plausible that Jack, who was close to his sister, would've been the one to protect her, not Stu.

And Jack had known his socio-fucking-path of a father meant it, that he wasn't bluffing. Jack knew Ian wouldn't blink at the idea of Rebecca going to prison for murder because she wasn't his daughter. Jack's mom, Rosalie, had a years-long affair with an old boyfriend. Ian found out when she got pregnant with Rebecca because he hadn't been in his wife's bed for a long time. He'd had his mistresses to see to those needs.

Unfortunately, things had gotten extremely unpleasant for Rosalie and Rebecca in the Devlin household. Ian threatened to make Rebecca's life miserable if Rosalie ever saw the old boyfriend again, which meant cutting Rebecca's real father out of her life. The guy didn't even know he had a daughter. And when Rebecca got older and learned the truth, she was forbidden from asking about him.

Over the years, they'd all heard things happening to their mom that no kid should have to hear, including their father forcing another pregnancy on her, just to prove he was a man.

Jack had tried to protect his mom and sister as much as he could from Ian and his brothers, who all seemed to be Ian replicas. But it was difficult to protect Rebecca from Ian because he hated her. Their father put up a front since appearances were so important to him, but he'd sell Rebecca down the river in a heartbeat if it came to it.

No need now, though, Jack thought, as he hurried up the steps to the front entrance of the sheriff's building.

Rebecca had done it herself.

Why?

After everything they'd both sacrificed for this lie … why now?

Striding into the building, Jack zeroed in on the reception desk where Rebecca was waiting with the new detective in town —Dahlia McGuire's man, Michael Sullivan. As soon as his sister saw him, she burst into tears and ran for him. Jack caught her slight figure as she burrowed into him, as if she couldn't get close enough. He squeezed his eyes closed as he felt how frail she was in his arms.

As she sobbed, Jack tightened his hold on her, wishing all that pain would just leak out of her and into him. When he opened his eyes, Detective Sullivan was standing in front of him, his expression carefully neutral.

"Jack Devlin?" he asked.

"Yeah, I'm Rebecca's brother."

"I'm Detective Michael Sullivan with the Criminal Investigation Department."

"I know who you are, Detective."

Sullivan nodded, his gaze dropping to Rebecca and then moving swiftly back to meet Jack's. "Your sister is free to go."

Confusion suffused Jack. "You aren't charging her?"

"A team is right at this moment looking for the body and the murder weapon. If we find those, we will charge Rebecca with aiding and abetting."

"Aiding and abetting? I don't—"

"Jack." His sister lifted her head, her eyes red and wet with tears. "I … let's go somewhere so I can explain."

Hearing the plea in her words, Jack gave her a tight nod.

JACK COULDN'T WAIT to get back to his place in South Hartwell. It was a nice house that Ian had insisted he move into after he "suggested" he sell his home in North Hartwell. Jack didn't sell but instead rented it out. It was as if he had some futile hope he'd get to return to it one day. Maybe even return to the man he used to be.

Pulling the car onto the side of the road, Jack switched off the engine and turned to his sister. "What is going on? What were you thinking?" It took everything within him not to rage at her.

Her blue-gray eyes, just like his, just like their mom's, brimmed with tears again. "Jack, I'm so sorry. I'm so sorry that this has taken so much from you … and I'm sorry you didn't know the truth. But Ian and Stu threatened me …"

A strange foreboding came over him. "What do you mean, the truth?"

Rebecca swallowed. Hard. "I didn't kill Caruthers."

Jack gaped at her, aghast. Colin Caruthers was the guy Rebecca had thought was just a tourist. He wasn't. He was wanted in four counties for several rapes. Ian discovered that after the fact, obviously.

Her mouth trembled. "Jack … he didn't *try* to rape me. He was raping me."

Rage and grief exploded through Jack as he watched the tears slip silently down his sister's cheeks.

No.

Fuck.

No.

Sick to his stomach, he shook his head as the guilt overwhelmed every other feeling. He should have been there. He should have protected her. "I'm sorry," he choked out.

"Stu came into the pool house. He said he'd been having a smoke by the pool and he heard me cry out for help. The next thing I knew, Caruthers had been pulled off me and Stu hit him repeatedly over the head with one of the dumbbells."

"Jesus fuck." Jack shook his head, trying to make sense of this new truth.

"He didn't mean to kill him." Her expression was so sad. "Jack, he was as shaken up as me. He'd just … he was trying to protect me." Fresh tears fell from her eyes. "He didn't know what to do. He was so scared. So he called Ian. And he took care of everything. He blamed it on me. Said I was a stupid whore for bringing Caruthers back to the house."

"He said what?"

"I … I *was* stupid, Jack. Looking for love in all the wrong places. But I never meant … I just thought we'd hang out."

"You were only seventeen. Of course that's what you thought! Do not blame yourself. Do you hear me?"

She nodded. "Stu was angry at Ian for saying that. He assured me he didn't blame me."

Disbelief moved through Jack.

Rebecca continued, "But Ian used it against us all, didn't he? Even Stu. He held it over him. Made him do things … like break into Bailey's inn."

"How do you know that?"

"He told me. You know he called me every month to see how I was doing."

"That doesn't excuse him punching her."

"I know. Stu knew that. Jack, he was so angry. He didn't know how to control it. So he got high whenever it got too much. He was high that night he broke into the Bailey's. But more than that, he had too much of Ian in him. He knew that too. He just let the anger turn him into his father. I ...I think I was the only person he was ever truly himself with."

Jack's chest tightened with too much emotion. He struggled to draw breath. "Why didn't you tell me? Why didn't *he* tell me? I could have helped you both."

"You couldn't. We both knew that. If I told the truth, Ian would manipulate it so that you went down for it. And Stu knew you wouldn't care about protecting him, but you would care about protecting me, so he suggested we lie about what happened. He knew Ian would figure out a way to take you down for it. Planting fingerprints on the weapon. Whatever it took."

"But Stu was ... we were constantly at each other's throats. Why didn't he talk to me?"

"He loved us in his own way. That's all you need to know. Everything else will just make you crazy with what-ifs. He'd want us to both be free now, Jack. And even if I have to do time for aiding and abetting, it doesn't matter. We've been in a version of prison for almost five years. I ... I've been ... there were some days I ... I didn't even want to be here anymore."

Horror suffused him. "Becca—"

"This is the only way I know how to live with it. Caruthers was an evil bastard ... but I can't live with the secret anymore and what it's taken from you. I feel lighter than I have in years." She offered him a sad smile. "And you ... you're free of all this now. You can leave Ian behind. Finally."

"You know Ian won't take this lying down."

"Yeah." She smirked. "So, you're telling me you haven't been keeping tabs on every dirty thing he's ever done?"

It surprised him he could laugh in that moment. His sister knew him too well.

"You have evidence, don't you?"

Jack's laughter faded into a smile. "And if I have?"

"Then I would suggest handing that evidence over to our friendly local detective. You can offer your cooperation in exchange for immunity."

The idea of being free didn't seem real. The possibility of seeing Ian brought down for all the shitty things he'd done to their family and this community over the years seemed like a dream. And there was only one thing standing in Jack's way.

"We do that, and it's not just Ian who goes down. Kerr goes down too. And what about Mom and Jamie?" Jamie, their youngest brother, was a freshman in college. Despite Ian's attempts to beat him down, he was proving to be more like Jack and Rebecca. In other words, he'd gotten a lot of Rosalie's genes.

"Kerr is just as bad as Ian. I couldn't care less if he goes down with our father. As for Mom and Jamie, we can protect them."

"And you?" He was heartsore from all that Rebecca had endured. "Who protects you?"

"I made a mistake," she whispered. "Over four years ago, I made a terrible mistake and trusted the wrong person. It happened, Jack, and I've tried to get over it and move on, but I couldn't live with the lie. Now, for the first time, I feel hope. I feel hope that I can finally let go of the past."

Jack unclipped his seat belt and did the same to Rebecca's so he could pull her into his arms. "I'm so sorry." His voice was hoarse as he tucked her head against his shoulder. Her fingers curled tightly into his suit jacket, pulling on the material as she shook. "I'm so sorry I didn't protect you."

"You thought you were." She pulled him closer. "Jack, you thought you were protecting me. But it's over. He can't hold this over us anymore. You can get your life back. You can tell Cooper everything."

Jack squeezed his eyes closed at the thought of his best friend.

Even if he told Cooper the truth, Jack doubted he'd ever forgive him for what had happened with Dana.

"You might finally settle down," Rebecca teased, pulling back to give him a sad smile. "Instead of breaking the hearts of all the eligible Hartwell females."

Jack was about to roll his eyes when her words sunk in.

If they could do what Rebecca thought they could—if they could take Ian down for good, Jack could have the one thing he'd wanted since he was twenty-eight years old.

It wouldn't be easy.

He'd burned that bridge a few times, and this morning was only proof of it.

But his sister's words played over in his head. *Now, for the first time, I feel hope.*

Hope.

Was that what was making his heart race and his fingers tremble?

The possibilities lifted something from his shoulders that had been weighing him down for years.

His hands still shook as he cupped his sister's face. "Thank you. Do you know how brave you are, Becs? Do you know how goddamn proud of you I am?"

Even though tears still shone in her eyes, she nodded. "That means a lot, Jack."

"I'm going to suggest something, and you will not bite my head off."

"Okay …"

"I want you to talk someone."

"A therapist?"

He nodded as he brushed his thumb across her temple. "A lot

of horrible things running around in this head, sweetheart. It needs to come out."

"I'll think about it."

"That's all I can ask. Second thing: you're staying with me. I have a tenant in the house in North Hartwell, but I thought I could give them notice and we'll move in there and move Mom into my place in South. Jamie, too, while college is out for the summer."

"Do you think they'll go for that?"

Jack knew his mom was intimidated by her husband. But he also knew she put up with most of his shit for the sake of her children. Stu's death had broken Rosalie. Knowing her husband was inadvertently responsible for her eldest son's murder ... Rosalie had grown implacably cold with Ian, and none of his blustering made a difference.

And he knew to never lift a hand to her again. Last time he'd hit Rosalie had been when Jack was twenty-two, and he'd knocked his father on his ass. Now that he thought about it, only Kerr had stood at his father's defense that night. Stu had sat back and watched the whole thing.

Jack had thought it was because he didn't care.

But maybe he'd enjoyed watching Jack take their father down.

His head spun as he began to see the past through fresh eyes.

One thing was for sure—it would be much easier to convince his mom to leave Ian now than it would've been a year ago. "I think Mom's been waiting for this chance for a long time."

16

EMERY

"The donations are finalized," Hague announced without a hello. The call from Hague as I closed the shop for the day was a welcome distraction.

I worried about Jack and Rebecca. News traveled fast in Hartwell, so no doubt I'd hear something soon, but the not knowing was infuriating. And I hated that I still cared so much about what happened to Jack Devlin.

This news from Hague lifted my spirits as I walked along the boards toward home. "That's wonderful."

"And it was all anonymous, just as you wanted."

"Excellent."

"As for what's left, I have some papers for you to look over and sign. I want to make sure you're happy with the stock options I've selected on your behalf. The money you're not investing has, as discussed, been split between several high-interest savings accounts, and we'll move those around depending on changing interest rates. Of course, we'll keep you apprised of any moves. And you still have all your grandmother's real estate investments in place. On that note, the estate is officially for sale."

"Thank you, Hague. I mean it. Really. I couldn't have done this without you." I let myself into the beach house, feeling at least one weight lift off my shoulders.

For years, I'd held on to my family's estate and continued as the major shareholder in the Paxton Group. However, I disliked that house, and I loathed that company. I hated what it had taken from me before I was even born. And while I didn't claim to be a climate change crusader, I wasn't comfortable being so directly complicit in air pollution.

The only reason I'd hung on to the estate and the company was because I'd promised my grandmother I would. But the weight of both had plagued me for years. It wasn't until I heard Jessica's and Dahlia's stories that I had an epiphany.

A few months ago, before Dahlia was shot trying to protect Ivy, she'd been reluctant to let Michael back into her life because of the guilt she carried over her sister's death. While Dillon's death hadn't been her fault, Michael was once in a relationship with Dillon, and that's really where Dahlia's guilt stemmed from.

To help her, Jessica had revealed her own past to us. Discovering what trauma Jess had been through, and how she'd thrown off the shackles of the past, had been enlightening. Jess was strong—she hadn't allowed her past to define her.

As much as my grandmother had been the only family to care for me, she'd also done her damage, to me and to others through me. The Paxton Group wasn't the legacy I wanted for myself. And I realized that I didn't owe my grandmother my future.

So, I had Hague begin the process of selling my shares. Most of the buyers were among current shareholders looking to increase their stake in the company. That I sold my holdings at cost made them go fast.

They were worth the kind of money most people could only imagine in their dreams.

I divided the bulk of it among my favorite charities. Mostly animal, children's, and women's charities. However, I also donated a phenomenal amount to a clean-air initiative. Talk about alleviating some guilt.

Hague insisted I keep enough for myself as a substantial security blanket, and I saw the wisdom in that.

But I was no longer a billionaire.

And it was wonderful.

People would probably think I was crazy. However, there was a difference between being a millionaire and being a billionaire. As a billionaire, I had to hide. Hartwell started out as somewhere to hide. Yes, now it was my home, but people knew me under a false name and identity. As a billionaire, it was hard to know who you could trust. It was hard to know if someone loved you or was just using you to get to your money, to siphon the power that comes from having so much.

It was exhausting.

It was lonely.

And I knew it was the major reason I didn't actively pursue a romantic relationship.

"Do you need me to come to the city to sign those?" I asked, picking up my mail from the floor as I wandered through the open space to my kitchen.

"No, I'll have them couriered over. If you have any questions, call me and we'll go over them."

"Great. Thank you, Hague."

"You're welcome, Emery. I hope this decision has brought you some peace of mind."

"It has." I was no longer shackled to that life. Truly. Anonymous. No longer of interest to the world.

"Good. We'll speak soon."

We hung up, and a slight smile played on my lips.

I was finally free.

~

I'D BEEN out on the porch, enjoying a mug of tea, when I heard the banging of the door over the sound of the waves.

So lost in thought about my new future, I startled badly and spilled hot tea on my lap.

Cursing under my breath, I moved into the house to the front door.

"Emery, you home?" Jack's deep voice sounded through the screen.

Part of me was relieved to hear his voice; another part was wary of him coming to me now. The part that worried about him won out, and I hurried to unlock the door.

Jack's eyes narrowed as soon as he saw me. "You okay? You took awhile to answer."

"I was out on the porch. I didn't hear you over the waves. Are you okay?"

He braced his hands on either side of my doorjamb. "Can I come in?"

On the one hand, I wanted to know how Rebecca was. On the other, I'd promised myself I'd never let him into my house again.

Sensing my indecision, Jack lowered his voice to a level of seduction that was completely unfair. "Please."

Just like that, I cursed my inability to deny him. I nodded, stepping back to let him in. He didn't take his eyes off me as he strode into the room. "You sure you're okay? You seem … I don't know. There's something different about you."

It unnerved me that he seemed to know me so well. I closed the door, giving him my back. "What's going on, Jack?"

When I turned around, his eyes narrowed again. "Em, what's going on with you?"

I strode by him. "I spilled hot tea on my leg just as you knocked." I pointed to my lap. Seeing the continued suspicion in his eyes, I pointed to the sectional. I didn't want to discuss my news with him. I wanted his news, and then I wanted him gone. "Have a seat."

He seemed relieved by the invitation and sprawled his long body across my sofa. I tried to ignore how masculine he seemed on my comfy sectional. I lowered onto the opposite end, as far from him as I could get.

Jack's lips pursed at the action, but he didn't mention it.

"Is this about Rebecca?"

The polite thing to do would have been to offer him a drink, but I didn't want to give him the impression that he was welcome to stay.

Jack nodded. Sitting forward, he braced his forearms on his knees. "I've been lied to, Em."

From there Jack told me the tale of what really happened the night that changed his family's lives. My heart ached for Rebecca and all that she'd been through, and I sensed Jack's confusion and turmoil over discovering a side to Stu he hadn't realized existed. I heard the conflict in his tone as he tried to reconcile the man who attacked Bailey with the man who had tried to protect Rebecca.

"It's not all black and white, Jack," I reminded him as he fell silent. "Stu wasn't all bad. That much is clear. But he still stood by and allowed your lives to be ruined to protect himself."

"And Becs." Jack sat forward. "He knew Ian would set her up for the murder instead—and me as her accomplice."

"How? The fingerprints on the weapon were Stu's."

"He'd plant hers instead."

I nodded thoughtfully. "Your father really is the phlegmy mucus on the pile of shit that lives on hell spawn, isn't he?"

Jack's lips twitched with amusement. "That is the most colorful insult I've ever heard. And yes, he is."

"I'm sorry. You can't feel guilty for any of it. All you did was try to protect your sister. And now you don't have to anymore.

You must be so proud of her for having the courage to come forward."

"I am." His voice was gruff and he lowered his gaze to the floor. "She could face time for this, and she's at peace with it."

"And what about you? What will Ian do?"

"He won't want to sully the family name any more than it has been. He'll let Stu take the rightful blame for the murder." Jack looked up now, his expression hardening. "But I'm going to take Ian down, Em. I have evidence."

My heart stuttered. "The kind of evidence that might implicate you too?"

"I'll only offer my cooperation in exchange for immunity."

I relaxed. "Good."

"Does that mean you still care what happens to me?"

I sucked in a breath. "Jack … I will always care for you."

He leaned toward me and licked his lips as if nervous. Which seemed strange because Jack was never nervous. "Em … when this is over, I'll be free. I … there wouldn't be a reason for us not to give this a shot."

Suddenly I understood his nervousness.

I wanted to throw my arms around him. The urge stemmed from a piece of me that clung to the hope of something developing between us. But he'd cut me to the quick last summer. I'd opened myself to him in ways I hadn't been sure I'd ever be able to again … and he'd rejected me. And then continued sleeping with Bailey's sister. And other women. Like the brunette at Winter Carnival.

His rejection and defection, no matter his reasons, hadn't just stung.

It had sliced me deeply enough to scar.

I used to trust Jack with my heart.

I couldn't explain why. I just had.

I … I didn't trust him like that anymore.

And without trust, what was the point?

"Em?"

"What happened to you not wanting anything permanent?"

"We both know I just said that to push you away. To protect you."

I lifted my gaze to meet his and something dark flashed in his eyes at whatever he saw in my face. His head jerked back a little, like I'd hit him. "I'm sorry, Jack. I'm happy that you'll finally get out from under your father's machinations. But our … this isn't the relationship you should try to mend. We're past that. I'm … I understand why you did and said the things you did. But I was left humiliated and rejected. Again. And it was clearly easy for you to forget me, as noted by the plethora of women you've been with throughout all this.

"I don't trust you with my heart. I'm sorry."

He looked away, the muscle flexing in his jaw as he clenched his teeth.

Seeing him struggle hurt.

"Go to Cooper." I stood abruptly, needing him gone. "Please go to Cooper and talk to him. Tell him everything."

Jack stood slowly with an angry storm in his eyes. "You think he'll forgive me when you can't?"

"Yes," I answered honestly. "You and Cooper have a history that goes beyond anything you and I had. Don't look at it like telling him is a chance for you to get something out of it—look at it for what it is. Cooper deserves the truth, whether or not he forgives you. He deserves to know why you did what you did. As much as losing him hurt you, don't you think it wrecked him? Don't you think he wonders every day what the hell made you do that to him?"

Bright emotion gleamed in Jack's eyes. After contemplating me for what seemed like a painfully lengthy time, he nodded sharply.

"Good luck, Jack." I strode to my door and pulled it open.

Bracing myself, I held my breath as he walked toward it. He didn't look at me.

Just when I thought he'd leave without saying goodbye, he stopped beside me.

Our eyes held, like two magnets clicking together.

A shiver skated down my spine.

"I'm sorry I broke what was between us," he said, voice gruff with feeling.

Pain lashed across my chest. "It was just attraction, Jack," I lied.

He gave me a mocking, anguished smirk. "Sunrise, we both know it was something far deeper than that."

Then he left, striding quickly out of the house and down the porch steps.

I closed the door, locking it.

As I listened to his car pull out of my drive, I let the tears fall and promised myself it would be the last time I shed them over Jack Devlin.

17

JACK

They found the body and the dumbbell. His father and Stu hadn't buried them in Hartwell at all. They were buried in the woods somewhere between Jimtown and Arabian Acres.

By some miracle, the sheriff kept the news of the find quiet.

A few days later, the forensics came back. Stu's prints were all over the weapon. They charged Rebecca for aiding and abetting, and Jack paid her bail.

That was the extent of the privacy of the investigation. Word was that the local paper caught wind of the story—it would be all over the front pages by morning.

Jack had spent the last few days ignoring Ian's phone calls and consoling his mother and Jamie. He felt bad not giving them a heads-up about what he was about to do. But he couldn't chance Ian finding out.

"So, what did you want to talk about?" Detective Sullivan asked. He sat on the edge of his desk, like he was preparing to move at any second.

They were in the detective's office. Jack hadn't stated this was official business when he'd asked to speak to the cop.

"A hypothetical," Jack replied casually, as though his heart wasn't racing a mile a minute.

Sullivan tensed ever so slightly. "Okay."

"For instance, if someone were to come to you with years of evidence that proved one of your citizens was guilty of multiple counts of racketeering, blackmail, fraud, and assault, but was perhaps complicit in those activities ... would you grant them immunity for their cooperation?"

The detective's eyes sharpened. Then he took a deep breath before he crossed his arms over his chest. "How it's supposed to work is that we'd need the district attorney to grant that person immunity. But we'd have to start proceedings first. That person would have to hand over what evidence they have without knowing whether we have granted the immunity."

Fuck.

"But ... if a police officer were to offer the promise of immunity to the witness, then the prosecutor would be forced to uphold that promise." He smirked ever so slightly.

"Are you saying that's a promise you would make?"

Sullivan's expression turned hard with solemnity. "That's a promise I would definitely make."

Taking a deep breath—and one of the biggest leaps of faith in his life—Jack reached down to his feet where he'd put the leather folder with three USBs and some paperwork in it. He picked it up and held it out to Sullivan. "There's enough shit in there to put my father, Ian Devlin, and my brother, Kerr, away for a long time. And you'll have my testimony in court."

The detective took the folder. "Then we better take this to an interview room. We need my promise of immunity officially recorded."

Jack at once relaxed and tensed. There was something reassuringly genuine about Sullivan. His gut instinct told him he could trust the guy. That didn't mean he wasn't apprehensive as fuck to get the ball rolling on putting Ian away for good.

He left the sheriff's station about two hours later, feeling drained.

They would arrest his father immediately.

After calling Rebecca to let her know and to warn her about the story in the newspaper tomorrow, Jack drove to Cooper's Bar. It took him fifteen minutes to talk himself out of the car, another five to open the door to the bar, only for Kit, one of Cooper's bartenders, to tell him Coop was at home because the doc was sick.

Jack worried about what *sick* meant.

Also, he didn't want to go near Cooper's house because the last time he'd been there, he'd been screwing Dana.

Shit.

The memory still made his stomach roil.

He couldn't do this.

"Don't look at it like telling him is a chance for you to get something out of it—look at it for what it is. Cooper deserves the truth, whether or not he forgives you. He deserves to know why you did what you did. As much as losing him hurt you, don't you think it wrecked him? Don't you think he wonders every day what the hell made you do that to him?"

As Emery's voice filled his head, Jack felt the sweet sharpness of it. She was right. His Em was awfully wise.

Wise enough to not want anything do with him anymore.

Getting into his car again, he distracted himself with thoughts of Emery Saunders and why it didn't feel like his chest was caving in knowing she didn't want to start a relationship with him. He pondered that thought all night until he realized the truth. He wasn't drowning in a bottle of whisky over Emery because he didn't really believe it was the end for them.

Jack had waited nine years to be with her.

He'd wait however long it took now to get her to trust him again.

Worrying over how he'd do that, Jack pulled up to Cooper's house. That familiar wave of nausea rolled right over him again.

Forcing himself out of the car, he heard Coop and Jess's dog barking from inside the house. His strides were slow as he walked along the drive, past Coop's truck and up the porch steps.

Just as Jack reached the porch, the door opened and Jessica stood there in her pajamas. Her skin looked pale and clammy.

He realized how goddamn selfish it was to have come here after being told Jess was sick.

"I'll leave," he said.

The doc's eyes narrowed. "Why are you here?"

"I … uh … I came to talk with Cooper, but if this is a bad time …"

Suddenly, the dog, a huge golden retriever, bounded past Jessica and ran straight for Jack. He chuckled as the beast threw himself at him, his paws landing on Jack's gut as he stumbled back under the force of the dog's enthusiasm.

"Louis, down," Jessica said weakly.

"You okay?" Jack asked, patting the dog as it tried to lick every inch of his hands.

"I'm fine. Cooper's upstairs running me a bath."

"I should—"

"Come in." She stepped aside. "Clearly you have something to say, so you should come in."

"He might not thank you for it."

"He won't get mad at me right now, so your timing is actually kind of perfect."

"Should I be worried about you?" Jack frowned as he passed by her and into the house.

It looked different.

Back when Coop was married to Dana, the furniture was sparse and modern. There wasn't clutter.

The house was earthy and cozy now, filled with photographs from Coop and Jessica's wedding. There were a lot of books lying around.

Jack smiled to himself.

This was definitely the kind of home Jack imagined for his best friend.

"Would you be worried about me if something was wrong?" Jessica asked as she closed the door.

"Jess! Who's here?" Cooper's voice called from upstairs.

"A visitor for you!" she called back.

"I'd be worried," Jack answered honestly when her gaze came back to his.

She smiled slightly. "I think I already knew that about you. But the evidence has been conflicting."

Jack nodded. "That's why I'm here."

Jessica raised an eyebrow. "Well then … I think I'll go take that bath and give you some privacy. Louis, come with me."

The dog followed the doc to the staircase, and that's when Jack noticed the slight swell of her belly in the tight pajama tee she wore.

"Doc …"

She looked back at him. "Yeah?"

He swallowed thickly, feeling a ton of emotions for his ex-best friend. "Congratulations."

Her eyes widened ever so slightly and she glanced down at her belly. "Shit." She gave a huff of laughter. "I've been wearing looser fitting clothes when I'm in public." Her expression turned wary. "We didn't want anyone but close friends to know. Until we're past the twenty-three-week mark."

"Your secret is safe with me."

"It better fucking be," Cooper growled from the stairwell.

Jack had been so busy looking at Jess, he hadn't even noticed Cooper appear.

"Uh … I'm going to take that bath." Jess hurried past her husband, giving his arm a squeeze as she went.

Cooper offered her a frustrated but loving look. "You call if you need me."

As soon as the doc and Louis were gone, Cooper walked down the remaining stairs and strode toward Jack.

Jack braced himself.

His stomach was a riot of nerves.

"You want to tell me what the fuck you're doing in my house?" Cooper asked casually. But his expression was anything but casual.

Jack exhaled slowly, forcing himself to hold Coop's steely gaze. "Rebecca has been charged with aiding and abetting in the murder of a man named Caruthers."

Cooper flinched back in surprise. "What?"

"A few weeks … fuck, I don't even know where to start." Jack dragged a hand down his face. "I don't know where to start, Coop."

There was a moment of silence and then something seemed to dawn on Cooper's face. "Are you here … are you here to tell me why?"

He swallowed hard. "Yes. I'm not looking for anything from you. I … just … I'm in the position to tell you the truth now, and you deserve the truth."

A muscle ticked in Cooper's jaw but he didn't respond.

Jack took that as permission to continue. "I'll start at the beginning … Dana."

His best friend's expression hardened.

"She'd been coming on to me for a while. Then one day she called me up and said she needed to talk about you. That she was worried. So, I came over and she gave me all this shit about how you were blaming her for not getting pregnant."

Cooper let out a huff of aggravation.

"I knew that shit wasn't true. You know I never liked her."

"And yet you fucked her."

Jack looked away, the memories of the past dancing across his eyes. "She grabbed my crotch. Tried to initiate sex. I got the hell out of there. I was on my way to tell you when Ian called. He said that Rebecca had killed a man who'd tried to rape her. And Stu helped her bury the body. She was only seventeen."

Cooper's features slackened with shock. "What the fuck?"

"You know she isn't his, Coop."

He was one of the few people in town who knew Rebecca wasn't Ian Devlin's daughter.

"He didn't give a flying fuck about her. But he knew I did. So he sent her away to school in England and blackmailed me into giving up my entire life and falling in line."

"Blackmailed you how?"

"He said he'd give Rebecca up to the police and plant evidence that it was me, not Stu, who helped her bury the body."

"Jesus Fucking Christ." Cooper stumbled to his couch, slumping down on it, his head in his hands. "Fuck, Jack. Fuck!" He glared up at him, outrage written all over his face. "Why the fuck didn't you tell me?"

Seeing and hearing the rage in Coop's voice, Jack's throat closed with emotion.

Emery was right.

His defection had wrecked Coop as much as it had wrecked him.

"I couldn't do that to you. I couldn't have this secret hanging over your life. Do you know what it was like for me, driving around this town, wondering where that fucking body was, wondering when the anvil would come crashing down to ruin Becs, me, my mom. And if you knew … you'd be complicit, Cooper, and it would take you down with us. I couldn't have that."

"So, what did you do?" Realization dawned on Cooper. "Huh? Say it."

"You kept asking me what was wrong. You kept pushing." Jack found himself getting agitated as he remembered. "You knew it was fucked up that I'd sold my company, started working for a man I hated. You wouldn't let it go. I knew you wouldn't stop. The only way to keep you safe was to push you out of my life. And Dana … I hated that you had no clue what a disloyal, conniving bitch she really was."

"So you showed me."

Jack flinched at the underlying rage in his ex-friend's voice. "I did what I thought was best for you."

"That's why I never saw you with her again. That's why you warned Jess about my license. Nailed Stu for hitting Bailey. Then what the hell was Vanessa, huh?"

He swallowed hard. "I had to keep tabs on her. When I realized she would go through with the sale … I convinced her to go with Tremaine's offer instead."

Cooper's head jerked in surprise. He stood, pointing a finger. "That stays between us. Bailey thinks her sister did the right thing in the end."

Jack sighed. "Maybe Bailey should know what her sister is capable of so she knows not to trust her."

"Jesus fuck," Coop repeated as he paced the living room. "And Rebecca? She's been charged?"

"They lied to me, Coop." Jack crossed his arms over his chest. "Rebecca was …" Saying it still made him sick with guilt. "The guy was raping her. There was no trying. He did. Ian found out later he was wanted for multiple rapes in different states."

Cooper looked as devastated as Jack felt. "Oh, hell. Little Becs."

Jack swallowed down the emotion threatening to explode out of him. He looked at the floor, taking a minute.

"What happened, Jack?"

"Stu heard her crying out for help in the pool house. He saw the guy raping her and hit him in the head with a dumbbell. Repeatedly." Jack looked up and found Cooper's expression surprised again. "He was just trying to protect her."

Coop nodded, dazed.

"Rebecca came home a few days ago and went to the sheriff. Confessed. They found the body and the weapon. It's got Stu's prints all over it. They charged Becs with aiding and abetting. She's out on bail."

"I can't believe this." Cooper shook his head. "I mean, I knew it had to be something, but murder ... fuck."

"I want you to forgive me." The words blurted out of Jack before he could stop himself.

Cooper's eyes narrowed.

"I don't expect it. I'm not asking you for it. But I want it."

His friend looked at him. Really looked at him. There was no hardness or anger. But there was a shitload of weariness in Cooper's eyes. "Before Dana, I considered you the truest man I had ever known."

Jack flinched.

"I'm glad you told me, Jack. However, that doesn't mean I understand your reasoning. We were brothers. I would've done anything for you. And maybe if you'd told me what was going on, I could have helped you figure it out. You devastated my life. You think I cared in the end that she cheated on me? No. I cared that she cheated on me with *you*. That *you* betrayed me. And now I find out it was all to push me away, protect me? I don't know if I get that. I don't know if I ever will."

Jack's hope deflated.

He hadn't realized how much he needed that forgiveness from Coop.

Neither he nor Emery trusted him.

Jack knew he deserved the consequences of his actions. Didn't make it any harder to swallow.

"I should let you get back to Jessica." Jack started for the front door.

"Jack."

He glanced over his shoulder at Cooper. His friend exhaled slowly. "If you had come to me before I met my wife, I would've kicked you out on your ass no matter what the truth was."

Jack waited as Cooper rubbed a hand through his hair.

"But I guess … I guess I don't know if I wouldn't have done the same thing—the pushing you away to protect you part, I mean. The sleeping with my wife part was just plain fucked up."

"I wasn't … It's not an excuse … I just … I wasn't in my right mind, Coop. I was in a messed-up place."

"Yeah, I can imagine." He took a step toward Jack. "Lucky for you, I've come to find a twisted sort of gratitude over the past few years for your actions. Because if you hadn't done it, I might have been with Dana when Jess moved to town."

That hope rose in Jack.

"I don't know if it'll ever be the same between us … but I forgive you, Jack."

Tears he tried desperately to fight back brightened his eyes.

Cooper saw and his own glistened, his lips pinching hard.

"I'm so sorry, Coop. I'm so fucking sorry," he choked out.

"Yeah, I can see that. I'm sorry too. For what happened to Rebecca. For what happened to you."

Jack gave him a grateful nod, afraid if he spoke, he'd start fucking bawling. He pushed out of Cooper's house and hurried down the porch steps.

He was just about to get into his car when Cooper called out to him.

Jack looked up to find his friend standing on the porch, a thoughtful frown marring his brow. "Yeah?"

"I can't make any promises … I … this shit will take time … but … why don't you come by the bar before it opens sometime. If you need to talk."

It was a generous offer.

And it made Jack miss his old friend even harder than before. "I might just take you up on that, Coop."

Cooper gave him a tight nod and strode back into his house to be with his pregnant wife.

His pregnant wife whom Jack knew he partly had to thank for Cooper's willingness to forgive.

18

EMERY

I barely slept that night. I fervently hoped that Cooper had been more receptive to Jack than I had been. Despite my need to protect my heart, I didn't want him to feel as though he wasn't worthy of forgiveness.

It was contradictory, I know.

However, as I drove to Ivy's rental place on Johnson's Creek, I considered offering friendship to Jack. It meant I could keep my heart safe from him but still extend forgiveness. An offer of friendship would let him know I didn't think he was beyond repute. That perhaps trust between friends could bloom again.

Like most of Hartwell, the houses on Johnson's Creek were all white clad with brightly colored awnings and old-fashioned porches. Except most of the houses were bigger than a lot of homes in Hartwell. Moreover, it wasn't actually a creek but rather a lake.

Like most of South Hartwell, this was where the money was. A few homes on Johnson's Creek were second vacation homes. Ivy's two-story house was one of the smallest, even though it was slightly bigger than my beach house. The front faced onto the neighborhood, like most of the houses, and the back faced onto the lake.

I parked on Ivy's driveway, and she'd opened the door before I'd even put a foot on the porch. To say she was surprised to see me was an understatement. She invited me inside, leading me through an open-plan living area much like my own, and out onto the porch facing the lake. Her house was perched on a slope over the water, and I could see she had her own private dock.

I sighed inwardly at the sun glistening across the water. She and I were both blessed to wake up to magnificent views.

After she returned with a cold lemonade for me, we sat at her white wicker bistro set and gazed quietly out at the lake. People water-skied in the distance.

"So, what brings you here, Emery? Did my mother send you?" Ivy asked.

I knew she and Iris hadn't resolved their issues. Although Ivy had stayed with her parents for months after her fiancé's death, and she'd returned to her parents after Freddie Jackson attacked her in her apartment, there was still an estrangement between them. Mostly because Ivy refused to tell Iris what exactly had gone on between her and Oliver Frost. She'd pushed her parents away before he died, practically cutting everyone out of her life. And then when he overdosed and it was all over the papers, Ivy had returned to Hartwell to hide.

It was a shame. She was a wonderful screenwriter. I'd seen the movie that she won an Academy Award for, and her storytelling abilities were magical. Iris had given me a list of all the films Ivy had written, and I'd loved them. She was somewhat fatalistic but utterly romantic at the same time. It was a compelling combination.

Intelligence and wariness shone in her large dark eyes. I blushed a little under their intensity. Ivy was stunning. Her eyes tilted slightly upward and then narrowed toward the corner.

She wore mascara today, making them appear even bigger. Her smooth, bronze skin was enviously perfect, her cheekbones movie-star high, and her mouth small but full. Since the attack, Ivy had cut her long, jet-black hair into a shoulder-length bob that now hung in tousled waves around her face. Iris and Ira didn't know much about Ivy's real parents beyond the fact that her mother was Filipino.

If I'd met Ivy at one of her star-studded events back in Hollywood, I wouldn't have been able to talk to her. She was the kind of beautiful that stopped you in your tracks. And when she was all glammed up, it was intimidating.

Even now, wearing jeans and a T-shirt, there was something untouchable about Ivy.

"Well?" She raised an eyebrow before taking a sip of lemonade. "You're blushing. My mother definitely put you up to this."

I frowned. "Why would Iris send me to see you?"

"Because I'm no longer under her roof and her nose is twitching." Ivy's lips quirked. "She's worried about me. All the time."

"Well, mothers are supposed to worry about their daughters. You should be grateful for that." I winced because I sounded almost accusatory.

"I am grateful. But I'm also a grown woman who doesn't need her mother sending over spies."

"I'm not a spy."

"Then why are you blushing?"

"I do that. Especially around people I don't know very well."

"Right. Actually, I already knew that." She studied me carefully. "I don't get it, though. I mean, you've seen you, right? You have Hollywood written all over you."

I huffed in embarrassment. "Oh, yes, I'm quintessential Hollywood."

She laughed at my sarcasm. "Not in personality. And I would

not recommend that world to anyone, let alone someone as shy as you, but you're beautiful and the camera would love you."

"Is that all it takes?"

Ivy frowned. "No. Not for most of the biggest, well-respected actors. You have to be able to act. But you also have to have that certain something. Charisma. You can't cheat charisma. Some of the most average-looking actors have charisma and it transcends good looks. You know … they're just naturally sexy. And nothing is hotter than a guy who can take what you've written and make it so real, your heart feels like it might burst out of your chest watching him." She gazed at the lake, smiling softly to herself.

"Did you date actors while you were out there?" I asked tentatively, not sure it was a subject she'd want to touch.

Ivy threw me a wicked smile. "Hell yeah."

I laughed and her grin widened.

After a moment of surprisingly comfortable silence, she asked, "So really, Emery, why are you here?"

"To invite you to lunch today." I sat up a little straighter. "The girls come to my store once a week for lunch. Jess, Dahlia, and Bailey. I thought you might like to join us."

Ivy contemplated me. "You know, my mom used to talk about you all the time." She looked a little sheepish. "I was jealous of you."

Shocked, I could only stare. "Why?"

"Silly, right? I was in LA. I had the kind of career very few people get to have in film. Hotshot fiancé. Fame. Respect. Blah blah blah. But I missed my family. I missed this place." She gestured to the water. "I missed my mom's sharp wit. And I missed Bailey and how she could turn the most banal event into a story that had you rolling on the floor."

We shared an affectionate smile for our friend.

"And Mom talked a lot about you. The sweet, shy bookstore

owner. I could tell she felt a motherly protectiveness for you, and I'll admit, I didn't like it. Childish, huh?"

Thinking of how I hadn't wanted to share my friends with Ivy, I shook my head. "I understand."

"I will say one thing for Mom … she's always right about people. She's got that gut instinct, you know. And if Mom thinks you're good people, then you're good people." Ivy stood. "I'd love to come to lunch with you."

I beamed, glad my decision to put myself out there with Ivy had paid off.

MY FRIENDS SAILED into the bookstore together, chattering madly with a cloud of intensity hovering over their heads. They stopped abruptly at the sight of Ivy standing on the stairs that led to the seating area.

"Ivy." Bailey walked to her first. "You're here."

"Emery invited me. I hope you don't mind."

"Of course I don't." She pushed Ivy toward the chairs and turned back to mouth "thank you" to me.

I smiled and shrugged as I grabbed a plate of sandwiches off the counter.

Jess approached and put her arm around me. "That was sweet of you," she whispered.

"She needs good friends." I eyed her carefully. Jess looked pale. "How are you?"

"I've been dealing with morning sickness, although I curse whoever named it that because it happens at *any* time of day. I'm feeling okay today, though. Ish." Jess lifted a rolled-up newspaper. "Have you seen this?"

I shook my head, my heart thumping with trepidation.

I thought I already knew what was in there.

"Drinks?" I asked everyone as they sat in the armchairs and

on the sofa, already diving into the sandwiches.

"We'll get those later." Bailey gestured to an empty chair. "Sit, sit. There is news afoot."

"What's going on?" Ivy took a bite of a canapé and moaned. "Oh my God," she said around a mouthful.

Dahlia chuckled. "Yeah, Em's lunches are the best."

"Yeah, you're not kidding. Emery, why aren't you catering? My God. These are better than what I had at glitzy LA parties."

"If you don't stop complimenting her, she'll burst into flames," Dahlia teased.

I shot her a mock disgruntled look.

"Okay, people, yes, Em can make a mean canapé ... can we concentrate?" Bailey gestured to Jessica. "Paper."

Jess opened and flattened it on the table.

Across the front page of the *Hartwell County Chronicle* were two photographs: one of Rebecca, the other of Stu. The headline read "MURDER ON HART'S BOARDWALK."

"Well, that's dramatic," I murmured.

"Dramatic." Bailey shifted forward in her seat. "Rebecca Devlin was raped nearly five years ago and Stu Devlin, trying to protect his sister, murdered the guy. She confessed to helping Stu bury the body and murder weapon. The guy was wanted for rape in multiple counties."

"It gets even more complicated." Jess sighed. "This stays between us."

The girls all nodded eagerly.

"Jack came to see Cooper."

I held my breath.

"He told Cooper everything. Including the fact that Ian Devlin knew about this." She gestured to the paper. "But they lied to Jack. They told him that Rebecca had killed Caruthers before he could rape her, that they covered it up and if Jack didn't fall in line, Ian would tell the police what Rebecca had done. And they'd lie and say it was Jack who'd helped her, not Stu."

"Holy shit," Dahlia breathed. "I shouldn't know this. If Michael knew, he'd have to arrest Jack for failing to notify the police about the crime."

Jess's eyes widened. "Oh, Dahlia … I—"

"You can't tell Michael." The words slipped out of my mouth before I could stop them. They flinched at the near hysteria in my tone. "You'd have to tell him I knew too."

"WHAT?"

I flinched.

Oh hell.

What had I just done?

"You knew?" Bailey said in between gaping at me like an oxygen-deprived fish. "How did you know?"

I couldn't believe I'd just blurted that out. What on earth was I thinking? I flushed hot and covered my eyes with my hand. "Oh, flea shit on a dog turd."

"Did she just say what I think she said?" Bailey whispered, shocked laughter in her voice.

"Emery?" Jess rested her hand on my arm.

I peeked at her through my fingers. "I've known for a year," I whispered.

Silence fell over the table.

"Okay. Sisterhood comes first," Dahlia announced. "Anything said in this room stays in this room."

"That's not fair to you," Ivy said. "Michael is your man. You shouldn't have to keep things from him."

"Although to play devil's advocate, clearly Michael kept this"—Bailey nodded to the paper—"from you. You didn't know about any of this before the news article, and it says in it that Michael is heading the investigation."

Dahlia contemplated this. "True. I mean, I knew something was up because he was distracted and told me he had an interesting case at work … but he didn't give me the details. But if you'd prefer me to leave, I can."

"You're not leaving." Bailey shook her head. "Unless you want to."

Dahlia's gaze came to me. "I'll stay. It's not like Jack or Emery were involved in the actual murder. And clearly Jack was being blackmailed, so …"

Everyone looked at me.

"I'll tell you after Jess finishes telling us about Jack and Cooper."

I wanted to know if Cooper had forgiven him.

"Right." Jess sighed. "Ian blackmailed Jack. That's why he gave up his business. And apparently, Cooper kept pushing Jack for the truth. Jack didn't want Coop to know because he didn't want him to be burdened with that knowledge. He was in a bad way." Jess frowned. "A really bad way and obviously not thinking straight. That's what I reminded Cooper. Anyway, Jack told Cooper that Dana was coming on to Jack before all this went down—"

"It's true," I interjected without thinking.

They all gawked at me in confusion.

Dammit. I was just blurting out all my secrets these days!

"I … uh … Jack and I spoke about it back then. He needed reassurance that telling Cooper was the right thing to do."

"You and Jack talked to each other?" Bailey threw up her hands. "What is going on? Am I in an alternate universe?"

"Okay, okay, clearly Emery is a woman of many mysteries," Dahlia said. "But let's allow Jess to finish."

Jess shook herself out of whatever thoughts she was having as she gaped at me. "Anyway … Before Jack could tell Coop about Dana, this all happened with Rebecca. Cooper was on Jack's case all the time about it, so Jack decided he needed to push Cooper away."

"Oh my God!" Bailey gasped loudly. "He set it up. He deliberately set it up so Cooper would walk in on him with Dana. Oh my God!"

"Yes, exactly."

"That is fucked up." Ivy shook her head, eyes wide with shock, even as she reached for another canapé.

"He thought he was protecting Cooper," I defended him.

Bailey's jaw dropped. "Okay, Jess, hurry up with your story because I am beginning to suspect that Emery Saunders is in love with Jack Devlin and I can barely contain myself."

I opened my mouth to deny the claim but Jess continued. "Well, Bails, you might not like the next part."

"Why?"

"Jack did warn me about Cooper's liquor license. He also did beat the shit out of Stu for hitting you."

Bailey's expression softened. "I knew it."

"But ..." Jess exhaled slowly. "He also slept with Vanessa to keep tabs on her. She was going to sell her shares to Devlin. Jack sweet-talked her into accepting Tremaine's offer instead."

Bailey's flushed cheeks paled. "What?"

"I'm sorry." Jess gave her a sympathetic look. "I thought you should know ... you should know that Vanessa can't be trusted."

Everyone was silent for a moment as Bailey glared at her lap. My heart hurt for her.

When Vanessa approached Ian Devlin with the proposal that he buy her shares in Hart's Inn, we all thought, by the fact that she ended up selling to Tremaine instead, that it had been her master plan all along to get Tremaine to step up for her sister. That she would never jeopardize Bailey's inn by actually selling to Devlin.

My heart also ached for Jack. I'd been so angry at him about Vanessa. I still was. But knowing he'd used her to protect Bailey shed new light over the situation.

"Right. Well." Bailey shrugged sadly. "I guess that shouldn't surprise me ... so ... what happened between Jack and Cooper?"

"Bailey—"

Bailey cut Dahlia off. "I want to digest this news later, if that's okay."

"Of course."

Jessica cleared her throat. "Right, well … Cooper." She smiled softly. "Cooper told Jack that if he ever needed to talk, he should stop by the bar."

That was wonderful news! "Really?"

Jessica smiled at me. "Cooper is a little confused by it all, but I talked it through with him … he's forgiven Jack and I think he wants to see if their friendship can be salvaged. He missed Jack. He grieved him. I think they both grieved each other. They have a bond, a connection. They might never get back the easiness of before, but I think Cooper would like to try. He doesn't want what happened with Dana to have power over his life. And as screwed up as Jack's thinking was, I think Cooper's trying to understand."

"That's wonderful," I said. I was so happy for Jack.

"It is," Bailey agreed, her expression sharpening. "So, Miss Saunders … why don't you tell us about you and Jack and why all the longing looks I've witnessed over the last few years suddenly seem to be part of a deeper story?"

I glanced around at my friends' inquisitive faces. Ivy looked curious. Dahlia was frowning. Jess appeared concerned. And Bailey looked ready to pounce out of her seat with excitement.

This was my own damn fault.

No matter what my heart told me, I couldn't seem to stop caring about Jack or wanting to protect him. What was wrong with me?

I exhaled slowly. "Well … I think it began the moment Jack and I met …"

19

JACK

"Jack, this is Agent Chen and Agent Underwood." Sullivan introduced Jack as he stepped into his office.

He'd called Jack to let him know that Ian's racketeering charges were federal crimes, which meant the feds were taking over the case from Michael and they wanted to interview Jack.

Agent Chen stepped forward. "Let's take this to an interview room."

The guy's demeanor was worryingly expressionless.

Jack threw Sullivan look.

The detective gave him a nod of reassurance.

Minutes later, Jack sat across from the two agents, his reflection glowering at him from the two-way mirror behind the feds. They went through the formalities of starting the formal recording.

Agent Underwood, a pretty, older woman with umber skin, leaned forward. "Mr. Devlin, we understand that you were promised immunity for your cooperation. Let me reassure you that the promise of immunity in exchange for your witness testimony still stands with the Bureau."

He relaxed ever so slightly. "Good to know."

From there he spent the next hour going over everything he'd already told Michael Sullivan. The experience wasn't any less draining. When they released him, Jack wanted nothing more than to go to Cooper's Bar and throw back a scotch. But he wasn't sure if Cooper's offer stood so soon after his confession.

The sound of Jack's name halted him just as he was about to open the door to leave. Turning, he watched Sullivan hurry down the steps.

"You okay?" he asked gruffly.

Jack nodded.

"Just a heads-up." Sullivan leaned in, lowering his voice. "The feds are working to freeze your father's and brother's assets, but for now, they posted bail."

Jack tensed. "What the fuck? I thought that bail would be set at an impossible amount."

Sullivan grimaced. "The bail judge was Judge Kent."

Anger coursed through him at the news. "I gave you evidence that Kent has been taking bribes from Ian for years. Why the hell would he be allowed to set bail?"

"Because the feds can't move on that evidence just yet. I'm sorry."

"How long until their assets are frozen?"

"It should happen today. It might already have happened. Once it does, they can say goodbye to their fancy defense attorney."

"Even so … they're still out until this goes to trial." Jack bit back a curse. "How do I protect my mother now?"

Rosalie had refused to move out of the mansion and into Jack's place in South Hartwell, terrified of Ian. Jack had hope that once his father was behind bars, he'd be able to convince his mom to take that step.

"Look, I'm not supposed to do this, but if your mom wants

to leave that house, I can accompany you to get her. In an *unofficial* capacity. As a friend."

Jack appreciated the offer but he couldn't put Sullivan in that position. "Thanks, but I … I'll figure it out."

"Be careful, Jack," Sullivan warned. "Ian knows the evidence is stacked against him and he seems like the kind of ruthless bastard that won't take this lying down. He comes at you, I want you to call me immediately. Don't deal with it yourself. Call me. I'll come and slap some cuffs on him with pleasure."

Jack nodded goodbye, his heart racing a little faster as he marched to his car.

"Fuck," he bit out in frustration when he reached it. And then something occurred to him. "Rebecca."

JACK BROKE the speed limit driving to his house in North Hartwell where he and Rebecca were staying. They'd already moved there, hoping Rosalie and Jamie would move into the South Hartwell home.

Practically flying out of the car, Jack took the porch steps three at a time and launched himself into the house. "Becs!" he yelled as he hurried through the lounge and into the kitchen. It was empty.

"Becs!"

No reply.

Shit.

Jack strode through the kitchen, planning to look upstairs, when a piece of paper pinned to the fridge caught his eye. He removed the tourist magnet holding it.

Gone for a walk along the beach. I have my cell if you need me. Becs xx

Jack reached into his suit pocket for his phone. He wanted her back here where he could keep an eye on her.

"Relax. There's nothing we can do to little sister now that hasn't already been done."

Rage, frustration, disappointment, all of it moved through him at the sound of his brother Kerr's voice.

Jack turned to face him.

Kerr leaned against the doorway to the kitchen, a smirk that didn't reach his eyes on his face. His fury was palpable.

Jack didn't care. Kerr was the eldest, the one who should have protected them from their father. But he was too like the old man. Selfish to the core. Probably why he'd never married. Thank God for that. Jack almost flinched at the sight of him. Of all of them, Kerr was almost the spitting image of Stu. And the memory of Stu filled Jack with guilt, regret, and confusion.

"No, despite her fucking everything up, I feel like little Rebecca has been through enough. And to be fair, she will probably see some jail time for this, and anything that happens to her in prison will be worse than what we could ever do to her." Kerr chuckled, pushing off the jamb. "Dad agreed."

Jack stared blankly at his brother, knowing his ability to not react pissed him off. "So? I'm supposed to be scared that you've come for me? The star witness in your case. Are you that fucking dumb?"

"You know you've royally screwed us, right?" Kerr glared. "We got the call that they froze everything. Mick Rooney, that fucking slimy bastard, is leaving us to swing in the wind."

Mick Rooney was their high-powered defense attorney. Jack smirked. "If you don't have the money to pay him, that's kind of the deal."

"You smug cocksucker." Malice flashed in Kerr's eyes. "That means we have nothing left to lose. We're going away for this. Probably for a long time … so we might as well take you down before we go."

"I'm not afraid of you, Kerr."

"No, I know that. Why do you think Dad hates you so much?

He can't stand that you're not afraid of him, that you don't respect him. I think you've finally pushed him over the edge, though, little bro. And since he knows you're not afraid of anything that might happen to you … we decided to hit you where it'll actually fucking hurt."

Fear flooded him. "Mom? Jamie?"

Kerr grimaced. "Why would Dad hurt Mom or Jamie? He still loves *them*."

"He's got a funny way of showing it." Jack's mind raced as he tried to figure out who Ian would go after. If he went after Cooper, Coop could take care of himself … but that wasn't the point.

"Look at you, scrambling to figure it out." Kerr snorted. "Let me help you. You thought your feelings for her were a secret, but Dad's PI caught you with her a few times over the years … and anybody with fucking eyes can see you mooning at her any chance you get. You big pussy."

Jack's stomach roiled. No. They couldn't possibly know about her.

"Tall, legs forever, ass a man would pay a lot of money to ride. Blond hair. Owns a bookstore … ringing any bells?"

He gave his brother no warning.

Jack jumped and used the force of the lunge to bring his fist down across Kerr's face. Blood sprayed out of his brother's nose, his head juddering on his neck.

Kerr fell to the ground with a sickening thud.

Knocked out.

Reaching for his cell, hands trembling, Jack dialed Cooper. He was nearer to Emery. It rang four times before his old buddy's voice filled his ears. "Hello?"

"Cooper, it's Jack." He huffed breathlessly as he ran out of the house to his car. "You need to get to Emery now. You're closer than I am. Ian's going after her to get back at me."

"Fuck!" Cooper growled. "On my way." He hung up.

Jack sped out of his driveway, fear unlike anything he'd ever felt before threatening to cripple him.

20

EMERY

After lunch, when the girls returned to work and Ivy followed Dahlia to her store (she'd started helping at the store when Dahlia was in her workshop), I closed the shop early. It wasn't something I typically did, but my mind was reeling after telling my friends the truth about my relationship with Jack. I'd even told them about last summer.

I could tell Bailey was dying to ask me a million questions, but she'd learned enough about me to know that an interrogation would only cause me to clam up. I told them what I was ready to share, and that was a surprising amount. Bailey, however, hinted at her curiosity about my experience with men.

I think she was trying to ask if I was a virgin.

I avoided those hinted questions because it would mean telling them about Tripp, and I wasn't sure I ever wanted to talk about him.

While Bailey seemed ecstatic about the idea of "Jack finding his redemption with Emery," like we were living in a romance novel or something, my other friends were less enthused. Jess and Dahlia were both concerned about my connection to Jack and urged me to continue to be cautious with him. Even Ivy, who wasn't as close to me, seemed a little perturbed and agreed. Bailey was annoyed with them all, especially when I promised them I was done with Jack Devlin for good.

I said the words—and I wanted to mean them—but they still hurt. It still ached deep inside me to think of never kissing Jack again. Even if it was best for me. I needed to remind myself continually how much it hurt to see him with those other women.

And I worried about him. I worried about his family's tragic tale being splashed across newspapers, becoming fodder for this town's gossips, of which there were many. Poor Rebecca. I didn't know her. However, I didn't want her to feel alone during all this. Perhaps I should talk to the girls about offering her support.

Or was that too intrusive?

Perhaps Jack's sister just wished to be left alone.

She might be like Cat, Cooper's sister. Jessica, apparently, had tried to invite Cat to many of our gatherings but as a single working mom, she was busy and had little free time. Jessica also suspected Cat was kind of a loner and liked it that way.

I sighed as I let myself into my house. This was why I closed shop early. My mind was so unfocused, jumping from one thought to the next.

That's also why I didn't sense his presence until I'd already stepped inside and closed the door behind me.

My heart lurched into my throat at the sight of the tall, distinguished, handsome older man standing on the edge of my kitchen, near my dining table.

Ian Devlin.

He had a gun pointed at me.

The first thought that crossed my mind was how I could reach inside the top drawer of the side table to my left. Inside that drawer was my loaded Glock.

My second thought was that Jack had been right all along.

Ian *was* spying on Jack. Otherwise he wouldn't be here, in my house, threatening me.

In retaliation for what his son had done.

Because that's what this was.

"You know why I'm here." Devlin glared icily at me.

"I-I know why. Although"—I let out a shaky exhale as I tentatively moved to the sideboard, pretending I merely wanted to put my purse down on it—"I don't know how you think this will help matters." I turned my back to him and sweat rolled down my spine beneath my dress.

"She speaks." Devlin snorted bitterly. "But she's stupid enough to put her back to a loaded gun."

Anger suffused me as I concealed my movements with my body and slowly opened the drawer. I winced as it made a slight grating sound.

"What are you doing? Turn around where I can see you."

God, he was such a cliché.

As quickly as I could, I reached in, grabbed the gun, and whirled around, clasping it expertly before me, pointing it at Devlin's chest.

He let out a chuckle of surprise but kept his gun trained on me. Lazily. With one hand raised. "You even hold that thing like you know how to shoot it."

I did know how to shoot it.

I knew how to shoot extremely well.

"A lady has to know how to protect herself," I replied. "Now, Mr. Devlin, I think it might be best if you leave before you make things any worse for yourself."

Fury flared in his eyes. "You don't get it. The feds took over the case against me. They froze all my assets. My attorney abandoned me. I'm *fucked*." He waved the gun dangerously, but I refused to flinch. I was ready to shoot if I needed to, even though the thought made me sick to my stomach.

"Mr. Devlin, stop waving the gun around or I will shoot you."

He gave a bark of laughter. "I'll believe that when I see it." Ian shook his head, despair leaching the anger from his face. "It's over. Betrayed by my own fucking blood. Do you know what that feels like?" His eyes turned worryingly blank. "I want to hurt him like he hurt me." His finger flexed on the trigger and mine twitched in retaliation.

The front door opened. I gasped at the sight of Cooper letting himself into the house. He saw me and my gun and hesitated. "Emery?"

I shook my head at him. "Get out, Cooper."

"Cooper!" Ian yelled viciously. "Get the fuck out of here or I will fucking shoot her!"

To my despair, Cooper threw back his shoulders, his face mottled with anger, and he strode into view, stopping at the sight of Ian holding the gun pointed at me. "You know, until this point, you've been a vicious bastard, but you've never been this dumb."

Ian sneered at him. "I've got nothing left to lose. I'm going away for a long time, boy. I might as well do something that my son will never forget."

"Jack doesn't care about Emery," Cooper said.

I tried not to flinch, wondering if he knew something I didn't.

"All you'll do is hurt an innocent woman. For nothing."

"What would you know about Jack?" Ian huffed, a bead of sweat rolling down his temple. "He wants this one. I've got the photographic evidence." He waved the gun at me. "Did you know she's a billionaire? My son is playing the long game with her. He's more like me than he wants to let on."

My heart rejected Ian's insinuation that Jack was only after my money.

But that little niggle of insecurity that would always be there made itself known.

"Bullshit." Cooper threw me a look. "Bullshit," he assured me.

And then the front door was thrown open again and Jack ran in, skidding to a halt beside Cooper who held up a hand to ward him off. Jack's clothes were askew, his hair disheveled, his skin damp with perspiration. His eyes moved between me and his father. He looked frantic.

"Don't do this," he spat at Ian.

Ian grinned.

And then, like people were wont to do, he underestimated me.

He swung the gun toward Jack. "Now I can't decide who I want to shoot more."

I narrowed my eyes, aimed at his hand that held the gun, and pulled the trigger.

Ian's roar of agony filled my home as he dropped his gun and fell to his knees, clutching his wounded hand.

I lowered my Glock, engaging the safety, and watched as Cooper kicked Ian's gun out of the way. He then pulled out his phone to call the police.

Jack was in my face, his grip tight on my biceps as he hauled me against him. I let him hold me for a few seconds before he pulled back to study me. "Are you okay?" he asked, his eyes roaming my body, as if searching for injury.

I nodded. I was a little in shock. My dress was soaked with sweat. But I was okay.

"Where did you learn to shoot like that?" Cooper asked as he stood guard over Ian who moaned like a wounded animal at his feet.

"My grandmother. She said a lady should know how to defend herself. I took lessons at her country club gun range throughout my teen years. I used to shoot competitively. I still visit a range every month. I'm pretty good with a crossbow too."

The information poured out of me as I stared at Ian as he frothed at the mouth.

Jack made a sound somewhere between laughter and a groan. My breath stuttered a little at his look of adoration. "You are full of surprises, Emery Saunders."

Cooper snorted and Jack looked over his shoulder at him. He still hadn't released his hold on me. "What?"

Cooper grinned knowingly at the two of us. "I think you're both full of surprises."

21

EMERY

It wasn't Michael who came to arrest Ian. It was Sheriff King himself and one of his deputies. Jeff King and Jack weren't exactly unalike in looks. They were both exceptionally tall (although Jeff was a little taller than Jack), loose-limbed, and had this great masculine swagger about them. They also shared a similar hard, rangy physique.

However, while Jeff was serious, gruff, and earnest, Jack oscillated between brooding and naturally charming.

Jeff bent his head to mine, his eyebrows creased in concern. "Are you sure you're all right, Emery?"

This close, I could smell his spicy cologne and saw that his blue eyes were a startling shade of aquamarine against his light olive skin. While the deputies of the Hartwell County Sheriff's Office wore khaki uniforms, Jeff's was black. It made his eyes pop.

Finding myself under his concerned scrutiny for the first time, my cheeks grew hot. His lips twitched as he took in the sight of my flushed face. He looked at me with something akin to tenderness.

"She's fine, Sheriff." Jack's voice was hard as he wrapped an arm around my shoulders and drew me tight to his side.

The sheriff and Jack stared at one another for an awkward beat. How was it possible for me to keep my cool while a man held me at gunpoint but then act like a freaking mortified schoolgirl around an attractive man? It was infuriating!

"I believe I asked Miss Saunders," Jeff said.

"I'm fine, Sheriff." And with Jack's arm around me and him sticking close even as Ian was marched out in handcuffs, I had felt fine. I felt safe and comforted with him here. I didn't want to feel that way, but I couldn't deny that I did.

"Well, if we need anything else, we'll let you know." Jeff cut me another look. "I can't tell you how glad I am to know you can protect yourself, Emery."

It sounded like a pointed comment.

Jack tensed next to me.

I tried not to smile. "Thank you, Sheriff."

As he walked out of the house, Cooper chortled.

He stood near the sectional. For a moment, I'd forgotten he was there, which seemed impossible. His eyes were on Jack. "I'd be careful there. I think someone thinks someone else is cute."

Jack huffed. "What, are we in middle school?"

Laughing under his breath, Cooper walked to us. "I need to get back to Jess. Do you want me to send the girls over?"

"Honestly, I'm exhausted now," I replied. "But if you could send them over in the morning, I'd appreciate it."

"You got it." Cooper then enveloped me in a tight hug. For a moment, I was too taken aback to do anything and then as the awesomeness of his hug set in, I closed my arms around him and held on. Tears burned in my eyes. "I'm glad, too, that you can shoot like nobody's business. I can worry a little less about you being here on your own."

He worried about me?

"Thank you," I whispered, my voice a little hoarse with emotion. "Thank you for coming to my rescue."

Cooper chuckled and released me but only to cup my face in his hands and grin. "You're welcome, darlin', though it isn't a hit to my reputation to tell the whole world it was Emery Saunders who rescued me and Jack."

I laughed softly as he stepped back and addressed Jack. "You okay?"

Jack held his hand out to him, his expression grim but grateful. "Thanks for being here for her."

Cooper slid his hand into Jack's. The vibe coming off them was intense. "I did it for you both."

"I won't forget it."

They released their handshake, and Cooper narrowed his eyes ever so slightly. "We'll talk?"

"We'll talk," Jack promised.

All the while, I watched them and tried not to grin with giddiness. I was so happy for Jack that Cooper was willing to give their friendship another go. It made me forget for a second that Ian Devlin had come here with the intention of shooting me.

Whoa. I just shot Jack's father.

Jack locked the front door behind him once Cooper departed.

"You can go, Jack." It sounded tentative because I didn't want it to sound like I was kicking him out. I just didn't want him to think I couldn't be alone.

He shook his head, staring at me incredulously. "You think I can leave you right now?"

"What about Rebecca?"

Jack cursed under his breath and then pulled his cell out of his pocket. "Give me your number."

"What?"

"Your cell. I didn't have your number tonight. Couldn't reach you. Couldn't warn you. That's not happening again."

Sensing he would not be budged and not entirely unhappy to provide my number, I rhymed it off. He then called my phone, which went to voicemail. "Now you have my number. I've gotta call Rebecca. Don't move," he told me before pressing a button and holding the phone to his ear. A few seconds later, he said, "Becs?"

Wanting to give him privacy, I strolled to the kitchen. I heard Jack's voice following me and realized he was shadowing my movements.

Hmm.

I filled the kettle, preparing to make tea, as Jack stood at my island and watched me while he talked to his sister and explained what had happened ... and that she shouldn't wait up.

I raised an eyebrow.

"Tea?" I asked as Jack hung up the phone. I reached up to a cupboard where I kept my scotch. Now and then, on a frigid winter's night, I liked to add a little whisky to my tea. I waved the bottle of Talisker at Jack. "Spiked tea?"

Although his mouth smiled, his eyes didn't. "Yeah, go for it."

We stood across from each other, the island between us.

"Kerr went to your house to taunt you about Ian coming for me?" I asked for clarification. It's what Jack had told the sheriff. He'd sent more deputies to arrest Kerr.

"Yeah," Jack bit out before taking a sip of the tea I'd slid toward him.

"Don't you think that's strange? It's almost as if he was giving you a chance to stop it."

His face darkened with fury. "No. He thought the deed was already done. He forgot Ian is a drama queen who likes to draw shit out. Luckily for us." Jack looked exhausted. "Shit, Em, I am so fucking relieved you're a secret markswoman."

I laughed a little. "Me too."

"I can't believe you can laugh about this. I'm sorry you got pulled into my fucked-up family drama." He shook his head. "How do I even apologize for what happened here tonight?"

"Jack, I don't hold you responsible. You tried to tell me that your father would attempt to use me in some way to get to you. You were right." One of the biggest reasons for keeping Jack at bay was because I'd been angry at him for rejecting me. But he'd only rejected me because he'd been trying to protect me. At the time, I thought it a pitiful excuse, one we both should've had a voice in. Yet he had been proven right tonight. This realization confused me. And made me more than a little tenderhearted toward him.

"I wish like hell I'd been wrong."

"It's done now. And I'm fine." I smiled to myself before I took a sip of tea. "People always underestimate me."

"I'll never underestimate you."

I nearly choked at the sincerity in his promise, at the emotion in his eyes as he gazed at me like I was his whole world. I remembered how frantic and scared he'd been as he burst into my house and saw Ian holding the gun. I'd never seen Jack lose his cool like that.

Ian's insinuation that Jack was playing the long game with me niggled at the back of my mind. I knew I shouldn't think that of Jack. Rationally, I knew his fear didn't stem from losing a chance at my billions but I wanted him to know the truth anyway. "I gave up the Paxton Group."

Jack raised an eyebrow at the abrupt change of conversation.

I took another fortifying sip of tea. Then I studied him, trying to decipher his feelings as I told him, "I sold my shares and donated most of the money to charity. I have no ties to the Paxton Group. I'm even selling the estate in New York. I'm ... I'm not a billionaire anymore, Jack."

I watched as he digested this news and then seemed to deflate with relief as he exhaled slowly. "Thank Christ for that."

Now it was my turn to be shocked. "Oh?"

"Do you know what kind of target all that money made you? It's a goddamn miracle no one found you hiding out in Hartwell. Emery Saunders isn't exactly a genius alias."

I huffed in indignation. "It worked for nine years."

"Like I said, a goddamn miracle."

"You're being annoying."

Jack chuckled. "The truth is annoying."

I harrumphed, pouting into my tea.

"You are so fucking adorable," Jack said softly. Our eyes met and his turned smoky and hot. "And beautiful. And kind. And naive. And wise. You're every contradiction under the sun … and I can't stop thinking about you."

It was the most wonderful thing anyone had ever said to me.

Then he was rounding the island, striding with purpose. Jack pulled me against his hard heat, my breasts crushed to his chest. My breathing grew shallow.

"Don't make me leave tonight, Em. I need to be near you."

"I—"

"Don't." He squeezed his eyes closed and rested his forehead on mine. "I know you can't make me any promises. But let me stay tonight. I won't hold you to anything in the morning."

My heart raced as I realized what he was asking.

Heat flushed through me, my lower belly trembled, and an intense ache grew between my legs. The truth was, I didn't want to be alone either, and I was tired of fighting how I felt about Jack.

Maybe I'd been too harsh before.

Clearly he cared about me.

Clearly the money wasn't an issue.

Jack.

I missed being touched. Being held. Being needed.

I kissed him on the lips. A soft brush of mouth against mouth.

He groaned, sinking into the kiss, his arms wrapping around me, crushing me against him. His kiss was hungry. Almost desperate. And the heat coating my skin abruptly felt like flames flickering across my body.

I broke the kiss, panting for breath, and Jack's fingers dug into my back like he was afraid I was pulling away for good. I swear my heart was about ready to burst out of my chest. My cheeks bloomed with warmth as I whispered, "Would you like to come upstairs?"

"Yeah, sunrise, I would like that very much," Jack replied hoarsely.

I took his hand and led him there, marveling at my bravery. Never in a million years did I ever think I'd have the courage to invite a man into my bedroom. But I guessed after being held at gunpoint and shooting a man, all I cared about was feeling close to Jack. It overruled every other thought and emotion.

We stopped by my bed and Jack didn't give me time to think. He was holding me tight, kissing me voraciously.

My emotions fed into the kiss as I wound my arms around his neck and curled my fingers into his soft, thick hair. I loved his hair. Our tongues stroked in desperation.

I pushed at his jacket, and he dropped his arms so he could shrug out of it. We didn't break the kiss, our mouths pulling at each other's.

Jack moved me back in the direction of the bed, and our lips didn't part until he lifted and then dropped me on my back across the middle of the mattress.

I laid there, panting, my entire body aflame. He kept me trapped in his gaze as he unbuttoned his shirt.

All I could do was watch in utter fascination.

This was nine years of longing finally coming to a culmination.

That ache between my legs became almost unbearable.

Jack tugged off his shirt and threw it behind him. Just as I'd imagined, he was all hard, lean muscle, and I'd barely had time to ogle him when he took hold of the hem of my long dress. Slowly, he pushed it up past my thighs, over my stomach, my breasts, and I raised my arms above my head so he could pull it off. His eyes devoured, raking over me as I lay under him in my white cotton bra and panties. I had a moment of insecurity. I bet Jack was used to women who wore fancy lingerie.

There was a twinge of pain near my heart.

I didn't want to think about Jack with other women.

"Whatever put that pretty frown between your brows, get rid of it," Jack whispered. "Because you are the most beautiful woman I've ever seen. You will always be the most beautiful woman I've ever seen. You need proof." He drew my gaze to the thick arousal stretching the fabric of his pants. "I'm a grown man and you do this to me with just a whisper in my ear."

I gasped at the thought, shivering with anticipation.

When I looked up, our eyes met.

"Do you want me like I want you?"

Butterflies fluttered wildly in my belly. I felt like a teenager. Like a virgin. But it didn't stop me from replying, "Yes, Jack. I want you very badly."

He closed his eyes for a minute, seeming to savor those words. And then when he opened them, I shivered at the stark longing and lust glittering in their blue-gray depths. Leaning over me, he grazed his knuckles across my stomach, his eyes following his fingers as they trailed along the edge of my underwear. I sucked in my breath at the sensation.

"Jesus, Em, I'm trying to be a gentleman, I want to go slow, make love to you …" His eyes moved up my body. "But I don't want to treat you like bone china either."

My nipples peaked against my bra at the dark arousal in his voice. "I'm not bone china, Jack. I don't want to be treated like I'm fragile. I'm not."

His gaze only intensified. Then his hand flattened on my

stomach and he smoothed it upward slowly, heading between my breasts. His touch was possessive, and I was shocked by how much it aroused me. He unclipped the front clasp on my bra and eased it off.

The cool air rushed over my breasts and they swelled under his perusal. My breath hitched as he stroked them softly, his thumbs brushing over my nipples. Jack held my eyes as he gently, slowly, torturously teased my breasts. "You're so fucking sexy."

I think I stopped breathing.

"Nine years. Nine years I've dreamed of this." He leaned over, his erection pushing insistently against my belly, and his lips whispered over mine. "Have you dreamed about me, Em?"

"You know I—" I gasped as he squeezed my breasts hard, sensation shooting between my legs. "Have."

He slid his body down, pushing my thighs open, and he thrust his cock against me. I groaned, feeling a flush of heat move up my body from deep and low in my belly.

My thighs parted in invitation.

In answer, he kissed me, and I wrapped my arms around his strong back, trying to draw him closer. His lips moved down my chin, trailing in soft caresses along my throat and breasts. The scratch of stubble made me shiver even harder. As much as I wanted his mouth all over me, I was desperate to explore him. I'd wanted him for so long. "Jack ... can I touch you?"

He groaned against my right nipple. "Sunrise, you don't have to ask. You have permission to touch me anytime you want."

"Can you lie back for me?"

Jack lifted his head at the request, eyes gleaming. And then he moved, shifting off me to lie on his back. His expression was charmingly cocky. "Come and get me," it said.

I moved to straddle him, rubbing against his erection while I trailed my fingers lightly down his abs. His hard stomach tightened under my touch, and there was an answering throb between my legs. Jack clasped my hips in his hands and groaned as I slid over him.

I kissed him, wet and deep, as I pumped my hips against his arousal. His groans filled my mouth, making it difficult to break away, but I wanted to explore. I kissed my way down his throat, enjoying the stimulation I felt at the mere prickle of his unshaven skin.

I nuzzled against him, inhaling the masculine scent that was all Jack.

While my lips journeyed down his chest, his hands stroked me—caressing my back, my breasts, my sides, my stomach, and coasting down to cup my buttocks. "God, your ass." He squeezed it hard.

I lifted my head from his nipple. "You seem to have a thing about my ass."

Jack grinned wickedly. "You have no idea."

Laughing a little giddily, I returned my attention to his nipple and sucked it between my teeth. His cock jerked against my stomach. Feeling his patience strain as my mouth continued its downward path, tasting every inch of his sculpted stomach, I was a little smug. I liked being in control.

I pulled back to unbutton his pants and shuffled off the bed to yank them down. I stood, taking a moment to drink him in, now only in his boxer briefs. His impressive erection made me a little nervous; his strong, lean, hard body made me shudder with need. "You're beautiful, Jack."

"No one has ever called me that." Humor tremored in his words. "But I'll take it, Em."

Then Jack hooked his fingers into his boxer briefs and pushed them down, his erection springing out. I studied it a moment. Thankfully, it wasn't overly long, probably just a little above average. Longer than Tripp. And thick. Much thicker. Worryingly girthy. It had been a long time for me, and I was a little concerned about the fit.

"You keep staring at it like that, I'm going to lose my mind," Jack teased.

The best thing for the unknown was familiarity.

Decision made, afraid if I didn't move now I'd lose my nerve, I crawled back onto the bed. Over his body, I came to a stop at his erection.

Without a word, I lowered my head and took him into my mouth.

His groan echoed around the room.

I wrapped my hand around the base of him and fisted it while I sucked. I found my rhythm quickly, growing more and more turned on as Jack's pleasure intensified. I hadn't done this in a while, and it was different this time around. It had never turned me on before, made me slick between my legs, but watching how much Jack appeared to relish my mouth on him made me hotter than I could have imagined. His chest heaved and his thighs were taut as his hips pumped upward, thrusting in and out of my mouth and fist.

"Emery," he gasped, and I squeezed my thighs together, desperate for my own relief. "Stop ... Em ... stop."

But I couldn't. I wanted him to lose control completely. I wanted to watch that.

Suddenly I was hauled up his body until I straddled him.

"I need inside you." He dipped his fingers beneath my panties. His eyes flashed. "And you're so fucking ready, sunrise. You're beyond ready."

I pressed down on his fingers as they slid easily inside my slick heat. "I liked doing that to you, Jack."

He looked pained. "I can tell. Fuck, I can tell. God, I can't believe you're real." He kissed me hard as he increased the strokes of his fingers inside of me, pushing me toward climax.

I dislodged his fingers and pushed my panties down, leaning on my side so I could slip them down my legs. Once they were gone, I straddled him again and wrapped my hands around him, bringing him to my center. Mindless with want, with need, with desire, I didn't think about anything else but feeling him inside me. I pushed down on him and pleasure-pain caused a ripple of shivers all over my body.

"Uh, fuck!" He grabbed my hips, his fingers biting into my skin, and my eyes flew open at his touch. "You're so tight, Em. You feel so fucking good." He muttered endearments and desires and expletives as I took a minute to adjust to his thickness inside me.

Our gazes held as I slowly began to ride him.

There was nothing else in the world but Jack's eyes gazing into mine, the feel of his heated skin beneath my touch, his hands gripping my hips, guiding me up and down him, the sounds of my pants, his groans, the smell of sex in the air…

The tension coiled tighter and tighter inside me, and I didn't think of anything beyond chasing ecstasy. My rhythm changed and I slammed down harder.

"Em," Jack grunted, his grip almost bruising. "Emery!"

"I know, I know, I know," I panted as I clung to his hips for balance.

Then I let out a surprised squeak as I found myself flipped onto my back. Jack pinned my hands at either side of my head.

"My turn."

He released one of his hands to dip it between my legs. His thumb pressing down on my clit while he was still thick inside me felt amazing. I moaned, throwing my head back on the pillow.

"Fuck, look at you. You kill me." He held still, not moving.

"Jack, please," I begged mindlessly.

My plea was swallowed in his deep, passionate kiss, and I reached up with my free hand to curl my fingers in his hair, kissing him back like I needed his kiss to breathe. His thumb continued to circle my clit, and I gasped into his mouth. Jack took over the kiss while I sighed and panted and murmured his name, my hips pushing into his touch.

My thighs trembled.

My stomach tightened.

I was close.

So close.

Jack's thumb slicked over me and took me right over the edge.

As my body succumbed to the powerful orgasm, Jack took my free hand and pinned it again. I cried out as he slammed inside me, my inner muscles clamping around him as he thrust deep.

"Emery." His eyes flashed with something I couldn't even contemplate in that moment.

He pumped harder, his fingers lacing with mine and holding me down so I was completely at his mercy. To my amazement, the pressure grew inside me again.

I moved my hips against his thrusts, and this seemed to lead to his complete loss of control.

He released my hands and got onto his knees, gripping my thighs, opening them wider. And then he pounded into me. I could feel him kissing my womb.

"Take me, Em." His words were guttural, rough, husky, sexy. "I'm yours. All of me is yours."

My heart lurched at his words while my body built toward a new release. Watching Jack pump his hips against me was the hottest thing I'd ever seen. When his hips stuttered, the muscles in his neck corded and his teeth gritted. I came seconds before he did.

"Em, sunrise, darlin' girl." His chest heaved and he released his bruising grip on my thighs to collapse over me. His body melted against mine as he tucked his face into the crook of my neck. He ground his lower body into me like he didn't want his climax to end.

Our chests moved against each other's as we tried to catch our breath, and Jack's warm hand coasted down my left side and then curled around the back of my thigh. He gently pulled on it and then the other until I wrapped my legs around his back.

Sated, replete, moved, and overwhelmed, I closed my eyes, breathing him in, feeling him breathe against me.

The utter satisfaction, peace, and contentment lulled me to sleep.

22

JACK

As Jack got dressed, his eyes never left Emery's sleeping form.

The sheets tangled around her, revealing one long, gorgeous leg and the rise of her breasts. She barely made a sound as she slept, a hand resting near her cheek, her glorious hair spilling across the pillow.

He loved her so much, it was almost painful to look at her like this. Jack wanted to crawl back into bed and make love to her until neither of them could move.

However, guilt rode him to hell as he buttoned up his shirt with quick efficiency.

Last night he had been a selfish bastard. Desperate to have her, to feel her beneath him, to know she was safe and he could be with her through the night, he'd taken advantage of Em.

She'd made it clear until yesterday that she did not want a relationship with him.

A woman didn't change her mind that quickly.

Jack expected to spend weeks, if not months, convincing Em to give him another shot.

And he'd pounced when she was at her most vulnerable. When she was shaken by the incident with his father. He knew her defenses were low, and he'd jumped on the chance to be with her.

Fuck, it was such an opportunistic thing to do. He tried so hard to be better than his father ... but he'd dragged Jack down in the mud with him. He feared maybe a little too much of Ian had rubbed off on him.

Feeling sick with the guilt, Jack drank in the sight of Em. He needed to give her space. He needed her to know he wasn't a total bastard.

But he *was* a total bastard because the primal urge to get back into that bed with her was so strong, he actually took a few steps toward her. Cursing inwardly, Jack caught himself and strode quietly out of her bedroom. He'd wait for her downstairs because staying in here with her was too much temptation.

Images from last night flashed through his mind, making him groan.

Every time he closed his eyes, he could see her. Mouth around him. Getting off on sucking him. Riding him. Getting off on riding him. Her hair brushing his chest, her breasts bouncing with her undulations. He could see her beneath him, her face flushed, her mouth parted to allow the moans to escape as he thrust into her.

Fuck, he was getting hard again.

Striding into the living room, Jack sat on the sectional.

He'd wait for Emery to wake up and he'd apologize, and he'd promise to never take advantage of her again. That he would wait. He wanted her to know her own mind. To know that she was ready to trust him. It wouldn't last between them otherwise, and Jack wanted forever with this woman.

A half hour passed. Jack made coffee and fiddled around with a stupid puzzle game app on his phone, waiting for Emery to wake up. At around 5:45 a.m., his phone rang in his hand, and Rebecca's name appeared across the screen. He answered quickly because (a) it was early for Becs to be calling, and (b) he didn't want to wake Em before she was ready.

"Becs?"

"Jack." His sister let out a shaky exhale. "Jack, I've been with Mom and Jamie all night. Mom's not good. She's ... she's a mess over what happened to me and she's freaking out about being fodder for the town gossips. She's locked herself in the bathroom and I'm terrified she's going to do something stupid."

Jesus Christ.

Jack pushed off Em's couch. Rosalie Devlin had always dealt with life with a quiet dissociation. She bottled up everything. Jack had attempted to talk to her about his father and brothers, but Rosalie clammed up. He'd known that one day, all those bottled-up feelings would need a release.

"I'm on my way." Jack hung up and glared at the staircase.

He didn't want to leave Em like this. He didn't want her to think he'd abandoned her. But his family needed him right now.

Jack searched for a notepad and pen. He eventually found one in the sideboard but he saw her Glock in there too. The memory of her facing his father, expertly clutching the Glock, hit him. Em had shot a hole through Ian's hand with startling accuracy. The knowledge that she used to shoot competitively made Jack's lips twitch. It shaved at his terror when he remembered the sight of Ian training his gun on her.

Em really was full of surprises.

He sighed as he leaned on the sideboard to write her a note.

Em, I wanted to stay but stuff with my family has come up that I need to take care of. I'll explain later. Just know I'm really sorry. I feel like I took advantage of you last night. I'm a selfish bastard.

I'll give you some space—

Jack's phone beeped midsentence. It was a text from his sister.

Hurry, Jack!

Goddammit.

He scribbled his name at the bottom of the note that didn't say all he wanted to say and left it on her island where she'd definitely see it. Regret, guilt, and worry pursued him as he hurried out and got into his car to race to the Devlin mansion.

23

EMERY

Seven weeks later

MY PULSE RACED as I lowered myself into the seat across from Jessica in her office.

Word was out that Jess was pregnant. Her bump was now too significant to hide. Her morning sickness had lasted longer than average, and she'd assumed she would struggle with it for her entire pregnancy. But miraculously, it stopped about a week ago. Unfortunately, she wasn't sleeping well, finding it difficult to get comfortable at night.

Despite her exhaustion, I'd never seen her happier.

And knowing what she was about to tell me, I wished I could say the same.

Jess took my hands in hers, leaning into me, concern creasing her brow. "You're pregnant, Emery."

I wanted to be brave.

I wanted to be cool, calm, and collected.

And maybe I would have been if it hadn't been Jess in the room. The one person I trusted.

I burst into tears and caught a brief flash of tears in Jess's before she enveloped me in her embrace.

"Oh, it's okay, sweetie, it's okay," she soothed, rocking me.

However, it wasn't okay. I'd always imagined that the day I found out I was pregnant, it would be the happiest day of my life. That I'd be sharing the moment with the man I loved.

Instead, I'd gotten knocked up by Jack Devlin.

And I kind of hated him.

I sobbed harder.

Jessica tightened her hold on me. "Oh, Em, sweetie." She choked up. "Talk to me. You have me so worried."

After a moment or two, I pulled myself together and out of Jess's hug. She reached for a box of tissues on her desk and handed them to me.

Five weeks ago, I'd missed my period. I was ashamed to admit that in the aftermath of sleeping with Jack and finding he'd abandoned me, *again*, I'd also completely forgotten that we hadn't used protection. Jack probably assumed I was on the Pill, but as a longtime single woman with no menstrual or hormonal issues, I'd never had to be on it. Still, we should have used a condom.

Because Jack wasn't exactly a monk.

This realization only hit me when I missed my period.

I'd had hope that it was stress. That had happened to me in the past, my period delayed because of stressful events in my life. I didn't purchase a pregnancy test. I was in complete denial.

Until the morning sickness.

I'd gone to Jess as my doctor but also because she was my best friend.

"What about the other thing?" I waved my hand at her computer screen. I'd asked Jess to give me a pregnancy test and a sexual health check.

"We'll know soon enough about those tests," she assured me. "Now, talk to me before I assume terrible things."

Remembering her past with her sister, I hurried to assure her. "Oh, Jess, no. It was consensual."

She exhaled. "Okay. Excellent. Big relief." Tears shimmered in her eyes and her lips trembled. "I'm sorry, sweetie, I don't mean to get emotional."

I laughed through my own tears. "Oh, I understand."

Jess gave me a sad, watery smile. "We're pregnant together."

A flicker of excitement cut through my fear and disappointment that this was happening so differently from how I'd imagined. I was going to be a mom. I had someone coming into my life that I could give all my love to. This little person. And I was determined to do a hell of a lot better than my parents did with me.

It didn't change the fact that the circumstances were less than ideal. "Yeah." And then I blurted, "I slept with Jack."

She didn't look surprised by this. "Emery."

"He left me," I sobbed before I could stop it, curling into myself.

He broke my heart.

Again.

My best friend hugged me fiercely. For the first time since I'd woken to find that stupid, goddamn note from Jack, I let out everything I was feeling.

I hadn't cried, even though waking to find myself alone in my bed was one of the worst feelings in the world.

I hadn't cried at all the last seven weeks.

I'd bottled up all my pain and humiliation and rejection and fear that I would never be loved by the people *I* loved.

Now it was flooding out of me and soaking Jess's shoulder.

Jack leaving me like that, deciding he'd taken advantage without even asking me how *I* felt, was just a reminder of all the times he'd done that. He didn't treat me as an equal. He decided for us. Time and again. And I'd been stupid enough to believe things would change now that Ian was out of the picture.

Still, that little kernel of hope lived inside me that Jack would realize what a self-righteous asshole he was being, hope that was smashed to smithereens when the town gossip wave rolled over me.

Everyone was talking about the murder. About Rebecca Devlin's rape and the charges she faced for aiding and abetting Stu in accidental homicide. About Ian and Kerr Devlin being charged by the feds for racketeering and more, and that Jack was the one who handed them over to the police.

And about how Rosalie Devlin was so devastated, Jack had packed up his mother, sister, and brother Jamie and moved them out of town. Word on the street was that Rosalie's older brother lived in Wilmington and had invited them to stay until they could get set up on their own.

Jack had left Hartwell.

He'd left me.

Without a word.

Without a goodbye.

I'd thought he'd left for good, no looking back. I was under that impression for the first four weeks.

My friends noticed my despondency. No one pushed me about it.

But one night when I'd joined them at Cooper's trying to get my mind off it, Cooper had caught me coming out of the ladies' restroom. I'd sensed him watching me cautiously all night. I knew why when he told me he'd been in touch with Jack. That Jack hadn't left Hartwell permanently. He was just making sure his family was situated before he returned.

I thought that would make me feel better.

It didn't.

Because I hadn't been worthy of knowing this. Of Jack taking the time to tell me.

And I knew he had a lot going on with his family, but … he made love to me and then left me.

Like it wasn't making love after all.

Like it was just sex.

Like I was just one of his casual tourist flings.

No word from him. Not after his father held me at gunpoint and I'd shot him. Not after Jeff informed me that considering there were three witnesses to Ian holding me at gunpoint, his defense had advised him to take a plea bargain. The case wouldn't go to court, thankfully, and Ian would serve eighteen months for the crime.

And where was Jack when I found this out? Not with me!

Oh my God. I was pregnant with Jack Devlin's baby.

A man I definitely did not trust with my heart.

"You have to tell him, Emery," Jess said gently.

I nodded. It wasn't something I'd keep from him, no matter how much I was afraid of being permanently connected to someone who could hurt me so badly.

"Cooper has his number if you don't."

I shook my head frantically. "No. I'm not telling him over the phone. I'll tell him if he ever comes back."

"If? He *is* coming back … Do you want to tell me what happened between you?"

I did.

Once upon a time, Jess had trusted me with her story. So I told Jess everything.

I even told her about Tripp.

"You can understand why I don't trust many people, Jess," I whispered after I was done. "And something told me I could trust Jack. Right from the start. But I can't. Every time I let my guard down around him … I just end up feeling stupid and *used*."

"I know you don't want to hear this, but I don't think that's Jack's intention. He didn't tell Cooper the details, but he mentioned that he felt he needed to give you space to think about what you really wanted. And I think he would be devastated if he thought you thought he'd used you."

"Why is he talking to Cooper about this and not me? Whether he is using me or whether he just thinks I'm a child who needs to be coddled, neither makes me feel very good about him," I said, hearing the bitterness in my voice.

She sighed heavily. "You're right. He's going about this the wrong way. But I know the way he looks at you. Even if it worried me … I liked that for you. And I do know he's spent all his life trying to protect his sister and mom and Jamie from Ian and his brothers. It's a habit he can't break. He's inadvertently hurt quite a few people to protect his family. It's noble and sad at the same time."

Jess was right. Jack would always put his family first. And how could I possibly find fault with that? I couldn't. I couldn't blame him for that. I couldn't hate him for that.

I *could* hate him for not trusting me, for making decisions about us without discussing it with me, and for abandoning me.

And I could decide not to want to be with someone who would never put me first.

It's what I wanted. Even if that was selfish. I wanted someone who would put me first because I intended to always put them first.

Just because Jack and I were having a baby didn't mean I needed to give up hope of one day finding a man who would make me his entire world. Like how Jess was Cooper's entire world. Like how Vaughn gazed at Bailey like she was miraculous. Like how Michael watched Dahlia as if he was afraid she might disappear.

I wanted what my friends had.

I wanted an epic love.

I wanted a piece of the legend of Hart's Boardwalk.

"I never imagined raising my child alone," I whispered.

"You won't be alone. One, you'll have me and the girls. We will be the best aunties ever." Jess squeezed my hand and touched her belly with the other. "Plus, your little one will be my little one's best friend."

That thought made me grin, dispelling some of my sadness.

"And second, Jack is many things, but he won't abandon his child."

"I know." I *did* know that. "But, Jess, I meant … I thought when this happened, I'd be in love and living with the father. It won't be like that. Jack and I will never … we're going to have to share custody." Tears welled in my eyes again, and I was more than a little nauseated. "I'm sad. I'm sad that it's happening like this. I can't help it."

"Oh, sweetie." Jess pulled me to her again. "It will be all right. We'll see you through this. I promise."

I held on to Jess and that promise. I held on so tight.

IRIS HAD BEEN PESTERING me for weeks to come to dinner. While she was trying not to push about why I was so low, I think she'd put Jack's absence and my mood together and come to her own conclusion. Now and then, she'd drop him into the conversation, as if trying to read my reaction to the mention of him.

I'd accepted her invitation because Ivy had promised she'd be there, and I thought maybe she'd take the heat off me. Of course, I'd made this promise before I knew I was pregnant. Having only found out a few hours ago, I really wanted to call it off, but I knew if I did, Iris *would* start pushing me to talk to her.

They lived in a comfortable four-bedroom house in North Hartwell, a few blocks over from Jess and Cooper. Like all the houses in Hartwell, the home was clad with white wooden shingles, had a brightly colored awning, and a porch to while away the summer evenings.

It was Ira who greeted me at the door with a kiss on the cheek and a glass of lemonade. Ever the host.

"Iris is in the kitchen," he whispered, "so I'll say this quick. Warning: she invited someone else to dinner."

A niggle of uncertainty moved through me. "Who?"

"Sebastian Mercier," Iris announced as she strode into the hall, wiping her hands on her apron. She shot Ira a look. "Husband, you know I have bat ears."

"I don't know how I could forget."

Her lips twitched as she turned to look at me. "Mercier is the chef who bought George's old place and converted it into The Boardwalk. No one knows anything about this man or his seafood restaurant. He hasn't attempted to get to know the rest of us boardwalk owners"—there was definite judgment in her voice—"so I thought I'd go over there, introduce myself, and invite him to dinner. His restaurant is opening in a month, and I think it's high time we got to know this man."

I frowned. "I thought you weren't concerned about his restaurant now that you know it's a seafood place." Iris and Ira had been anxious about another restaurant opening on the boards. They already had competition from Cooper's with his pub grub, Paradise Sands with its fancy European restaurant, and Bailey's inn catered dinner for its guests. However, they were less anxious about the competition now that they knew it was a far cry from a pizzeria.

"Oh, she's not," Ira said dryly.

"What am I missing?"

"I just thought it would be nice to get to know him."

"And matchmake." Ivy appeared in the doorway to the sitting room. "Hey, Emery."

I smiled because it was nice to see her. "Hey." Then her words hit me. "Matchmake?"

"Pfft. Lies." Iris waved a hand at Ivy and wandered back into the kitchen.

Ira shook his head at me and mouthed "truth."

Uh-oh.

Following father and daughter into the sitting room, I asked quietly, "What's going on?"

Ira and Ivy exchanged a look, and Ivy sighed as she curled her feet under her on the couch. "Mom took one look at this chef and decided he was the perfect distraction for one of us."

There was that sinking feeling again. "For one of us?"

"Yup. She thinks he'll definitely decide he likes the look of you or me and it'll be a distraction for whomever he chooses."

Hearing the sarcasm in Ivy's voice, I smiled despite the uncomfortable situation I was about to find myself in. "And did it occur to her that both of us might like him and that might cause problems between us?"

Ivy grinned and shook her head. "I don't think she thought that far ahead."

I rolled my eyes and sat down beside Ivy. "I'm not really in the market for a distraction."

"Neither am I." She chuckled. "Let's hope he doesn't like either of us."

"Impossible," Ira said. "I've got two of the prettiest girls on the East Coast right here. No man can resist either of you. His problem will be choosing."

Ivy shook her head, a fond smile on her face. "Dad, do you not see how backward it is to have a man come over to dinner to choose from your prettiest girls?"

Ira winced. "Well, when you say it like that, it sounds backward."

Ivy and I shared a look and burst into laughter.

It was much-needed relief from an exhausting, emotional day.

I noted Ira watching us with a pleased gleam in his eye and suspected he was happy we'd become friends.

Iris came bustling back into the sitting room with a tray of snacks and placed them on the coffee table before us. "Some predinner munchies." She stood and placed her hands on her hips, her eyes coming to me. "You look a little pale, sweetheart. You okay? Is it the dinner guest? Did I go too far?"

"No," I assured her. "Although I'm not in the market for a French chef. I just haven't slept well these past few days."

"Well—" She was cut off by the doorbell ringing. "Oh, there he is."

As she and Ira both moved to answer the door, I looked at Ivy. "I'm surprised he agreed to this. He's been so mysteriously absent."

"Like a ghost. Bailey's curiosity is through the roof. People have only caught glimpses of him coming and going from the restaurant," she whispered.

A deep, masculine voice sounded from the doorway. With an American accent. Huh.

As if Ivy read my mind, she leaned in to whisper. "He's French American."

Ah, okay. I nodded and stood with her to greet the Greens' guest as they led him inside.

Oh boy.

That was one very handsome man.

"Sebastian, I'd like to introduce you to my daughter, Ivy."

Ivy moved forward to shake his hand with cool aplomb. Sebastian smiled, and there was a little flutter in my chest. He had the most gorgeous smile, a bright flash of white teeth, smooth brown skin, dark eyes that glittered beneath Iris's ceiling lights, high cheekbones, and a rugged, angular jawline. His dark hair had been shaved into a fade, accentuating the masculine angles of his face. Standing at least six feet with strong shoulders and a narrow waist, Sebastian Mercier was handsome with a capital H.

Like clockwork, my cheeks grew hot as we greeted one another.

Iris noted the blush and grinned like the Cheshire Cat.

Dammit.

Not long later, we were seated around the Greens' dining table, and I was taken aback by Sebastian's warmth and friendliness. Between not reaching out to the town upon his arrival, and the fact that he was this fancy chef from Boston, I'd expected him to be a little aloof. Silly of me, of all people, to assume such a thing.

"My family used to vacation here when I was a boy." Sebastian answered Iris's question about why he'd chosen Hartwell to open a restaurant. "My family owned a French restaurant in Essex, and my mother didn't like to leave it unattended. My father could only convince her to vacation here since it was close enough to hurry back if they needed to. It was the only time we had our parents' entire focus for a full week. I have a lot of fond memories here."

"And are you married, Sebastian?" Iris asked.

Ivy rolled her eyes and I hid my smile in a forkful of pasta.

"I am not. Running a restaurant is literally a full-time job. There isn't much time for dating." He took a bite of food and once he'd swallowed, he commented, "This is delicious. I can see why Antonio's is always busy."

It was the right thing to say. Ivy and I shared a grin as the Greens preened beneath the praise.

"I'm sorry if I haven't introduced myself to all the business owners on the boardwalk." Sebastian cut me an apologetic look. "There just always seems to be something to do at the restaurant and time gets away from me."

"Oh, that's understandable." Iris waved off his apology as if she hadn't been complaining about his "lack of manners" for months.

"So, you're single, then?" Ira pulled the conversation back to Sebastian's personal life. "And looking?"

Oh my God. Ivy groaned under her breath.

Sebastian's lips twitched. "Not right this second. I have the restaurant to focus on. Plus, I have a teenage daughter. She's with her mom in Boston, but she'll be joining me for a few weeks before summer's out. I try to make sure she has all my attention when she's with me. Although she doesn't seem to enjoy spending that much time with either of her parents at the moment."

"You look a little young to have a teenage daughter," Ivy said.

"Thank you. She's fifteen. Her mother and I had her when I was twenty-five."

"You're forty?" I blurted out in disbelief. He looked ten years younger than that.

He grinned at me. "Is that old?"

"No, no." Now I was blushing. "You just … you look about thirty."

His grin turned flirtatious. "Well, thank you."

"Those are some good genes," Ivy added.

Sebastian laughed, and it sounded a little embarrassed now. "If I'd known I would spend the meal being complimented by beautiful women, I would have arrived earlier."

"Oh, I like him," Iris decided, making us laugh.

My laughter was cut off, however, when a wave of nausea rolled through me.

Oh no.

I took a breath, trying not to be obvious about it … but the tide rose anyway.

"Excuse me." I shot from the table and hurried to the back hall to the Greens' powder room. Seconds later I was on my knees, throwing up my meal in the toilet bowl.

Groaning, I wiped my mouth with toilet paper and then flushed it all away.

"Emery?"

I looked up from the floor to find Iris in the doorway.

"I think I ate something bad yesterday," I promptly lied.

She nodded. "I knew you were looking pale."

"I'm sorry, Iris. I need to go home."

"Ira will take you."

"No, I brought my car. I don't want to have to come back for it."

"Ira will get it to you."

"Iris, I can drive myself home."

Her eyebrows rose.

I'd never used that tone with her. "Sorry."

"Don't be sorry." She crossed her arms over her chest. "I like you assertive."

I smirked and pushed to my feet.

Once I'd said goodbye to the concerned Greens and Sebastian Mercier, I felt guilty for feeling so relieved about getting into my car. But I just wanted to be alone.

Feeling exhausted and looking forward to curling up in bed, the last thing I expected when I pulled up to my driveway was to see an unfamiliar truck already sitting in it. I looked from the truck up to the porch and another wave of nausea hit me.

Oh my God.

Jack.

Jack was back.

Today of all days.

I trembled as I got out of the car, watching as he strode down the porch steps, a wary look on his face. He looked like himself again. Like the Jack I'd known when I first moved here.

Driving a truck, wearing a flannel shirt, worn jeans, and construction boots.

Our eyes locked, his soulful as ever.

I didn't trust that look.

As attracted to him as I'd always be, as much as I'd always care what happened to him, Jack Devlin had finally, truly broken my faith in him.

"What are you doing here?" I skirted past him, making sure

we didn't touch, and hurried up the porch steps. My keys shook in my hand as I opened the screen door.

"Em." I heard his footsteps behind me and whirled to glare at him.

My expression stopped him in his tracks. I knew I had to tell him I was pregnant. But I wasn't ready to. I'd barely had time to digest the news myself.

"I'd like you to leave."

He scowled. "We need to talk. It's been seven weeks."

"Oh, I'm well aware."

"Didn't you get my note?" He looked confused. "I told you I wanted to give you space—"

"Jack."

He shut up.

"Get the fuck off my porch." I unlocked my door and let myself in, slamming it and the screen door behind me. I'd caught the look of shock on Jack's face just before I turned my back on him.

It wasn't satisfying.

None of this was.

I was exhausted.

Emotional.

Drained.

I flopped down on my sectional, kicked off my shoes, and curled into a ball. The tears leaked from my eyes as I listened to his truck pull out of my drive.

24

JACK

Jack backed out of Emery's driveway but he didn't take his new truck very far. He parked on Main Street and strode along the boards to Cooper's Bar.

Agitation pumped through him.

Worry gnawed at his gut.

Fear made him feel a little sick.

Leaving Emery the way he had was a massive mistake. When Cooper called to check on things, his old buddy had tried to tell him things weren't right with Em. But Jack had been so sure giving her space to figure things out was what she needed.

Oh, clearly, she'd figured them out. And she wanted not one thing to do with him.

He winced remembering that angry coldness on her face and in her words.

Jack had never heard Em talk like that. Never to him.

Fuck.

Every time he thought he was doing the right thing, it was always wrong. He was always hurting the people he least wanted to hurt. But that morning, weeks ago, when he turned up at the mansion to deal with his mom, he saw Rosalie Devlin truly broken for the first time. She'd endured a lot in her marriage, but discovering the depths of darkness within the family, the hurt inflicted on her kids, hurt Ian had used against them, broke her.

She'd railed on about being a terrible mother, about not protecting them. How the whole town was talking about her. How she'd never be able to leave the house again for the shame of being such a mother. When she'd finally fallen asleep under their careful watch, Jack knew he had to get his mom out of town. Being here was no good for her. It was Rebecca who suggested they get in contact with Rosalie's brother.

As far as Jack knew, her family cut off contact a few years into the marriage when they realized what an asshole Ian was.

Rosalie had awoken, overhearing his conversation with his sister, and she told him to phone her brother, Heath. Apparently, he and Rosalie had kept in touch all these years. Heath sounded worried about his sister. Said he'd tried calling since seeing the news. He offered them a place to stay in Wilmington. Thankfully, Rosalie didn't take much convincing. Jamie neither as he was too concerned about his mom, and he said he didn't care about leaving Hartwell. He'd made a new life at college.

Once they settled at his uncle's, Jack had looked into their finances. He was trying to figure out how they could continue to pay for Jamie's tuition. The Devlin businesses that were important to Hartwell's economy were still running, including Ocean Blue Fun Park and the Hartwell Grand Hotel. While the staff could be paid, any other monies made were to be detained while his father's assets were frozen. Jack maintained contact with management at both properties, but he assumed that once his father was sentenced, they'd lose those businesses.

Jack had savings, but not enough to send Jamie to school and take care of his mom.

One day his uncle found him stewing in despair over

spreadsheets during a brief respite from phone calls, and he'd frowned. "Why can't you use Rosie's money?"

The question had confused Jack. "What money?"

His uncle gestured to the large home they were in. Jack had been somewhat taken aback to discover his uncle stayed in a wealthy town north of Wilmington called Greenville. His wife and two college-age daughters, who were spending their summer vacation in Europe, lived in a house that wouldn't look all that out of place in the movie *Home Alone*. "Where do you think this came from?"

"I assumed your family's money." Jack knew his mother came from a wealthy background. Rosalie didn't talk about it, so years ago he'd searched for information on his grandparents. Rosalie's father had inherited the largest fishing company on the East Coast, and he'd sold it for a tidy sum. But Jack's grandparents had died not long after Rosalie married Ian. When his grandmother passed away after a battle with cancer, his grandfather had a heart attack and died only days later.

Jack wondered if Ian thought by marrying Rosalie, he'd get his hands on her money?

It hadn't worked out that way.

They'd cut her off.

"Yeah. Family's money. But I have a sister," Heath said pointedly.

"I don't understand."

"Jack, do you know how much my parents adored us? Adored Rosie?" He sighed and sat down on the desk. "They hated Ian Devlin. Saw him exactly for what he was. They gave Rosie money when they married and found out he convinced her to buy the hotel and fun park in Hartwell. They lost their shit. It was supposed to be for their daughter. So, they cut her off. But they didn't want to leave Rosie with nothing. It was in their will. They left her fifty percent but entrusted it to me. I'm basically the guardian of Rosalie's fortune. It was so Ian couldn't touch it, but she'd have it if she needed it."

Shock had moved through Jack. "Are you telling me that Mom is rich?"

Heath grinned. "I'm a finance guy. She trusted me to invest it, and those investments have paid off. She has more now than she had to begin with. I can sign over whatever you need now for Rosie to get on her feet. I'd like her to stay in Greenville. She can afford a place here. And as soon as she divorces Ian, all the money will be signed over to her."

Relief swamped Jack. "Ian doesn't know about the money?"

"Not at all."

Jack shook his head. "We can't make any lavish purchases like houses until he's behind bars. If he thought for a second Mom had money, he'd blackmail it out of us to pay for his attorney."

Heath's expression darkened. "He really is a son of a bitch, isn't he?"

"You have no idea." Jack sat back. "What if we just rent a place for her and Becs and Jamie … we do it through you and pay you back afterward? That way Ian will think you're taking care of the financial burden."

Heath nodded. "That's no problem. But everyone is welcome to stay here for as long as needed. This is a big house."

And Jack had appreciated that.

"I'd look into the hotel and the fun park, Jack. I remember a conversation with Rosie about those purchases. My sister isn't dumb. Ian needed her signature to hand over that money. She co-owns those businesses. She made sure of it."

This revelation had Jack on the phone to their family's financial and business manager. He sent over what they asked for. And sure enough, the deeds to both properties had his mother's name on them. Rosalie Devlin co-owned the businesses. After several weeks of conversation and investigation he did not enjoy putting his mother through, the feds were satisfied his mom had nothing to do with his father's racketeering charges. So, they hired a lawyer. They had enough evidence to prove that the businesses rightfully belonged to Rosalie since the money to purchase them was hers. It might take awhile, Ian might already be in prison by then, but they were going to win those businesses back.

Which meant they were important enough for Jack to continue to oversee. In fact, Rosalie wanted to sign them over to him as soon as she legally could. It hadn't been the career Jack planned for, but the hotel and park were important to Hartwell, and Jack could think of worse jobs.

Moreover, they'd keep him close to Emery.

He hadn't left Greenville until his mom and Rebecca were settled into a picturesque rental near Heath. Jamie had just returned to college, which Rosalie could now afford. After a few weeks of Rebecca spending every second with their mother, Rosalie seemed in a better place. Both mother and daughter had started seeing a therapist, which Jack hoped would help.

It was still weird leaving them there. It hadn't been easy, but Heath promised to watch over them.

It had taken a ton of willpower not to contact Emery over his seven-week absence, to give her space while he got his family into a better place. Memories of their night together was both a pleasure and a pain.

And when Cooper called and said Emery was looking a little low these days, Jack's gut tightened. He'd questioned himself. But then thought *no*. She didn't need him in her space, muddling her head. And he had so much to deal with, he thought it best to stay away. Jack wanted to be able to give her his entire focus when they next spoke.

Now he knew that way of thinking was fucked up. He'd screwed up with her. Again.

Pushing into Cooper's place, Jack caught sight of his friend behind the bar chatting with Bailey Hartwell and Vaughn Tremaine. He looked over at Jack and gave him a friendly nod.

That tightness in Jack's chest caused by Em's anger loosened a little. Never did he think he'd be welcomed at Cooper's again in his life. He sensed eyes on him as he walked across the bar, but he ignored their curious looks. The gossip mill would start grinding soon, and before anyone knew it, it would be all over Hartwell that not only was Jack Devlin back in town but Cooper had welcomed him into his bar.

Jack slid onto the empty stool next to Bailey. She turned to give him a soft smile.

"Hey, Jack, how are you?"

He'd always had a soft spot for the middle Hartwell. She was gregarious and open, so you always knew what she was thinking. "I've been better. How are you?" He looked past Bailey to Vaughn, who watched him cautiously. Jack gave him a nod of greeting.

"Um … stressed," she answered honestly and shot Vaughn a tired smile. "Our wedding is in four days."

"Oh, right."

"I sent you an invitation," she said. "But I sent it to your South Hartwell house."

"I haven't been there in a while. Sorry."

"There's still time to RSVP."

No, there wasn't. She was making an exception for him. And Jack knew turning down her invite would be rude, considering he didn't deserve it in the first place, but he'd be stupid not to go. Not if he wanted to start over here, which he did.

"I'd be honored to be there, Bails, thanks." His voice was a little gruff with emotion.

"We're happy to have you there," Vaughn said, not sounding happy at all, but Jack didn't take it personally. He knew Tremaine hated Ian Devlin and would naturally be wary of his son.

"What can I get you, Jack?" Coop asked.

Ellen Luther, a local sitting a few stools down, made a surprised gurgling sound in the back of her throat at Coop's congenial question.

Jack and Coop shared a lip twitch. "Whatever's on tap, thanks."

He exchanged small talk with Bailey about the wedding as Cooper got his drink. He pushed the pint across the bar toward him and asked, "You seen Emery?"

Jack stiffened. "Yeah."

"And?"

He could feel Bailey listening intently. "It couldn't have gone any worse."

"Shit. I'm sorry."

Jack shrugged. "I'll figure it out. Once I can get her to talk to me."

Bailey nudged him with her elbow. "You do realize you're sitting next to one of Emery's best friends."

He sighed. "I heard something to that effect."

She grinned. She might be one of Em's best friends, but she didn't know what had happened between her and Jack. If she knew, she wouldn't be smiling at him.

This was confirmed when she said, "I know you two had a thing last summer, and you pushed her away to protect her, but I'm pretty sure you could convince Emery to come around."

"Maybe Emery doesn't need to come around." Vaughn cut Jack a dark look. "If my woman was held at gunpoint by my father, I wouldn't skip town for seven weeks after the event, leaving her unprotected."

Yeah, Tremaine definitely didn't like him.

"One, I don't know if you heard, but Em can protect herself. She's a crack shot," Jack said with pride. "Two, you don't know what the hell you're talking about."

Bailey made a face at Cooper and then turned to Jack. "Okay, yes, not cool to leave after that happened, even if Em is Lara Croft. Jeez, she's like a coin block in *Super Mario Bros.*, except instead of coins coming out every time something hits her, secrets do." She frowned. "That was one too many video game analogies. Anyhoo ... we all know why you left, and looking after your family is noble." She shot Tremaine an admonishing look before turning back to Jack. "Something I'm sure Emery completely understands."

"Yeah?" Jack sipped his beer. "Is that why she told me to get the fuck off her porch?"

Bailey's eyes widened. "She said that? The word 'fuck' and everything?"

Jack nodded.

She burst out laughing. Vaughn grunted with amusement at her side.

"Thanks," Jack muttered sarcastically.

"No, I'm sorry." Bailey patted him on the shoulder. "It's just, I'm a little proud of her." Her eyes bugged out at Tremaine. "A *lot* proud of her."

Her fiancé gave her an affectionate, loving smile that transformed him.

That's what women did to you.

Turned you from a badass, alpha male into a lovesick idiot. Jack would scoff at it, if he hadn't already experienced the effects of being a lovesick idiot for the last nine years.

"You should write her a letter," Bailey announced.

"What?"

"If she won't talk to you, then write her a love letter." She leaned into Jack. "Emery is a romantic. You want a chance with her, then you need to lay your cards on the table. Be completely honest with her. Write it all down. I promise ... no woman can resist a love letter."

"Is that so?" Tremaine murmured.

"Yes, that's so." She cocked an eyebrow at him. "So, your vows better be something else."

His eyes gleamed. "No pressure, then."

The couple bent their heads toward each other. Jack turned away, Cooper watching him warily.

"What do you think?" Jack asked.

Cooper leaned in, lowering his voice. "I think … maybe something else happened between you … Otherwise Emery wouldn't have told you to fuck off. Because the last time I saw you both, she didn't look too unhappy about having your arm around her."

"I didn't … We were together. And then Rebecca called after and I had to leave. Em was still asleep," he muttered. "I left a note about giving her some space to think—"

"You did what?" Cooper grimaced at him.

"I'm getting the strong feeling that was the wrong move."

His old buddy sighed heavily. "You've screwed around with more women than I can count, and somehow you still don't know the first thing about them."

"Then tell me what to do." Jack clenched his jaw in self-directed anger. "Tell me how to fix this with her."

"Answer one thing first."

He nodded.

"Do you love her?"

Jack's gut twisted. "Since that night I first saw her, Coop."

At his raw honesty, Cooper grinned. "Then maybe Bails is right. I wouldn't know how to write a letter, but if it was what it would've taken to get Jess, I'd have written a fucking letter."

A love letter.

Jack exhaled slowly.

Right.

25

EMERY

"You did what?" I gaped at Bailey in disbelief.

She was my first customer of the morning, popping by before the store was even open. Standing casually with a to-go cup in each hand, one for her and one for Dahlia, Bailey smiled at me like she had done nothing wrong.

"You invited Jack to your wedding?"

"I did."

"And he said yes?"

"Of course, he said yes. It would be rude to say no."

I felt a flicker of nausea and took a deep breath to stem the tide.

"Em, it's not that bad. You're a bridesmaid so you'll hardly get the chance to interact with him." Her eyes twinkled with mischief.

I narrowed my eyes. "Do you think I'm a moron? I know what you're up to, Bails."

"Moi?" She pointed innocently to herself, all wide-eyed and cute. "I'm merely making sure that everyone who deserves it feels welcome to attend our wedding."

"Deserves it?"

"We're not overly persnickety. As long as you're not a home-wrecking sociopath, a backstabbing sister, a murderer, or are currently in jail on federal charges, we're pretty happy to extend an invitation."

"So, no Dana, then?" I teased, despite my upset.

"Absolutely not. And she's livid." Bailey grinned wickedly. "The biggest wedding this town has seen in fifty years, and she didn't get an invite. And no one blames me. They understand how awkward it would be for me to have my pregnant bridesmaid's husband's ex-wife at my wedding. So, I don't even look like a bad person for not inviting her. I'm taking an enormous amount of petty satisfaction from the whole situation."

Not as much as me. Dana Kellerman was not my favorite person. I chuckled wearily at Bailey's naughty grin. "You're awful." But I said it like I thought the opposite.

My friend laughed. "Oh, come on, Em. Don't worry about Jack. There will be plenty of other eligible bachelors to catch the eye. Vaughn has invited some friends he actually does like from his Manhattan life. A few are single, rich, and handsome."

I rolled my eyes. The last thing I needed right now was to date. "I think I'll pass for now."

"Oh, no you won't. You're twenty-nine, Emery, and you've never had a serious relationship. Don't you want to change that? And what would be more romantic than falling in love at your best friend's wedding?"

It was on the tip of my tongue to blurt out that I was pregnant.

I wouldn't.

One, Jack needed to know first.

Two, I was only seven weeks. I didn't want to announce anything at all until further along in the pregnancy. As much as I was in turmoil about what my future looked like as a single mom, I'd quickly fallen in love with the idea of being a mother.

I'd have a son or daughter. To raise, protect, and love. And although I'd never planned to do it this way, I wanted it now. And I wanted nothing to take that away.

But I knew things could happen. I knew babies could go away. Seven weeks was too soon to tell anyone. It might jinx my pregnancy. I could almost hear my grandmother scolding me for such a superstitious thought (after scolding me for getting pregnant out of wedlock, that is). Yet I couldn't change how concerned I was. I'd hold off telling anyone until it got too hard to hide. I'd have to ask Jack to do the same.

My stomach roiled again at the thought of telling Jack.

I needed to tell him soon. I had planned to.

Yet now that I knew he'd be at the wedding, I wasn't sure I wanted to be stuck at the same event with him if he knew the truth.

"You look a little pale suddenly. Are you okay, Em?"

"I had food poisoning yesterday." I perpetuated my lie. "Still feeling a little off."

"Oh, sweetie, that's not good. Why don't you just close the store today?"

"I'd rather work through it." I couldn't look at her as I lied. "So, are we all ready for the big day?" I changed the subject.

"Yes. All set. My parents arrive tomorrow and are no longer giving me a guilt trip for rescinding Vanessa's invite." At my look of concern, Bailey waved me off. "She was never going to show anyway. And it's better I know the truth. Am I sad? Yes. But I won't let it ruin my wedding. Mom and Dad and Charlie get it. So, they'll all be here tomorrow, and Vaughn's dad and the rest of his guests will arrive the night before. They're all booked into the hotel. The staff are working harder than ever because it's the boss's wedding, so I feel like we're in excellent hands." She smiled. "And all you need to do is show up at the inn on the eve of the big day."

"I can't wait."

I was also glad Vaughn and Bailey had had their bachelor and bachelorette parties months ago. There had been much drinking involved. At least this way, I could avoid a glass of champagne if Bailey had wedding-eve drinks without it being weirdly noticeable.

"Me neither."

As soon as Bailey left to deliver Dahlia's coffee, I let out a shaky exhale.

I couldn't tell Jack about the baby. Not until after the wedding. That way, I wouldn't be trapped in the same room with him for hours while he had that knowledge.

26

EMERY

Bailey and Vaughn had taken over Main Street.

Literally.

They'd gotten permission to block the street, and car owners were asked to move their vehicles the day before in preparation for the wedding. Why? Because the ceremony was taking place at the gazebo at the top of Main Street. The many guest chairs were set out in front of the gazebo, down onto the street. It meant anyone who didn't get an official invite could watch from a distance.

The chairs wore white linen coverings and bows the color of pink cherry blossoms. A white aisle strewn with cherry-blossom petals had been laid between the chairs and all the way up to the gazebo and altar. The gazebo's pillars had been wrapped in fresh-flower garlands of white roses and pink peonies.

The sun shone brightly.

The waves sparkled in the distance.

Tourists wavered on the boardwalk, cameras out, taking shots of the beautiful bride and groom as they recited their vows.

Sitting in the front row beside Jess, Dahlia, and Ivy in our matching pale-pink bridesmaid gowns, I stared up at Bailey and Vaughn feeling a strange mix of joy and envy. The way he gazed at her was awe-inspiring. Like he couldn't believe she was real and that she was his.

I wanted that for Bailey. I was overjoyed for her.

Yet, I was afraid I might never find the same.

Shrugging off my worries, I smiled through blurry tears at the couple. Vaughn, as always, looked striking, no matter what he wore. In a tux, he looked like a movie star.

And Bailey ... she was a beautiful vision in golden ivory. The Jenny Packham gown fitted perfectly to Bailey's elegant figure and had a 1930s vibe to it. The bodice was embellished with hand-sewn beads. It had sheer cap sleeves and a plunging V-neckline. A delicate silk ribbon accentuated Bailey's small waist and tied into a small bow at the back. The silk-chiffon skirt pooled in elegant layers around her feet.

The stylist had coiled Bailey's bright auburn locks into a complicated updo. She wore a simple, elegant, beaded vintage headpiece that matched the dress perfectly.

A hush fell over the guests as the officiant, Kell Summers, invited the bride and groom to recite their vows.

Vaughn's father, a very distinguished, handsome man who was way too charming for his own good and made me blush up a storm, handed his son Bailey's wedding band. Taking her left hand in his, Vaughn gently guided the band down her finger until it nestled beside her impressive engagement ring. Then he clasped her hand between both of his, gazing deep into her eyes.

"It is an understatement to say that I never expected you, Bailey Hartwell."

Bailey beamed at him as we all tittered, remembering how at odds they'd been before they pulled their heads out of their asses and realized they cared about each other.

Vaughn stared lovingly at her as she smiled that glamorous

smile of hers. "How could I anticipate someone like you? How could I hope that someone like you existed?"

Tears welled in my eyes as Bailey's brightened with emotion.

"I spent torturous hours trying to find the perfect vows, the perfect words. Cursing myself for being a man who is not great at expressing his feelings. Knowing how important it is that you understand the depth of what I feel for you. Then a wise man reminded me that I don't need to be a poet to do that." Vaughn drew her closer so he could hold their joined hands to his chest. "There is nothing and no one in this world who means what you mean to me. And I want you to know that my every action, my every decision, my very purpose in life is to protect what we have. To love you. To make you happy. To make sure you never regret a single moment spent by my side."

I swiped a tear off my cheek as Bailey leaned in to kiss Vaughn. A sweet, soft, intimate kiss given as if she'd forgotten they had an audience.

Another tear fell down my cheek, and as I moved to wipe it away, there was a hot tingling sensation on the back of my neck that had nothing to do with the morning sun.

A shiver chased the tingle down my spine. I turned my head.

My gaze cut through the seated guests, transfixed by the couple in the gazebo as Bailey recited her vows.

I was about to turn back to listen when my eyes locked with his.

Jack.

He sat on the other side of the aisle, about seven rows back, next to Cat and Joey Lawson. His gaze was fixed on me, his expression searing.

My belly knotted.

Joey saw me looking in their direction and waved exuberantly.

Despite my heavy worries, Joey always made me smile. I grinned at him and waved back before turning around.

I caught Jess's eyes as I did, and she gave me a sympathetic smile. She reached for my free hand, the one not wrapped around a bouquet of peonies, and squeezed it tight.

I squeezed hers right back.

~

NOT LONG LATER, I was momentarily distracted from my concerns about bumping into Jack. The photographer took so long with the pictures on the boardwalk, at the inn, and on the beach, Jess felt faint and Bailey excused the bridesmaids from the rest of the photo shoot.

Dahlia, Ivy, and I walked Jess back to the hotel where Cooper, Jeff King, Michael, and Jack were waiting together. The sight of Jack standing among them, looking sexy in his tailored suit, brought my earlier worries crashing back.

"You okay?" Jess asked as we approached the men.

"Why are you asking Em if she's okay?" Dahlia frowned. "You're the one who was about to pass—oh, Jack, right? Gotcha."

"I'm fine." I gave them all a strained smile.

"That was the least convincing fine I've ever heard," Ivy commented.

Cooper strode toward us, a deep scowl on his face. "You all right?" He took Jess from us, running his hands down her arms. "I was just saying they had you out in that sun for too long."

"I'm fine, I'm fine." She rested against him, looking wilted. "I just need a glass of water and some shade."

Before any of us could say a word, Cooper escorted Jess into the hotel.

Michael and Jeff approached.

"Do you need us to stay with you?" Dahlia asked under her breath.

"I need to talk to Jack alone."

"C'mon, dahlin', let's get you girls a drink." Michael took hold of Dahlia's hand and gestured for us all to go inside.

"I'll be right in," I said. Michael nodded and wrapped his arm around Dahlia's waist.

For a moment, I was a little taken aback at the way Jeff gazed so fiercely at Ivy. She stared up at him like she'd never seen him before. To be fair, he looked incredibly handsome in his suit.

"Drink?" he asked her.

"Sure."

He held out his arm, and she took it.

They never broke eye contact the whole time.

Interesting.

My attention moved past them to Dahlia and Michael. As they neared the hotel entrance, Michael whispered something in Dahlia's ear that made her laugh.

My gut twisted, watching him grin as he opened the door for her.

Ivy and Jeff followed them inside.

Finally, I couldn't avoid him any longer. Especially since he was walking toward me.

"You look beautiful," Jack said, sincere and sexy.

I scowled at him.

His lips twitched like he thought I was cute, which was more than mildly irritating. I was hot, a little nauseated, and I wasn't allowed to drown my sorrows in champagne. And I loved champagne. It would be a bad idea to piss me off.

I tilted my chin up and straightened my shoulders as I forced myself to meet his gaze. "I just wanted to say that I'd like to enjoy my friend's wedding without having to deal with this." I gestured between us.

"Em—"

"We'll talk after the wedding. Just … leave me be for now. Please."

Jack exhaled slowly, shaking his head a little. I could feel his exasperation. But then he nodded, his soulful eyes boring into mine. "I can do that."

I sighed with relief. "Thank you."

Once inside, the hotel's air conditioning cooled my heated skin, offering me a small reprieve from physical discomfort. If only its powers extended to my emotional agitation. Seeing Jess and Dahlia with their guys and Ivy and Jeff standing together near Cat and Joey, I hurried over to them. While Jess and Joey drank water, everyone else had a flute of champagne in hand.

"Emery?" Cat held one out to me.

"You know, I'm a little hot. I think I'll just have some water."

Jess reached behind her on the table at their backs and grabbed a glass for me. I gave her a grateful smile.

"You look pretty, Emery," Joey said, gazing up at me with his usual bright adoration.

As always, it made my heart feel a million times bigger.

"And you look very handsome in that tux."

He beamed at me. "Will you dance with me first? A guy's gotta stake his claim."

I struggled not to laugh. As did everyone else. Except Cat, who shot Cooper an amused but accusatory glare.

Cooper chuckled. "Why am I getting the look?"

"Because where else would he have heard something like that?"

"Oh, it wasn't Uncle Coop." Joey shook his head. "I read it in one of those books you like so much. The ones with the motorcycles on the cover."

Cat paled. "You did what? Did you take my e-reader?"

"Yeah." He shrugged.

"Joey, what have I told you about that? When we get home, we're going to have a discussion about privacy and not touching things Mom has expressly forbidden you to touch. And I also want to know how much you've read."

Joey looked chagrined, his gaze downcast. "It was a chapter. You came back into the room before I could read much of it."

"Joey …" She sighed heavily.

He winced at her disappointed tone.

"Hey." I smiled down at him, trying to distract them both. "Of course, you can have the first dance."

His melancholy melted away and he hugged into my side, his arm around my waist. I held him to me as I took a huge gulp of water. Joey was a bit of a contradiction. Exceptionally bright, a gifted musician, he knew more about the world than other kids his age. He was precocious and confident. At the same time, he was still innocent and affectionate.

"What's with the books?" Dahlia asked Cat.

"They're romance novels." Cat worried her lip. "Dark romance novels. With the kind of stuff in it I don't want my kid reading. Jesus. Can you put a password on an e-reader?"

"Yeah," I replied. "I'll show you how."

Cat seemed surprised by my offer but smiled gratefully. "Thank you."

"Jack," Cooper said, and I turned to see Jack striding across the lobby. He slowed but didn't stop, his eyes dropping to where Joey clung to my side. His expression warmed as he shot me an tender look before turning to Coop. "Drink?"

Jack shook his head. "I better get inside, grab my seat."

"Sure? The happy couple might be a little while yet."

He flicked a look at me before replying to his friend. "I'll catch you later."

Guilt suffused me. I knew there was probably nothing more Jack wanted than to hang out with Cooper, but he was abiding by my wishes to avoid me today.

Unfortunately, his abidance didn't last long.

~

"EMERY, Joey, I hate to cut in, but I'm going to." Bailey pulled up beside me and Joey on the dance floor. She was glowing with bliss. And a handsome, dark-haired man around my height with dreamy bedroom eyes accompanied her.

"Emery, this is Soren Michaelson. He's an old college friend of Vaughn's and lives in Manhattan. Soren, Emery used to live in upstate New York but now owns the boardwalk bookstore."

Oh, hell no.

I hadn't believed Bailey would try to play matchmaker at her wedding. But why not? It was definitely something she was capable of.

And she was doing it!

"Do you mind, Joey?" She asked.

Joey glared at Soren Michaelson. "I'll allow it. But don't get your hopes up, buddy. I've staked my claim."

Soren grinned. "I respect that."

"Hmm." Joey cut me a look. "You want to dance with this guy?"

It was one of the hardest things I'd ever had to do, holding in my laughter. "If you're okay with it, Joey?"

"Sure. Mom says I shouldn't monopolize your time."

"Will you dance with me?" Bailey held out her hand to him. "I *am* the bride."

"Yeah, so you're already claimed."

"Come dance with me, Joe-Joe." He took her hand. "While we dance, Aunt Bailey will explain to you how girls aren't something you can just claim like a ball from the lost-and-found. Mmm'kay?"

Soren chuckled. "He's a character, huh?"

I nodded. "He's wonderful."

"Dance?" He held out his hand.

Seconds later, I was in this stranger's arms, still smiling about Joey.

"You can't blame the kid," Soren teased, eyes dancing over my face. "He has great taste."

My cheeks heated. "Thank you."

"So"—Soren swayed us a little more, his hand tightening on my back—"things I already know about Emery Saunders: Vaughn is protective of you."

My eyes flew to his. "How do you know that?"

His lips twitched. "Because he threatened to castrate me if I, and I quote, 'didn't treat Emery with the respect and manners a lady deserves and attempted any funny business with her.'"

Vaughn said that?

Soren's amusement grew at my shock. "He obviously cares about you, and it takes a lot to make an impression on Vaughn, so I'm already intrigued. I also know you run your own business, you have men falling in love with you before they're even in high school, and you are the most beautiful woman in this room."

A person could roast marshmallows on my cheeks, I grew so uncomfortable with his flattery. "And you do not know how to take a compliment." He laughed and drew me closer until my chest brushed his.

Before I could respond, a shadow fell over us.

"Can I cut in?"

Jack.

We stopped dancing under the scowling façade of the father of my unborn child. The father who still didn't know. The father who had promised he'd avoid me tonight. The father who was glaring at Soren Michaelson like he wanted to rip off his head.

And because I did not want to cause a scene at Bailey's wedding, I murmured, "Of course."

Disappointment clouded Soren's expression. His grip tightened ever so slightly. "Later?" he asked me.

As nice as that sounded, as much as I'd love the opportunity to find someone who could drive Jack Devlin out of my heart, I was not on the market for a relationship.

Other than the mother-child kind.

I gave him a vague smile and nod, and he released me.

Seconds later, I was in Jack's arms.

I tried to keep a distance but he pulled me close. Despite my struggle to keep thoughts of our night together out of my head, the memories flooded in. Although it had ended disastrously, I couldn't deny that sex with Jack was beyond my wildest imaginings.

Gazing anywhere but at his face, I whispered, "You promised."

He bent his head to mine, his lips brushing my ear and setting off a cascade of shivers down my neck. "Don't make me stand by and watch you flirt with someone else."

I jerked my head away and glowered. "Why? You've done it to me for nine years."

Remorse and pain flooded his eyes. "Em ..."

"I don't want to dance with you, Jack, but I don't want to make a scene. Will you please let me go?"

"Okay." He loosened his hold to tilt my chin up, forcing my eyes to his. "But only right now. In this moment. I can't let you go beyond that. I can't." Jack shook his head solemnly. "We're not done, sunrise."

No, we weren't.

Just not like he thought.

Tears threatened to choke me, so I hurriedly pulled out of his grasp and walked away, trying to look calm as I made my way off the dance floor.

Unfortunately, the scene I'd tried to avoid found me anyway.

It was hours later. Our group of friends were crowded near a table at the back of the room. Bailey and Vaughn stood with their arms around each other, laughing and joking. Vaughn's dad was dancing with Bailey's mom, while Bailey's dad had coaxed Cat and Joey onto the dance floor. Iris and Ira were laughing uproariously at something Old Archie and Anita were telling them a few tables over.

Dahlia, Michael, Jess, Cooper, Ivy, Jeff, Jack, and I stood in a huddle. It was a mark of how deep the connection between Cooper and Jack must have been that they seemed to fall so easily back into their friendship, despite their jagged past.

I attempted not to act overly aware of Jack's presence as we all chatted.

We were having a wonderful time.

Until it took a terrible turn.

A waiter stopped by with a tray of drinks. Vaughn took one for Bailey, for himself, and then held another out to me. I waved it away. "I'm fine, thanks."

"Oh, have a drink." Bailey took it from her husband and gestured to me with it. "Cut loose. It's our wedding."

"I'm really fine."

"Not everyone needs to have a drink to have fun," Jess teased, trying to rescue me.

"I know, but Em loves champagne." Bailey mock scowled at me. "You haven't had a drink all night. And you wouldn't take a drink last night at the inn, either. If I didn't know any better, I'd think you were pregnant."

Panic froze me to the spot as my cheeks bloomed fiery hot and an awkward silence fell over us.

It was moments like these that birthed the phrase "pregnant pause."

Fuck.

"Oh my God." Bailey inhaled sharply.

Jack stared at me in shock.

"Oh. My. God." Bailey glanced between the two of us.

I was going to be sick.

Right all over her designer wedding gown.

"No fucking way," Vaughn bit out. He held out his glass to Bailey. "Hold this."

Bailey took it and before anyone could blink, Vaughn punched Jack.

"Oh my God!" I rushed to intervene as Jack reeled. It took him mere seconds to get over the sucker punch before he straightened. His face darkened with fury as he lunged at Vaughn.

"Why does my husband keep punching people at weddings?" Bailey cried.

"Jack! Vaughn!" I reached them just as Cooper restrained Jack and Michael pushed Vaughn away.

"You son of a bitch," Vaughn growled. "I knew it. I knew you couldn't be trusted."

"He doesn't know." I pressed my hands to Vaughn's chest to hold him back. I sagged, exhausted as I turned to Jack whose expression clouded with a mixture of anger, incredulity, and accusation. "I mean … he didn't know."

"You're pregnant?" Jack growled, pushing Cooper away so he could come to me.

I nodded, mortified. Now everyone would know. The whole town. "I just found out."

Jack hesitated, as if he didn't know what to say.

"If you even think about asking her if it's yours, I'll kill you," Vaughn warned.

"Of course it's mine." Jack bared his teeth at Vaughn like he was thinking of preempting the groom's threat. He turned to me, his expression dark and foreboding … and worryingly satisfied. He held out his hand. "We need to talk. Now."

Eyes wet with tears, I turned to Bailey, trying to ignore the hush beneath the band's music. Everyone was watching us. "I'm so sorry, Bails."

"Don't be silly." She pulled me into her embrace. "I'm sorry I outed you." I shook my head and Bailey released me. "Are you going to be okay?"

Before I could answer, Jack's strong hand wrapped around my wrist, gently pulling me away. "I'll make damn sure of it," he vowed.

It was as I'd feared.

On the one hand, Jack seemed awfully calm about the news of his impending fatherhood, which was a relief. On the other hand, he also seemed to have assumed that this baby meant he now had an in with me.

And I was not looking forward to dispelling him of the idea.

27

JACK

Emery was pregnant.

Em. His Em. With his kid.

Pregnant.

Jack didn't know what emotion to grasp on to first. For the first time in his life, he was feeling a rush of many. It was overwhelming.

He was worried about Emery.

He was scared shitless.

He was strangely satisfied.

And grateful that an accidental pregnancy happened between him and the woman he loved and not some woman passing through town.

Angry at fucking Vaughn Tremaine for sticking his nose in, acting like he was Em's protective big brother.

Thankful Cooper had asked if he was all right instead of shooting him condemning looks like so many of the wedding guests had, like he'd violated the town virgin.

And Jack was nervous. Nervous about the way Emery wouldn't meet his eye as they sat across from one another in her beach house. She still wore her bridesmaid gown. It was a light pink that looked great against her skin and hair. Em's lashes were dark with mascara, but that was all he could see of her eyes.

Look at me.

He wanted to gaze into those startlingly pale, beautiful blue eyes and attempt to work out what Em was thinking.

Was she scared?

Did she hate him?

Did she not want the baby?

Fuck, that didn't even occur to him. What if she didn't want the baby?

"Em, I'm going crazy over here. Talk to me."

"I *was* going to tell you about the … the baby." She slowly lifted her gaze to meet his. There was so much anxiety and concern in her eyes, Jack couldn't pin down if she was worried he thought she hadn't planned to tell him, or she was freaked out about the whole thing. Probably both.

He sat forward on his seat. "I know that. You told me we'd talk later, remember?"

Relief flickered across her face. "Yeah. I just don't want you to think I would keep this from you." Anguish darkened her expression. "Now everyone will know."

"Let's forget about that for now. First … I'm sorry. I'm sorry for leaving that stupid note that—"

"Jack, don't." Emery stood, touching her temples like she had a headache. The pale-pink dress was the classiest bridesmaid dress Jack had ever seen. It was sleeveless with a high neckline, tied around the neck in a big bow that made a man's fingers itch to pull it loose. The dress clung to her gorgeous figure, and all that was revealed of her skin was her arms and back. He wondered if those women realized when they picked this dress out for Em that it was sexy as fuck.

Her belly was flat. By Jack's calculations, she was only seven weeks along. No sign of the baby yet.

Heat flushed through him. That possessive feeling he had about Em, the feelings he tried to stomp down because he didn't want to act like a caveman dick, roared through him a hundredfold. When he saw her dancing with that preppy-looking asshole at the wedding, he wanted to rip the guy's arms off.

If he'd known then that she was pregnant with his kid, Jack might have just done that.

And he didn't know how to feel about it.

He didn't like that side of himself.

But he couldn't deny that Emery made him territorial as hell. Jack knew he had to work on softening the edges of those feelings or he'd push Emery even further away.

"Tell me what you want," Jack coaxed, watching her pace the living room.

Em stopped pacing to face him. She wrapped her arms around her waist, almost protectively, and Jack wanted nothing more than to go to her and put his arms around her too.

He knew by the stubborn glint in her eyes that such a gesture would not be welcome at this juncture.

"I'm keeping the baby."

Jack sagged with relief. Terror wasn't far behind, but that was probably normal for any soon-to-be father. Right?

"You can be involved if you want, but I can take care of this child alone, emotionally and financially, so you don't need to feel obligated to do so."

It was like being sucker punched for the second time that night but this time by a fucking butterfly—you never anticipated the impact of a flutter of its wings. "What?" he bit out.

She looked uneasy. "I'm just saying—"

"I'm in this." Jack flew off the couch, gesturing to her belly. "That's my kid. *Our* kid. Fuck! I don't need to feel *obligated*? What the fuck is that?"

"I just meant that you weren't expecting this. So I don't want to hold you to anything."

"Oh yeah? Were *you* expecting it?"

"Of course not!"

"Were you the one who forgot to put on a condom?"

"Jack—"

"I was gone for you." His voice grew hoarse as the memory of that night seven weeks ago filled his mind and his dick. "So lost in you, I didn't even think. That's on me."

"It's on us both." She glared at him. "I'm a grown-up, Jack. It's up to me to make sure I'm protected during sex too. I'm not on the Pill. I've never had to be. And then I didn't … think."

"Fine, we both forgot. Now we have a kid on the way." He took a tentative step closer, not wanting to spook her. "I don't know about you, but as much as I am scared shitless out of my mind"—he threw her a shaky smile—"I'm also excited about it."

Her beautiful eyes grew round with surprise. "You are?"

"Aren't you?"

She nodded slowly.

He wanted to touch her. He wanted to touch her so badly, but he quelled the urge. "I know we have things to work out, but I want to be with you. I want us to be a family."

And just like that, a guard slammed down over Emery's expression. Jack watched it happen with alarming trepidation. She retreated from him.

Shit.

"Jack … I'm sorry, but that will not happen."

"Em—"

"I don't trust you."

Fuck!

"Em—"

"You can't change my mind. And I-I can't change that you're the father of my baby—"

"You'd want to?" he cut in angrily. Hurt. So fucking hurt, it was like she'd plunged a knife through his chest and yanked it upward.

"I never imagined having a baby with someone I wasn't in a relationship with."

"That's why I'm suggesting we get in a relationship."

"Not for the sake of a baby."

"Em, it's not for the sake—"

"Jack." She held up a hand to stop him. "No. I … I can't take it anymore."

He swallowed hard against the desire to yell, to be angry, to plead. "Explain."

Emery shrugged wearily, and Jack hated it. He hated that she was not even thirty years old and she was weary. Because of him. "I feel like I've been left here to wait for you for nine years. And I know it's not that simple," she hurried to add. "I know you had your reasons and a part of me even understands them. But you've never prioritized me, Jack. And maybe you didn't owe me that. But that's what I'm looking for. I'm looking for a guy who hasn't used other women to push me away, to remind me of what we're not … so many women"—her eyes glistened with hurt that killed him—"that I had to ask Jessica to *test* me."

Suddenly Jack felt sick.

And unclean.

And like a dirty piece of shit for touching her.

He lowered his head, hands on his hips. "I … I've never not worn protection … until you."

"I know. My tests came back clean."

Jack wanted to get out of there. He wanted to get away from her and get very fucking drunk.

"I'm not saying this to hurt you."

He scoffed, cutting her a dark look that made her flinch.

"Jack." She took a step toward him. "I'm not. I … I'm just trying to be honest. I know you never promised me anything, and I don't blame you. You've been honest from the start with me, if a little confusing in some of your actions. But I want to be with someone who doesn't rush away in the morning after making love to me, leaving me a shitty little note."

Indignation cut through him. "I admit the note was shitty and it wasn't all I intended to say, but Becs had called and my mom was melting down. I had to get to her."

Emery nodded. "I know. For the past—what—five years, you've put your family first. And that's admirable. I'm not blaming you for that. What I'm telling you is that I want to be with a man who sees me as his family first. Who puts *me* first. That's never been you, Jack."

As much as her words killed him, Jack couldn't argue.

He'd done that.

He'd put his family first before all things.

Including Cooper. Including her.

A choking feeling wrapped around his throat.

He'd failed her.

"I'm not willing to give up on the idea of finding the right person because we got pregnant. I'm happy for you to be as big a part of our child's life as you want to be … but it won't be as a family." Her eyes gleamed with sadness. "It'll be with a shared custody agreement."

Shared custody?

Meaning dropping off his kid to the woman he loved after only seeing that kid every other weekend? Watching Em raise his kid with whatever lucky bastard she deemed right for her?

No.

No!

His life was a piece of shit because of his father. He was thirty-eight years old and having to build a new life for himself, start over, and Emery Saunders was the one thing he wanted in his life more than anything.

Had he made mistakes with her? Oh, hell yeah, he had.

Yet Jack couldn't give up.

They hadn't even gone on a date but Jack knew that she was his and he was hers, and he felt that deep in his fucking soul.

It had eaten at him for years not being with her.

"I ..." He swallowed through the choking sensation. "I've been pretty messed up in the head for the last five years. I said and did things that I regret. I ... I'm trying to make amends, Em."

"I know." Her expression softened. "And you should ... I want that for you. You have no idea how happy I am to see you and Cooper trying to rebuild your friendship. I want that for you, Jack. I just ..." Her hand rested on her belly. "I have someone else to think about now. I have to lead by example. For years, I've accepted the very little that I was given by the people who were supposed to love me. I don't want my child to think that's okay." Her voice cracked and she looked away but not before he caught the heartrending sight of tears in her eyes. He wanted to go to her. He wanted to hold her. Forever. "I ... I don't want my kid to think it's okay to accept the least that people are willing to give. I want my kid to know they deserve to be loved unconditionally. I can't just say it. I have to show it and live by example."

Jack didn't know how to tell her that giving him a shot *would* be living by example.

He didn't know how to tell her that he would marry her in a heartbeat because he was so sure he'd never want anyone else for the rest of his life.

He didn't know how to tell her that her pain was his pain, and that he'd do anything to take it away. That he hated whoever had hurt her before he'd even walked into her life.

He didn't have those words.

Bailey had suggested he write a letter.

But Jack realized that even if he did, Emery wasn't in a place to believe him.

Yeah, he knew his girl was a romantic, but there was something deeper here. He knew it went back to her family. To something that happened to her as a kid. Maybe even with a boy. Em hadn't been a virgin when they'd slept together. Someone else might have broken her heart before he ever unintentionally broke it too.

No. For the first time in her life, his romantic Emery didn't need words.

She needed actions.

And they were having a baby together, which meant he had a legitimate excuse to monopolize her time.

In fact, Jack had about seven months.

Seven months to prove through action that he could deserve her. That he loved her beyond reason or doubt. That he would lay down his life for her and his kid.

That he wasn't going anywhere.

No more prioritizing his family over her. She was right. He'd done what he could for them. Now Emery and the baby growing in her belly were his family.

"Okay."

Her wet eyes flew to his in shock. "Okay?"

She'd been expecting a fight.

He wouldn't do that.

His fight for her heart would be the stealthy kind.

"This isn't about me or what I want. This is about you and our kid." He sighed heavily. "You don't want to be in a relationship, then fine. But I will be involved like any father would be. I'm talking doctor's appointments, picking out shit for the nursery, answering my cell at two in the morning because you can't sleep or you have a craving for pickles and mint chocolate chip ice cream."

She opened her mouth, looking ready to protest.

He cut her off. "I mean it, Em. This is my kid too. I want to be there for all of that."

Jack waited anxiously for her to agree. She had to agree.

Finally, she nodded. "Okay."

He tried not to look too relieved. "Can I get you anything now?"

"No, I'm fine. I … uh … I'm tired, actually."

"Then I'll leave you be. But I'll be back, Em. I'm not going anywhere."

28

EMERY

It came as no surprise that Iris was the first person at my door the next day. The store was closed on Sundays, so I thankfully didn't have to face the gossips just yet. I had missed calls from my friends, which I intended to return.

Especially when I saw Iris on my porch.

I knew the girls (excluding Bailey who was probably already at the airport on the way to her honeymoon) would be worried enough to descend on my house in Iris's wake.

"You okay?" Iris demanded as she strode into the house.

"Yes."

"The sickness at my place?"

I nodded sheepishly.

Iris sighed.

"Do you want tea?"

She shook her head and crossed her arms. I gestured for her to sit but she stayed standing. "So ... how long has this thing between you and Jack been going on?"

I felt like the real answer was nine years. But when I thought back, this thing really started just before Devlin blackmailed him. "About five years."

Iris's eyes widened. "Holy … what?"

I sighed and sat. "Can you sit? I don't want to crane my neck looking up at you the whole time."

"Pregnancy comes with an attitude, huh?" Iris teased, sitting on the sectional.

"Oh, you of all people know there is an attitude buried under the blushing," I huffed. "I think the pregnancy is just making me care less." That wasn't entirely true. I still cared. I was anxious about becoming gossip fodder for the Hartwell masses.

"Five years, Emery?" Iris insisted.

"On and off." I shrugged. "Mostly off. I'd decided it was definitely off last summer and then everything happened with his father and I realized Jack's reasons for staying away from me were legitimate and then we slept together and he left me to go deal with his family, which is fine but not right after you sleep with someone!" My rambling anger echoed around my house. It surprised me.

"Em?"

I shook myself out of my hurt. Or I tried to. "He's not right for me is the conclusion."

"Does he want to be right for you?"

An ache, deep and hot and painful, seared my chest. "He … wanted us to be a family for the baby, but I said no. And he was fine with that."

Completely fine.

Bastard.

I knew it was contrary of me, but I was mad at him for not even putting up a fight. It proved I was right about him. Jack Devlin was not *the one*. *The one* would fight. He would fight for me.

"Emery?"

My pain must've shown in my eyes because Iris frowned with concern. "We'll all take care of you. And one day, you'll find someone. The right someone."

"Oh yes." I waved away the thought because I couldn't even think of romance right now. "But you don't have to worry about me, Iris. While Jack and I aren't going to pursue a relationship, he is very insistent on being a part of our baby's life and the entire pregnancy."

Iris harrumphed. "Well, we're still here if you need us."

"I appreciate it."

"Now, outside of Jack, how are you feeling about becoming a mom?"

Iris chatted for over an hour, taking me up on that offer for tea. When she got up to leave, I clasped her hand in mine before she could open the door.

"I know you're not much for sentimentality, Iris," I teased. "But I don't think I've ever thanked you for giving me a safe place to turn to the moment I got here. I think of you as family. I hope you know that."

Iris squeezed my hand right back. "The feeling is mutual, my girl." She leaned in and kissed my cheek. "Now, you call if you need me. I'll be mad if you don't." She pointed to my belly. "That kid in there is gonna call me Nana Iris so I've got rights."

I laughed, some of my melancholy easing, as I waved her out the door.

Nana Iris. I touched my still-flat stomach. That had a nice ring to it.

It wasn't too much long after Iris left that I got a call from Jess, followed by one from Dahlia. They wanted to come to the house but I told them both I was exhausted. The truth was, I just … I just wanted to wallow for a while.

Wallow in the utter disappointment that was Jack Devlin.

While I was wallowing, I began internet researching. I sent for a bunch of books on pregnancy. Maybe it was too soon, but I liked to feel prepared and since it was apparently impossible to feel prepared for parenthood, I had to do something.

In the middle of a freak-out about the impossibility of

preparedness (because who knew there was a situation outside of death in which you could not prepare yourself!), I got a text from Ivy.

Had a drunken one-night stand with the sheriff. Thought it might take your mind off Bailey outing that you're having a baby with the town lothario. On that note, how are you feeling?

I spit out my tea on a surprised bark of shocked laughter.

I hit the call button.

Ivy answered after two rings. "You okay?"

I smiled. "I'm fine. How are you?"

"Oh, Em, would it be self-absorbed to ask God why I keep making stupid decisions?"

"She asks the pregnant girl," I joked.

Ivy chuckled. "Was Jack Devlin a stupid decision?"

"Five years' worth."

"Ouch. Okay, there is a bigger story here obviously."

"Yes, there is, but you texted me to get my mind off my problems. Was Jeff a stupid decision?"

"Can you keep a secret? I mean, Bailey already knows but … can you?"

"Of course."

"Jeff moved to Hartwell when I was sixteen. He was twenty-two, a deputy at the time, and he moved here because he fell in love with Kelly Aikman. She was beautiful and sweet and I envied the hell out of her the moment I caught sight of Jeff." Ivy laughed. "I spent my last two years in Hartwell mooning over a married man who didn't even know I was alive. Then I left, and crushes fade, you know … but Bailey would keep me informed. That he got elected sheriff. That Kelly died. Fuck, that broke my heart. I envied her for so long, and then … she had so little time. And she was the sweetest woman. Oh gosh, I hurt for him, you know. Losing her so soon. And you would have thought it would wake me up." She seemed to be talking to herself now. "But, no, I kept on going, making stupid mistake after stupid mistake, as if we're granted a never-ending supply of chances. Which we're not.

"I'd just started dating Oliver when Bailey told me Jeff and Dahlia were a thing. I was jealous. Isn't that ridiculous? I didn't even really know Jeff. He was just a crush. I guess … I guess I was jealous of more than that. Dahlia was Bailey's new best friend. She was dating Jeff. She … she was living a life maybe I'd missed out on … that was all my fault, I guess."

"Ivy …" I said her name just to remind her I was there.

She cleared her throat. "Anyway, Jeff and I talked for real for the first time when that whole thing with Freddie Jackson went down. And then last night, he was very attentive."

"Of course, he was." I smiled to myself. "Ivy, you're …"

"I'm what?"

"Well, you're not only the most stunning woman I've ever met in real life, you're … you're not the easiest person to get a lock on." My own honesty surprised me. Words were just blurting out of me these days.

"In what way?"

"This is the most you've ever told me about yourself."

She chuckled. "Emery, I know nothing about you except that you're pregnant with Jack Devlin's baby, so pot, meet kettle."

"I didn't mean it in a bad way. I just mean that I could see how a man like Jeff would be intrigued to know more. You don't give everything away up front."

"Well, I gave some things away last night."

I laughed. "Were you very drunk?"

"Nah. I knew what I was doing, which is even worse. But when your teen crush gives you sexy eyes, it's hard to say to no to that. Even when you should."

"Why would you say no? Jeff King is a wonderful man, Ivy. You could do a lot worse."

"First, he just wanted sex. When men are really into you, they don't do one-night stands."

I flinched, thinking about Jack.

"And second, I don't know if I'm staying in Hartwell. Oh wait, someone is knocking at my door. It's probably Mom here to give me the third degree—oh shit!"

Hearing the shock in her voice, I asked, "Ivy, are you okay?"

"Uh ... Jeff is here. And he ... Okay, he looks mad."

I grinned. "Did you, by any chance, run away while he was sleeping?" As soon as the words left my mouth, I winced. Jack had left me sleeping seven or so weeks ago.

"Maybe. Why is he here? Oh shit, he saw me. I have to open the door."

"Good luck!"

"You don't have to sound so cheerful," she huffed. "I'll call you later."

The line went dead.

Ivy had done what she'd hoped to do. She successfully distracted me from my own problems.

My phone beeped.

Bailey this time.

Are you okay?

I texted back that I was fine.

At the airport. When I get home, we'll talk. Just know we're here for you. Me and Vaughn.

I thought of Vaughn punching Jack at his own wedding in my defense. As much as I hated seeing Jack hurt, it was nice that Vaughn felt a brotherly protectiveness toward me.

Thank you. Don't worry about me. Enjoy your honeymoon! We'll talk when you're home.

The extraordinary weight of worries on my shoulders lightened a little as I moved out onto the porch to sit on my swing. The beach was busy with families and couples enjoying the summer morning. The waves lapped gently at shore. The gulls cried above.

I eased back on the porch swing and took a deep breath.

No matter what happened, I had a family here now. I had people who cared.

And I was no longer afraid to let them care and to care about them in return.

I trusted them.

Even if I couldn't trust Jack, I found comfort and joy because Hartwell really was a place I could call home.

DRIVING to Millton the next morning, I spoke to my car. "Call Ivy."

After four rings, she picked up, sounding a little groggy. "Hullo."

"Did I wake you?" That surprised me. It wasn't too early in the morning. I closed the store every second Monday morning to volunteer at a therapy center, Balance, in Millton, but the children's group didn't come together until ten o'clock.

"Uh, yeah. Give me a second."

I could hear a shuffling around. A second turned out to be a few minutes.

"Sorry, sorry." Ivy came back on the line. "I had to switch on my coffee machine. Useless without it."

"No problem. Are you okay?"

"Oh God, Em, I suck." She groaned, sounding exhausted.

"What happened?"

"Jeff spent the entire day here yesterday. He was pissed at me—coffee's ready, one second."

"Is this a writer thing … building my anticipation?"

I heard her chuckle down the line followed a few seconds later by the slurp of her drinking.

"That's better. Okay. He was pissed at me for running out on him. Apparently, what I thought was a one-night stand was not a one-night stand. I tried to tell him it needed to be a one-nighter, but he kind of ignored me. It was bizarre. The next thing I know, he's making lunch and we're sitting out on the porch, chatting. Then lunch turned into me making dinner. We talked. All day. And then we … oh my God, Emery." She groaned. "God, we had sex all night. Like … the best sex of my life."

I smirked. "And that's a bad thing?"

"I … I just … I don't have a great track record with men. I just—I'm not ready for anything serious and it is now clear to me that Jeff is that guy. You know, Mr. Monogamy Guy. He pretty much said that outright."

"Well, evidence suggests he's telling the truth." It was true. I'd never seen the sheriff serial date. At all. Dahlia was the second woman he dated after his wife died. They dated awhile, and he was definitely more into her than she was into him. Since Dahlia, he'd attempted a few relationships, but they never lasted. Having talked to Dahlia about her relationship with Jeff, however, I knew it had started pretty normally. She said she knew he was serious because they went on seven dates before they had sex.

I remembered the look on Jeff's face when he saw Ivy at the wedding.

It was an intense look.

"I shouldn't have slept with him again. Multiple times." She sighed. "He woke up early to leave for work and whispered in my ear that … that what happened between us meant the world to him and this was just the beginning for us. Who says that?"

A romantic.

"He doesn't even know me, Emery. If he knew the truth, God, he'd run away and never come back. He has no idea that he is way too good for me."

My breath caught. "Ivy, don't say that. It's not true."

"It is, Em." She sounded defeated. "I let a rotten guy do awful things to me for a long time." Her breath hitched. "Anyway, I gotta get ready for my day of avoiding the sheriff. You okay?"

"I'm fine—"

"Okay, good. Bye."

My heart raced. This was the closest I think anyone might have gotten to Ivy opening up about her dead fiancé. Shit. "Call Balance."

Ahmad, the young receptionist, answered.

"Hey, it's Emery. I am so sorry, but I can't make it this morning. I'm sorry for the last-minute call, but something just came up. Are the other volunteers on their way?"

"They're already here. It's good. The kids will miss you, though."

Guilt suffused me. I'd never missed a group. But my friend needed me. "I'm so sorry."

"Not at all. I hope everything's okay."

I hoped so too.

DECIDING to grab some bagels to take to Ivy's, I stopped in at Lanson's on my way to her place. I was in the bread aisle, deciding over which type of bagel Ivy might like. I opted for a few kinds and as I was just about to move on to fillings, I heard my name.

I stopped in the middle of the aisle and stared to my left. Whoever it was, was in the aisle next to mine.

"He should be shot for touching that girl."

"She's not a girl, Ellen. She's a grown woman. And she had to know Jack's reputation before she jumped into bed with him."

Nausea rolled over me. It was starting.

The gossip.

"Do you think she did it to trap him?"

"Absolutely." A new voice joined in. One I recognized.

"Oh, Dana, I didn't see you there. You heard, then?" I was pretty sure that voice belonged to Ellen Luther.

The third voice, the one I didn't recognize, said, "It's unbelievable. It's always the quiet ones."

My cheeks were on fire.

"She's always been a manipulative, pretentious little bitch," Dana said acidly. "No one else could see it. But I did. And she's had her eye on Jack for ages."

The audacity of it. Dana Kellerman. Cheater. Mistress. Manipulator. Gossiping about me?

"So, you think she's trying to trap him?" the unknown voice repeated.

"Absolutely. But I know Jack. He won't fall for it. They'll raise that child separately."

We would. And people would think it was because he didn't want me. Not the other way around. Small, narrow little minds.

"I don't know. I think you might have it the wrong way around. Word is that Emery Saunders comes from a lot of money. He's a Devlin. Maybe he deliberately used her naivety against her and got her pregnant to get his hands on her money," Ellen said.

I grimaced, aghast.

Why did it never occur to people that maybe two people slept together because they had feelings for one another?

Why was there always a dark, hidden agenda?

Why did everyone always assume the worst of everyone else?

"Jack wouldn't land himself with a prissy virgin for money. He likes sex too much," Dana gloated. "Emery Saunders can't give a man like Jack what he needs."

"Well, you would know," Ellen retorted slyly.

Dana huffed. "I'm just saying. She'd bore him to tears."

Done listening to them, I strode up the aisle and around the corner as they continued to shred Jack and me to pieces.

Ellen Luther, Dana Kellerman, and Sadie Thomas stood huddled in the magazine aisle. Ellen noticed me first and blanched with shame. Sadie prattled on about "the poor kid born from this scandalous mess" and Ellen nudged her to shut her up.

"What?" Sadie looked at her and then finally caught sight of me.

Dana sneered, enjoying that I'd overheard.

Dana, the cheater.

Sadie Thomas, who slept around. A lot. Not that I judged. But I judged her judging me when she was used to people talking about her and knew it wasn't nice or fun.

And Ellen Luther, whom I'd always thought better of.

But people liked their gossip.

I stared at every single one of them with a disdainful disappointment I'd learned from my grandmother until even Dana squirmed.

Without a word, I turned on my heel, dumped my basket at the door, and left Lanson's.

By the time I got to Ivy's, I was worried I needed her support as much as she needed mine.

"Em?" Ivy opened the door, looking a lot brighter than I'd expected considering her mournful tone on the phone. "Are you okay?"

"That's what I came to ask you."

Ivy scrutinized me for a second and stepped aside to gesture me into her home. "What happened?"

It was on the tip of my tongue to tell her. To let it all burst out. But I was afraid if I did, I would cry, and those awful women didn't deserve my tears. Instead, I focused on the original purpose of my visit. "I'm worried about you."

"Em—"

"What did you mean? About Jeff not deserving you … about a rotten man, doing awful things?"

She exhaled shakily. "Shit."

"Ivy?"

"Coffee?"

"Ivy—"

"I'm not deflecting. I just need more coffee."

"I'll have water." I made a sad face and pointed to my stomach. "I'm only allowed so much caffeine now."

She gave me a commiserating smile. "Right."

Not too long later, we settled on her porch, overlooking the lake, coffee and water in hand, eating leftover pastries that Jeff had brought over the day before.

I waited patiently for her to speak first.

Finally, while I was halfway through a cinnamon bun, she spoke. "I haven't told anyone this. I wasn't even sure I could."

I noted her coffee mug tremble and felt a lurch of aching empathy in my chest. "You don't have to if you're not ready."

"When I got off the phone with you, I realized I'd said to you out loud what I've been telling myself for years. And I've been telling myself those things because it's the things *he* used to tell me. And yet, I know deep down I don't believe them." Something like loathing filled her eyes before she glanced away. "'*You're worthless, Ivy. What would you be without me? No one would care about you. I made you. I can unmake you. You don't deserve me. I could have anyone.*'" Her words gathered more anger as she spewed out what I suspected was the abuse she'd received from Oliver. "'*Don't even think of fucking leaving me. No one leaves me. I'll fucking kill you before you leave me.*'"

Tears built in my throat and stung my eyes. "Ivy."

Hearing the choked way I said her name, her head whipped to me. "Don't cry for me, Em. I'm not sure I deserve it."

"Don't say that."

"I'm Iris and Ira Green's kid. Can you, in any stretch of the imagination, imagine my mom putting up with that shit?"

No. But many women did. "You were scared," I guessed.

"He … once he locked me in our walk-in closet for nearly two days. I tried to find a way out but I … I pissed my own pants." Bitterness curdled the last few words and my tears escaped, hearing the humiliation in them. "Another time, I wanted to leave this party we were at because he kept flirting with this twenty-year-old actress right in front of me. He dragged me into a bathroom and held a paring knife he'd found in the kitchen to my throat. He told me that the next time I made a scene, he'd take me home and hold a knife at my throat while he 'showed me the only thing I was good for.'" She released a breath and it shook so badly, it almost felt like the porch trembled with the force of it.

"You know, he was actually nicer to me when he was high. You ever heard of the like?" Her dark eyes found mine. "I stayed in that nightmare, cutting out my mom and dad, because I was ashamed I'd let myself get into that mess. And I didn't want my mom to know." With an abruptness that shouldn't have startled me but did, Ivy bowed her head and sobbed into her hands.

Crying silently for her, I got out of my chair and lowered to my haunches, my arms sliding around her. I pulled her into me. Ivy didn't resist. She let me take her weight and her pain.

29

EMERY

"Bailey will be so pissed I told you first," Ivy said wryly as she sipped at a fresh mug of coffee.

It was awhile after her confession and the tears that had followed. She'd gone inside to clean up while I made her a fresh pot and tried to push down the rage I felt toward a dead man.

I chuckled at the idea of Bailey finding out Ivy had confided in me first. "Yeah."

"I just feel like I can trust you. Not that I can't trust Bailey, but … timing is everything, I guess."

"You *can* trust me," I promised her.

She nodded.

"Ivy, you need to tell your parents. They know and suspect something like this anyway … and they would never be ashamed of you. He did what all abusers do. He made you feel you were to blame for his actions. But you aren't."

"I know that," Ivy whispered. "Deep down, I know that. I knew it while he was doing it. I … just … I was planning to get away." She glared at me. "Believe me. I planned that shit every day for two years."

"I do believe you. Ivy, do you know how many good, strong

women are victims of domestic abuse each year in this country? The statistics are frightening. You are not alone."

"I'm not strong."

"You bashed a gunman over the head with an Academy Award statuette to protect Dahlia. If that isn't badass, I don't know what is."

Ivy grinned, though it didn't quite reach her eyes. "That *was* pretty badass. Is it wrong that that's what I think of now when I look at it instead of the screenplay I won it for?"

Laughing, I shook my head. "No, that just makes me like you even more."

Her expression darkened. "Would you still like me if I said I was relieved when Oliver died?"

There it was.

The root.

"You feel guilty," I surmised. "You feel guilty because his death freed you."

She nodded, swallowing hard.

"That is a natural response. It does not make you a terrible person."

She huffed. "I … I don't know if I'm a terrible person or if I'm stupid or weak … but … who entangles themselves with an honorable man when they're this fucked up? I should never have let Jeff touch me."

I thought on this a moment. "Are you surprised that you could? That you wanted him?"

Her eyes flew to mine. "Yes, actually."

"Maybe you have better instincts than you think. Maybe you've honed them since meeting Oliver. You trusted me and I can assure you I am trustworthy." I smiled. "And you trusted Jeff to be the first man you've slept with since Oliver. And you can trust him. I doubt there is a man in the entire state of Delaware who you can trust more than Jeff King. Okay, there's Cooper, Vaughn, and Michael, but they're all taken so they don't count."

She tilted her head, her gaze wandering curiously over my face. "Jack doesn't count?"

My heart ached. "I used to think so."

"Until he slept with Dana?"

I shook my head. "I still trusted him then. I still believed in him."

"Not now?"

"Not now."

"You don't trust easily either, do you?"

I thought of Ivy confiding her secrets to me. "I trust you."

She smiled gratefully.

"Can I tell you a story? Only Jess knows it. It's the reason I … well … it's part of the reason I am the way I am."

"You can tell me anything."

So I did. On a warm Monday afternoon, I told Ivy Green my story.

Afterward, we sat in silence for a while.

Until eventually I turned to her and said, "Please tell your parents about what you went through with Oliver."

She closed her eyes briefly and took in a deep breath. "I will. I promise."

"And if you care about Jeff, don't push him away. If you can't start something with him, I absolutely understand, but tell him why. You won't regret it."

"He'll look at me differently."

"I doubt it, but if he does, then you'll know for certain he isn't the right guy for you."

"When did you get so wise, Emery Saunders?"

"I have no idea," I answered honestly, smiling as I settled a hand on my belly. "Maybe my kid is full of wisdom and leaking some of that goodness into me."

"Your kid," she muttered. "You're going to be a mom."

Fear, excitement, and anticipation caused a swooping sensation in my belly.

"If I stay in Hartwell, do I get to be Aunt Ivy?" she teased.

I didn't tease when I replied, "You get to be Aunt Ivy no matter where you are."

Her eyes brightened and her voice sounded a little thick as she said, "I think maybe I'll stay right where I am. It feels like a good place to be."

30

JACK

Jack's patience was wearing thin.

He'd texted Emery Sunday and Monday and hadn't heard a thing back. Not a single reply.

That shit was not right.

Which was why Tuesday morning, he swung his car into a parking space on Main Street and marched down the boards to Emery's store. It was morning. It was coffee rush hour, even if it was the end of August and already eighty degrees outside at eight o'clock in the morning. Jack expected he'd have to wait in line and wouldn't be able to question Em about her ignoring him in front of customers.

What he saw through the door was Em sitting in an empty store with her head in her hands.

"Sunrise, what's wrong?" he asked as he pushed through the door.

She raised her head at the tinkle of the bell and his accompanying question. The look in her beautiful eyes matched the crease of concern between her brows. Em gestured to her empty store. "No one has come in this morning. No one."

What the hell?

She shook her head in disgust. "I was closed yesterday. And I overheard Dana, Ellen, and Sadie gossiping about us in Lanson's."

"What did they say?" Jack bit out angrily as he strode to the counter. He reached for her hand but she pulled back, which only increased his agitation.

"They're wondering which of us deliberately trapped the other."

Fury mowed over his anger. "What?"

Em flinched at his bark. "Was it the shy, virginal bookstore owner who wanted to catch herself a man?" She gestured sarcastically to herself. "Or mercenary Jack Devlin who found out Emery Saunders comes from money?"

"They said that?"

"You can imagine what Dana was saying. How I trapped you but you'd never fall for it, that someone like me couldn't keep your interest since I'm sexually inexperienced and we'll be raising the baby separately."

"I'm going to kill her." He pushed back off the counter, ready to march into town and blast the hell out of them for gossiping about Emery like this. She didn't deserve it. They'd practically run his mother out of town because of their gossiping shit, and he wouldn't let them hurt Emery.

"Don't." Emery reached over the counter, grabbing his arm.

He covered her hand with his, seeking contact.

"Jack, don't." She tried to let go, but he took hold of her hand and held on. "I just want to get through this without giving them anything more to be scandalized over."

His heart beat too fast. He had pent-up aggression he wanted to dole out on someone. Preferably someone who had hurt Em.

"Please." She squeezed his hand.

Taking a deep breath, Jack nodded.

"Can I have my hand back now?"

He shook his head. "Not until you tell me why you've been ignoring my texts."

"Your texts?" Emery scowled. "I haven't received any—oh my gosh." She covered her mouth with her free hand, her eyes filling with sheepishness. She dropped her hand and grimaced. "I blocked you. When you didn't call or text for weeks ... I blocked your number."

Disappointment and self-directed anger twisted his gut. He tightened his hand around Em's, feeling her silver rings bite into his skin. "How about you unblock it now?"

"Of course. I'd do it now if I had both hands free."

At her teasing, Jack released her. He watched as she pulled her cell out from under the counter and tapped on the screen.

"When is your next doctor's appointment?"

"This week. It's my first prenatal visit."

"I want to be there."

"Jack, it's not a big deal. Why don't you come with me for the first ultrasound?" She looked up from her phone and waved it at him. "Unblocked."

He ignored that. "I want to be at every appointment."

She sighed, sounding a little exasperated. "Jess says I'll have an appointment once a month until twenty-eight weeks. And then it'll be every two weeks and then every week. Do you really want to come to every single one?"

Jack leaned in, hoping proximity would somehow make the words sink in. "Every. Single. One. Every appointment. Every scan. And I'm going to be around, Em. I'm going to make you dinner. We're going to hang out. We're going to become the bestest fucking friends during your pregnancy, so help me God."

To his surprise, her lips twitched with amusement. "The bestest fucking friends?"

As cute as her amusement was, Jack was deadly serious. "We're going to raise a kid together, and you said you don't trust me. I'm going to be the father of your child, Emery. I know you don't want me the way I want you, but I have to earn your trust either way. For my kid. If you don't trust me, you do realize our kid will eventually sense that. Do you want that? Because I don't."

Her eyes grew adorably round, her skin flushing a gorgeous pink. "I … you're right. I don't want that."

Jack relaxed a little. "I can't snap my fingers and say 'Em, trust me.' It doesn't work like that. I get it. I get that I screwed up with you. But for the sake of co-parenting, please give me the chance to earn your trust. The only way I can do that is to spend time with you."

She studied him before she asked, "Just friends?"

It took everything within him. In fact, Jack had to swallow down a growl of indignation at the mere thought. And then, for the first time, he intentionally lied to Emery. "Just friends."

After contemplating him a moment, Emery gave him a small, tentative smile. "My prenatal visit is at Hartwell County General on Thursday at two o'clock."

Jack mentally noted it so he could make sure his schedule was clear. "Where will I pick you up? Here or at your place?"

"Oh, we can just meet there."

He glared at her.

Her lips twitched again. "Here. One thirty."

"Good." Jack flashed her a pleased smile. "Thank you."

The pink staining her cheeks turned a delightful strawberry. Jack's body reacted to her blushing. Seemed like a good time to get gone. "I'll take two Americanos to go."

While she busied herself making the coffees, Jack couldn't help but watch her. She wasn't showing. Not yet. But she had their baby growing in her belly. Tied to him forever through the beautiful kid they'd made. Jack was going to be a father. She would be his kid's mom. The possession that was becoming so familiar roared through him. Heat built in his blood, traveling south with dangerous speed.

Trying to divert his thoughts, he said, "Don't worry about the gossips. They'll find something new to talk about it."

"I'm not worried about the gossip." She slid the coffees toward him. "I'm worried that people are so judgmental about this pregnancy that they don't want to come through my doors."

That was the part Jack didn't get. He knew Cat was treated like shit when she got pregnant with Joey out of wedlock, but only by a small pocket of the most conservative members of the community. Hartwell, in general, was not a conservative place. It was strange that no one would venture into Em's store because of this.

Concern niggled at him.

"I'll look into it."

"You think there's something more going on?" She worried her bottom lip, drawing his attention to her mouth.

He needed to get out of there before he did something stupid, like kiss the anxieties right out of her. "We'll see. Stop worrying. I'll take care of it."

"If someone is trying to sabotage me, Jack, I want to know. They think they can walk all over me because I'm quiet, but they can't. And they should know that."

Jack knew that for a fact. "When I find out what's going on, I'll let you know. And we'll take care of it the way *you* want to take care of it."

Em's expression softened and she gave him a small nod of thanks. "Coffee is on the house."

His chest ached with the urge to kiss her. The ache traveled into his throat and choked a response right out of him. Instead, he lifted his cups to her in thanks and got the hell out of there before he ruined his stealthy plan of attack.

And even though Jack was running late for a meeting with his hotel manager, and that wasn't exactly the impression he wanted to give his staff first week in, Jack knocked on Cooper's door. The bar wasn't open yet, but Coop was sometimes there early doing inventory and cleaning up.

It was Jack's lucky morning that Coop was the one who opened the door.

He held out the second Americano to his friend. "Got a quick minute?"

Cooper took the coffee and gestured Jack inside. The bar's air-conditioning offered relief from the sultry morning.

"What's wrong?"

"No one is at Em's. It's like they're boycotting the place. Have you heard anything?"

Cooper grimaced. "There's been gossip. I know we have some conservatives in town who wouldn't like her being pregnant out of wedlock but not enough she wouldn't have any customers. It's not like she's the first unmarried woman in Hartwell to get pregnant."

Yeah, exactly Jack's thoughts. "Em heard three women gossiping yesterday in Lanson's. Some wondered if I was after her money and deliberately got her pregnant—others are thinking she tried to trap me and failed."

Cooper sighed in exasperation. "Yeah, that's the shit we heard too. I had to stop Jess from marching through town with a megaphone screaming her outrage. It's got her stressed so I can't imagine how Emery's feeling, and the last thing we need is our pregnant women worked up right now. Thankfully, a scandal only lasts until the next one comes along."

"My family has given this town plenty to chew over these last few months." Jack followed Cooper as he pulled a chair out at a table. He took a seat across from him, disbelieving how easily Cooper had let him back into his life.

The problem was, he suspected something, and he was afraid airing it might sour things between them again.

"Fuck," he muttered under his breath. "I hate to ask this, Coop, but it's too important."

"Ask what?"

Jack forced himself to meet his friend's gaze. "Dana was one of the women bitching yesterday. She was spreading it around that there was no way I'd be interested in Emery, that she couldn't satisfy me, and Em was trying to trap me."

Cooper's expression darkened. "Why am I not surprised?"

"I … man, I hate coming to you for your opinion on this, but do you think Dana might spread that shit far and wide? Vilifying Em? I gotta say, I was surprised by how many people seemed to come to my side after the shit with Ian went down. Maybe someone is telling them Em took advantage. Is that a stretch?"

"One—" Cooper took a sip of coffee as if to gather his thoughts. "Dana is a part of our history. We'll never get past that if we tiptoe around any mention of her. She doesn't deserve the awkwardness or the tension. Truth is, Jack, I feel like I was married to her in another life. I'm so disconnected to that time now. Going forward, I'm just holding on to the memory of the guy who beat the shit out of an older kid for beating the shit out of me. To the guy who took care of my mom's funeral arrangements because I was too fucked up. Who stood at my side and cried with me at her funeral."

Jack's throat tightened.

"I'm holding on to the memories of the guy who was once the truest man I'd ever met. Because I believe he's still in there." Cooper pointed at Jack's chest. "Or I wouldn't be sitting here with you."

"Coop …" Jack's voice was hoarse.

"So, she's not a part of us anymore. I'm letting it go because you deserve a second chance." Cooper sipped at his coffee again, giving Jack time to control his emotions. "As to your question … yeah, I think Dana has been pissed at you a long time, and it would not surprise me if she took it out on Em by spreading shit."

"If I warn her off, I give her the attention she wants."

"Yeah, that's true."

"Em wants to know what's behind no one coming to her store. I told her I'd tell her if I found out."

"She doesn't need that stress."

"But maybe she needs to be the one who stands up for herself."

Cooper smirked. "I will not lie—I'd like a front-row seat to shy Emery Saunders tearing Dana Kellerman a new one."

Jack chuckled at the thought. "Me too."

"How are you? You scared shitless like me?" Cooper asked.

He grinned. "You know it."

"Our kids will be almost the same age."

Something warm moved through him. "They'll grow up together?" He didn't mean it to come out a question, but it did.

"Yeah, they will," Cooper promised. "And you and Em? You said you loved her."

"There are some people in this town who will think that I don't. That I just used her. But they're wrong." Jack rubbed a hand over his head, feeling a little exhausted. "I love her, Cooper."

"I believed you the first time you said it. I think I believed it that first night she walked into my bar, and you looked like a fucking angel had fallen from heaven just for you." That was just like Coop. To know his friend so well. To know Jack had been taken with Emery from the moment he saw her. "Did you feel that way about Jess?"

A small, satisfied smile prodded Cooper's lips. "We ran into each other in the rain, right outside the bar. And I got that funny feeling on the back of my neck."

Jack grinned. He knew about all Cooper's "funny feeling." While Jack had great gut instincts about people, Cooper had a weird sixth sense. Anytime something important was about to happen in his life, he got a strange tingle down the nape of his neck. "So you knew, huh?"

"I knew it meant Jess wasn't just a gorgeous tourist passing through. I knew it meant I should make an effort to get to know her. And I'll never ignore that feeling again." He took another sip of his coffee. "Have you told Emery yet? About how you feel? Did you write that letter Bails suggested?"

"Nah. Em doesn't trust me. If I said that now, whether to her face or in a letter, she wouldn't believe it. I have to show her. She thinks I just want to be friends. So we can co-parent. I told her I want to be at every appointment and that we're going to hang out. Become best buds."

Cooper's grin was slow and wicked, and Jack knew he understood. "You're in it for the long game. Stealth attack."

Jack grinned back. "You know it."

"I've just realized I can't tell Jessica any of this shit, can I?"

"Absolutely not."

"Fuck." Coop made a face. "The woman can smell it when I'm keeping something from her."

"Then wear more cologne." Jack narrowed his eyes. "They're best friends, Coop. Jess can't tell Em what I'm planning or Em will run in the opposite direction."

His friend heaved a giant sigh. "I won't tell her. I promise. But you owe me."

"So every time we have a secret from our women, we owe each other for not telling them?"

Cooper burst out laughing.

"What?" Jack frowned.

It took awhile for Coop's amusement to die down and then he stood, smacking Jack on the shoulder as he passed. "It's cute you think you'll have secrets from Em once you're together."

Jack rolled his eyes at his buddy's smugness. But it didn't bother him. Not at all. Because his friend seemed certain he and

Emery were a sure thing … and that gave Jack the reassurance he needed.

There was a part of him that still wondered if he should leave Emery to some guy who deserved her more.

But if Coop, the best guy he knew, could forgive him and still think he was worthy of Emery Saunders, then Jack didn't feel so selfish about it anymore.

After all, he couldn't imagine anyone could love Emery the way he loved her.

With every molecule of his entire existence.

And he was already far gone for the kid growing in her belly.

Scared? Yeah. Worried about starting over with a new career at his age and having enough money to care for his new family? Definitely. But excited.

And so fucking in love he could barely stand it.

31

EMERY

The next day, during lunchtime, when my place was usually busy with locals looking for their caffeine fix, only tourists popped into the store to buy books. When Jess and Cat walked through my door, I struggled but won the fight against bursting into worried tears.

Jack had just called and told me he'd been asking around and found out what was going on. Dana Kellerman had been working her deceitful little mouth. She was the full-time receptionist at Jennifer's Hair & Beauty, a salon where she used to be the part-time receptionist when she was content to live off Cooper's money. Did that sound bitchy? Did I care? The woman was vicious!

"Apparently," I relayed to Jess and Cat as they sat across from me in the store's reading nook, "Dana has been telling anyone who cares to listen that I trapped Jack. And how awful that is after everything Jack's been through with his family. She's made me the villain. No one will come into my store. I mean, some people were already appalled because I'm pregnant out of wedlock. It's like it's 1959 or something."

"That happened to me," Cat commiserated. "Single woman

getting pregnant. They weren't happy. Judgmental assholes. But they forgive pretty quickly. It's hard for them to hold on to a grudge in a town where most people are pretty liberal and understanding about these things. Give it a week or so."

My blood boiled with outrage. "I don't want forgiveness," I snapped. "I didn't do anything that requires forgiveness."

Cat raised an eyebrow. "You're absolutely right. And have I mentioned I like pregnant Emery?"

My gaze shot to Jess's. "I think I need to confront her."

"Who?" Jess's expression tightened. "Dana?"

"Yes. In front of everyone."

"Oh, Emery, I don't think that's a good idea. You shouldn't stress yourself like that … and I wouldn't want you creating more scandal that might hurt you."

"Would you sit back and let people say these things about you? What have I done to deserve them all assuming the worst about me? Nothing. I've had enough." I really had. It felt like if I didn't finally stand up for myself, I'd break. I didn't want my child to go through his or her life like I had, letting people take advantage without speaking up. "Bullied at school because I was shy. I let them walk all over me. They stole a scenario straight from a movie—had a cute boy invite me out on a date and then they all ambushed and threw eggs at me."

Cat and Jess looked horrified. "Oh, Em."

"Even my grandmother walked all over me. *Don't do this. Don't say that. Be this way. Be that way*. And don't even get me started on Tripp and Jack!"

"Em." Jess reached for my hand. "Em, please, sweetie, you need to calm down."

"No." Cat touched Jess's wrist. "She needs to get this out." Her eyes rested on me. "Em, if you want to confront Dana, then I'm coming. I've got your back."

Gratitude moved through me. "Thank you."

Jess let go and heaved a sigh. "Then I am too."

"No." I shook my head. "You're pregnant. I won't stress you out."

"You're pregnant too and I'm your doctor. I'm coming."

Cooper would likely kill me, but I recognized that stubborn set to Jess's chin. "Fine. Let's do this."

"Oh, we're going now?" Jess looked comically wide-eyed as Cat and I stood. "Okay, yes, let's get it over with."

Indignation, hurt, and fury fueled me as we locked up my store, marched down the boards, and hurried along Main Street to Jennifer's salon. It used to be called Heidi's but Heidi fell in love with a firefighter from Wilmington and sold the place to Jennifer Kwan. From all reports, Jennifer was an excellent stylist and the girls she had working in her beauty department were awesome too. However, I traveled to Essex, the largest city in Hartwell County, to get my hair trimmed, to have my nails done, just to avoid Dana Kellerman.

"Are you sure about this?" Jess hurried to catch up.

I slowed my marching. "I'm sorry. We should not be rushing a pregnant woman."

Jess guffawed. "Again… You do realize you're pregnant too."

"Of course. I just … you look it."

Cat chortled at my comment.

I winced. "That came out wrong."

"Did it?" Jess gave me a reassuring smile. "You're not wrong. But you'll look it, too, in a few weeks."

"I don't know. I think Emery will be one of those annoying women who only has a bump and doesn't get pregnant anywhere else," Cat opined.

"Are you saying I look fat, Cat?"

Cat shot her sister-in-law a wry look. "I'm saying you look pregnant. Obviously, you have a bump but your cheeks are fuller and your tits are huge. I was the same."

"Don't get me started on these breasts." Jess sighed. "Your brother can't keep his hands and mouth off them."

I snort-laughed, slapping my hand over my mouth at Cat's foul look.

"What did I say to deserve that?"

Jess tilted her chin in the air and gave a haughty sniff. "You said my cheeks were fuller. I am aware my pregnancy is attaching itself to every part of my body, including my ass, but it does not need to be pointed out!"

Cat threw an arm around Jess, pulling her into her side. "Babe, I didn't mean those cheeks, and I didn't mean it's a bad thing. You look gorgeous."

"You do," I agreed.

Jess exhaled slowly. "I'm a little sensitive because my jeans don't fit anymore. And I know I'm pregnant ... but will they ever fit again?"

"Mine didn't." Cat shrugged. "I'm a size bigger now than I was pre-Joey, and I never got back to it. Little bugger's worth it, though."

Jess frowned. "You have a beautiful figure."

"So do you. And Jess, you'll be gorgeous no matter what size you are. My brother thinks so too."

"I know this is about Emery ..." Jess put her hand on my arm as we approached the salon. "And I know Cooper is entirely indifferent to his ex-wife, but sometimes it galls that she's so beautiful."

Oh. I hadn't even thought about that. How selfish of me. "Jessica, you don't have to come in."

"Yeah, she does." Cat stopped us, scowling at Jess. "I hope what just came out of your mouth is pregnancy hormones because you know, I know, Em knows, and Cooper for goddamn sure knows that Dana Kellerman is a pile of shit frosted in diamonds. Don't even think about feeling insecure about her looks. She's the devil."

"She's just so smug." Jess crossed her arms over her chest.

"What does she have to be smug about? You're walking

in there with Coop's ring on your finger, the kid you guys made in your belly, and the whole town has followed your love story like it's a goddamn fairy tale. Nearly every woman in Hartwell watches the way my brother looks at you, and they envy the hell out of you. Me? I look at the way you watch my brother, and I am so grateful he ended up with you. He's a great guy, a wonderful brother, a fantastic uncle ... but he and I both know you're not the only lucky one in this scenario. *He's* so lucky to have found *you*. And she"—Cat pointed to the salon—"deep down knows that no man will ever feel about her that way because she will end up with someone just as selfish as she is. Any good man she ever meets will eventually see right through her."

The sisters shared a loving, affectionate look, and I finally had to clear my throat.

I mock glared at Cat. "Are you just going to use up any and all material I can use against Dana?"

"What?"

"A pile of shit frosted in diamonds. And that last thing you just said about men—maybe I wanted to say those things to her face."

Cooper's sister snorted. "If I'd known how fun you were, I would've made more of an effort to get to know you." Her smile died. "You know what, I'm sorry, Em. I am one of the people you should be calling out. I *should* have made an effort to be your friend."

"It goes both ways, Cat."

"True. But I have the advantage of not being shy." She turned to face the salon. "Are we going to do this?"

"Now I'm nervous." I wrung my hands, my heart racing. "I lost my momentum."

Jess looked remorseful. "I'm sorry. That was me. I made it about me."

"Don't be silly. I'm dragging you into a salon to face your husband's ex-wife."

Cat sighed. "Let's stop yammering and go in. People are looking."

It was true. Some ladies inside the salon were peering curiously out at us.

"Emery needs a plan," Jess argued.

"I have a plan." I threw my shoulders back, feeling nauseated but determined. "I plan to call her out." I marched to the door.

"Oh, we're going in, we're going in!" Cat hurried Jess along behind me, sounding way too excited.

Entering the salon, my eyes zeroed in on Dana who was standing in front of Sherry, the owner of Sherry's Trousseau, chatting to her as she sat under the hood dryer. Her eyes flew to the door and she froze.

I stopped, feeling Cat and Jess nudge into my back with the abrupt movement.

Dana smirked and sashayed toward us.

All eyes were on me.

I felt them.

I sensed their judgment.

Dana's gaze moved to Jess, darkened with hatred, and then to Cat. They flickered a little warily … and I realized she might be afraid of Cat.

Good.

"How can I help?"

The hairdryers in use by Jennifer and her other stylist quieted. Both women watched me. I now had every person in that salon's attention. I swallowed hard, feeling my knees shake.

My cheeks were on fire.

When I looked at Dana again, she saw my blush and sneered.

"Do you speak?" she snapped.

I could do this.

I straightened my shoulders. "Jack and I were told you're

spreading a vicious rumor about us. I came to demand that you desist."

To my shock and gratitude, my words came out strong and stern.

Tension moved through the salon as Dana raised an eyebrow. "Excuse me?"

"You heard me. I'm losing business because of your slander. If you do not desist, I'll be forced to take legal action." I had no idea that's what I would say, but out it came.

I heard Jess make a gurgling sound behind me and Cat muttered, "Fucking awesome."

Dana's jaw dropped. "You can't do that. You have no evidence I've said anything."

"We have witnesses. People who have come to us and told us you're telling anyone who will listen that I tried to trap Jack by deliberately getting pregnant." Despite my flaming cheeks and shaking legs, I grew more confident. "It's lies." I moved my attention from Dana to all the people in the salon. I looked them all in the eye, and they flinched a little at my obvious disappointment.

I returned my gaze to Dana. "Why anyone would believe someone like you, someone known to lie and cheat, I have no idea. But if my business doesn't pick up because of the lies you're spreading about me, I will take you to court."

"You can't." She huffed in outrage. "You can't do that. I've never heard of that."

I shrugged casually and smirked. "Slander isn't an easy charge to prove, but I have so much money at my disposal, I can afford to try. Can you afford to defend yourself?"

"Oh my God, I'm going to pee my pants, this is so good," Cat muttered under her breath.

I tried not to laugh as I stared Dana down.

"I'm going to have to ask you to leave," Dana demanded, gesturing to the door.

"And I'm going to have to ask you to desist spreading gossip and rumors or you'll be hearing from my lawyer. I'm not leaving until you make it clear you understand."

"I'm not dumb," she snarled.

"Contrary to all evidence." I crossed my arms over my chest. "I'm afraid I must insist on you saying the words."

"Huh?"

"I, Dana Kellerman, do vow to stop spreading vicious gossip and lies about Emery Saunders and Jack Devlin." I spoke as condescendingly as possible and watched a few of the women nearest me look down, covering their smirks.

I felt a flicker of uneasiness. I wasn't a bully. It wasn't in my nature to get off on making someone feel small. Unfortunately, I was on that side of the situation now—it was back down and lose this war against Dana, or proceed and feel guilty later about being a bitch.

I chose the latter.

"Well?"

"I'm not admitting to anything because I haven't done anything. And I won't. I won't say shit about you or Jack. Like I care about you getting knocked up by that useless manwhore."

My eyes narrowed and I took a step toward her.

"Em?" Jess's hand rested on my back.

"You're talking about the father of my child, and I'll thank you not to insult him."

"Whatever." Dana shook her head and waved her hand at us. "Just take yourself and your stupid little posse and get out and don't come back."

"Oh." Cat glowered at her. "Then I guess I'll need to find a new hair salon."

"What?" Jennifer yelped from the back. She glared at Dana before yelling at Cat, "Don't listen to her. She's just my receptionist."

"Then you might want to think about getting a new receptionist," Cat offered. "I know more than a handful of women who don't come in here, Jen, because they don't want to deal with Dana. They all go to Essex instead."

"That's true," I added. "*I* go to Essex."

Jennifer's jaw clenched as her eyes narrowed on her receptionist.

Dana looked ready to kill us.

And I took that as our cue to leave.

We did so quietly and with dignity, and I waited until we were out of sight before I asked, "Did we take that too far?"

Cat burst into raucous laughter. "Oh my God, no. It was the best thing ever! You're my new hero!"

I looked at Jess who grinned at me.

"I felt kind of mean."

"That's because you're a good person." She squeezed my hand.

"Don't feel mean," Cat huffed. "Neither of you have lived here all your life, so let me tell you a little something about Dana Kellerman: that egg thing that happened to you in high school? Take that and times it by a million when it comes to the shit she pulled on girls in high school. She tortured kids. When Cooper told me he was dating her, I tried to warn him. He told me she'd grown up a lot since then." Cat snorted. "Uh, yeah, no. She's still pulling that crap."

"Well, your brother learned that the hard way," Jess defended him gently.

"Yeah. But my point is"—Cat turned to me—"don't feel guilty about embarrassing her in there, making her feel small, because she has lived her life getting off on other people's misery. If she loses her job, great. Maybe she'll fuck off and go torture another town with her selfish, catty, nasty, downright-mean attitude. They say people have a reason for being the way they are, and I believe that. I do. But some people are just born selfish to the core, and Dana Kellerman is one of them. Don't feel bad. Feel proud that you stood up for yourself and for Jack."

A little stunned by Cat's passionate speech, I exhaled slowly and nodded at her. "Okay. I will."

"Good. And next time you want to stand up for yourself, please invite me. That was the classiest put down I've ever witnessed."

We shared a warm smile and my unease faded a little in light of my newfound friendship with Cat Lawson.

32

JACK

With a very deliberate hand on Emery's lower back, Jack walked at her side as they moved through the corridors of the medical building next to Hartwell County General in Essex. He'd picked her up thirty minutes ago for their first prenatal appointment at the OB/GYN offices there. Em and Jess had decided it would be better that Em saw the same doctor throughout her entire pregnancy, and Jess wasn't available to be that doctor because she'd be on maternity leave soon.

Every day it all got a little more real that Jack was going to be a father, and he was scared, excited, and a whole load of emotions in between. But it was also surreal. Like it hadn't sunk in as reality yet.

Emery was a little stiff beneath his touch at first. He thought about letting her go but then she seemed to relax. Jack was glad. He was afraid if he didn't try to create familiarity between them, Em wouldn't ever take down that wall she'd erected to keep him out.

"Here." She gestured to the reception desk. The older woman behind the desk was on the phone. She held up a finger for them to wait.

Emery sucked in a shaky breath and Jack increased the pressure of his touch on her lower back as he leaned in to ask softly, "You okay?"

He inhaled that singular scent of hers—like a wave of flowers in the ocean—as she turned to look at him with her spectacular eyes. "I'm fine."

"No nausea?"

"It seems to have abated pretty quickly for me." She lifted her crossed fingers and gave him a stiff smile. "We'll see."

The stiff smile bothered him. He knew she was trying. But it was shit that what was once so easy between them seemed a little forced now.

"Can I help you?" the nurse asked as she hung up the phone.

"We have an appointment," Emery said, and Jack took encouragement from the "we" part. "Emery Saunders."

The nurse checked her computer. "Okay, just take a seat. Dr. Britt will see you soon."

As they seated themselves in the waiting area, Jack had to let go of Em.

She turned to speak to him and Jack bent his head toward her. Her lashes fluttered rapidly at their proximity and he took heart from it. "Did you schedule plenty of time off work? Jess said the first prenatal visit is usually the longest."

"Don't worry about it."

Nodding, Em looked away. Jack studied her as she nibbled on her lower lip. At the same time her fingers twisted together on her lap. Today she wore a long, pale-pink dress with full sleeves and a loose silhouette. Despite its looseness, when the breeze blew it back against her waist as they'd walked across the parking lot outside, it revealed that her stomach was still flat.

Jack was looking forward to the bump.

"Hey," he said softly as he reached for her hands. He peeled them apart by curling his fingers through one of them. He squeezed her hand tight. "Are you nervous?"

She stared at their clasped hands for a second and he waited, his heart picking up speed while she decided whether to pull away. He held his breath as she proceeded without letting him go. He sighed inwardly in relief. Her gaze met his. "A little."

"No need." He flashed her a grin and took encouragement from the way her cheeks flushed. She liked his smile. That was obvious. He intended to use it against her. "Any woman who can stand up to Dana Kellerman can handle her first prenatal visit."

Emery blushed even harder, but she returned his smile.

"You know how proud I am, right?"

"You said as much."

He had. Word had reached him at the hotel about Emery's salon standoff with Dana. He'd called her to get her version of events and had grinned so hard through her retelling, his cheeks hurt.

The best thing was people had started coming back in for their coffee at Em's now that she'd set the record straight. Shit, Jack would've loved to have seen Dana's face when Em threatened her with a slander lawsuit.

"Emery Saunders."

They both looked up to find a woman around Em's age in a white doctor's coat, waiting patiently for them.

"I'm Doctor Madeline Britt. I'll be your obstetrician throughout your pregnancy."

Jack felt a pull on his hand as Emery tried to drop his. He tightened his grip and gently pulled her to her feet. He let go so they could shake the doc's hand and introduce themselves, but he reached for Em's hand again right after.

"Jack, I don't need you to hold my hand," she complained under her breath as they followed Dr. Britt.

"Yeah, but I need you to hold mine," he teased, throwing her a boyish smile.

She rolled her eyes but that pretty pink stained her cheeks again as she did it.

The doctor led them to a private hospital room. She aimed her gaze at Em. "I'm going to do a breast and pelvic exam. Some women prefer to get those over with first and have their partner"—she gave Jack a benign smile—"wait outside."

Jack looked down at his girl. She squeezed his hand.

"Can you wait outside?"

"Of course." He kissed her temple and backed out of the room.

As soon as he was out of there, Jack sensed he would not be asked back in. Emery didn't want him there, and she'd use this as an excuse to keep him at a distance. He didn't blame her but he felt useless outside. All he could offer right now was support as she went through this experience. Jack wished she'd lean on him.

It surprised the hell out of him then when Dr. Britt stuck her head outside the door and told him to come back inside.

It was encouraging.

Maybe Em just wanted to include him … or maybe she *did* need him.

Jack hoped it was both.

He smiled as he came to stand by her side at the bed. She was back in her dress and sitting up. He took her hand and this time, she let him without a word.

"Okay." Dr. Britt smiled at Jack. "Keeping Dad up to date, the breast and pelvic examinations are done. We'll get the results on the Pap test soon."

He knew he looked stunned. And it was because no one had called him Dad yet.

Fuck.

It felt really good.

It felt amazing.

Emery seemed to sense the reason for his expression and gave him a tender, understanding smile. Christ, she was the sweetest woman on the planet. Even when she was disappointed in him, she still found a way to be kind.

"Right, as I explained before you came in, Jack, I'm going to ask Emery questions about her medical history."

"Okay."

The doc asked Em if she had any medical or psychosocial problems or had ever had any. That was a no. She took her blood pressure, her height, and her weight, which he was glad to see she had no problem with him knowing. It made him laugh inwardly that she could blush at his mere smile and yet discuss her last menstrual period in front of him without turning even a hint of pink.

"Birth control?"

"Well, clearly none," Em huffed.

Jack swallowed a snort.

Dr. Britt's lips twitched. "I meant in the past. The Pill or otherwise?"

"Oh. Just condoms."

Which reminded Jack that he did and did not really want to know who Emery had been with before him. If she hadn't been on the Pill, then that suggested she'd never been in a long-term relationship.

"Any hospitalizations?"

"When I was seventeen. Car accident. I broke a few ribs."

Jack's chin jerked back in surprise. He hadn't known about any car accident.

"Have you had any pain or problems with your ribs since?"

"No. Is it an issue?"

"No. But sometimes there can be stress on the ribs during pregnancy and I just want to make sure there are no underlying issues we need to know about."

"Okay." Em bit her lip.

Dr. Britt placed a reassuring hand on her arm. "It's nothing to be concerned about."

Jack tightened his grip on Em's hand and she seemed to relax.

"Are you taking any medications?"

"Does copious amounts of caffeine count?" she joked, making Jack chuckle.

The doctor raised an eyebrow. "Yes. You'll need to cut the caffeine intake. One cup a day at the very most."

"I was joking. I knew that." Em looked up at him solemnly. "I knew about the caffeine thing. I've been cutting back."

Smiling and trying not to laugh at the same time, Jack wrapped an arm around her and pulled him into his chest. His tone was filled with humor. "I believe you, sunrise."

"Any allergies to medication?"

"None that I know of."

Dr. Britt asked a few more questions about Em's family medical history. Whether she'd been experiencing any bleeding or cramping, which thankfully was a no.

"I see from the records your doctor sent over that you've already had all the tests for sexually transmitted infections done, so we'll just take a blood sample and do some screens. I'll explain what they're all for as we go along."

The reminder that Emery had Jess run STI tests was an unwelcome one. They needed to have a real conversation about that. But obviously now wasn't the right moment.

Just as Em was beginning to look a little pale and tired, the real discussion started about ... well, it felt like everything. They talked about what medications Em could take, things like prenatal vitamins and supplements, as well as exercise and expected weight gain. Emery asked questions about her diet, about who she should call if she had questions, what she should do if she *did* experience bleeding or cramping, what did the doc consider an emergency, what miscarriage precautions she could take, how the doctor felt about natural childbirth, what was the doctor's policy on labor induction …

It went on and on, and Jack realized that for all his worries, Emery was carrying about a million more.

He was woefully un-fucking-prepared.

And he needed to do better.

Listening intently, attempting to retain every bit of information the doc gave them, Jack realized he had a lot of reading to do.

He didn't want Emery shouldering the burden of these worries alone.

"I should buy some books," he said after five very long minutes of silence as they walked out of the building.

"What?" She frowned in confusion.

"Books. I realized in there that I have no fucking clue about any of this. I need to do some reading."

"I have books," Em offered. "You can borrow those."

"That would be great." He studied her carefully as they stopped at his truck. "You doing okay?"

"Tired," she admitted. "It was a lot of information. And I'm hungry. I only had a rice cracker this morning."

"Antonio's," he said, opening the door for her and giving her a hand up.

"Antonio's?" she queried once he was in the driver's seat.

"I'm taking you there. Now. For something to eat."

"You don't have to. I can just go home and make a sandwich."

"You could."

She let out an exasperated laugh. "I'll take that to mean we're going to Antonio's."

"Good food, and you can relax there." Iris wouldn't let anyone bother or gossip about them in her establishment. Emery was like a second daughter to her. He knew because she'd been glowering in his direction ever since she found out he'd gotten Emery pregnant. In fact, he was a little surprised she hadn't yet searched him out just to annihilate him. Jack was bracing. He was pretty sure a "talk" from Iris Green was in his future.

Antonio's was busy despite it being that awkward point in the day between lunch and dinner. It was August, so there were still plenty of tourists kicking around Hartwell, taking advantage of good Italian food right on the boardwalk. As Jack held the door open for Em, he saw her attention laser focus somewhere beyond him. He turned to look and saw Ivy Green sitting at a table for two with none other than their good sheriff Jeff King. Jeff was in uniform, but his body language, the way he leaned over on his arms so his head was bent toward Ivy's, suggested this was more than just a casual meeting.

"Table for two?" the hostess asked.

"Please."

She grabbed a couple of menus and led them into the noisy chatter of the restaurant. Ivy and Jeff looked over. Emery waved at Ivy who returned her smile while Jack and Jeff shared a subtle lift of the chin in greeting. It was afterward that Jack became aware of the locals in the restaurant. They seemed like they didn't know who to gawk at—Ivy and Jeff, or Em and Jack.

He knew by the stiff way Em held her shoulders that she'd noticed too.

Oh, they'd all be gossiping about the four of them and what the two couplings meant. There was no getting around that.

"You don't want to say hi?" Jack asked Em as they took their seats, trying to distract her from the folks who were staring.

She shook her head. "No."

Jack eyed Ivy and Jeff again and watched the way Ivy responded to Jeff with a flirtatious smirk. Then she reached out and ran the tips of her fingers over his knuckles as she talked.

Okay, then. "Since when did they become a thing?" Jack asked.

Em looked unsure for some reason.

Then he realized she wasn't sure she could trust him to share about her friend's relationship.

"Never mind." He looked down at his menu, feeling fucking exhausted all of a sudden. "What do you feel like eating?"

"They're taking it slow."

Jack looked up at her.

"Jeff and Ivy. They're taking things slow. It's not public knowledge." Em shot them a wry look. "Though they're not exactly being discreet at the moment." She turned back to Jack. "But they *are* a thing."

Relieved she'd trusted him with that, Jack nodded. "I hope it works out. Jeff deserves a good woman."

"He does. And Ivy deserves a good guy."

"Well, well, well." Iris appeared at their table as if out of nowhere. She eyeballed him. "Jack Devlin."

He grinned at her. "Iris Green."

She narrowed her eyes. "Don't think you can flash me that boyish smile of yours, Jack Devlin, and get away with … stuff."

"Stuff?" he teased.

"Stuff." She gestured to Emery.

"I don't think Emery appreciates being referred to as stuff."

"I'm trying not to be indelicate."

"You're doing a fine job."

Emery snorted, and Jack struggled to keep a straight face.

"Don't be a smart-ass with me, Jack. All I'm going to say." She dipped her face to his and lowered her voice, "You better take care of my girl and this kid, or I will hunt you down, flatten you, and bring you here to give the very large pizza oven in my kitchen back there a new purpose in life."

Seeing Emery cover her mouth and choke on her laughter, Jack's eyes twinkled into Iris's. "You've given this some very *graphic* thought."

"Don't think you can charm your way out of this. You need to take responsibility for your actions."

That dispelled Jack's humor. "Iris, I know Emery means something to you so I'm not going to tell you to mind your own business, even though that's really what I want to say. Instead, I'll assure you that there is nothing more important to me than Emery and our kid."

She harrumphed but straightened. "Okay, then. What do you want to eat?"

After they'd ordered and Iris had left the table, Em sighed as she glanced around the restaurant. "I know she means well, but she just made them all stare again."

"They'll stop, Em. Once they get used to us, they'll stop."

"We're none of their business."

"Agreed."

"They've come back to the store."

"You told me." He cocked his head, confused by her melancholy tone. "That's a good thing."

She wrinkled her nose, her expression adorably petulant. It made him want to kiss her. Everything she did made him want to kiss her. "I'm still mad at them for believing the worst in me, Jack."

"Coming from someone who had to live with them thinking the worst of him for years, I can honestly tell you that it's best to just let it go. Forgive them. They're not worth that eating at you."

Emery's eyes brightened with sympathy. "I'm sorry. That was totally insensitive to say to you. And you're right. I shouldn't let what they did fester. I have a bad habit of holding on to things."

Tell me about it.

"Do you ever let them go?"

"Sometimes." She shrugged. "Most of the time. I only tend to hang on if it's me I'm mad at, not someone else."

"What do you ever need to be mad at yourself for? You're perfect."

She guffawed. "I'm not perfect, Jack."

"No, but you're perfect in all your perfection and imperfections. So, you're still perfect." He smiled.

"Iris is right." Em rolled her eyes. "You are such a charmer."

"But I always speak the truth," he promised.

She seemed unable to meet his gaze after that. Instead she fiddled with her napkin and blurted out, "Do you forgive your dad?"

Jack was a little taken aback by the question, but he wanted to share everything with Em. Even the difficult stuff. "I don't know. That's the honest truth. I just know that I don't want him to have any part of my life or my decisions going forward. I can't wait for his trial to come along, be over with. I guess I'm trying to forgive him. But not for him—for me. For my family."

"How are they? Your family?"

"Mom and Rebecca both started seeing a therapist, and they're growing closer every day. They've even talked about getting in touch with Rebecca's biological father when they're both ready. Mom seems like a completely different person away from Hartwell and Ian." It was true. Rosalie had started going out again. She wasn't socializing a great deal just yet, but she was shopping, taking walks, hanging out with his uncle and his family—this was all a huge step in the right direction. "I'm a little worried about Becs and the upcoming trial. But she's assured me she's ready."

"I meant to say that, um, I know you probably have legal counsel for Rebecca, but because of contacts in the Paxton Group, I know the best defense attorneys in the country. If you need an introduction, I can help."

Jack gave her a grateful smile. "I might take you up on that."

She nodded. "So … when is your father's trial?"

"Four weeks."

"Jack, you should've told me." Em seemed put out that he hadn't.

He held her gaze and whatever she saw in his made her go extremely still. "I didn't tell you because I've been focusing on you. On the baby."

Making you a priority.

"Oh. Well ... of course I appreciate that, but your father's trial is a big deal. Do you have to go on the stand?"

"Yeah."

Her brow puckered with worry. "That's so hard for you."

"Not really. He deserves what's coming to him."

"You know ..." She looked down at the table, fiddling with the silver bracelets on her wrists. Her long lashes covered her expression from him. "I know things aren't ... I know ... ugh." She covered her eyes now with her hands and took a deep breath.

"Em." He reached out to touch her wrist, gently prying her hand away from her face.

She uncovered her eyes, and he saw her sad confliction. That expression caused a flare of feeling near his heart. "I know we're trying to be friends," she finally pushed out. "And that means I'm here. If you need to talk."

The pain eased a little. "I might just take you up on that one day. It goes both ways, you know."

She nodded but didn't respond.

Jack fell into silence easily, enjoying it because it meant he got to look at her. He tried not to grin at how she found numerous ways to avoid his intense regard. Until finally her eyes flew to his, her cheeks bright pink, and she huffed, "Stop looking at me."

I can't, sunrise. There's nowhere else I want to look.

Instead he smiled and made her blush even harder.

Finally, sensing she'd reached her quota on squirming under his flirtatious attention, he asked something that had bothered him since their hospital visit. "You were in a car accident when you were seventeen?"

It was amazing really.

How fast it happened.

How quickly Emery's entire expression tightened, then smoothed out into perfect blankness. "It was nothing," she replied coldly.

And before Jack could question her abrupt change in demeanor, Iris returned with their food. She stuck around a bit, thawing Emery's iciness.

But when she left, silence descended over the table again, and Jack didn't know how to breach it. That wall Em had put up was now covered in barbed wire and volts of electricity. Her one-word answers drove him crazy.

She seemed relieved when they left, and she didn't want him to walk her down the boards to her beach house.

Jack walked her home anyway.

He said goodbye as she mumbled it in return and hurried into the house, locking the door behind her.

He studied the door that stood between them.

Something happened to Em when she was seventeen. Something important. And that gut instinct he used to rely so heavily on told him he needed to know what that was. Knowledge of Em's past could only help him figure out a way to convince her that *he* was her future.

33

EMERY

As beautiful as warm mornings were in Hartwell, I often enjoyed the dull, gray days just as much. That morning, I'd gone outside with my mug of hot water and lemon and curled up on my giant porch swing to watch the energetic waves push against the shore. Soft gray clouds hinted that it might rain later.

It was the end of September. Most tourists had returned home to the normal routine of life. Schools were back in session, and Hart's Boardwalk's low season had begun.

I hadn't slept well the night before. Not because of the baby, who seemed to be giving me very little trouble so far. We estimated I was only twelve weeks along, and Jack was on his way over to pick me up to take me for our first scan.

Every time Jess asked how I was feeling, I felt incredibly guilty because I was great. Jess had been plagued by sickness in the first half of her pregnancy, and now she was plagued by swelling. By the end of every day, her feet, legs, and fingers were swollen and uncomfortable. Plus she'd had to go through most of her pregnancy during the summer heat. At thirty-four weeks, she was almost ready to pop, and she looked it. She was irritable, exhausted, and ready for Baby Lawson to arrive. Cooper was taking it all in his stride, even though he absorbed the brunt of her irritation.

"How are you coping?" Bailey had asked him one Saturday afternoon when we were all hanging out at Jess and Coop's. Jess was in the bathroom peeing for the hundredth time, which was really making me anxious about those last few weeks of pregnancy.

"My wife is carrying our kid," Cooper had replied. "She's exhausted. She's sore. She's worried constantly about doing something that will make us lose our baby ... so I can take it. It's nothing compared to what she's going through right now."

Jack had shot me a look in that moment that told me he understood Cooper completely.

It'd made my stomach somersault and that familiar ache score across my chest.

Jack Devlin was a major problem.

I'd discovered that just because you told yourself someone wasn't good for you didn't mean your heart would feel the same way. And when it came to Jack, my heart most definitely didn't want to acknowledge that Jack was bad for it.

Attraction was a problem too, especially now that I had an increased sex drive.

Every time he was around, my body came alive. I'd look at his lips or his hands and I'd feel my breasts tighten and that tug low, dirty, and deep that made me want to rip his clothes off and have my wicked way with him. I looked it up. Apparently, hormones could make some women extra *needy* during pregnancy. Lucky me.

If only there were someone else who incited such feelings in me.

But no.

Just Jack. With his big knuckles and long, graceful fingers. Big man hands I wanted on my body.

And it wasn't just physical attraction.

Every time he threw that sexy, wickedly boyish smile my way, I melted. Every time he did something considerate, which was all the time (holding doors open for me, bringing me snacks just because I mentioned a craving earlier, sliding an extra pillow behind my back anytime I shifted uncomfortably on the couch), I wanted to jump him. I wanted to throw caution to the wind and scream, "Screw it!"

However, that would not be fair to Jack. Despite his continued flirtations, he'd taken me at my word about us just being friends. If I initiated sex between us, that would confuse things.

Not that things weren't already confused.

My heart ached for him.

My head told me that five weeks was not enough time to determine whether I could trust Jack Devlin with my heart.

My vagina was unhappy with this logic.

I sighed heavily as I gazed out at the water.

"You sound like you have a million things weighing you down."

I started at Jack's voice and looked to my right to find him standing in the porch doorway. I'd given him a key to the beach house for emergencies. I raised an eyebrow at his appearance.

"I knocked," he assured me. "You didn't answer."

"Oh. Sorry."

"You okay?"

His expression was tender. When he looked at me that way it got me every time. And why did he have to be so gorgeous? His blue-gray eyes squinted against the dull light, causing attractive laugh lines. His cheeks were unshaven, and he wore a beautifully fitted dark gray shirt and black suit pants.

Running the hotel and fun park had become Jack's full-time job. Between his mother's lawyers and my contacts through the Paxton Group, Jack had gotten his mother's case for full ownership of the businesses pushed through before his father's trial. Which started tomorrow. Once Ian lost the businesses to Rosalie, she signed it over to Jack. He tried to argue with her about it, but in the end, she convinced him she didn't want anything to do with Hartwell.

However, the hotel and park were a big part of the community here and they'd finally have a decent owner in Jack. Once she explained this, I convinced Jack to accept her gift graciously. I'd also asked Hague for advice about finding the best defense attorney he knew. I then gave the woman's number to Jack for Rebecca. She was a New York lawyer and Hague assured me she had an outstanding win percentage. It turned out she cost a heck of a lot of money. I wanted to offer to help, but Jack said Rosalie had her own money and would pay for Rebecca's defense.

Poor Jack had been rushed off his feet with these matters, trying to get up to date on where the hotel and park were financially while implementing changes to both. And he was trying to be there for me. I was worried he was exhausting himself.

"Em?"

I stopped ogling him and looked out at the sea. His change in work clothes were not unwelcome. While I liked him casual, there was something about Jack in a shirt and trousers, no tie, collar open showing off that strong, tan throat of his that appealed to me.

It made me want to nuzzle my face in his throat and pull his shirt out of his pants, unbuckle his belt—

"I'm fine." I cut off my wayward thoughts. "Is it time to go?"

"Yeah. You sure you're okay?"

"Absolutely." I gave him a tight smile and got up off the swing.

Jack's eyes dropped down my body. I was wearing jeans and my favorite white blouse that had oversized balloon sleeves. "No bump yet?"

It was on the tip of my tongue to tell him to examine me closer.

Jesus!

What was wrong with me?

I scooted past him into the house. "There's a little swell."

I could feel his intense regard as he followed me inside. "Why are you blushing?"

"I'm not," I lied. I threw him a quick look. "We should go."

In an effort to distract him as he pulled away from the house and headed to Essex, I decided to tell him something else that was on my mind. "I'm going with you tomorrow. To the trial."

Tension fell between us, thick and fast. A different kind from the usual sexual tension. "Absolutely not."

I bristled at his overbearing tone. "I wasn't asking."

He cut me a dark look. "You're not going."

Hurt, I wanted to go ice queen on his ass and give him the silent treatment. But I needed to know why he didn't want me there more than I needed to pout. "I want to be there for you."

"And while I appreciate that, you're pregnant with our baby and I would rather you (1) stay away from stressful situations, and (2) stay as far away from my father and brother as possible."

"The trial is not going to stress me out to the point I'm endangering our child, and I think I'm the best one to decide that. You need support."

"I said no."

Fury built inside me, fast and boiling.

THIS!

It flooded out. "This is why we're not together! Your total lack of respect for my ability to make sound decisions for myself!"

Jack hit his right signal and pulled off onto the side of the road. He turned to me, eyes blazing. "What the fuck does that mean?"

I refused to be intimidated by the heated energy pouring off him. "Our entire relationship, if you can even call it that, has been you making all the decisions for both of us."

"Not fucking true," he growled. "If that were true, you'd be in my bed every fucking night."

"Argh!" I raised my fists at either side of my head in frustration. "That's such a male thing to take from this! My point is"—I glared at him—"you made all the decisions in the past. We couldn't be together because it wasn't safe for me. Was I given a voice in that discussion? Was I allowed an opinion? NO!" I yelled, and Jack flinched back in surprise. "I am so tired of you deciding what's best for me without asking me what *I* think is best for me. And that, Jack Devlin, is another reason you and I will be *co-parenting*."

His face was mottled with anger, his eyes like fiery blue chips. His throat worked as if he was attempting to halt words from pouring out of his mouth.

It didn't surprise me when he whipped his head back around and pulled back onto the road without another word.

We drove the rest of the way in seething silence.

Through my anger, sadness filled me. I saw a future of handing our child over to Jack every second week. That meant a future of twenty-six weeks a year of utter loneliness. Alone without our kid and without Jack. The image of a faceless woman standing beside Jack as I dropped off our child made my gut twist.

Would we have a son who looked like Jack?

Would our child be angry at me when they eventually found out *I* was the reason Jack and I weren't together? Would our kid resent me for it?

Would I resent me for it?

I wondered all the time what our baby would look like. Be like. I was excited to find out. I was excited for days on the beach, holding tight to a little hand, watching chubby little legs take their first steps in the sand.

Yet, I realized ruining all my excitement was not just the fear of being a bad parent, of not being prepared, but anger. I was so mad at Jack for giving me reason to distrust him. And I was so mad at myself for not being able to get over it.

When we pulled up to the hospital buildings, I got out of the truck before Jack could help me down. I hurried toward the entrance of the building that hosted the OB/GYN offices, but he caught up quickly. He wrapped his strong hand around mine and I glared up at him in surprise. He glowered at the building, not meeting my eyes.

I tugged on my hand, but he wouldn't release it. "I'm mad at you," I stated the obvious. "I don't want to hold your hand."

Jack scowled. "I'm mad at you, but I *always* want to hold your hand. Therein lies the difference between us."

Pain and guilt hit me fierce and quick, and my eyes filled with tears before I could stop them. I looked away and stubbornly refused to let the tears fall.

"Sunrise." Jack squeezed my hand, his tone remorseful.

"Forget it." I jerked away from him as we reached the elevator and hit the button for our floor. How come I was always the bad guy? I wasn't the one trying to force decisions on us.

Aren't you? a little voice whispered. *Aren't you the reason you won't forgive and forget?*

Yes. But I had my reasons. Jack had just proven that in the truck.

We stepped inside, alone in the elevator.

The tension was palpable.

He didn't reach for my hand again.

If the technician who came out to greet us noticed the aggravation between me and Jack, she didn't show it. She introduced herself as Amy and hopefully took our strained smiles and quiet demeanor for nervousness. It was our first baby scan after all.

Once I was situated on the bed, Amy asked me to lift the

hem of my top and unbutton my jeans. I did, feeling intensely aware of Jack's eyes on me. I chanced a look at him and saw he was staring intently at my belly.

"You're not showing too much yet," Amy said, "but that's normal for week twelve. Although that's what we're here to determine. If you *are* twelve weeks." She smiled and then gestured to my belly. "As for the bump, you're tall with a longer abdomen, which might mean you're not going to show for a while."

I nodded. I'd already looked that up. Apparently, some women with longer abdomens had more space for the uterus to develop upward rather than outward, which meant a smaller bump.

"Okay, let's get started."

I jumped as she gently pressed the ultrasound wand to my belly. I turned my head to look at the screen set up by the bed.

Amy moved the wand across my stomach. My whole body was tense as we waited to hear—

My breath caught at the whooshing sound of a rapid heartbeat.

"There we go. There's the heartbeat." Amy smiled.

And it hit me. Like a tidal wave.

I was really, actually, truly going to be a mom.

I was going to have this tiny little person to love and raise and show them everything my parents hadn't shown me.

I'd finally have a family.

Although I'd thought about this from the moment I'd found out I was pregnant … it *hit* me. There was a little person growing inside me.

Tears filled my eyes, spilling down my cheeks. And suddenly, I could smell Jack's cologne, I could feel his lips whispering sweet kisses across my temple and down my cheek, catching the tears. His fingers curled tight around mine.

Turning my head on the pillow, I looked at him, his face

close, and through the wet in my eyes, I saw his were bright with emotion too. As if he couldn't help himself, he pressed his lips to mine, and I let him.

In fact, I kissed him back.

It was the sweetest kiss of my life.

"Sorry," he whispered hoarsely as he broke away. "Caught in the moment."

I squeezed his hand to reassure him it was okay and then saw our tech beaming at us. She clearly thought we were a loving couple. It hurt that we weren't.

Looking away from her, I turned back to the screen to listen to that beautiful heartbeat.

Not long later, we left with an envelope filled with scan snapshots that we could share with our friends and Jack's family. Rosalie was itching to meet me, and Jack and I were putting it off because we didn't want to deal with any questions about why we weren't together. I knew neither of us could put off that meeting much longer.

"March," Jack said. It was the first word either of us had uttered since leaving the hospital.

"Yeah." Our baby was due March 1. I was definitely twelve weeks along. I clutched at the envelope with the images. "We're going to be parents, Jack."

"I know, Em. I still don't think it's fully hit me. I'm getting there, but ..."

"It hit me harder, hearing the heartbeat ... But I know what you mean. I don't think it will fully hit us until the little one is here."

"Yeah," he agreed. And then he said, "You're right."

I looked at him and he flicked me a remorseful look before turning his eyes back to the road.

"You're right, Em. I have made decisions for us both without taking your opinion into account. I never even thought about it like that. I just ... you have to know that wasn't me being a controlling, bullying bastard." He glowered, but I knew it wasn't directed at me. "I'm not my father. I thought I was protecting you."

Sympathy and exhaustion hit me at the same time. "Jack, I know you're not your father. That's not what I meant."

"I know. But I need you to know that it came from a place of good. Pushing you away … I did that for you. If I'd made those decisions for me, we would've been together a long time ago. I was trying to be unselfish, and protecting you is just something my instincts scream at me to do. But somehow, I've ended up being high-handed. I'll stop doing that. If you want to come to the trial, then that is absolutely your prerogative."

Relief flooded me. It wasn't the first time Jack had admitted when he was wrong and vowed to do better. And he'd proven last time that he meant it. "I do. I want to be there for you. You're my friend."

His hands tightened around the wheel. "Yeah."

This need for him to assure me that he wasn't his father bothered me, though. For weeks, I'd been concerned that my decision not to be with Jack because I didn't trust him romantically was still causing him to think he wasn't worthy of trust, period. I'd known that when he suggested we spend time together because I had to learn to trust him if he was to be the father of my child. I'd agreed at the time, but afterward, it bugged me that he thought I wouldn't trust him to be a good dad.

"Jack?"

"Yeah?"

"You know you're a good man, right?"

He frowned. "What do you mean?"

"I mean, *I* know you're a good man. Cooper knows. Jess. Your mom and sister and brother and uncle. Everyone who matters knows you're a very good man."

Jack flicked me a soft look. "Okay."

"But do you know that? Do you feel that?"

Understanding crossed his expression. He let go a long exhalation before he replied, "I've had a lot of time to think about it these last few months. Despite my past concerns, I know I'm not my father. If I were my father, I wouldn't have been miserable living the life he wanted for me. I've made mistakes. A lot of them. But I know I'm a good guy. I know my intentions." He cut me another look. "But if *you* know that … then why don't you trust me?"

Despite the topic of conversation, I hadn't been expecting him to ask me that, nor so bluntly. "It's not that I don't trust you —I just don't trust you romantically."

"See, that makes no sense to me."

Hearing his frustration, I knew that words were not enough, that if I wanted him to understand my stance between us, I'd have to tell him the truth. Now. I'd have to open the store a little later than usual, but it was time I told Jack everything. "Do you need to get back to work right away or can you make some time to talk?"

"I'll make time."

I smiled nervously. "Then when we get to my place, you should come in. I have some things to explain."

Jack looked taken aback but relieved. "That'd be good, Em."

Yeah, not really for me. It was not a trip down memory lane that I particularly enjoyed.

We were seated on the sectional. I was curled in the corner while Jack lounged a few seat cushions away, his long legs sprawled, his arms resting along the back of the couch.

A cup of coffee sat on the coffee table, opposite my cup of decaf.

Untouched.

Jack was laser focused on me.

So, I began. To get to the root of our problem, I had to start at the beginning. I told him about my parents, their negligence, about their death, which he already knew a little about. I explained about my complicated feelings for my grandmother. How she gave enough of a shit to teach me some manners, but how she stifled me. How I knew it was partly overprotectiveness and partly her controlling nature.

"I had no friends. The one time I snuck out to be with a boy, it was part of a cruel joke and my grandmother found out and ..." I sighed, looking away from Jack's concerned expression. "I was sixteen, had never been kissed, had no one to talk to, and I was vulnerable. Enter Tripp Van Der Byl. He was twenty years old. A junior at Columbia. He was the son of the CEO of Paxton Aeronautical." My gaze returned to Jack's; his expression was tight, like he knew whatever I was about to tell him wasn't going to be good. "At first, I just saw him like every boy in our circle. Preppy, arrogant, that clean-cut kind of handsome that made me want to mess up his hair and unbutton his collar."

Jack grinned.

I smirked, but it fell away as I remembered what it was like to be sixteen and think I was falling in love. "It was summer, and he was home from college. We were always invited to the same stuffy dinners. Knowing how strict my grandmother was with me, he would talk to me whenever her back was turned. As we got to know each other, he didn't seem like any of the boys I went to school with or had met. He seemed as exasperated by the pretentiousness and suffocation of our privilege as I was. We liked the same books. He made me laugh. He told me he couldn't believe how much more mature I was than the girls he went to college with. It was innocent at first. But then we started to sneak around. He was my first kiss." I blushed and looked at the carpet. "He was my first everything."

"He slept with a sixteen-year-old?" Jack bit out.

Hearing the indignation in his voice, I looked at him. I nodded. "I didn't think there was anything wrong with that. He was only four years older. I looked older, I acted older. And I just ... I wanted to be loved, Jack. He told me he loved me."

"You were sixteen." He looked angry. "A four-year age gap isn't a lot at other times in life, but no way when I was twenty years old would I have dreamt of touching a sixteen-year-old, no matter how goddamn smart and beautiful she was."

I shifted uncomfortably. "Well, Tripp did. We had a secret relationship behind our families' backs for almost a year."

"Jesus."

"Then one night, not long after spring break, I lied to my grandmother and told her I had a study session at school I couldn't get out of. There was a session—she checked. I just didn't go to it. Tripp came home and took me out that night. He left his cell on the table of this little out-of-the-way restaurant we were at and it went off while he was in the bathroom. I shouldn't have looked, but I did."

I remembered that awful, sickening feeling in the pit of my stomach when I saw the text from some girl called Freya. "It was an explicit message from another girl that sounded like he was cheating on me. So, I confronted him. We argued, but he convinced me she was a girl he'd met who wouldn't take no for an answer. That she was harassing him. I was so stupid." I laughed bitterly at myself. Tripp had been so mad at me for being faithless. He'd been so desperate. He'd pulled the car off to the side of the road and begged me to believe him.

"I love you, I love you so fucking much, don't you get it?"

We'd had sex in the car. It was not our first time. And frankly, back then, sex hadn't been a big deal for me. It was okay. I did it because Tripp liked it so much and I loved him. But his intensity, his passion for me, had excited me that night. It was the first time he'd made me come during sex.

I was so naive. For minutes after that moment, I'd felt guilty for not having faith in him.

"I believed him. Ten minutes later, a car came careening around the corner too fast and slid onto our side of the road. Tripp swerved to avoid it and we hit a tree. He sustained a concussion and a broken arm, and I had broken ribs. And our families found out about us."

"What happened?"

"Somehow, and I do not know how because Tripp's car was totaled, but my grandmother found out that a"—I looked away and sighed in half embarrassment, half frustration—"used condom was recovered from the vehicle. She asked if we were having sex, and I said yes. She asked for how long. I told her. And I also explained that I loved him." I turned to Jack. "She lost her ever-loving mind. She said he was just using me to get his claws into the Paxton Group. That his father was a ruthless, ambitious bastard she'd been trying to oust from Paxton Aeronautical for eighteen months. She called the police."

"Shit."

I shook my head, remembering the mortification and guilt and shame she'd made me feel. "She wanted Tripp charged with statutory rape, but since I was seventeen, the police couldn't do much. And I wouldn't admit to them what I'd admitted to her about our relationship starting before then."

"Em."

Hearing his censure, I narrowed my eyes. "I stand by it, Jack. She tried to have him charged with rape but rape didn't happen. Should he have pursued a relationship with me? No. Maybe I was mature in other ways, but I was a lonely, vulnerable kid, and he took advantage. But I wasn't going to ruin his life over it by slapping a sex offense on his record."

He sighed heavily. "Okay, sunrise."

"It didn't matter anyway. She told me she'd prove he was just trying to use me." I reached for my decaf, needing something in my hands. Although the pain had faded, I still remembered how much it hurt to realize my grandmother was right. "She got us all in a room together. Tripp, me, his father. And she offered to back Mr. Van Der Byl from now on as long as he promised to keep his focus on Aeronautical and no other part of the company. And then she offered Tripp $20 million and a high position in any area of the Paxton Group he wished to take after graduation … so long as he stayed away from me."

"Holy shit." Jack sat forward, anger darkening his gaze.

"He took it. And not just because his father immediately urged him to. Tripp didn't even look at his dad or me. Wearing this smug little smirk like he'd won, he just said, 'I accept your terms, Mrs. Paxton.'"

"And just like that …" Emotion clogged my throat. "I was alone again."

"Fuck … Em—"

"Oh, it gets worse, Jack. My grandmother made me get tested for STIs. I naively told her, with much embarrassment, that we'd always used protection. And I had to sit through the most uncomfortable, mortifying reminder given by my *grandmother* that you can catch an STI from oral sex." I gave him a pained smile, and Jack shook his head in sympathy.

"Sunrise …" He sounded just as pained for me.

"Yup." My smile fell. "He gave me chlamydia."

Understanding dawned and the muscle ticked in his jaw as he looked away.

"It's not evidence that he cheated. He could've had it from before … but between that text I found and the proof that he'd been using me all along, I think he was most definitely cheating on me the entire time."

Jack rested his elbows on his knees and held his head in his hands. "You think I'm just like him?"

"No," I rushed to assure him.

Jack's head flew up and he gave me a disbelieving glare. "You think I'd fuck around on you."

"That's not what I'm saying. I'm trying to explain why I find it so hard to trust people." I stood, my agitation making me restless. "For so long after moving here, it wasn't just my shyness that stopped me from letting people in. It was the fear of being hurt again ... because he broke my heart, Jack." Tears filled my eyes. "Everyone I'd ever loved before moving here had broken my heart. And I know now that my feelings for him were borne from the desperation of a kid who needed someone to love her. I know that now. But it doesn't change the way I felt back then. Or how easily he fooled me."

"Em—"

"No, let me explain." I held his hurt gaze even though it filled me with remorse. "When we met, all those fears just ... I didn't feel them with you. There was something about you I instinctively trusted. I once told you that you have the kindest eyes of any man I've ever met. I spoke the truth. And I wanted to believe in them, in you. And even though I told myself it was stupid, I couldn't help it. I wanted to trust you. I wanted ... I wanted you."

Something soft, something like awe, filled his eyes. "Sunrise."

"But you kept hurting me, Jack, whether you meant it or not. The other women. Pushing me away. Vanessa. Abandoning me after we made love, hours after your father held me at gunpoint."

He squeezed his eyes closed again, as if he couldn't bear to hear anymore.

"The purpose of me telling you all this isn't to berate or hurt you. But you said weeks ago that I had to learn to trust the father of my child." I took a step toward him. "I know you, Jack. I know you spent years of your life miserable to protect your sister. That you abandoned me to protect your mom. That you, as wrong as it was, pushed Cooper away to protect him too.

You've sacrificed so much for other people, and I think you are honorable and true. I think my baby is lucky to have you as a father."

When he opened his eyes, they blazed fiercely with feeling.

"Trusting you as a father, as a friend, is something completely different from trusting you as a lover," I finished softly. "And there's just too much hurt between us in that respect."

Jack quickly looked at the floor.

I watched him swallow hard.

After what seemed like minutes of agonizing silence, he finally cleared his throat and stood. When he met my gaze, I was relieved to see he didn't look angry. Or hurt. There was understanding there. "Thank you for trusting me with this. I get it now."

I relaxed. "Okay. I'm glad."

"You're still my best friend," he said, the words a little hoarse. "Even if I'm not yours."

Emotion choked me. I didn't know what to say.

"I'm going to head to work." He moved around the coffee table and stopped by my side. "Will we drive to the trial together?"

More relief moved through me. "Absolutely."

Then my breath stuttered as Jack's head dipped and he pressed a soft but electrifying kiss to the corner of my mouth. "See you tomorrow," he said casually as he pulled back. "Call me if you need me."

"I will," I pushed out, watching him leave.

The corner of my mouth still tingled hours later.

34

EMERY

There were parts of the day in court that I couldn't remember, mostly because my focus had been solely on Jack. I watched him constantly. When he moved to take the stand, it was the only time my attention drifted to his father. Ian sat on the other side of the courtroom, at the front with his attorney and Kerr. Father and son were being tried together since Kerr was intrinsically tied up in the crimes, and surprisingly he hadn't let his father take the blame by accepting a plea bargain.

I could only see Ian's profile. But his jaw was tight and his skin pale. His eyes narrowed as Jack took the stand.

Holding my breath, I relaxed a little when I realized the prosecution would question Jack first. Jack answered their inquiries, confirming evidence he'd provided to the prosecution, that he'd witnessed and been party to his father's blackmailing and racketeering. They got into individual examples and my stomach twisted as I listened to the awful things Jack had knowledge of. Knowing him, it must've been eating away at him for years.

The prosecution asked Jack why he'd worked for his father,

and Jack replied that his father was abusive toward his mother and sister and it was made clear that his loyalty and obedience would save them from that abuse.

Jack had warned me this would be his answer. That his mother and Rebecca had discussed it and they'd agreed to be deposed, backing his claims. The prosecutor mentioned this, handing over Rosalie's and Rebecca's written statements.

My stomach churned for Jack when the defense attorney stood. I knew the state provided this attorney, but that didn't mean he might not be an excellent litigator. As he interrogated Jack, trying to insinuate that Jack had a lot more to do with the racketeering charges than he claimed, my skin flushed with indignation. The urge to jump to Jack's defense was real, even more so when the defense moved on to Jack's claims that he was protecting his mother and sister.

"Other than this written statement, we have no other evidence that these claims of abuse are true. No hospital records, no police reports. And frankly, a written statement from a young woman facing charges for aiding and abetting a murder is hardly reliable. Isn't it true, Mr. Devlin, that you are lying about your father abusing your mother and sister to cover up the fact that you were a willing partner in your father's business ventures? That *you* were the one who convinced your father to take more unlawful steps forward in the business?"

I guffawed in outrage as the prosecutor called, "Objection! Leading the witness. And might I remind the court that Mr. Jack Devlin has been cleared of all charges and he's not the one on trial here."

The judge nodded. "Sustained."

The defense gave a nod of acknowledgment. "Let me rephrase. Mr. Devlin, are you lying about your father abusing your mother and sister?"

Expression hard as flint, Jack's gaze moved toward Ian. The loathing was difficult to miss. "No. I'm not lying. Ian Devlin mentally, emotionally, and physically abused my mother and sister for years. I did what I could to protect them. As you can see, neither of them is here today because they can't stand to be in the same room as Ian."

The court rang with that truth.

The defense attorney quickly changed tact and began trying to trip Jack up on specific incidents of racketeering and blackmail he'd recorded in his witness statements. Jack remained stoic and unflappable. But I wished I could be up there, holding his hand.

When that day's session ended, I waited for Jack outside the Wilmington courthouse. He wore a strained expression as he walked to me in his tailored suit. He'd shaved off his scruff, and I missed it. What I didn't miss was the exhaustion that pervaded him.

"I could drive," I offered as he approached.

Jack shook his head as he reached for my hand. I let him take it without resistance, slipping my fingers through his and holding on tight.

"Are you sure?"

"I'm sure, Em."

I pressed into his side as we walked toward the parking lot. "You did brilliantly, Jack. You were so calm and collected."

"It took a lot," he admitted gruffly. "I wanted to throw a punch at his smug face."

"I wouldn't have blamed you. I wanted to punch him too."

"You already shot him," Jack reminded me with a wry smile.

I grinned, glad to see some lightness in his eyes. "I did, didn't I?"

Jack pulled open the passenger door of his truck and helped me up. "I'm just glad you don't have to face him in a trial for that."

Me too.

"Are you hungry?" I asked as Jack got into the cab and

started the engine. "We could go to The Boardwalk. I haven't dined there yet, but Bailey and Vaughn said the food is great." Other than my eventful dinner with Sebastian at Iris and Ira's, I hadn't seen the chef out and about at all. It would appear he'd been telling the truth when he said he was a workaholic.

"I'm wiped, Em. But if you're hungry, we could grab something and take it back to yours."

"Okay."

Silence fell between us as Jack drove home. It was comfortable, although I was worried about him.

He looked so melancholy and distant.

I didn't like it.

We stopped at a drive-through sandwich place closer to town and then Jack drove us to my place. Despite my concern about how distant he was being, I didn't want to push him. And I thought after a day of constant interrogation, the last thing Jack needed was someone badgering him with questions. Instead, I offered to turn on the sports channel—Jack shot me a tender look. I handed him the remote.

And although I didn't want to appear as if everything was about me, when we sat on opposite sides of the sectional with our food, I voiced my concerns. "If there's even an infinitesimal part of you worried about how I feel about what I heard in there today—about the blackmail and everything—Jack, I don't blame you. All I kept thinking was, God, it must've been awful for you, being forced to be a party to those things. I hurt for you. I wish I had known back then so I could've been a comfort."

His tired eyes moved to me from the screen and something eased in his expression. "You were a comfort."

We shared a small smile. Sensing we were okay, that Jack was genuinely exhausted, I let silence fall between us. Once we'd eaten, I removed all my jewelry and placed the silver on my coffee table. I caught Jack watching me. He did this a lot—

watched me take off my jewelry. As if the familiarity satisfied him in some way.

I ignored that possibility because it made me feel weirdly needy for him.

I casually reached for my e-reader and while I read, Jack watched a rugby game between New Zealand and Wales. My father liked rugby. I remembered him taking me to a match when we were in England as part of a European summer vacation. I was ten. Dad had done a ton of business while we were abroad that summer, so the game was my fondest memory of my father. It was one of the few times he was focused on me, trying to teach me the rules of the game. My mother thought rugby was inappropriate for a young girl, and I don't recall my father ever taking me again after that.

As I was talented at doing, I drowned out the TV and fell into my book.

I didn't know how much time passed before I realized I needed to use the bathroom. Uncurling myself from the sectional, I glanced over at Jack and faltered.

I'd missed him stretching his long body on the couch and he'd fallen asleep on his side, his head on an oversized cushion. My sectional had deep, wide seat cushions, and the urge to tuck myself in beside him was real. He'd taken off his suit jacket and tie when we'd come into the house. The buttons of his collar were opened, and he'd rolled up his shirt sleeves, revealing his tan, corded forearms.

I felt more than a tingle of need in all my good places and glanced away guiltily. The last thing Jack deserved was me ogling him. With a sigh, I got up quietly and went to the restroom. The art deco clock on the wall above the dining table said it was only eight forty-five. It was still fairly early and yet, it might as well have been midnight for how tired I was. On my return, I yawned as soon as I looked at Jack.

That urge to curl up beside him and sleep grew stronger.

My hand automatically moved to my stomach.

The three of us cuddled up together sounded so nice, tears pricked my eyes.

Scoffing inwardly at my nonsense, I put the emotion clogging my throat down to the difficulty of the day. Being pregnant, I did find myself in need of more naps than normal. There was absolutely nothing wrong with taking a nap with Jack. It would be my way of offering him comfort, even in his sleep.

Mind made up, practically itching to feel him pressed against me, I switched off the television and tentatively laid down beside Jack. I held my breath, worried I'd wake him. But Jack must've been completely out of it because he barely even moved as I pressed my back to his front and rested my head on the cushion beside his. His chest pushed gently into my back as he breathed.

It was nice.

More than nice.

I closed my eyes and listened to Jack breathe and followed him quickly into sleep.

35

JACK

It took awhile for the warm, soft body pressed against Jack in his dreams to pull him out of unconsciousness and gradually into waking.

Before he opened his eyes, he felt the soft curves of her ass against his groin. His arm was settled over a slender waist, his fingertips touching what he discerned was the lower curve of a breast.

Her scent invaded him.

Emery.

Jack's eyes flew open, adjusting to the dark.

Where am I?

Then it hit him. Crashing at Em's after the trial because he was so exhausted.

His lips and nose were settled in Emery's soft hair. Her shoulders rose and fell with light breaths as she slept.

He remembered lying down on her couch as he watched rugby. He must've fallen asleep.

Which meant Em had deliberately curled up beside him.

Feeling her breast sit heavily on his fingertips, her magnificent ass against his pelvis, inhaling her, memories of their night together flooded him.

Blood rocketed to his dick and his erection pushed against his suit pants and into the crest between Em's ass cheeks.

Jack turned his head into the cushion to muffle his groan of need.

Then he heard it.

The swift intake of breath, seconds before she pushed her ass into his dick.

"Em," he grunted, cupping her breast in his hand and squeezing the full, lush globe.

She whimpered and clutched his hand, drawing it away from her breast and down her stomach. If it was possible, he hardened even more at the feel of the gentle rise of her belly where their baby was growing. She moved his hand over and down to the tight gap between her closed thighs.

Euphoria and arousal made his voice hoarse. "Is that where you need me, sunrise?"

She tensed. And then Jack felt a cool breeze waft over him as Emery flew to her feet. She swayed as she whirled around to glare down at him.

"What the hell are you doing?" Her cheeks were flushed hot.

Indignation rushed through him. "Me? I didn't fall asleep with you next to me, darlin', you did that."

"That wasn't an invitation to stick your"—she gestured to Jack's still-visible erection—"in my ass."

God, the very thought of doing just that only made him harder. He sat up and pressed his fingers to his eyelids. "Fuck, Em, could you not?" Then he dropped his hands and glared up at her. "Why do I feel like a bad guy here? I woke up, you were in my arms, that tends to make me hard, yeah … but I wasn't the one who rubbed her ass into my dick or put my hand between her legs."

In the moonlight spilling through the windows, he could see

she was bright red with mortification. "I was asleep! I thought I was dreaming!"

Oh, really? "So, you dream about me?"

"Screw you, Jack!" she yelled with a lot more anger than Jack felt the situation warranted. "You can see yourself out!" Before he could reply, Em rushed through the doorway that led to the staircase.

Jack launched himself off the sectional and hurried after her. "Em, why are you making a big deal out of this?"

"Don't follow me!" she screeched.

Jesus Christ.

Jack followed her. "Sunrise?"

"Don't come in here," her voice commanded.

Jack ignored her and strode into her bedroom where she stood, arms crossed over her chest, glowering at him.

It was a cover.

She was embarrassed. She was mortified she'd touched him.

What the hell?

"Em, what's going on? So you were dreaming ... okay. Fine. Disappointing for me," he teased, "but it shouldn't embarrass you. Or make you pissed at me."

Remorse softened her expression. "I'm sorry ... I'm just ..."

"You're just what?"

Emery threw her hands up. "I'm frustrated!"

Confused, he frowned. "Frustrated?"

She glanced around the room, like she couldn't meet his eyes. "Frustrated. As in ... sexually," she whispered.

And Jack was fighting not to get hard again.

Fuck me.

"Apparently it happens with some women when they're pregnant. And it's happening to me. A lot. So much. Nearly all the time."

The woman he loved, who was carrying his baby but didn't

want to be in a relationship with him, was standing there telling him she was horny.

So this was what hell looked like.

"I see," he choked out.

Her eyes moved back to him reluctantly. "I think we should take some space."

No fucking chance. "Nope."

"But you're the problem," she blurted.

"Excuse me?"

"It's you!" She gestured to him in exasperation. "With your throat and forearms and sexy hands and that swagger."

Thrill coursed through Jack as he approached her. "Are you telling me you're horny, Em, or that you're *horny for me*?"

"I hate that word." She slapped her hands over her face to cover her mortification and groaned.

Jack grinned as he approached, heat flushing through him. He gently peeled her hands from her face. "Don't be embarrassed, Em. I am unbelievably flattered. And more than happy to be of use."

Her jaw dropped. "Meaning?"

"I can't have my favorite girl walking around all frustrated, now can I?" He maneuvered her toward the bed.

"But Jack ..." Her chest rose and fell with excitement as her expression moved between desire and uncertainty. "It wouldn't change anything between us."

"I know that," he lied. "I'm just a friend helping another friend out. No strings attached."

Emery bit her lower lip. "I don't know."

That she was even considering it meant she really fucking wanted him.

She was hormonal, her sex drive had kicked into top gear, and it was Jack she wanted. Even if Emery couldn't see what that meant, he could. And he was not above using the situation to further his case: Jack vs. Emery's heart.

"You wet, sunrise?" he asked, voice gruff as he itched to slip his fingers inside her and find out for himself.

"Jack." She stumbled against the bottom of the bed and raised her hands to rest on his chest.

"Are you wet?" he repeated against her mouth.

Emery was panting now. She nodded slowly, cheeks high with color.

"Let me give you what you need," he whispered. "For however long you need it. No promises, no owing me anything."

"Jack ..."

"I want to kiss you, Em." He brushed his mouth over hers. "Not just here"—another brush—"but where you need it most. Right on that pretty little pussy of yours."

She gasped, her fingers curling into his shirt. And then, "Oh, screw it," she panted, and pulled him down to her mouth.

Thank you, God! Jack sent up an exultation as he sank into Emery's deep, hungry kiss. Quickly he took it over and she swayed in his arms.

"Dress off," he pulled back to say.

While Em whipped it up and off, Jack divested himself of all his clothes, watching as Em threw her dress to the floor, standing there in nothing but her lace underwear.

"You're so beautiful, I can barely stand it," he said.

"Jack, hurry."

But Jack didn't want to hurry.

He wanted to make love to his pregnant Em.

With light strokes, Jack learned every inch of her with his touch—her ribs, her waist, her belly. His fingers trailed over the slight swell, and possessiveness roared through him. Her ass was next. He fondled and squeezed until Em was squirming and muttering with impatience.

"Jack, please."

Smiling at her with promise in his eyes, Jack unhooked her bra and nudged the straps down her arms. It fell to the floor.

The cool air whispered over Em's breasts, making her nipples pucker into tight, needy buds.

"You sensitive?" he asked.

She made a throaty sound that Jack took for an affirmative.

Jack cupped her sweet tits in his hands, and she reacted instantly, moaning and arching into his touch. Jack fought a growl of arousal, watching her face flush. She was ready to go off like a firecracker. Her hips undulated as he played with her breasts, sculpting and kneading them, stroking and pinching her nipples. She thrust forcefully into his touch, whimpering her need for him as her fingers bit around his biceps.

"Mouth, Jack. Mouth," she commanded harshly.

Wanting her wound so tight, she'd explode, Jack gave her his mouth but not where she wanted it. Instead, he kissed her. Em melted into his kiss, sliding her hands up his arms, over his shoulders and around his neck to pull him deeper into the kiss. Her mouth opened, inviting him inside.

He slid his tongue against hers, licked at it, sucked on it, all the while pinching her nipples between his fingers and thumb.

"Jack." She broke the kiss. "Please."

Deciding he'd tormented her enough, he bent his head to her chest and lifted one soft globe to his mouth. Her sigh of absolute pleasure sang through him as he wrapped his lips around her nipple and sucked. He moved between her breasts, licking and laving and sucking deep.

She tensed. And then her moan of release rang out into the room as she shuddered against him.

Jack lifted his head, disbelief passing through him as he watched the aftermath of Emery's orgasm. His hand slipped between her legs, sliding through her soaked heat.

"You just came?"

Her eyelashes fluttered as her eyes slowly opened. She still swayed against him.

"You came with just my mouth on your tits." His fingers bit into her ribs.

"Yes," she panted. Her hands moved down his chest, her fingers catching on his nipples. She kissed him there, her touch trailing possessively down his abs. "It's not enough," she whispered in frustration. "Jack, it's not enough."

Holy fuck.

This was the best night of his life.

Jack slipped his fingers into her wet again, his thumb finding her clit, and her fingers dug into his waist. "This what you need, Em?"

Her head fell back so she could look up at him through desire-fogged eyes. "Yes." She pressed her hips into his touch as tears of need pricked her eyes. "Jack, please."

Tenderness added a tinge of desperation to his desire. "I'm going to take care of you. I'm here." *Always.*

He nipped at her lips. Playful kisses. Sweet kisses. He rubbed his thumb over her swollen clit. Taking one thigh in hand to open her wider, Jack slipped two fingers inside her tight channel.

"Oh God." Her head fell back. She clutched at his waist and undulated against his touch.

"Open your eyes, Em. I want to watch it build."

She gave him those spectacular eyes, hooded with lust, and he didn't break his gaze as she climbed toward climax.

"How long have you needed this, sunrise?" he asked roughly.

"A while."

"You've been fantasizing about it?"

She nodded on a gasp.

"You've been sitting next to me in my truck, wet and needful, and I didn't know?"

"Yes!"

Jack felt like he might blow without her even touching him.

"Jack!" She tensed and then her muscles throbbed around his fingers, more wet soaking them as she came.

Not even giving her a chance to come down from it, Jack nudged her onto the bed. He hooked his fingers into her underwear and yanked them down her long, gorgeous legs. He discarded them on the floor and stood gazing at Emery spread out for him on the bed. His eyes zeroed in on that gentle rise of her belly again.

His erection strained toward her, but he ignored it and bent his head to her stomach. Her belly trembled against his touch as he planted soft kisses all over it.

"Jack," she whispered.

He looked up and saw the tender tears in her eyes.

Eyes on her, he kissed his way down the swell until he reached the apex of her thighs. Then he took hold and pushed her legs apart.

"Oh my God!" Her head flew back on the bed, breaking their gaze.

But not their connection.

Em lifted her hips, inviting him in, and he took the invitation with relish. He licked at her distended clit, pressed his tongue down on it, and then sucked.

"Oh God, I can't take it." She squirmed beneath him, and he realized she was sensitive from her two previous orgasms. Jack gripped her hips tight, keeping her right there, and devoured her.

It took a little longer this time, but when Em broke, she screamed his name, her hips jerking with the violence of her climax.

And Jack was done with foreplay.

He needed inside her.

He lifted her under the arms and slid her farther up the bed. She was still gone. Still recovering from the orgasm that had just ripped through her. Still trembling and shivering in the aftermath. And Jack wanted to feel it. Spreading her thighs, hands braced at either side of her head, he nudged against her wet heat and pushed his throbbing dick inside her.

"Fuck." He groaned, long and hard. Although his Em was wet, her muscles were swollen from orgasm and resisted his presence. Em whimpered as her inner muscles pulsed around him. Her pussy clutched his dick as her hands gripped his waist, her fingernails biting into him.

Heaven.

He was in goddamn heaven.

Jack's breathing grew stuttered and he realized it wouldn't take long. He was so hot from how hot his Em was.

And then their eyes locked. Her fingers bit into his waist, her lips parted to release her pants, and she lifted her hips to meet his gentle thrusts.

"Em." He glided in a little faster, a little harder.

"Jack." She clung to him. "I feel you everywhere. I feel you everywhere."

His balls drew up and his hips stuttered as shivers chased down his spine, heat gathering deep ... "Emery!" The orgasm *wrenched* out of him, the bliss making his eyes roll back in his fucking head as he poured himself inside her.

He tried to hold himself up as he continued to pulse and throb, clutched in her tight heat.

Then it was too much.

He collapsed over her, his forehead pressed to her throat as she caressed his damp skin, her hands moving soothingly over his back.

"Sunrise." He shuddered, grinding his lower body against her, wanting her to wring every last drop of cum out of him. "Fuck me."

He heard a hitch in her breathing and then she said, sounding amused, "As soon as you're ready to go again, I will."

Jack groaned through his lusty laughter.

36

EMERY

My selfishness strapped me to the bed.

I was pinned by it as Jack got up and walked his gorgeous, naked ass into my bathroom.

We'd had sex all night.

Jack had been gentle, even when I demanded he not be. But he was being careful of the baby. The only time he'd let it get a little rough was when I was on top. I rode him hard.

Cheeks flushing with the memories, I groaned and covered my face with my hands.

The man had the ability to make me lose all inhibition.

Jack had woken me to tell me he had to leave to get ready for court. I'd been unable to speak as I realized what I'd done. Last night, I'd let my hormones take over. I had no idea it was so possible to let your desires control you like that. I mean, they always kind of controlled me when it came to Jack … but this was next-level irresponsible. They had driven all rational thought from my head.

Jack strode back into the bedroom a few minutes later, his smoldering gaze on me. He was so tall and delicious, despite my self-directed anger, I wanted to climb him. Forcing myself to look away, I finally unpinned from the bed and sat up, clutching the sheets to cover my chest.

I didn't know why.

Jack had seen and kissed every inch of me.

"First thing's first. I'm clean. I got tested after our first little chat about that."

Remembering how badly he'd taken that conversation the first time, I felt guilty. "Jack—"

"Don't. It's fine, Em. You should know I get checked regularly. I would never fuck around with that."

"Okay." I believed him.

"Wish I could stay and have coffee with you, sunrise, but I need to be back in Wilmington soon." Jack began to dress.

"Do you need me there?" I offered without thinking.

He shot me a tender smile. "No, Em. I'm not on the stand today. You should open the store."

I barely nodded.

"Hey." He stopped buttoning his shirt and put his hands to the bed so our faces were close. "We okay?"

Mine crumpled with anxiety. "Oh, Jack, I'm so sorry. I shouldn't have ..." I gestured between us.

Jack's expression hardened a little and he pushed back off the bed to finish dressing. "And why not?"

Was he kidding?

"Because ... because we're not together and this ... I was selfish last night. This blurred the lines. So badly."

Jack's hands went to his hips as he contemplated me. I tried not to think of what those hips could do to me.

Jesus.

I looked down at the bedsheets because looking at Jack was dangerous to my libido.

"I thought we agreed this was just sex. Anytime you need me, I'm here for you."

My eyes flew to his. "But … you wanted more between us. It isn't fair to you."

"Did you or did you not come down on me for making decisions for the two of us without taking your feelings into account?"

Another guilty flush heated my cheeks. "Yes."

"Am I or am I not a grown man capable of making my own decisions?"

I narrowed my eyes at his condescending tone. "Yes."

His lips twitched at my snippy tone. "Then, Emery, I don't need you to protect me. You want sex, I'll give you sex. Nothing wrong with that." He flashed a wicked grin. "Honest to God, best sex of my life. Why the hell would I turn down the opportunity to have more?"

"Because it's not that straightforward, Jack, and you know it."

"Well, I'm a guy." He stated the obvious. "I can have great sex without it being more. So, the only reason not to do this is if you can't have sex without letting your feelings develop into something more."

I was at once hurt by his insinuation that he could detach his feelings from the act of making love and irritated that he'd trapped me. Now if I said no to the friends-with-benefits situation, I'd be suggesting I had deeper feelings for him.

I shrugged, feeling petulant. "I can have sex without needing more from you."

He studied me a moment, an undecipherable look in his eyes. "Good." He put a knee to the bed and leaned in and gave me the kind of kiss that was a prelude to dirty sex. I slid my fingers into his soft, thick hair and held on for the ride.

When Jack finally let me up for air, my entire body tingled. He pressed a sweet kiss to my nose and tried to pull away, but I held on to his neck. "You don't kiss a girl like that and leave her wanting more, Jack," I whispered. "It's exceptionally rude. Didn't your momma teach you any manners?"

He smiled a smile that was at once cocky and regretful. "I've got places to be, sunrise."

My grip on his nape tightened, pulling him down as I laid back down. "Then you should have thought about that before you kissed me."

Jack grinned, tugging the sheet down between us. "Guess I've no recourse now but to apologize for misplacing my manners."

"Don't worry." Heat flushed through me as all that rational thought flew from my mind and I unzipped his suit pants. "I'm very good at accepting apologies." I slipped my hand inside his underwear and gripped his hardening length, loving the way he groaned, deep and wanting. "In fact, I predict my acceptance will be on your mind all day."

I thought I heard him mutter, "Then it'll be nothing new," but I couldn't be sure and his fingers were between my legs, chasing away all thoughts of anything but him and his hands and his mouth and his … well, you know …

"BAILEY, I love you, but if you tell one more story about your luxury three-week, five-star honeymoon across Europe, I'm going to scream," Jess said, tucked into a large armchair in her sitting room with her feet up on a plush stool. Her cheeks were full and flushed, there were dark circles under her eyes, and I could see why Coop and Jess had asked repeatedly for their OB to check if they were having twins. She was huge.

They weren't having twins, though.

They were just having a Lawson, and clearly he or she was going to be built like a Lawson.

Poor Jess, I thought. Her pregnancy had been uncomfortable from the start.

Bailey shot me, Ivy, and Dahlia a guilty look. "Have I been talking about it a lot?"

No. She hadn't. This was the first time since her and Vaughn's return that she'd even mentioned Europe. I gave her a reassuring shake of my head.

"I can't think of you and Vaughn or anyone gallivanting freely across Europe, doing nothing but sightseeing, eating at nice restaurants, drinking champagne and cocktails, and having great sex *all* the time. I haven't been able to find a comfortable position to sit or sleep in, let alone have sex in, for the last four months."

More guilt suffused me.

I'd just had a night of epic sex.

Such epic sex, I was in denial about how out of control this situation with Jack could get. I didn't want to think about it. I only wanted to contemplate the next time I could get him naked.

It was so unlike me.

And yet there was something freeing in not caring about the future and only living in the moment.

Probably a terrible point in my life, i.e., about to become a responsible parent, to indulge in such a philosophy.

But my baby wasn't here yet, so it didn't count.

Right?

"I'm sorry, Jess." Bailey gave her a sympathetic look.

"No, I'm sorry." Jess glowered at the wall beyond us. "I'm an irritable, unpleasant human to be around. Dahlia and Em closed their stores to come here so I didn't have to come to you, and I'm being horrible."

"You're thirty-four weeks pregnant with what I can only assume is a future NBA player," Dahlia retorted. "You're allowed to be irritable."

"Emery isn't irritable."

Oh God, don't bring me into it.

"Look"—Jess gestured to me, bringing me into it—"twelve weeks pregnant and you wouldn't even know it. I bet you're going to have a cute little bump and stay long-legged and beautiful and comfortable throughout the whole thing."

"Let's focus on the future," I urged. "And how our children will be so close in age, they'll grow up as best friends."

"And," Bailey jumped in, "if one is a boy and the other a girl, they might grow up as childhood sweethearts. How adorable would that be?"

"That *would* be adorable," Jess agreed with a smile.

All four of us sighed with relief that she liked the idea. It was her first smile of the day.

"What about you and Vaughn?" Jess asked Bailey. "Have you had the kid talk yet?"

"We know we don't have a ton of years to put it off, but we've decided we'd like at least a year, maybe two, where it's just us."

"I get it," Dahlia agreed. "Michael and I talked about having kids just after I got shot. I wanted to know it was an option. But now Michael is talking about it *a lot*, as if he wants it all and he wants it all as soon as possible. I just want him for a while. I didn't have him for so long, and as selfish as it sounds, I don't want to share him just yet."

"Have you told him that?" Ivy asked.

"No, I don't want him to think I'm selfish."

"I don't think he'll think that's selfish at all," I assured her. "In fact, I think it'll probably make him want to have sex with you."

"Watching paint dry would make that man want to have sex with her," Bailey teased.

Dahlia grinned, and it was smug. "You're not wrong."

"And what about Ivy and Jeff?" Bailey gave Ivy a mischievous smile.

"Oh hell, we are nowhere near that."

"Well, the entire town is talking about the good sheriff mooning after our Academy Award-winning Ivy Green. They're anxious that she'll break his heart by returning to Hollywood."

Ivy gaped at Bailey. "Are you kidding me? Are people really saying that?"

"Of course, they are. Between Emery and Jack hanging out all the time, and you and Jeff, the tongues are a-wagging."

If they knew what Jack and I had been up to last night, the gossips would lose their minds.

"Jeff and I are very new. We're just enjoying each other's company."

"But are you staying in Hartwell?" Bailey pressed. "Because the gossips want to know."

"The gossips can go take a flying jump off the boardwalk."

"I mean me, Ivy," Bailey huffed. "Your best friend wants to know."

Ivy's expression softened. "I just sold a screenplay I wrote awhile back, and I've started working on a book."

Melancholy moved through me at what this meant. Was Ivy leaving us?

Bailey's face mirrored my feelings. "You're going back."

"Nope." She shot us a dazzling grin. "I can still write scripts and not live in Hollywood. People still want to work with me. Plus I've always wanted to write a book, and my agent thinks it's a superb idea. I can do that anywhere. So, I'm staying in Hartwell. I'm happy here."

Bailey flew off her chair with a girlish squeal and threw her arms around Ivy. She laughed and held on to her friend, and my heart ached with the genuine joy I saw on Ivy's face. After all she'd been through, it really seemed like she was going to be okay.

Dahlia and I took turns hugging Ivy.

"I'm so glad you're staying," I said with feeling.

Ivy cupped my face in her hands in a way that reminded me of Iris. She whispered, "You helped me so much, Em. I'm so glad we met."

Tears filled my eyes, but the sweet moment was broken when Jess cursed. "Goddammit! I can't even get out of the damn chair to hug a person!"

Sure enough, she was struggling to push herself up and out of the armchair. Ivy rushed to her feet to go to Jess instead.

"I swear to God," Jess huffed after she was done hugging Ivy. "If he doesn't go on to do a job that requires him to be physically huge, this kid will owe his mother!"

We all stared at her in shock.

"What?" She glared at us.

"He?" Bailey took an excited step toward her. "You're having a boy?"

Jess's face paled. Then her head flopped back on the chair. "Aw shit, Coop's going to kill me."

37

EMERY

I was assaulted with nervousness.

The fact that Jack's hand was on my ass as we walked up to the front porch of the huge Colonial-Georgian house was not helping. "Jack, your hand."

He shifted so it was pressed to my lower back, but his long fingers still touched the top of my butt.

"Do you want your mother to think we're together?" I turned to face him before we reached the door. "This is confusing enough. We do not need to mislead her."

With a patient expression, Jack settled his hands on my hips and bent his head to mine. "Sunrise, I've explained the situation to my mom. She knows we're not together."

"You can't call me sunrise." I pushed his hands off my hips. "And you can't touch me with sexual familiarity in front of her. Or anyone." Or they might figure out we've been screwing each other's brains out almost every night for four weeks.

"One, I'm pretty sure they can tell I'm sexually familiar with you." He nodded to my bump. "Two, then you shouldn't have worn that dress."

With temperatures cooling, I'd worn a long-sleeved, ankle-length jersey dress I loved. It clung to my figure but the material was stretchy, so it gave over my little baby bump and my somewhat bigger-than-normal breasts. Despite the clinginess, with its tight sleeves and high scoop neck, I'd thought it was conservative. Until I opened my door to Jack and his eyes turned smoky and *wanting*.

Apparently, he told me, I'd worn a similar dress the first time he ever saw me, and it did wonderful things for my ass. The man was incorrigible.

I'd plaited my hair into a fishtail braid and I'd forgone a ton of bracelets for a few necklaces of varying lengths. Silver and amethyst drop earrings Dahlia had crafted hung from my ears, and as per usual, nearly every finger had a ring on it.

I wasn't sure what kind of woman Rosalie Devlin was, but I was determined to be myself. Silver and all. Even if I was a nervous wreck about it.

"Em, you look beautiful. You always look beautiful, and not just because you have a Helen of Troy thing going on with your face." He grinned. "But because your goodness shines out of you, sunrise. My mom and Becs will see that, and they're going to be grateful that my kid's mom is an outstanding woman. End of story."

My cheeks heated at his compliments. "Jack," I whispered, gazing up into soulful eyes and seeing he meant every bit of it. My stomach somersaulted at the intensity of his expression.

The sound of a door opening broke the moment between us. "I thought I heard voices."

Yanking my eyes from Jack's, I saw Rebecca Devlin standing in the doorway to Jack's uncle's home. I recognized her from her photograph in the newspaper. Apparently, when she'd arrived back in Hartwell months ago, she was painfully thin and wan looking. While Rebecca was still very slender, Jack had mentioned she'd put on a little weight and now she had a healthy glow.

We weren't just at his uncle's house to introduce me to his family—we were there to celebrate. Four weeks ago, Ian and Kerr Devlin were sentenced to thirty years for three counts of racketeering. They'd probably serve less time than that, but it still meant they'd be inside for a long time. Kerr was in his forties now, which meant he'd lose the best decades of his life. As for Ian, he would be an *old* man before he ever breathed free air again ... if he lived that long. According to Jack, this news, along with the news that she would become a grandmother, had given his mom a new lease of life.

We were also celebrating the fact that the shark of an attorney Hague found had gotten Rebecca off with nothing more than community service in her aiding-and-abetting charges. She wouldn't have to face prison, much to Jack's utter relief.

And Jack and I were privately celebrating (along with the rest of our friends) the news that Dana Kellerman had left her rental apartment behind and departed Hartwell for Boston, where she'd accepted a job with an old college friend.

Yay!

The Wicked Witch was leaving Hart's Boardwalk for good!

"Becs." Jack rested his hand on my waist and led me to the door. He only released me to hug his sister tight. "You look great."

She studied me as they hugged, her eyes only returning to her brother when they released one another. "Thanks. I feel great. An enormous weight has been lifted. In more ways than one."

I also knew from Jack that Rosalie and Rebecca were seeing a therapist and that both were feeling the positive effects of those sessions. No decision had been made yet about Rebecca meeting her real father, though I knew from Jack, it had been much discussed these past few weeks.

"I'm glad, sweetheart." He turned his attention to me. His

smile was easy. Almost proud. "Becs, I'd like you to meet Emery."

Rebecca didn't return my shy smile. Her eyes were on my belly as she stepped forward and offered her hand in a somewhat formal gesture. "Hello."

Not sure how to take her cool reception, I shook her proffered hand. "Hi. It's nice to meet you."

Her eyes moved to my face, which I was pretty sure was tomato red with uncertainty. Something softened in her expression. "You too. Come on in."

As we followed her inside the large, traditionally decorated home, I caught Jack's eyes. They filled with reassurance as his hand returned to my lower back. This time I didn't ask him to remove it. I needed that touch. I desired the comfort of his proximity. These people would be in my life because of my child, and I wanted to like them. Rebecca's reception had been slightly off, and I didn't know why.

"Mom, Jack's here!" Rebecca called as she strode away from us. We'd entered a large entrance hall with a wide staircase directly ahead. The walls were open at either side of us; to the right, a large dining room; to our left, a massive sitting room. Rebecca strode through the sitting room and Jack ushered us after her.

"Perfect timing." An elegant woman with thick, dark blond hair stood from a comfortable armchair at the end of the room. A man and woman seated opposite her on a huge sectional stood too.

The woman was tall and willowy. She strutted across the room in a pale-blue silk blouse tucked into a high-waisted, knee-length pencil skirt. Her heels were pale blue and black leather, matching her outfit perfectly.

Jack released his hold on me as the woman embraced him. "Darling, it's lovely to see you," she murmured.

This was Rosalie Devlin?

I'd anticipated a diminutive, nervous wreck of a woman.

She was nothing like I'd expected. Ian Devlin, for what a gigantic bastard he'd been, had been a tall, good-looking man. I could only imagine he'd been even more so as a young man. It saddened me that he'd swept Rosalie off her feet. But I guess she got her sons out of it. I wondered what Rebecca's real father was like and if Rosalie had loved him.

Rosalie pulled out of Jack's embrace but held on to his arm as she turned to me.

"Mom, this is Emery."

Just like Rebecca, her eyes dropped first to my belly. They stayed there awhile before returning to my face, bright with tears. I stiffened, not sure what those tears meant.

"Emery. May I hug you?"

Relief loosened my tense muscles. In answer, I moved to embrace her, and she gave a teary little laugh in my ear as we hugged. She smelled of expensive floral perfume. When she pulled back, she cupped my face in her hands, studying me with a small, delighted smile that definitely reached her eyes. "Look at you. Aren't you perfect."

Of course, I blushed.

"Mom, stop, you're embarrassing her," Jack said without conviction, sounding like he was enjoying my discomfort. The bastard. The look I cut him only made him grin harder.

Rosalie bit her lip and released me. "I'm sorry. I just …" Her gaze dropped to my belly again. "I can't believe I'm going to be a grandmother. It's wonderful. And she's so lovely, Jack." She turned to her son, touching his chest.

"I know," he agreed with the kind of deep feeling that made my heart ache.

"Hi, Emery." The man, just as tall as Jack, approached. "I'm Jack's uncle, Heath. Nice to meet you." He held his hand out to shake. Studying him, I saw quite a bit of resemblance between him and Jack.

"Likewise." I smiled shyly and shook his hand. And then did the same when he introduced his wife Amelia.

"We have two daughters, Rosie and Leila, but, like Jamie, they're at college," Amelia said.

I nodded, discomforted to be center of attention.

Jack sensed it and tucked me into his side.

"How are you feeling?" Rosalie asked, her eyes moving between my face and my bump.

"I'm good," I assured her quietly, touching my rounded stomach. "I've been lucky so far. I feel great."

"How far along are you?" Amelia asked.

"Sixteen weeks."

She raised an eyebrow. "You don't look it. In fact, if you were to turn around, no one would know you were pregnant at all."

"I was the same," Rosalie offered. "It's perhaps our height. My bump was a little bigger with the boys but not with Rebecca. I was very neat with Rebecca. Perhaps you're having a girl." She seemed delighted by the notion.

A little girl.

My goodness.

The thought filled me with longing. But so did the idea of having a boy.

"We find out in a few weeks what the sex of the baby is," Jack said.

"So, you don't want it to be a surprise?"

Jack nodded at me to answer since I was the one who wanted to know. Jack didn't mind either way. I grinned at Rosalie as I thought about Jess. "One of my best friends is pregnant. In fact, she's a week past due." Poor Jess. "And she's having a boy. We've both got this ridiculous notion in our heads that if Jack and I have a girl, then she might grow up to fall in love with Jess and Cooper's boy." I blushed because saying it out loud to strangers made us sound so infantile.

To my surprise, however, Rosalie brought her hands

together, her eyes bright with happiness as she looked at Jack. "Cooper's boy?"

Jack nodded.

"Oh, wouldn't that be wonderful?" She squeezed her son's arm. "I like that idea very much. Okay. Then we'll all pray for a girl!"

Not long later, Jack led me into the dining room for dinner. We were far enough away from his family for me to murmur, "Your mom seems in great spirits, Jack."

"I haven't seen her like this in years. I told you she was excited to be a grandma."

"Then we'll need to make sure she gets to see her grandkid a lot."

Jack seemed to stumble over his own feet, and I pressed a hand to his chest to support him. That hand fell away as if burned when I saw his expression.

He looked at me …

Like Vaughn looked at Bailey.

Like Michael at Dahlia.

Cooper at Jess.

Oh my God.

It occurred to me it wasn't the first time Jack gazed at me as if he loved me. In fact, there were times these past few weeks that he'd looked at me this way as he *made* love to me.

I just hadn't wanted to admit I knew what his expression revealed.

"As beautiful as Emery is, darling, the food is waiting to be consumed," his mother teased from her place at the dining table.

Jack tore his eyes from mine and led me to my seat. I blushed at the knowing smiles on his mom's and aunt's and uncle's faces. But when my eyes moved to Rebecca, I only saw her frown.

~

DINNER WENT WELL.

Jack must have prepped his family because no one asked me about mine. They had questions about my store, and Rosalie asked about my favorite books and for recommendations. We talked about the baby and the scans. She and Heath and Amelia regaled me with stories of parenthood that made me laugh and put me at ease and distracted me from my feelings for Jack.

The only person who didn't was Rebecca, who spoke sometimes, but mostly seemed to observe for the evening.

Observing me.

And I got the feeling she didn't like what she saw.

After we'd moved back to the sitting room for drinks (decaf tea for me), I excused myself to use the restroom. It was down the hall behind the staircase, near the enormous kitchen at the rear of the house. I had to walk past a wall of photos, and I'd noticed pictures of Jack and his siblings on the wall. Considering Heath had no part in their lives until recently, this surprised me.

I used the restroom and returned to the photographs. There was one of Jack and Rosalie on their own together. Jack was in his football gear, so he must've been in his late teens and already a few inches taller than his mom. They were standing outside the Devlin house. He had his arm around his mom's shoulders, and she was tucked into his side, happy to be there. Pride shone from her eyes. Jack grinned at the camera, unabashed to be taking a photo with his mom.

Knowing their history, I could see why Heath would frame this photo. It was evidence that his sister had a child in her life who obviously adored her.

"Mom sent them photos."

I jerked my head around to find Rebecca standing in the hall. I hadn't even heard her approach I'd been so lost in my thoughts.

She gestured to the wall with the photographs. "All that time,

Uncle Heath and Aunt Amelia had us, but we never had them." Rebecca approached me. "It might have helped to have them in our lives back then. They're wonderful people."

I nodded. "I can tell."

Her eyes narrowed and I tensed. "I don't know you, Emery, so don't take this personally—"

Oh hell.

"But I don't like the way you're stringing my brother along. I'd like it to stop. Especially since there's a child involved." She nodded to my belly.

Had Jack and I been that obvious? "I don't know how to take that if not personally?"

"Okay, so it *is* personal. Jack told me everything. How long this thing between you has been going on. That he got you pregnant and that you don't want to be in a relationship with him because you don't trust him." She scoffed at that. "My brother. The guy who sacrificed his whole goddamn life for others. He's, like, the noblest guy in the world, and you don't trust him."

Guilt shimmered through me. But also defensiveness. "You have no idea what's between me and Jack."

"What I know is, is that I'd do anything for Jack." She took a final step toward me. "I want my brother to have everything he wants. And he wants you. And frankly, it pisses me off that you don't think he's good enough for you. Who is to say that it's not you who isn't good enough for him?"

Indignation roared through me and I straightened my shoulders. "How dare you," I whispered. "How dare you presume things about me or my feelings for Jack?"

Whatever she heard in my tone made her flinch. Rebecca sighed heavily. "You're right. I'm sorry. I just ..." Her expression turned pleading. "Don't break his heart, okay? He's been through enough."

Understanding flooded me.

Rebecca felt guilty. She felt like Jack had given up a part of his life for her. And as she said, she wanted Jack to have everything he wanted.

Remembering the look on his face when we'd walked into the dining room, I realized I couldn't keep willfully ignoring reality. Our sexual relationship was tying the bond between us tighter and tighter, and if I didn't stop it soon, there was no way I could end it without hurting Jack.

Or myself.

38

JACK

It had taken an annoying amount of coercing to get Emery to agree to dinner with him. Jack was pissed but trying *not* to be pissed. Ever since Emery had met his family, she'd been acting distant. He'd been sleeping in her bed nearly every night for the past four weeks, but she'd told him the night of his family's dinner that she was tired and wanted to sleep alone. And then she'd been weird when he'd stopped by her store for coffee the next morning. Em had then put him off about seeing each other later that night.

The only reason he had her in his company now was because she'd promised he could be a part of the prenatal checkups, and they were due for an appointment. On the drive back from Essex, Em had said she wanted to be alone, but uneasiness gripped Jack and he couldn't let it go.

Emery was pulling away from him.

He could feel it deep in his gut.

So he insisted they have dinner at The Boardwalk.

"I can't eat seafood, Jack," she complained.

"You wanted to eat there only a few weeks ago because you *can* eat seafood." He'd researched what Em could and could not eat. "Anything high in mercury is out, but seafood is great for omega-3. As long it's cooked properly, we'll be good. I'm pretty sure there will be non-seafood options on the menu if you don't want to take the chance."

She gaped at him as they walked to the restaurant. She looked unbearably sad. "You really have read all those pregnancy books, haven't you?"

Jack stopped on the boards and pulled her into his arms. "Em, what's going on?"

"Jack, don't." She tried to pull away. "I don't want people to get the wrong idea about us."

"People ... or me?" he bit out impatiently.

Emery pressed her lips tight and glowered up at him.

It was irritating how fucking cute she was when she was pissed when he was pissed back at her. Grabbing hold of her hand, Jack led her into The Boardwalk without another word.

The restaurant wasn't huge. It had been completely transformed from the shabby beach gift store George Beckwith used to run. Shining, wide-planked hardwood floors, crisp white walls, copper light fixtures, and simple, modern seating gave the place a warm but uncluttered feel. Black-and-white photographs of Hartwell hung on the walls, which Jack thought was a nice touch.

A young hostess approached and told them they had a fifteen-minute wait. There was a small seating area near the front of the restaurant, and Jack led the silently fuming Em over to it. Sadie Thomas was already sitting there with some guy Jack didn't recognize. She gave them a breezy smile that Em completely ignored.

It could've been because she wasn't over Sadie talking trash about her or because she was too angry at Jack to notice her.

They sat in silence the entire wait, and Jack ignored the speculative looks Sadie kept throwing their way. Em shifted uncomfortably beside him and Jack used the situation to take hold of her hand and clasp it on his lap. She must've seen Sadie's eyes narrow on their clasped hands because Em didn't pull away.

Even when Jack turned her hand over and traced the backs of her rings with his fingertips before moving onto her palm. Her arm jerked a little and he looked at her.

"Tickles," she whispered.

He stared into her gorgeous eyes and found a smile in them, despite the tension between them. Jack wanted to rail at her for being so fucking stubborn. They were perfect together. It was easy and comfortable, but not so comfortable it wasn't still exciting as hell to be around her. They'd taken the prospect of parenthood together in stride with no drama.

They could talk about anything. They'd always been able to talk about anything.

And the sex.

Fuck.

The sex was out of this world.

He knew Em wasn't as experienced as he was, and if it wouldn't remind her that he'd slept around, he'd yell at her about how sex like the sex between them came around once in a blue moon.

The urge to say those words was strong, but thankfully, the hostess returned to lead them to their table before Jack said anything stupid. As they walked through the small restaurant, Jack noted the glass wall beyond the bar counter. It revealed exactly what was going on the kitchen. Only a chef who had nothing to hide would install a feature like that.

And the kitchen was state of the art. It gleamed like a brand-new penny. Jack's eyes danced over the people in chef whites, noting one of them, a big, tall guy, was watching them go by. Jack's gaze moved forward to watch Em walk ahead of him, her gorgeous ass swaying. She was wearing another clingy dress that made him think about doing very naughty things to her.

Aunt Amelia was right. You could not tell Em was pregnant from the back. But then she turned to take her seat and he took in the sight of her small bump pushing against the fabric of the stretchy black dress.

She was seriously killing him with these tight dresses.

Pregnant Emery did it for him like no woman had ever done it for him.

Emery caught the look in his eyes as they took their seats, and her cheeks turned a little pink. She read him like a book. "Stop it," she murmured under her breath before looking down at her menu.

"Emery?" a deep, masculine voice said before Jack could reply.

They looked up to find the chef who'd been watching them behind the glass now standing by their table, gazing down at Em with a smile on his face. The chef was tall, though not as tall as Jack, and broad-shouldered. Jack would go out on a limb and say he was also a *handsome* guy.

And he was smiling the whitest smile Jack had ever seen at Emery.

Like he knew her.

Like he liked what he knew.

What the hell?

"Sebastian." Emery grinned back at him in familiarity. "How are you? I'm so sorry it's taken me this long to come to your restaurant."

Sebastian.

Sebastian Mercier.

The guy who owned The Boardwalk.

How did he know Em?

Jack watched as the chef put his hand on the back of Emery's chair and leaned into her a little. He watched, and he didn't like what he was seeing.

"Well, you seem to have an excellent excuse." His dark eyes dipped to her belly. "Congratulations."

She blushed prettily.

Like how she blushed for Jack.

Jealousy roared through Jack before he could stop it. "I'm the father," he bit out.

They both looked at him in surprise, as if finally remembering he was there.

Sebastian caught the ominous look in Jack's eyes and pushed away from Emery. He held out a hand to Jack. "Sebastian Mercier. Head chef and owner of The Boardwalk."

Reluctantly, Jack shook his hand. "Jack Devlin."

The chef raised an eyebrow. "No relation to Ian Devlin?"

"Yeah, what of it?" he snapped.

"Jack," Emery reprimanded.

"Oh, I meant no offense," Sebastian said casually, as if unaffected by Jack's sharp tone. "Can I help you with the menu? Recommendations?"

Before Jack could politely tell him to fuck off back to his kitchen, a voice cut through the restaurant.

"Emery, Jack!"

Seeing Em's eyes widen to a spot over his shoulder, Jack turned to watch Cat Lawson hurrying through the restaurant, her cheeks flushed, her hair wild with the wind, her eyes filled with worry.

"Are you all right?" Sebastian stepped into her path as she approached. Jack was already rising from his seat.

Cat threw Sebastian a startled look, her eyes growing round as she took him in. She seemed struck mute for a second before she said, "And who are you, handsome?"

Sebastian grinned and opened his mouth to respond, but Jack cut him off. "Cat." He took hold of her arm. "What's wrong?"

Cat jerked her blue gaze from the chef to Jack. "I was

hurrying to my car and I saw you guys in here. Quick, we gotta go. Jess's water broke!"

Jesus Christ.

Jack immediately moved the three of them into action. They created a bit of hubbub getting out of the restaurant, Jack wanting to hurry but not wanting to hurry Em. As they strode quickly down the boards to Main Street, Em asked Cat where Joey was.

"Piano lessons. I was at Antonio's when Coop called. I'll pick up Joey first and meet you at the hospital." She hurried to the opposite side of the street where Jack's truck was parked. Stopping at her Ford, she yelled across, "Hey, Em!"

"Yeah?" Em called back as Jack yanked open the passenger side door for her.

"Who was the tall drink of sexy back there?"

Emery grinned. "Sebastian Mercier!"

"The chef?"

"Ladies," Jack growled impatiently.

"Yeah!" Em ignored him. "You like?"

"I'd have to be dead not to!" Cat called before she hopped into her car.

Jack rolled his eyes, even though he enjoyed hearing Em's laughter. Once he'd helped her up into the truck, he rounded it and slammed into the vehicle.

"You're jealous," Em observed as he pulled out onto the street.

"How do you know him?" Did they have a past Jack didn't know about?

"Iris invited him over for dinner a few months ago. She was trying to set him up with either Ivy or me. Clearly that didn't go well."

His hands tightened around the wheel. "Didn't it? He was flirting with you."

"No. He smiled at me."

"You blushed."

"I always blush when a good-looking man smiles at me. You know that."

"Guess I thought that was just for me," he muttered, feeling weirdly hurt.

She didn't reply.

That was beginning to sting like a motherfucker when she whispered, "Your smile does more than make me blush, Jack."

He liked that. A lot. He would've liked it a lot more if Emery hadn't sounded heartbroken when she said it.

COOPER CALLED him on the way to the hospital and seemed relieved to hear Jack was already on route. It soothed his agitation, knowing he and Coop were in such a good place again that he wanted Jack by his side for this big moment.

When they arrived, they discovered Bailey, Vaughn, and Dahlia already there.

"Cat's picking up Joey first," Emery explained to Bailey. "Where are Michael and Ivy?"

"Michael's working," Dahlia replied.

"And Ivy is having dinner with her parents and Jeff tonight." Bailey ran a nervous hand through her hair. "It's a big deal and I didn't want to interrupt that, but more than that, if I tell Ivy, she'll tell Iris and Iris will turn up and …" Bailey shrugged, looking uncertain. "Jess doesn't seem like she wants a lot of people crowding in."

"Good call," Jack assured her.

"Jack."

He glanced over his shoulder as Coop strode down the corridor, looking more than a little concerned. Jack hurried to meet him, and to his shock, Cooper embraced him, thumping his hand on his back.

"You okay?" Jack's voice was gruff.

Cooper's face strained with anxiety, his eyes alarmingly bright.

Fuck.

"They took her away."

"Away? What the hell for?" Jack could feel their friends surrounding them.

Cooper took a step to the side to address them all. He looked ready to throw up. "Baby went into distress. Something about late decelerations in his heart rate. Late returns to the baseline heart rate after a contraction. Long story short, Baby isn't getting enough oxygen. They took Jess into surgery."

"Emergency C-section?" Em stepped forward to grasp Coop's hand.

He squeezed it tight and nodded.

"She'll be okay, Jack," Emery assured him, sounding pretty certain. "It's the best thing for Jess and your boy."

Something about her reassurance seemed to break Coop, and he turned away from them, one hand covering his face while his other held on to Em's.

Emotion choked Jack, seeing his friend so worried and vulnerable. He placed a hand on Coop's shoulder and squeezed.

"Can I get you anything, bud?"

Coop shook his head. His voice hoarse, he replied, "Just don't go anywhere."

Jack's was equally so. "Never, Coop."

"Mr. Lawson."

Every single one of them jerked around to stare at the doctor smiling at Cooper.

Cooper shot out of the uncomfortable waiting room chair. "Are they okay?"

The doctor grinned. "Both mother and baby are in very good health. Would you like to meet your son?"

Relief and joy flooded Jack as he watched Cooper hang his head with probably the same feelings times five million. A sob burst out of Cat, who'd been sitting next to Coop for the last hour. It seemed to surprise the heck out of Dahlia and Em, but Jack had known Cat her entire life and knew she was a big softie under that cool-as-cucumber facade.

Joey moved from Em (his second-favorite person in the world) to go to his mom.

"I'll be back," Coop threw over his shoulder as he followed the doctor.

A hand slipped into Jack's and he turned to look at Em, who'd moved to the seat beside him. She smiled, her eyes bright with happiness.

And Jack was done.

He was done with all the bullshit games, trying to stealth seduce the woman he loved into agreeing to make what was between them real and permanent. When Emery gave birth to their baby, Jack wanted to kiss her breathless in gratitude for giving him the best gift in the world.

He wanted to do that knowing they were going home together with their child.

Raising their child together in the same house, day in, day out.

Till death do they part.

39

JACK

Light burst into the room, waking Jack at the crack of dawn. He'd forgotten to shut the curtains when he brought Em back to her beach house the night before. To his relief, Em didn't ask him to leave. She let him take her upstairs, help her undress, and she even let him hold her while she fell asleep, exhausted by the day's events.

They'd been allowed to go in twos to see Jess and the baby.

Cooper had a son.

It was surreal.

But fucking great seeing how happy it made his friend.

Jess and Cooper had named their boy Tyler Joseph Lawson.

Apparently, the umbilical cord had wrapped around Tyler's neck, causing oxygen deprivation. When Cooper told them that, Jack had pulled Em so tight into his side, he was probably gripping her too hard. But that shit was terrifying. The thought of it happening to their little one scared the hell out of Jack.

As for Tyler's size, he was long and big at eight pounds and eight ounces. No wonder Jess had been uncomfortable for most of the pregnancy.

Seeing how tired Jess was, they'd excused themselves and

promised they'd be back in the morning to visit since Jess would have to stay until the doc said she was okay to be discharged.

An exhausted Emery hadn't said much in the truck on the way home, and Jack had known that it wasn't the right time to bring up the status of their relationship.

Turning his head on the pillow, every part of him ached as he took in the sight of Emery lying beside him. God, he wanted this for the rest of his life. Waking up to her.

The thought of losing it ... it was worse than any grief Jack had ever experienced in his life.

Em had kicked the duvet off during the night. She'd been getting especially hot in her sleep lately. That's why he'd helped her into a cami-and-short set for bed, despite the cool fall temperatures.

The cami had risen up Em's stomach, revealing the cute little baby bump. Unable to resist, Jack reached out and smoothed his hands over it. Sometimes when he touched the bump, he felt like a kid who'd just been told Santa was real. It was awesome, magical, that there was a baby, a little person, growing inside Emery. A little person made up of him and her.

Jack hoped their kid had Em's eyes. It would be a dying shame if Em didn't pass on such beauty to her kids.

Kids.

Jack wanted more than one.

And he wanted them with Em.

Because if he didn't have them with her, he wasn't having them at all.

Suddenly her hand, bare of the silver rings he'd helped her remove last night, covered his. His gaze moved from her belly to her face. She was awake, a soft, sweet look on her face.

"Morning."

"Morning, sunrise," he whispered.

At his words, Emery got this unbelievably beautiful, tender look in her eyes. A look she couldn't stop, couldn't hide.

A look that said she loved him.

And it caused Jack to blurt out, "I'm so goddamn in love with you, Emery Saunders."

Her eyes widened, any sleepiness disappearing.

Then she sat up, fast, panicked.

Jack sat up too, his heart beating a mile a minute. "I'm in love with you," he repeated, now that it was out there. "I've been in love with you for years."

Emery shook her head, her cheeks pale. "No."

That one word was like taking a fucking bullet. "No?" Jack pushed off the duvet and dove out of bed. He stood over her. "What the hell does that mean?"

She stared up at him, aghast.

No.

She was scared.

Emery was looking at him as if petrified.

"Why?" Jack shook his head, not understanding. "You know we're great together. Are you holding back to punish me?"

"No." Em slipped out of bed so the sizable piece of furniture acted as an obstacle between them. "But we had an agreement. You promised that sex would change nothing."

"An agreement we both knew was bullshit."

"Jack, you can't love me," she snapped.

"Well, tough shit, because I do." He rounded the bed and scowled as she backed away from him. Jack stopped moving. He held up his hands like he was dealing with a frightened animal. And he got it. He got from everything she'd told him that Emery was terrified to love anyone ever again. But she was already doing it. With her girls. With Iris. With Joey. With the baby in her belly. And whether she wanted to admit it, with Jack.

"I know you're scared. I know people who were supposed to love you didn't treat you the way you deserved. And I know I've made my mistakes. But you know me, Em. You *know* me. We've known each other from the moment our eyes met across Cooper's Bar nine years ago."

He held her gaze, begging her silently to tell him that she loved him too.

Instead, those gorgeous eyes of hers filled with tears and she whispered, "I'm sorry, Jack."

Agony tightened its awful grip around his chest, like a hot, burning demon with vicious claws that wouldn't let go. Unable to bear looking at her, Jack dressed quickly and got the hell away from her before he said something he'd later regret.

40

EMERY

It was a good thing Ivy had agreed to drive.

We would never have gotten to Balance in Millton otherwise. In fact, it was a surprise to me that the kids were able to take my mind off the horribleness of the last week.

"Does it hurt?" Angeline, a seven-year-old girl whose mother was receiving cancer treatment, asked as she stared at my belly. I'd been answering her questions about my pregnancy for the last five minutes.

I shook my head, wearing a slight smile. "No."

"Do you feel it moving?"

"Sometimes I feel like there are bubbles in my belly, but I won't feel Baby really move for maybe another few weeks."

"How did it get in there?"

Oh crap.

"Emery!" Ivy called my name far louder than necessary since she was right next to me. "Bring Angeline over. Casey here needs a card-playing partner."

I knew she was trying to save me from the awkward questions. "Cards? You're teaching Casey to play cards?"

Casey was a rambunctious eight-year-old who'd had childhood leukemia. He was in remission, but his parents felt he should be around kids who had either gone through the same or had family members who had. His near-death experience had made him a little more mature than other kids his age, and they were afraid he was struggling to make friends he could connect with.

"Poker, to be exact," Casey replied.

I made a face at Ivy who smiled sheepishly.

When I told her about my volunteer days at Balance, she'd expressed an interest in volunteering with me. I wasn't sure, however, the parents would be happy about us turning their kids into card sharks.

Still, I could forgive her.

Because on the way here, she'd helped me come to a realization that a supposedly smart woman like me should've reached long ago.

"So, you were quiet at Jess's yesterday," Ivy had said as soon as I got in her car that morning.

Jess was out of the hospital, home and recovering from her C-section. Tyler, so far, was turning out to be an angel baby who slept most of the time, and when he was awake, he was quiet and adorable. Yesterday had been the first day Cooper left the house for the bar, knowing all us girls were there to watch Jess. Jess complained that he was hovering.

We told her what we'd witnessed at the hospital—Cooper's obvious emotion and fear when she was rushed in for the C-section. Jess's eyes brightened and she murmured something about letting him hover after all.

"Was I?" I replied to Ivy's leading question.

I knew I'd been quiet.

I was quiet because Jack Devlin had told me he loved me. That he'd loved me for years. And instead of euphoria, I'd felt paralyzed by fear. Jack had stormed out, and other than clipped, short texts checking in about my well-being, I hadn't seen or heard from him since.

A week of no Jack.

It was miserable.

"How are things going with you and Jeff?" I asked, trying to distract her.

Ivy threw me a smug smile. "Fantastically."

"In all the Jess, Cooper, Tyler excitement, I never asked how dinner went with your parents?"

"Oh, Mom was her typical embarrassing self, asking Jeff questions about marriage and kids and all those scary, forever topics that we have not broached."

I groaned on her behalf. "I'm sorry."

"It's fine. Jeff has a great sense of humor. We laughed about it afterward."

"So, you're still taking it slow?"

Ivy gave a little huff of laughter. "Trying. I know he's trying to."

"What does that mean?"

"It means he's intense. Not in a bad way," Ivy hurried to reassure me. "I know the signs for intense in a bad way. I just mean we're trying to go slow, but we enjoy being around each other. We really, really love sex with one another. And we can talk, Em. We really talk about stuff. Things I never thought I'd ever be able to talk about with a man."

"That's great, Ivy."

"Yeah. I just hope we're not rushing in too fast. I can't seem to help it with him." She grinned, her smile all the more beautiful for how happy she looked. "It's like having a crush on a really hot famous guy, meeting him, having him miraculously crush on you back, and even more miraculously turn out to be the best guy ever."

It made me so giddy for her. And giddy for him. He deserved

someone great to feel that way about him. "I'm glad for you both."

"Don't tell anyone I said all this to you. I don't want to jinx it."

"I won't," I promised.

"So, you and Jack?" She dove right in.

After all Ivy had confessed to me, I had to trust her. She deserved trust to be reciprocated. "We've been having sex."

"Oh. Okay."

"A lot of sex. It was supposed to be no strings attached."

"Yes, because that kind of arrangement makes total sense with the man whose baby you're carrying."

I ignored her sarcasm. "He told me he loved me. The morning after Tyler was born. And I didn't say it back. We haven't spoken since."

"Why didn't you say it back?"

The million-dollar question. I'd had time to think on it this past week. "Because … You know my past, Ivy. You know what's happened when I dared to love someone. I survived all that. I survived my parents' lack of love, for goodness' sake. I survived Tripp. But Jack." I looked at her, emotion welling inside of me. "Jack has been and always will be the person I want most in the world. And I already know what it feels like to be hurt by him. If I allow myself to admit to him … to start an actual relationship and then he turns around and stops loving me … How do I survive that? And I don't just have me to think about anymore. I have my baby. I can't fall apart over a broken heart when I have a child I'm responsible for."

"Why would Jack stop loving you?" she asked.

"Because people stop loving each other all the time."

"Okay. Then let me pose another question. Say you do push Jack away because you're terrified of being hurt. It doesn't change the fact that you love him. And then he eventually settles for some other woman since he can't have you. You'll have to drop off your kid to Jack and this other woman who will help raise your kid. With Jack. How does that make you feel?"

Anytime I imagined that hypothetical, my chest burned like it was on fire from the inside. "Heartbroken," I whispered.

"So, let's look at the math. You tell Jack you love him, you create a real family together, and somewhere down the years, there might be a 0.1 percent chance that Jack falls out of love with you and you get your heart broken. Or … you let Jack go now. He meets someone else. There is a 100 percent chance it will break your heart. I don't know about you, but I much prefer the percentage of the former."

"Ivy, 0.1 percent is being generous."

She threw me a wry smile. "Em, do you know what we've all been talking about behind your back for weeks?"

I stiffened. "What?"

"You and Jack. And how it makes our stomachs flutter just witnessing the way he watches you." Ivy fanned herself comically. "Seriously, Em. If I thought for one second Jeff was looking at me like that, I'd never let him out of bed. Even Bailey, who has Vaughn treating her to his smoldering intensity all the time, said no guy she's ever met has ever quite looked at a woman the way Jack looks at you."

I gaped at her, my heart racing. "How does he look at me?"

She gave me a quick, somewhat misty-eyed smile. "Like he's just waiting to jump in front of a moving car for you. Or take a bullet to protect you. Like he couldn't live without you."

Tears brightened my own eyes. "Ivy."

"Like you're the reason he exists. It's intense, Em. But it's a good intense. I would never say this if I didn't mean it … But you should tell Jack you love him and give it a shot. So, there's a tiny, tiny chance it doesn't work out between you. Is that slight chance worth losing out on being with a guy who looks at you with such longing, it makes my heart hurt?"

I sucked in a deep, shaky breath.

And I knew she was right.

I knew if I let Jack slip away, I'd regret it for the rest of my life.

"Goddammit," I huffed. "Now I really just want to find Jack."

"Take a minute, breathe," Ivy advised. "We'll go to the group. You can get your head together and think about what you want to say to him when we get back into town."

So that was the plan.

And I was a jittery, distracted mess as we hung out with the kids.

Leaving Ivy to teach Casey solitaire, which was a much less controversial alternative to poker, I was walking across the room to where the kids were playing a video game when I felt a painful squeezing sensation in my belly. It was like a period cramp.

Even though my heart sped up at the feeling, I tried to shake it. But when I took another step, I experienced another painful squeeze.

Concern made me flush hot from head to toe. Excusing myself, I hurried to the restroom and locked myself inside a stall. My mind raced to the worst-possible reason for the cramps, and I unbuttoned my jeans.

There on my underwear was my worst fear. A few spots of blood.

Terror ricocheted through me at the same time another cramp did, and I let out a little whimper.

"Em?" Ivy's voice rang out through the room, and I realized she'd followed me. "Em, are you okay?"

My entire body shaking, I pulled up my panties and jeans and hurried out of the stall.

One look at my face made Ivy pale. "What's wrong?"

"We need to go to the hospital."

41

EMERY

I could still hear Ivy's voice as she called Jack. She'd called him as we rushed out of Balance. Her words echoed around in my head.

"Jack, you need to get to Hartwell General. I'm taking Em there now. She's cramping ... and bleeding ... I know"—her voice broke a little—"but I've got her, okay?"

I wondered what he'd said.

But I didn't ask.

I was too busy being petrified out of my mind about losing our baby.

Ivy must've broken every speed limit to get us to Hartwell. She kept cool and calm when we arrived at the hospital, her voice authoritative as she explained to the emergency room nurse what was wrong.

They took me into a private room right away. Five minutes later, Dr. Britt arrived. I remembered answering her questions as if on autopilot. She examined me. Ran tests. But it was like I was outside of myself. Fear had caused some kind of dissociation. Fear that not only would I lose this baby ... but in losing my baby, I'd also lose my Jack.

Before I ever got the chance to have him.

"Em, your heart rate is high. I need you to calm down."

She'd just finished saying those words when Jack appeared, striding through the door. The sight of him was like a rubber band snapping at my nose. I felt present again. No less fearful, but present.

He reached my side, grabbing my hand between his. "Sunrise."

"You're here," I whispered, relief flooding me to feel his firm hand around mine.

"I always will be," he vowed, his voice gruff.

"Good timing, Dad," Dr. Britt said with a smile on her face. "The baby is fine. Heart rate is normal."

"But—"

"The bleeding was merely spotting. And the cramping happens sometimes for no nefarious reason. I'll have you monitor things and come back in if you have any heavier bleeding, but I'm not concerned. And I don't want you to be."

The terror that had been building inside me unleashed in a fit of sobs.

Jack's arms wrapped around me, the bed depressing as he slid onto it so he could hold me as close as possible. "Shh, sunrise, you're killing me," he said hoarsely. "Please, please, Em, you're okay. We're all okay."

"I'll give you a moment," I heard Dr. Britt say.

We were all okay. Jack kept whispering it over and over until it began to sink in.

I needed to tell him. I needed to tell him before it was too late.

"Jack." I pulled my face out of his throat and clasped his cheeks in mine, feeling the prickle of his stubble tickle my palms.

His blue-gray eyes were bright with concern and love, and so much more.

I saw it.

I saw what Ivy was talking about.

God, Jack Devlin adored me.

And I adored him right back. "I wanted to see you this morning." I moved my hands to his throat and down his shirt, curling my fingers in tight. I was afraid he'd disappear. Disappear before I had the chance to tell him. "Jack, I love you too. I love you so much more than I ever thought I could love anyone."

His arms tightened around me, hope beaming through his concern. "Em, don't say it just because we got a scare this morning."

"It's not that." My fingers curled around his collar, pulling him to me so his mouth almost touched mine. "Ivy asked me how I felt about the idea of you with someone else, raising our child with some faceless woman," I spat out the word *woman* and saw Jack's lips twitch with amusement. "I wanted to throat punch her. The hypothetical woman. Not Ivy."

Now he was just flat-out smiling. "This hypothetical woman is in a lot of danger from you."

"I'm not joking, Jack. I'm sorry I've hurt you." My face crumpled as the tears came again. "I'm such a coward," I sobbed. "I'm so sorry."

"Hey, hey." He lifted my chin. "You are not a coward."

"I am. I thought I was going to lose our baby and then I'd lose you too."

Disbelief filled Jack's expression. "Let me make one thing clear. No matter what happens, there is nothing in this world that could tear me away from you. God, Emery, don't you know by now that I fucking *live* for you? I don't care what that says about me. It's how I feel. You make living worthwhile and if it had taken me ten, thirty, or fifty fucking years to convince you to give me a shot, then that's how long I would've waited. There will never be another woman for me. Never. It wouldn't be fair to any woman to share my life with them when I belong so completely to you."

Fresh tears fell down my cheeks, but these were good ones. Happy ones. Brave ones. "I've never loved anyone like I love you. I've been in love with you for nine years," I admitted, and he reacted by holding me impossibly tight. "There's no one else for me either, Jack. There never will be."

A wide, ecstatic, sexy-as-hell smile spread across Jack's face. "So, we're doing this? We're going to be a real family?"

His joy and excitement were infectious. "Yes," I promised.

"About damn time!" I heard Ivy shout from outside the doors.

I laughed and Jack cupped my face in his hand, watching me. "God, I hope our kid gets your eyes and your laugh."

I didn't get a chance to reply.

Jack was too busy kissing me.

A deep, tender kiss that tasted like a vow.

EPILOGUE

EMERY

Waking my husband up by making love to him was one of my favorite things in the world. And considering I'd woken up an hour before our alarm was set to go off, I took advantage of this fortuitous situation.

While I'd finally relinquished control on the bookstore café and hired a full-time employee to help me out, Jack's workload had only increased. Going into business with Cooper and taking over Germaine's, a club on Main Street that had gone up for sale six months ago, meant he and Jack were buried with work. They'd decided the club needed updating and had closed it for renovations. Between their other businesses, it meant neither Jess nor I had seen our husbands much lately.

We got it.

We supported them.

But I missed Jack.

I shared this in the kisses I trailed across his chest. I licked at his nipple and felt him stir with a slight groan. Slipping my hand inside his pajama bottoms, I took a hold of him and he hardened as I kissed my way down his abs.

"Sunrise," he growled.

I looked up at him and saw the sleep in his eyes obliterated by heat.

"Get up here."

I did as I was told. But first, I yanked his pajama bottoms down far enough for access. Then I climbed over him.

I was already naked.

Straddling Jack, I pressed my breasts to him, undulating as our lips met. He slid his hand into my hair, fisting it to hold me to him as he kissed me hungrily. Feeling him ready—I'd been ready since I woke up and started ogling him—I shifted my hips until he was right where I wanted him and drove down.

As Jack entered my body, we both moaned, breaking the kiss.

I pressed my hands to his chest, gazing lovingly, hotly into his eyes as I rode him.

Jack gripped my hips, watching me with deep, male satisfaction. Our pants were deliberately restrained, my cries choked in my throat as the tension coiled tight and low in my belly.

"Em," Jack groaned, his hands moving to my ass. "Fuck."

"Shh," I reminded him.

In answer he sat up, changing the angle of his thrusts and catching my pleasured cry in his mouth. Wrapping my arms around his shoulders as he pulled me tight to him, kissing me hard, deep, our mouths fighting to stay together as I rode him, I moaned helplessly against him.

I missed being able to scream his name as I came, and I knew he missed it too.

His hand moved between us, his thumb pushing down on my clit. "I'm close, sunrise. I need you with me."

He rolled his thumb on the bundle of nerves between my legs and I slammed my mouth down on his so he could swallow the sound of my climax. Then I was taking his grunts of release. He throbbed inside me as my pulsing sex wrung him dry.

"Fuck," he muttered, pressing kisses down my chin, my

throat. I arched my neck, sighing blissfully as he captured a taut nipple in his mouth and sucked.

"Jack ..." I undulated against him again, my fingers curling in his hair at the nape of his neck. "Baby—"

"Daddy!"

Jack released my nipple and pressed his forehead to my chest.

"Mommy!"

"I'll go," I whispered.

Jack lifted his head. "It's okay." He gave me a squeeze.

"No, you don't have to get up for another half hour. Sleep." I gently pressed him back to the mattress as I lifted off him.

His jaw clenched and he grunted as he lost me. "Fuck, I miss my sunrise."

"I'm right here." I grinned at him as I rolled out of bed.

I could feel his eyes on my ass as I moved across the room to where I'd thrown my nightie.

"You know what I mean, Em," he murmured.

Turning around, I pulled on my robe just as our daughter yelled for me again. We could tell by her tone it was not urgent, she was not hurt. She was just ready to get up and face the day.

"You're launching a business. It takes time."

"It's not worth losing time with my two favorite girls. That's the first time we've made love in three weeks."

I knew that.

I was counting.

"We'll talk about this later." I threw him a reassuring smile and hurried out of the bedroom.

When we were deciding about where we would raise our kid, we'd decided on the beach house, even though Jack's house in South Hartwell was larger. I told Jack to continue with the sale, and while he was at it, sell his place in North Hartwell too.

Despite only having three bedrooms, the beach house was in the perfect location.

Thankfully, it also had land on either side of it because we would need to build an addition. And I didn't want to move.

Hurrying down the hall, I pushed into Tabitha's room. Our daughter was turning four in three months' time. However, first, her archenemy, Tyler Joseph Lawson, was turning four today.

We had such high hopes that those two would hit it off.

But they fought like cats and dogs and had done this since they could walk.

The problem was they were both too bossy for their own good.

It seemed my child had inherited her grandmother's sass.

Despite our differences, it made me smile to think of my grandmother looking down on us and feeling smug that she'd passed along some of her traits to her great-granddaughter.

Tabby was sitting on the floor of the bedroom her father had worked with painstaking attention to detail to put together. He'd built custom shelving for all her books and toys. Even her bed was custom built by Jack and his old boss Ray. It had storage underneath for more toys. An old-fashioned armoire that Jack had sanded down and repainted stood in the corner, filled with more clothes than any kid needed, as was the matching dresser.

Surrounding our daughter on the carpeted floor were her cuddly toys and dolls.

"We're having breakfast," she announced in her cute, high-pitched voice as she gestured to her toy companions. "And I got hungry for real."

My lips twitched. "Is that so?"

She gave me a look that said "well, yeah" that reminded me a lot of her father. Tabby was a wonderful mix of us both—she was a miniature version of me in looks but had her father's mannerisms and sense of humor.

And his appetite.

"C'mon, then." I reached down, hooked her under the arms, and lifted Tabby. It amazed me how one day she was this tiny little thing, and now I had toned upper arms and shoulders from carting her around everywhere. She wrapped her little legs as far as she could around me and clung to my neck.

Burying her face in my throat, she kissed me and whispered, "Morning, Mommy."

Love, the kind of love I didn't even know I was capable of or existed in this world, filled me. I loved Jack. I knew without shame in admitting it that I'd lose something essential to my very existence if I lost him. But the love I had for our daughter was so mammoth, so consuming, there were no words for it. Or the way it filled my entire being to the point it was painful. Like I was incapable of containing the size of it. I lived in this constant and indescribable place of pure joy that she existed and pure terror that something might one day harm her.

I knew Jack felt the same way because we'd spoken about it since the moment she'd entered this world.

"Morning, baby," I replied as I carried her downstairs. "What do you want for breakfast?"

Thus began the usual twenty-minute conversation in which Tabby couldn't make up her mind.

We'd finally decided on blueberry pancakes when Jack strode into the room. He'd thrown on a T-shirt with his pajama bottoms, but he still had sex hair. I shivered, wishing we'd had time for more.

"Morning, Daddy!" Tabby yelled from her seat at the table. She loved sitting with the grown-ups, so we'd put a booster seat on one of the dining room chairs for her.

Jack grinned and lifted her into his arms for a cuddle and a kiss. "Is that how you're wearing your hair for Ty's party?" he teased her.

Her white-blond hair was a tangled cloud of silk around her face.

She wrinkled her nose. "No!"

Jack chuckled. "Why not? It's cute."

"Do I have to go?" Tabby pouted.

Seriously. Those kids. Jack and I shared a look before he gave Tabby a squeeze and returned her to her chair. "Tyler's important to us. To you too. Even if you don't get along all the time. Would you want him to miss your birthday?"

"Uh ... yeah."

She said it like she was forty, forcing me to choke back my laughter.

Poor Jack struggled not to laugh too. "Baby girl, that's not nice. It's Ty-Ty. We love Ty."

"I told him I didn't want to give him a present for his birfday and he told me"—Tabby turned in her seat to aim the conversation at me too—"he told me that he's gonna wrap Louis's dog poop up and give it to me for my birfday."

Wow. Their mini war was getting colorful.

"I told him," she said, panting now, her voice getting louder, "I told him, I told him that he's stupid because I would do the same but wouldn't tell him! He ruined poop surprise!" She gesticulated her exasperation with a pointed outstretching of her arms.

"As true as that is, we don't call people stupid." Jack stood from his haunches and ruffled her hair before he wandered into the kitchen toward me.

He was wearing a sexy, lazy smirk that widened when we heard Tabby mutter, "Then stupid people shouldn't be stupid if they don't wanna be called stupid."

I rolled my eyes as Jack wrapped his arms around me, pulling me away from the pancakes. "She has a point," he muttered against my mouth before he took it in a very, very nice good-morning kiss.

"Ugh." Tabby's voice cut through it.

I laughed against Jack's mouth and pulled away. "I think it's safe to say she didn't inherit my romantic nature."

My husband chuckled before pressing a sweet kiss to my nose. He released me and then gently nudged me toward the table. "Go, I'll finish up." He moved to the pancake that was seconds from burning and flipped it expertly.

I grumbled under my breath because I couldn't do the flippy thing but made my way over to Tabby to explain what a stalemate was and why she needed to enact one with Tyler today.

"I STILL THINK they'll grow up and fall in love," Bailey offered.

Jess and I cut her a disbelieving look before returning our attention to our kids.

Tyler's birthday party was underway in Jess and Cooper's substantial backyard. They'd hired a magician dressed as Iron Man. Jess and Cooper had spoken to Tyler about being on his best behavior with Tabby, and there had been no fights when the kids congregated around the performer.

They were, however, wearing grumpy faces and shooting each other death stares now and then.

"I'm telling you," Bailey insisted. "They're like a kid version of me and Vaughn when we first met."

"We'll see," I muttered uncertainly. I still had that worrying poop-gift story on my mind.

"Where *is* Vaughn?" Ivy asked, her eyes searching the backyard.

"He and Michael are putting Lily and Jenna down for a nap." She jerked her head to the house.

Lillian Tremaine, or Lily, was Bailey and Vaughn's thirteen-month-old daughter. They named her after Vaughn's beloved mom who died when he was young. Jenna was Dahlia and

Michael's sixteen-month-old daughter. For now, we were surrounded by girls.

The men didn't seem to mind.

They were all a bunch of doting, protective fathers.

"Mimosa, ladies." Dahlia crossed the yard to where we huddled in the shade. In her hands was a tray of champagne flutes filled with orange juice and champagne.

Bailey took two, passing one to Jess who waved it off. Her gaze was firmly trained on the kids and the magician. All the kids' parents were around, so it wasn't like we didn't have an eye on things, but that was Jess. And she was excellent at multi-tasking, which meant she could still enjoy a conversation with us while keeping her eyes on the kids.

Ivy reached for a glass, her simple engagement ring and wedding band flashing in the sunlight.

"Em." Dahlia held a glass out to me.

I waved it off. "Too early in the day for me." My eyes moved across the yard, sensing someone's attention on me.

Jack.

He was standing with Cooper, but he was looking at me.

His eyes narrowed in thought.

I gave him a flirty smile, and he grinned.

"I miss Coop," Jess abruptly announced, her eyes still on Tyler and the kids.

"How so?" Bailey frowned.

Jess flicked a look at me. "I'm sure Em knows. I've barely seen Cooper for the last month."

"Yeah," I agreed. "But we knew launching a business would take up a lot of time."

"We did. And I support them. But if I don't get my husband back soon, I won't be happy."

"Have you spoken to him about it?" Ivy frowned.

"Do you hassle Jeff for working long hours?" Jess asked pointedly.

"No. I knew what I was getting into when I married him."

"Exactly. You support your spouses in all their endeavors," she grumbled.

I chuckled at her surliness.

That chuckle was abruptly halted by, "I'm pregnant again. I'm thirty-nine. I had complications with my last pregnancy, and Cooper and I discussed it. Tyler was supposed to be an only child." Jess cut us a worried look. "He doesn't know. I'm scared he'll be mad. And I need him."

"Oh my goodness, Jess, you need to tell him." Bailey squeezed her shoulder. "And congratulations."

We all went to congratulate her, but she hushed us. "He knows something's up. He's mad at me for being distant. We had a huge fight this morning in bed." She buried her face in her hands.

I wanted to speak.

I wanted to offer reassurances.

But I could not believe what I was hearing.

All I could think was ... how weirdly in sync we were.

My heart rate increased.

"Uh, Jess ..." Ivy tried to warn.

However, having seen his wife looking visibly distressed, Cooper was marching determinedly across the yard in our direction with Jack at his back.

"Ladies," Coop said as Jess's head snapped up at his voice, "can you watch the kids for a minute?"

"Of course."

"Sure."

"Absolutely."

Cooper took hold of Jess's hand, pulling her out of the lounger. They disappeared into the house, hand in hand.

"Where's Cat?" Bailey asked, trying to defuse the sudden tension and worry among us.

"Late." Dahlia rolled her eyes. "Jess said Cat's been cagey about the party ever since she heard Seb got an invitation."

Seb, as in Sebastian.

"He's not here either," I observed.

"When are those two going to pull their heads out of their asses?" Bailey muttered dryly.

"Sometimes it takes time," I replied, smiling at Jack. "It took us nine years."

"Oh God, I can't take a nine-year Cat-and-Seb drama. Uh-uh, no way." Bailey sipped at her mimosa. "I may have to intervene."

"You have a child," Dahlia reminded her. "A child who needs her mother to be alive. And if you intervene, Cat Lawson will kill you. You're scrappy. But she's tougher."

"Truth," Ivy muttered.

"Where's Jeff?" I asked my friend before Bailey could act on the glare she was shooting Dahlia, who only made matters worse by laughing into her drink.

"Working. He'll be here after the kids' party for the barbecue."

"I could take Cat," Bailey huffed.

"Take me where?"

We turned to see Cat coming down the steps with a birthday gift in hand. Joey was noticeably absent. He was a teenager now, one who looked like a miniature Cooper, and the kind of teenager who could befriend anyone. He hung around with kids from all different cliques, which meant he was always on the go doing something.

Or dating someone.

Once I married Jack, Joey moved on to girls his own age.

"Nowhere," Bailey answered quickly.

"Give me a glass of that," Cat huffed, gesturing to the mimosas. "My brother depresses the crap out of me. It's his kid's fourth birthday party, and he and his wife can't keep their hands off each other long enough for even that."

My lips twitched at her mock-disgusted glower.

"They're going at it in the bathroom." Her smirk turned wicked. "That is, they *were* going at each other. Until I hammered on the door and told them I was calling the cops for public indecency."

We chuckled, but my laughter died when I saw Cat case the backyard as if she were searching for someone.

"He's not here," I told her.

She shrugged. "Who isn't?"

Letting her have it her way, I stayed silent as she strode across the yard to her nephew.

"I'm telling you, it'll be another nine years unless I intervene," Bailey muttered.

"Intervene in what?" Vaughn's voice called to us.

We turned to see him and Michael striding down the steps toward us, baby girls in their arms.

"I thought they were napping?" Bailey said as she reached for Lily.

He held his daughter close. "I've got her," he assured her.

Dahlia reached up for Michael's free hand. Jenna was curled in his other arm, her head resting sleepily on his shoulder.

"Uh … I don't think Coop and Jess knew we were in the house." Vaughn's lips twitched. "We thought it best to give them some privacy."

"Jess is pregnant," Bailey explained.

"We heard. There was some yelling … but ultimately Coop seems to be taking the news well," Michael murmured.

"I don't know why," Dahlia said. "Her pregnancy was the worst."

We shot her reproving looks and she glared at us. "Uh, please, like you all weren't scared shitless of her when she was pregnant the first time."

We grumbled. But it was true.

"Another baby." Ivy grimaced. "This is just going to make Jeff so broody."

"I thought you wanted kids?" Bails frowned in confusion.

"I do. And I know we should start soon." She shrugged. "But I'm enjoying my time alone with the sheriff. I quite like being able to have sex with him whenever I damn well please."

Jack and I shared a look, and I knew we were both thinking about this morning and the fact that it was the first time we'd had sex in three weeks. That wasn't a huge amount of time in the grand scheme of things, but it was unusual for us.

He'd just been so exhausted lately.

And … well … I had a lot on my mind.

A little while later, Cooper and Jess returned to the backyard looking disheveled and pleased with themselves. They explained they wanted to keep the pregnancy just between us so as not to take away from Tyler's big day. So we didn't make an enormous deal out of congratulating them, but I was over the moon for my friend. And I really, really hoped her second pregnancy was easier than the first.

"Can we talk?" Jack whispered in my ear, his hand closing around my wrist.

Hearing the seriousness in his tone, I nodded. We excused ourselves, heading into the house. Jack led me upstairs to Tyler's room and closed the door behind us.

"What's going on?" I asked.

He rested his hands on his hips, his expression unreadable. "When were you planning on telling me?"

I blinked in confusion. "About Jess?"

"No." His expression softened. "No, sunrise, about you."

The light of knowledge in his eyes caught me completely off guard. "How do you know?"

"I enjoy having sex with my wife, so I tend to keep track of your period. And then I saw you waving off that mimosa …"

Before I could stop it, a smile pushed at my lips. Excitement unfurled in my belly. "I haven't been to see Jess yet, but I took two tests. Both positive."

The word 'positive' was barely out of my mouth before I was in my husband's arms as he kissed the life out of me. His big hands went to my stomach as we kissed. Then he abruptly broke away. "Me and Cooper need to figure out a way to do business without losing so much time with our families."

"Yes," I agreed.

"But right now, we're going to ask our friends to watch Tabby so I can take you home and celebrate our fan-fucking-tastic news in bed."

My thighs quivered at the mere thought. "Really? Can we do that?"

"Fuck yeah. We'll tell them why."

"Should we do that?"

"They're going to know soon enough."

Jack grabbed my hand and hurried me out of the bedroom and downstairs. Thankfully, our closest friends were still huddled, although now Cooper was holding baby Lily.

Ivy took one look at our faces and frowned. "What's going on?"

My eyes flew to Jess's. "Well … I just told Jack my news. It looks like you and I will be pregnancy buddies again." I said this a little warily because I didn't want to steal the spotlight and I also remembered how good I'd had it with my pregnancy with Tabby compared to Jess's with Tyler.

Jess barely contained her squeal as our friends tried to lower their voices and their surprise. "I can't believe this."

"I know!" I jerked my thumb between Coop and Jack. "It's like these two can't do anything if it's not together."

The two best buddies grimaced at my crack while Vaughn and Michael ribbed them.

"Enough," Jack said, waving them off. "You guys mind watching Tabby for an hour?"

Every single one of them got a knowing gleam in their eyes.

"Go." Cooper sighed. "At least one of us should get a shot at something better than a quickie in the bathroom."

Jess smacked his arm while I blushed beetroot. This only made Jack give a bark of laughter. I was about to rescind my capitulation to copulate when he abruptly took hold of my hand and hauled me around the side yard to the exit.

"Tabby?" I hissed at him in semi-exasperation as I heard our friends laughing behind us.

"She won't even notice we're gone, Em."

This was probably true.

"An hour," I reminded him as he helped me into his truck.

Jack flashed me that wicked, wicked smile of his that had gotten me knocked up again in the first place.

WE WERE LONGER THAN AN HOUR.

In fact, Jack took his sweet time making love to me for a blissful two hours that afternoon.

Afterward, we returned to the party to discover Tabby had not noticed we were gone because the détente between her and Tyler had ended, and she was wrapped up in their mini war. Jess assured me Ty started it by telling Tabby her dress was ugly and he didn't want her at the party.

Unlike other little girls who might cry at this, Tabby had told him "he could stick his party where the sun didn't shine."

I blamed Jack for that one.

Jess said it was hard to reprimand her when most of the adults were choking on their laughter.

As the other kids went home, leaving only the Lawsons' closest friends at the barbecue, Ty and Tabby settled down once they had the focus of Iris and Ira. The Greens might not have been blood, but they were definitely doting grandparents to our kids.

It was a splendid night.

Tabby fell asleep in the car, and I took pleasure in watching Jack carry her up to her bed. She was so small in his arms. The sight of them together always made my chest ache with love.

I was in our bedroom undressing when Jack strolled in and purposefully shut the bedroom door. There was a scorching tenderness in his eyes that I knew well.

I waited as he came to me and rested my hands on his chest. He cupped my face in his warm, roughened palms. "You've given me everything, sunrise."

"The feeling is mutual, sweetheart."

"Do you know how much I love you?" he asked, his voice hoarse, his gaze searching my face for the answer he already knew.

"I do." I looked up at him with all the love and belief I had inside of me. "It's the truest thing I've ever known."

ACKNOWLEDGMENTS

Hart's Boardwalk readers, thank you so much for your amazing support and love for this series. Without it, the third and fourth novel in this world might never have happened. Thankfully they did because I know many of my HB fans have waited for Jack and Emery's story since book two. Jack has been one of my favorite characters from the very beginning because I knew he was a true hero behind the façade of anti-hero. It was so much fun to finally reveal all, including his secret relationship with Emery. I hope their love story was everything you wanted it to be.

For the most part writing is a solitary endeavor but publishing most certainly is not. I have to thank my wonderful editor Jennifer Sommersby Young for always, *always* being there to help make me a better writer and storyteller.

And thank you to my bestie and PA extraordinaire, Ashleen Walker, for handling all the little things and supporting me through everything. I appreciate you so much. Love you lots!

The life of a writer doesn't stop with the book. Our job expands beyond the written word to marketing, advertising, graphic design, social media management and more. Help from those in the know goes a long way. A huge thank you to Nina Grinstead at Valentine PR for brainstorming with me, for your encouragement, your insight and for going above and beyond. You're amazing and I'm so grateful for you.

Thank you to my review team, to every single blogger, instagrammer and book lover who has helped spread the word about my books. You all are appreciated so much! On that note, a massive thank you to all the fantastic readers in my private Facebook group *Sam's Clan McBookish*. You're truly special and the loveliest readers a girl could ask for <3

A massive thank you to Hang Le. You've created the most beautiful covers that fit perfectly with the story. You're wonderful and so incredibly talented, my friend.

As always, thank you to my agent Lauren Abramo for making it possible for readers all over the world to find my words. You're phenomenal and I'm truly grateful for all you do.

A huge thank you to my family and friends for always supporting and encouraging me.

Finally, to you my reader, the biggest thank you of all.

BLACK TANGLED HEART

To my siblings, Jane was a friend. A pseudo-sister, the girl we grew up with.
To me? She was everything.
Our passion consumed us.

When our world fell apart, I thought our love would be the thing that held us together.
She was the love of my life. But she abandoned me when I needed her most.
And I'll never forgive her.

For years I've been planning my revenge against the people who took everything from me.
Jane won't be an exception. I'm coming for her.
She knows it.

She says she wants to help me serve my version of justice on the people who hurt me.
I'll let her.
She probably thinks it will save her from me.

It won't.

Black Tangled Heart is a complete standalone. *The Play On* series are books connected by the theme of the arts industry, not by characters, and can be read in any order.

"Readers are in for a thrilling and emotional ride with this one! The storyline is engrossing, the characters are complex, and the chemistry is off-the-charts palpable. It's my favorite book by Samantha Young to date." -- K.A. Tucker, international bestselling author of *The Simple Wild*

Buy it now or read it free with Kindle Unlimited

CPSIA information can be obtained
at www.ICGtesting.com
Printed in the USA
LVHW030139071120
670844LV00015B/1656

9 781916 174078